Emelie Schepp is an international bestselling Nordic crime author with a career in marketing, publicity and project management. Her Jana Berzelius series has sold nearly 1 million copies around the world. Schepp lives with her husband and two children in Sweden. You can find her on Twitter @EmelieSchepp, on Facebook and Instagram, and at www.EmelieSchepp.com

MARKED FOR LIFE

LIFE

Emelie Schepp

ONE PLACE. MANY STORIES

This novel is entirely a work of fiction. The names, characters and incidents portrayed in it are the work of the author's imagination. Any resemblance to actual persons, living or dead, events or localities is entirely coincidental.

HQ
An imprint of HarperCollinsPublishers Ltd
1 London Bridge Street
London SE1 9GF

This paperback edition 2017

1
First published in Great Britain by
HQ, an imprint of HarperCollinsPublishers Ltd 2017

Emelie Schepp asserts the moral right to be
identified as the author of this work.
A catalogue record for this book is
available from the British Library.

ISBN: 978-1-84845-537-5

Printed and bound by
CPI Group, Croydon CR0 4YY

To H.

CHAPTER
ONE

Sunday, 15 April

'112, WHAT IS YOUR EMERGENCY?'

'My husband's dead . . .'

Emergency operator Anna Bergström heard the tremor in the woman's voice and glanced at the clock in the top corner of her computer screen: 19.42.

'Could you give me your name, please?'

'Kerstin Juhlén. My husband is Hans. Hans Juhlén.'

'How do you know he is dead?'

'He isn't breathing. He's just lying there. He was lying there like that when I came home. And there's blood . . . blood on the carpet,' the woman sobbed.

'Are you hurt?'

'No.'

'Is anybody else hurt?'

'No, my husband is dead.'

'I understand. Where are you now?'

'At home.'

The operator took a deep breath.

'Can I have your address please?'

'Östanvägen 204, in Lindö. It's a yellow house. With large decorative urns outside.'

Anna's fingers raced across the keyboard as she zoomed in on Östanvägen on the digital map.

'Help is on the way,' she said in a calming voice. 'And I want you to stay on the line until they get there.'

Anna didn't get any answer. She pressed the headset to her ear, straining to listen.

'Hello? Are you still there?'

'He's dead.' The woman sobbed again. Then the sobs became hysterical, until all that could be heard was a long anguished scream.

Detective Chief Inspector Henrik Levin and Detective Inspector Maria Bolander stepped out of their Volvo in Lindö. The cold sea air from the Baltic caught Henrik's flimsy spring jacket. He pulled the zipper up to his neck and put his hands in the pockets.

On the paved driveway there was a black Mercedes together with two police cars and an ambulance. Some distance from the cordoned-off area were two parked cars emblazoned with the logos of the town's two rival newspapers. Two journalists, one from each paper, were straining against the police tape in an effort to get a better view.

'Nothing I hate worse than an upmarket crime scene.' Detective Inspector Maria Bolander, or Mia as she preferred, shook her head in irritation. 'This one's even got statuary.' She stared at the granite lions, then caught sight of the huge urns next to them.

Henrik Levin offered no response as he set off up the pathway to Östanvägen 204. Discreet lighting illuminated the snow that had settled on the grey edging stones. He nodded to the uniformed officer, Gabriel Mellqvist, who stood sentry at the front door, then he stamped the snow off his shoes, opened the heavy door for Mia, and they both went in.

The house was a hive of activity as Forensics systematically examined the scene. Judging by the coating of powder on various surfaces, including the door handles, they had already dusted for fingerprints. A couple of technicians were collecting and bagging evidence while others checked for signs of blood spatter on the walls. Every few moments the flash of a camera lit up the tastefully furnished living room where a dead body lay sprawled on the striped carpet.

'Who found him?' Mia asked.

'His wife, Kerstin Juhlén,' Henrik said. 'She apparently found him dead on the floor when she came home from a walk.'

'Where is she now?'

'Upstairs. With Hanna Hultman.'

Henrik Levin looked down at the body. The dead man, Hans Juhlén, was head of the department dealing with asylum cases at the Migration Agency's local office. Henrik stepped around the body, then leaned down to study the victim's face – the powerful jaw, the weather-beaten skin, the grey stubble and greying temples. Hans Juhlén's name often cropped up in the news, and based on the photos that accompanied those articles, Henrik had been expecting a younger man. The deceased was wearing neatly pressed trousers and a light-blue striped cotton shirt, now saturated with blood from the wounds to his chest.

'Look, but don't touch,' forensic expert Anneli Lindgren cautioned Henrik from her vantage point next to the large window.

'Shot?'

'Yes, twice. Two entry points from what I can tell.'

Henrik glanced around the room, which was dominated by a sofa, two leather armchairs and a glass coffee table with chrome legs. Paintings by Ulf Lundell hung on the walls. The furniture didn't appear disturbed. Nothing was knocked over.

'No signs of a struggle,' he said and turned toward Mia, who was now standing behind him.

'No,' said Mia, her gaze focused on an oval sideboard. On it lay a brown leather wallet with three five-hundred-kronor bills sticking out. She felt a sudden urge to pull them out – or at least one, but she stopped herself. Enough, she told herself; pull yourself together.

Henrik's eyes wandered to the windows which looked out on to the garden. Anneli Lindgren was still checking for fingerprints.

'Find anything?'

Anneli Lindgren looked up at him from behind her spectacles.

'Not yet, but according to the victim's wife, one of these windows was open when she came home. I'm hoping I'll find something other than her prints on it.'

As she went back to her slow, painstaking work, Henrik turned to Mia.

'Shall we go upstairs and have a few words with Mrs Juhlén?'

'You go up. I'll stay down here and keep an eye on things.'

Upstairs, Kerstin Juhlén sat on the bed in the master bedroom with a cardigan draped around her shoulders, staring vacantly ahead of her. Officer Hanna Hultman, who had been keeping an eye on her, withdrew as soon as Henrik entered, closing the door behind her.

On his way up the stairs, Henrik had imagined the victim's

wife as delicate and elegantly dressed. Instead he found a heavyset woman dressed in a faded T-shirt and dark stretch jeans. Her blonde hair was styled in a blunt bob; the dark roots were showing through, suggesting she was overdue for a visit to the hairdresser. Henrik's eyes scanned the bedroom, taking in the chest of drawers and then the wall of photographs. In the middle of the wall hung a frame with a large faded photo of a happy bride and groom. He was aware that Kerstin Juhlén was watching him.

'My name's Henrik Levin, and I'm the Detective Chief Inspector,' he said softly. 'I'm sorry for your loss. I realize it's a difficult time, but there are a few questions I need to ask you.'

Kerstin dried a tear with the sleeve of her cardigan.

'Yes, I understand.'

'Can you tell me what happened when you came home?'

'I walked in and . . . and . . . he was just lying there.'

'Do you know what time it was?'

'About half past seven.'

'Are you sure?'

'Yes.'

'When you entered the house, did you see anybody else?'

'No. No, only my husband, he . . .'

Her lip quivered and she buried her face in her hands.

It was obvious an in-depth interrogation would be pointless at this stage, so he decided to keep it brief.

'Mrs Juhlén, we've sent for victim support, but in the meantime there are questions I must ask.'

Kerstin removed her hands from her face and rested them on her lap.

'Yes?'

'I understand that a window was open when you came home.'

'Yes.'

'And it was you who closed it?'

'Yes.'

'You didn't see anything amiss outside as you closed it?'

'No . . . no.'

'Why did you close it?'

'I was afraid someone might try and come back in.'

Henrik put his hands in his pockets and pondered for a moment.

'Before I leave you, is there anyone you'd like us to call? A friend? Relative? Your children?'

She looked down, her hands trembling, and whispered something in a barely audible voice.

'I'm sorry, could you repeat that?'

Kerstin shut her eyes, then raised her tear-stained face toward him. She took a deep breath and answered him.

Downstairs in the living room, Anneli Lindgren adjusted her glasses. 'I think I've found something,' she said. She was examining a handprint she'd captured on the window frame. Mia went up to her and noted the very clear form of a palm with fingers.

'There's another one here,' Anneli pointed out. 'They belong to a child.'

She reached for her Canon EOS and adjusted the focus. By the time Henrik returned she was busily snapping a series of photos to document her find.

Anneli beckoned him over. 'We've found some fingerprints,' she said, raising the camera in front of her face again to zoom in and take another shot. 'They're small,' she added.

'So they belong to a child?' Mia clarified.

Henrik looked surprised and leaned close to the window to get a better look. The prints made an orderly pattern. A unique pattern. Clearly from a child-sized hand.

'Strange,' he mumbled.

'Why is it strange?' said Mia.

Henrik looked at her before he answered.

'The Juhléns don't have children.'

Monday, 16 April

THE TRIAL WAS OVER, AND PROSECUTOR JANA

Berzelius was satisfied with the result. She had been absolutely certain the defendant would be found guilty of causing grievous bodily harm.

He had kicked his own sister senseless in front of her four-year-old child and then left her to die in her apartment. No doubt it was an honour crime. Even so, the defendant's solicitor, Peter Ramstedt, looked rather surprised when the verdict was announced.

Jana nodded to him before she left the courtroom. She didn't want to discuss the judgement with anybody, especially not with the dozen or so journalists waiting outside the court with their cameras and mobile phones at the ready. Instead, she made her way towards the emergency exit, pushed the white fire door open and ran down the steps.

Avoiding journalists had become a matter of routine for Jana Berzelius. Three years earlier, when she started in the prosecutor's office in Norrköping, it had been different. Then she had appreciated the coverage and praise the media gave her, revelling in articles that celebrated her 'meteoric rise' and dubbed her 'the next prosecutor-general'. Her mobile phone vibrated in the pocket of her jacket, and she paused in front of the entrance to the underground car park to look at the display before answering. As she checked the caller ID, she noticed the clock was showing 11.35.

'Hello, Father,' she said, passing through the door to the heated car park.

'Well, how did it go?'

'Two years' prison and ninety in damages.'

'Are you satisfied?'

It would never occur to Karl Berzelius to congratulate his daughter on a successful court case. Jana was accustomed to his taciturn ways. Her mother, Margaretha, was much the same. Though she'd been warm and loving during Jana's childhood, housework had always won out over playing games. She'd fold laundry rather than read stories, or clean the kitchen rather than tuck her daughter into bed. Now Jana was thirty and she treated both parents with the same unemotional respect with which they had raised her.

'I am satisfied,' Jana answered emphatically.

'Your mother wonders whether you're coming home on the first of May? She wants to have a family dinner.'

'What time?'

'Seven.'

'I'll come.'

Jana ended the call, unlocked her black BMW X-6 and sat down behind the wheel. She threw her briefcase on to the leather-upholstered passenger seat and put her mobile on her lap.

Jana's mother was also in the habit of phoning her daughter

after a court case. But never before her husband did. So when Jana felt her mobile vibrate as she was expertly manoeuvring her car out of the tight parking space, she answered without checking the display.

'Hello, Mother.'

'Hello, Jana,' said a male voice.

Jana braked and the car jerked to a halt. The voice belonged to Chief Public Prosecutor Torsten Granath, her superior. 'Well?' he prompted.

Surprised that he should be so eager to hear how the case had gone, Jana gave a swift recap.

'Good. Good. But I'm actually calling about another matter. I want you to assist me on an investigation. A woman has been detained in connection with the death of her husband. He was the official in charge of asylum cases in Norrköping. According to the police, he was shot dead. Murdered. You'll have a free hand in the investigation.'

Jana remained silent, so Torsten continued:

'Gunnar Öhrn and his team are waiting at the police station. What do you say?'

Jana looked at the dashboard: 11.48 a.m. She put the car in gear and got moving again.

'I'll drive straight there.'

Jana Berzelius strode in through the main entrance of Norrköping police station, and took the lift up to the third floor. The sound of her heels echoed in the wide corridor. She looked straight ahead, acknowledging the two uniformed officers she passed en route with the briefest of nods.

The head of CID, Gunnar Öhrn, was waiting for her outside

his office. He ushered her into a conference room overlooking the Norrtull roundabout, which was already clogged with lunchtime traffic. The opposite wall was taken up by a vast whiteboard and a screen. A projector hung from the ceiling.

Jana approached the oval table where the team sat waiting. She exchanged greetings with DCI Henrik Levin, then acknowledged the others present – technician Ola Söderström, Anneli Lindgren and Mia Bolander – before sitting down.

Mia Bolander gritted her teeth, folded her arms and leaned back in her seat as Gunnar Öhrn welcomed the new arrival. She'd been seething since the moment it was announced that Berzelius was to oversee the preliminary investigation of the Hans Juhlén case. Though the two women were contemporaries and had worked together in the past, Mia considered the prosecutor a rival rather than an ally. There was no camaraderie with Jana Berzelius; she was too stiff, too formal. Most people made an effort to be social, to get to know their colleagues, perhaps share a beer or two after work. But Jana rebuffed even the most casual enquiries about her private life and showed no interest in anyone else's affairs.

In Mia's opinion, Jana Berzelius was an arrogant fucking diva, looking down her nose at everyone. She represented everything Mia detested: old money, privileged upbringing, no idea what it was to be mortgaged to the hilt – the antithesis of Mia with her working-class background and mounting debts. Unfortunately, nobody else seemed to share that view. On the contrary, they were all nodding appreciatively as Gunnar congratulated Jana on her latest triumph.

Out of the corner of her eye, Jana noted the hostile stare of the female inspector on the team but chose to ignore it. She opened her briefcase and pulled out a notepad and pen.

Gunnar Öhrn drank the last few drops from a bottle of mineral water, then handed out folders containing copies of all the data they had gathered so far: the initial report; photos of the crime scene and the exterior of the house; a floorplan of the Juhlén house and diagrams showing where the victim, Hans Juhlén, had been found; along with a physical description of Juhlén and a few biographical details. There was also a log recording the investigative steps that had been taken since the victim's body was discovered.

Gunnar pointed to the timeline on the whiteboard as he summarized the report filed by the two officers in the patrol car dispatched to the scene in response to Kerstin's 112 call. They had been the first to interview the victim's wife – or at least, they had attempted to interview her. When they arrived at the house she was screaming hysterically. Apparently incapable of speaking coherently, she started to hyperventilate when questioned and kept repeating over and over that she didn't kill her husband, she just found him in the living room. Dead.

'So do we suspect her?' said Jana, aware that Mia was still glaring at her.

'She is certainly of interest. Since she doesn't have a verifiable alibi, we've detained her.'

Gunnar thumbed through the folder.

'OK, to summarize: Hans Juhlén was murdered sometime between 15.00 and 19.00 yesterday. Perpetrators unknown. The forensic experts confirm the murder took place in the house. That is, the body had not been transported from anywhere else. Correct?'

He looked to Anneli Lindgren for confirmation.

She nodded. 'He died at the crime scene.'

'The body was taken to the medical examiner's lab at 22.21 and inspectors continued to go through the house until after midnight.'

'Yes, and I found these . . .'

Anneli spread out ten sheets of paper with a single sentence written on each. 'They were hidden in the back of the wardrobe in the victim's bedroom. They appear to be threatening letters.'

'Do we know who sent them and to whom they were addressed?' asked Henrik as he reached across to examine them. Jana jotted a note in her notepad.

'No. I got these copies from forensics in Linköping this morning. It'll probably take a day or so before they can get us more information,' said Anneli.

'What do they say?' asked Mia. She pulled her hands inside the sleeves of her knitted sweater, put her elbows on the table and looked at Anneli with curiosity.

'The same message is on each one: *Pay now or risk paying the bigger price.*'

'Blackmail,' said Henrik.

'So it would seem. We spoke to Mrs Juhlén. She denies any knowledge of the letters. She seemed genuinely surprised.'

'They hadn't been reported then, these threats?' said Jana and wrinkled her brow.

'No, nothing has been reported by the victim himself, his wife or anybody else,' said Gunnar.

'And what about the murder weapon?' said Jana.

'We haven't found one yet. Nothing was near the body or in the immediate area,' said Gunnar.

'Any DNA traces or shoe prints?'

'No,' said Anneli. 'But when the wife came home, a window

was open in the living room. That could be how the perpetrator gained entry. The wife closed it, unfortunately, which has made things more difficult for us. But we did manage to find two interesting handprints.'

'Whose prints?' said Jana, her pen poised to note down a name.

'Don't know yet, but everything points to these being the prints of a child. The strange thing is, the couple don't have any children.'

Jana looked up from her notepad.

'Is that significant? Surely they know someone who has children. A friend? Relative?' she said.

'We haven't been able to ask Kerstin Juhlén about it yet,' answered Gunnar.

'Well, that must be the next step.' Jana took her diary out of her briefcase and flipped through to today's date. Reminders, times and names were neatly written on the pale yellow pages. 'I want us to talk to her as soon as possible.'

'I'll phone her lawyer, Peter Ramstedt, right away,' said Gunnar.

'Good,' said Jana. 'Get back to me with a time as soon as you can.' She put her diary back in her briefcase. 'Have you questioned any of the neighbours yet?'

'Yes, the nearest ones,' said Gunnar.

'And?'

'Nothing. Nobody saw or heard anything.'

'Then knock on every door in the street and all the surrounding streets. Lindö has many houses with large drawing rooms overlooking the street.'

'Yes, I imagine you would know that,' said Mia sarcastically.

Jana locked eyes with Mia.

'What I am saying is, somebody must have seen or heard something.'

Mia's eyes flashed with anger, then she looked away.

'What more do we know about Hans Juhlén?' Jana went on.

'He lived a fairly ordinary life, it seems,' said Gunnar, referring to the notes in the folder 'He was born in Kimstad in 1953, which makes him fifty-nine. Spent his childhood there. The family moved to Norrköping in 1965, when he was twelve. He studied economics at university and worked for four years in an accounting firm before he got a position in the Migration Agency's asylum department and worked his way up to become the head. He met his wife Kerstin when he was eighteen and they married in a registry office one year later. They have a summer cottage by Lake Vättern. That's all we've got so far.'

'Friends? Acquaintances?' Mia said grumpily. 'Have we checked them?'

'We don't know anything about his friends yet. Or his wife's. But we've started tracing them, yes,' said Gunnar.

'A more detailed conversation with the wife will help fill in the blanks,' said Henrik.

'Yes, I know,' said Gunnar.

'His mobile phone?' Jana wondered.

'I've asked the service provider for a list of calls to and from his number. Hopefully I'll have it tomorrow latest,' said Gunnar.

'And what have we got from the autopsy results?'

'The medical examiner will be sending us a preliminary report later today. In the meantime, all we can say for certain is that Hans Juhlén was shot and died where he was found.'

'I need a copy of the ME's report,' Jana said.

'Henrik and Mia are going to the morgue straight after this meeting.'

'Fine. I'll tag along,' said Jana, and smiled to herself when she heard a deep sigh from Inspector Bolander.

THE SEA WAS ROUGH SO THEY WERE CONFINED DAY
and night, making the stench grow even worse. The seven-year-old girl sat
in the corner. She pulled at her mama's skirt and put it over her mouth.
She imagined she was at home in her bed, or rocking in a cradle when
the ship rolled in the waves.

The girl breathed in and out with shallow breaths. Every time she
exhaled, the cloth would lift above her mouth. Every time she inhaled,
it would cover her lips. She tried to breathe harder and harder to keep the
cloth off her face. Then one time she blew so hard it flew off and vanished.

She felt for it with her hand. In the dim light she caught sight of her
toy mirror on the floor. It was pink, with a butterfly on it and a big crack
in the glass. She had found it in a bag of rubbish somebody had thrown
on to the street. Now she picked it up and held it in front of her face,
pushed a strand of hair away from her forehead and inspected her dark
tangled hair, her big eyes and long eyelashes.

Somebody coughed violently in the space, and the girl gave a start.
She tried to see who it was, but it was difficult to distinguish people's
faces in the dark.

She wondered when they would arrive, but she didn't dare ask again.
Papa had hushed her when she had asked the last time how long they
would have to sit in this stupid iron box. Now Mama coughed too. It was

so hard to breathe. A lot of people had to share what little oxygen was inside the box. The girl let her hand wander along the steel wall. Then she felt for the soft cloth from her mama's skirt and pulled it over her nose.

The floor was hard, and she straightened her back and changed position before continuing to run her hand along the steel wall. She stretched out her index and middle fingers and let them gallop back and forth along the wall and down to the floor. Mama always used to laugh when she did that at home; she'd say she must have given birth to a horse girl.

At home, in the shed in La Pintana, the girl had built a toy stable under the kitchen table and pretended her doll was a horse. The last three birthdays, she had wished for a real pony of her own. She knew she wouldn't get one. She rarely got presents, even for her birthday. They could barely afford food, Papa had told her. Anyway, the girl dreamed of a pony of her own that she could ride to school. It would be fast – as fast as her fingers galloping back up the wall.

Mama didn't laugh this time. She was probably too tired, the girl thought, and looked up at her mother's face.

Oh, how much longer would it take? Stupid, stupid journey! It wasn't supposed to be such a long trip. Papa had said when they filled the plastic bags with clothes that they were going on an adventure, a big adventure. They would travel by boat to a new home. And she would make lots of new friends. It would be fun.

Some of her friends were travelling with them. Danilo and Ester. She liked Danilo; he was nice, but not Ester. She liked to tease and poke fun in a mean way. There were a couple of other children on the journey too, but she didn't know them; she had never seen them before. None of them liked being in a boat. Especially not the youngest one, the baby – she cried all the time. Except now she'd gone quiet.

The girl galloped her fingers back and forth again. Then she stretched to one side to reach up even higher, then down even lower. When her *fingers reached all the way into the corner, she felt something sticking out. Curious, she screwed her eyes up in the dark to see what it was. A metal plate. She strained forward to try and study the little silver plate screwed into the wall. She saw some letters on it and she tried to make out what they said. V . . . P . . . then there was a letter she didn't recognize.*

'Mama?' she whispered. 'What letter is this?' She crossed her two fingers to show her.

'X,' her mother whispered back. 'An X.'

X, the girl thought, V, P, X, O. And then some numbers. She counted six of them. There were six numbers.

CHAPTER FOUR

THE AUTOPSY SUITE WAS BATHED IN THE GLARE OF fluorescent ceiling lights. A shiny steel table stood in the middle of the room and on it, under a white sheet, the contours of a body were visible.

A long row of plastic bottles marked with ID numbers were lined up on another stainless-steel table along with a skull saw. The metallic tang of raw meat permeated the room.

Jana Berzelius went in first and stood across the table from the medical examiner, Björn Ahlmann. As they exchanged greetings, she pulled out her notepad.

While Henrik took his place next to Jana, Mia Bolander chose to stand near the exit door. Henrik too would have liked to remain at a distance. He had always struggled with autopsies and could not for the life of him understand the pathologist's fascination with corpses. Though Henrik's job brought him in contact with death, he still found its effects on the human body hard to witness up-close. Even after seven years, he had to force himself to maintain his composure when a body was exposed.

Jana, on the other hand, didn't seem in the least bothered. Her face betrayed no sign of revulsion or horror, and Henrik found himself wondering what it would take to make her react.

Knocked-out teeth, poked-out eyes, chopped-off fingers and hands didn't do it. Nor tongues that had been bitten to shreds, or third-degree burns. He knew this because he had witnessed these things in her presence, and while he'd had to fight waves of nausea until he emptied the contents of his stomach, she invariably appeared unperturbed.

Then again, Jana's face never gave much away. He couldn't recall seeing her show signs of stress or exhaustion, or happiness for that matter. She rarely smiled and should a smile happen to cross her lips, it was more like a line. A strained line.

Henrik didn't think her austere personality entirely matched her appearance. Her long dark hair and big brown eyes gave off a warmer vibe, though she took pains to ensure this was countered by the navy blazer, three-quarter-length skirt and ever-present high heels. Combined with her unflappable demeanour, this 'uniform' marked her out as a no-nonsense professional, the image she was intent on projecting in order to secure the respect of her colleagues. Perhaps she let out her personal feelings outside work . . . Or perhaps not.

Björn Ahlmann carefully folded back the sheet and exposed Hans Juhlén's naked body.

'Right, let's see. We have an entry hole here and we have an entry hole here,' said Björn, indicating two open wounds on the chest. 'Both seem perfectly placed, but this is the one that killed him.'

Björn moved his hand and indicated the upper hole.

'So there were definitely two shots?' Henrik commented.

'Exactly.'

Björn picked up an image from a CAT scan and clipped it to the light box.

'Chronologically, it seems he first received a bullet in the lower part of his ribcage, and fell backwards, striking the ground. This resulted in a subdural haemorrhage at the back of his head. You can see it here.' Björn pointed at a black area on the image. 'But he didn't die from that first shot or from the heavy fall. No, my guess is that when Hans Juhlén collapsed, the perpetrator moved in close and shot him again. Here.'

He pointed at the second entry hole.

'This shot went right through the cartilage of the ribcage and through the pericardium, the membrane surrounding the heart. Death was instantaneous.'

'So he died from bullet number two,' said Henrik.

'Yes.'

'Weapon?'

'The cartridges found at the scene came from a Glock.'

'Then it won't be easy to trace,' said Henrik.

'Why?' said Jana. There was a faint buzz as her mobile phone vibrated in her pocket. She ignored it and asked again, 'Why?'

'Because, as I'm sure you are aware, the Glock is a very common weapon, used by military and police personnel all over the world. So the list of people with legitimate licences will be a long one and every name on it will need to be checked,' he said.

'Then we'll have to see that the task is entrusted to somebody with patience,' said Jana. Once again the phone vibrated in her pocket. The caller must have left a message.

'Any indication that the victim tried to defend himself?' Mia asked from across the room.

'No wounds of that nature – no scratch marks, no bruises or marks from a stranglehold on his throat. He was shot. Plain and simple.'

Björn looked up at Henrik and Jana.

'The blood has settled in a manner consistent with his having died and remained in the same place, and yet—'

'Yes, Gunnar told us,' Mia interrupted from across the room.

'Indeed, I talked with him this morning. But there are—'

'No fingerprints?' she said.

'No. But—'

'Narcotics then?'

'No, no drugs. No alcohol. But—'

'Broken bones?'

'No. Will you let me finish now?'

Mia fell silent.

'Thank you. The thing that caught my attention was the path the bullets took through the body. One of the entry holes' – Björn pointed at the higher of the two – 'is nothing out of the ordinary. The bullet passed through the body in a straight line. But the other bullet went diagonally. So, judging by the angle, the perpetrator must have been kneeling, lying down or sitting up when he or she fired the first shot. Then, as I said earlier, once the man was down, the shooter went up to him and fired a final shot right through his heart.'

'Execution style,' said Mia.

'That's for you to judge, but yes, it would seem so.'

'So he was standing up when bullet number one hit him,' said Henrik.

'Yes, and he was shot at an upward angle from the front.'

'You're saying somebody knelt or lay down and then shot up at him from the front? It makes no sense,' said Mia. 'I mean, how could somebody be sitting on the floor right in front of him and manage to shoot him? Wouldn't he have had time to react?'

'Perhaps he did react. Or perhaps he knew the murderer,' said Henrik.

'Or it was a bloody dwarf or something,' said Mia and laughed.

Henrik let out a sigh.

'You can discuss it among yourselves later. According to my calculations, that is how Hans Juhlén died. My findings are summarized here.' Björn held out copies of the autopsy report. Henrik and Jana each took one.

'He died sometime between 18.00 and 19.00 on Sunday. It's in the notes.'

Jana thumbed through the report; it appeared to be as comprehensive and detailed as she'd come to expect from Ahlmann.

'Thanks for the summary,' she said, pulling her phone from her pocket to listen to the voicemail.

Gunnar Öhrn's message was crisp and concise: 'Interview with Kerstin Juhlén, 15.30.'

Jana slipped the phone back into her pocket.

'Interview at half past three,' she said quietly to Henrik.

'What?' said Mia.

'Interview half past three,' Henrik repeated for Mia's benefit.

The medical examiner adjusted his glasses. 'Are we done?' he asked.

'Yes,' Jana told him.

As he started to pull the sheet back over the body, Mia opened the door and backed out to avoid contact with Jana.

'We'll get back to you with any questions,' said Henrik to Ahlmann as they left the autopsy suite.

'Please do. You know where I am,' Björn called after them, but his voice was drowned out by the thrumming of the ventilation pipes in the ceiling.

★

The Public Prosecution Office in Norrköping consisted of twelve full-time employees headed up by Chief Public Prosecutor Torsten Granath. Fifteen years earlier, when Granath was appointed, his first act had been to set about getting rid of staff members who were no longer pulling their weight. Several long-serving employees had been encouraged to retire, lazy administrators had been fired and under-utilized specialists had been invited to find new challenges in other areas of their profession.

At one stage there were only four employees remaining, but when the office was asked to cover a larger geographical area, dealing with crimes in the adjacent municipalities of Finspång, Söderköping and Valdemarsvik, Granath was forced to recruit. He set about filling the vacancies with new hires who boasted impressive track records. Jana Berzelius fit the profile.

Now sixty-two, Granath had slowed down a little and occasionally found his thoughts straying to the well-kept greens of the golf course. But his heart still belonged to his profession; this was his mission in life and he would keep on with it until he reached pensionable age.

His office was surprisingly cosy; on his desk were gilded frames with photos of grandchildren, there were curtains on the windows and a green woolly rug on the floor. He always paced back and forth on the rug when he talked on the telephone. And that was what he was doing when Jana Berzelius entered the department.

As soon as she spotted Jana, the office administrator, Yvonne Jansson, began waving a yellow Post-it note.

'Mats Nylinder at *Norrköpings Tidningar* wants a comment on the murder of Hans Juhlén. He said you owe him a few words after sneaking out of court this morning. He waited more than an hour for you, hoping for a statement about the judgement.'

When Jana didn't answer, Yvonne went on: 'Unfortunately, he isn't the only one who's been trying to get hold of you. Somehow the media have found out you're in charge of the preliminary investigation. This murder has every paper in Sweden interested. They all want something to put in their headlines tomorrow.'

'And I'm not going to give them anything. You'll have to refer them to the police press officer. There will be no comment from me.'

'OK, no comment it is.'

'And you can tell Mats Nylinder that too,' said Jana as she continued into her office, her heels clicking on the parquet floor.

The furnishings were spartan but not without a touch of elegance. The desk was teak and so were the bookshelves that held row upon row of bound case files. The right-hand side of the desk was occupied by a three-tier silver letter tray. On the left-hand side there was a laptop. Two white orchids in elegant pots stood on the windowsill.

Jana closed the door behind her and hung her jacket over the back of her leather-upholstered chair. She'd had the desk positioned so that she sat with her back to the window, preferring the view through the glass wall that separated her from the office corridor. While she waited for her computer to start up she riffled through a tall stack of summonses to be adjudicated, then glanced at her watch. Only one and a half hours before the interview with Kerstin Juhlén.

Suddenly tired, she leaned forward and began to massage the nape of her neck, her fingertips tracing the uneven skin. When she was done, she arranged her long hair so that it covered her neck and flowed down her back.

After looking through a few of the summonses, she got up to fetch a cup of coffee. When she came back, she left the rest of the paperwork untouched.

THE INTERVIEW ROOM WAS BARE EXCEPT FOR A
table and four chairs, with a fifth chair in a corner. One wall
had a window with bars; on the opposite wall was a mirror. Jana
sat next to Henrik with her pen and notepad in her hand. She
watched in silence as he turned on the tape recorder. They'd
agreed that she would let him handle the questioning. Mia
Bolander pulled up the extra chair behind them. Henrik waited
until she was seated before reciting Kerstin Juhlén's full name
and personal identity number, commencing the interview with
a preamble for the benefit of the tape.

'Monday, sixteenth of April, 15.30. This interview is being
conducted by DCI Henrik Levin, assisted by DI Mia Bolander.
Also present are Public Prosecutor Jana Berzelius and Solicitor
Peter Ramstedt.'

Kerstin Juhlén had been detained as a possible person of
interest, but had not been charged with any crime. She sat next
to Peter Ramstedt and placed her clasped hands on the table. Her
face was pale and she wore no make-up. Her hair was uncombed,
her earrings removed.

'Do you know who killed my husband?' Kerstin Juhlén asked
in a whisper.

'No, it's still too early in our investigation to say,' said Henrik, watching her intently.

'You think I've done it, don't you? You think I was the one who shot him.'

'We don't—'

'But I didn't do it! I wasn't home. It wasn't me!'

'As I said, we don't know who shot him as yet. We are still investigating the circumstances surrounding his murder and trying to determine what happened. Which is why I need you to tell me everything you remember about Sunday night.'

Kerstin took two deep breaths. She unclenched her fists, rested her hands in her lap and straightened up in the chair.

'I came home . . . from a walk.'

'Did you walk alone, or was somebody with you?'

'I walked by myself, to the beach and back. When I got home, I took my coat off in the hallway and I called out to Hans, because I knew he ought to be home by then.'

'What time was it?'

'About half past seven.'

'Go on.'

'When I didn't get an answer, I assumed he'd been delayed at work – he always went into the office on Sundays. I carried on into the kitchen to get a glass of water and saw a pizza box on the kitchen counter. That was when I realized Hans must be home. We usually eat pizza on Sundays. Hans picks it up on his way home. Yes, well . . . I called out again, but got no answer. So I went to check if he was in the living room and what he was doing and . . . I saw him lying there on the floor. In shock, I called the police.'

'When did you phone?'

'Straight away . . . soon as I found him.'

'What did you do after you phoned the police?'

'I went upstairs. The emergency operator said I mustn't touch him, so I went upstairs.'

Henrik studied the woman in front of him. Her eyes shifted nervously, never meeting his gaze. Her restless fingers gripped the cloth of her light-grey trousers.

'I've asked you before, but I must ask again: did you see anybody in the house?'

'No.'

'Outside?'

'I noticed that the front window was open so I closed it. In case someone was still lurking out there. I was frightened. But no, I've already told you. I saw no one.'

'No car on the street outside?'

'No,' Kerstin answered in a loud voice. She leaned forward and rubbed her Achilles tendon, as if relieving an itch.

'Tell us about your husband,' said Henrik.

'What about him?'

'He was head of the asylum department at the Migration Agency here in Norrköping, correct?' said Henrik.

'Yes. He was good at his job.'

'Can you elaborate? What was he good at?'

'He worked on all sorts of things. In the department he was in charge . . .'

Kerstin fell silent and lowered her head.

Henrik noted that she swallowed hard, he imagined, to prevent tears from coming.

'We can take a little break if you like,' said Henrik.

'No, it's OK. It's OK.'

Kerstin took a deep breath. She glanced at her lawyer who was twirling his pen on the table, and then she started talking again.

'My husband was head of department. He loved his job and had worked his way up, devoting his life to the Migration Agency. He is . . . was the sort of person people liked. He was kind to everybody, regardless of where they came from. He didn't have any prejudices. He wanted to help people. That was why he liked it there so much.

'The Migration Agency has come in for a lot of criticism recently,' Kerstin said, then paused before continuing.

Henrik nodded. During a routine examination of procedures for arranging accommodation for asylum seekers, the National Audit Agency had uncovered a number of improper practices. Over the last year, the Migration Agency had spent fifty million kronor on accommodation; of that, nine million kronor had been spent on direct agreements, which contravened guidelines. The Audit Agency had also found illegal contracts with landlords. And in many cases there were no contracts whatsoever. Details of the audit's findings had been published in the local press.

'Hans was upset over the criticism. More refugees had been applying than they had anticipated. He'd had to arrange accommodation for them in a hurry. And then it went wrong.'

Kerstin fell silent again. Her lip quivered.

'I felt sorry for him.'

'It sounds as if you know quite a bit about your husband's work,' said Henrik.

Kerstin didn't answer. She wiped a tear from her eye and nodded.

'Then there were the problems at the asylum centre,' she said.

A number of assaults and thefts had taken place at the accommodation unit for asylum seekers. Given the stress of their situation, it was hardly surprising that arguments often broke out among the new arrivals. Temporary staff brought in to run the centre had struggled to maintain order.

'Which also made the local papers,' said Henrik.

'Yes,' said Kerstin and straightened her back again. 'Many of those who arrive at the centre are in poor mental condition. Hans did everything he could to make their stay as comfortable as possible, but it wasn't easy. Somebody kept setting off the fire alarm in the middle of the night and people got scared, so Hans had no option but to hire more staff. My husband was very committed, he put his very soul into his work.'

Henrik noted that Kerstin didn't look quite so miserable now. Something had come over her in the last few minutes, perhaps a pride in her husband's work; perhaps a sort of relief.

'Hans spent a lot of time at the office. He often worked late of an evening, and every Sunday he left home after lunch and didn't come back until dinnertime. I never knew what time he would be home, what time to have dinner ready, so he always used to pick up a pizza on the way. Just like yesterday. As usual.'

Kerstin Juhlén hid her face in her hands and shook her head as the anguish and grief came flooding back.

'You have the right to take a break,' said Peter Ramstedt, gently placing a hand on her shoulder.

Jana was watching his every move. Ramstedt had a reputation as a ladies' man and seldom hesitated to physically console his female clients. Given half a chance, he'd take it further.

Kerstin raised her shoulder slightly in discomfort, which was evidently enough to make the solicitor remove his hand. He pulled out a handkerchief and offered it to her. Kerstin accepted, and loudly blew her nose.

'Sorry,' she said.

'That's all right,' said Henrik. 'So if I've understood you correctly, your husband had a difficult job.'

'No, I mean . . . yes, but I don't know. I can't say exactly . . . I think . . . it would be best if you were to speak with my husband's PA.'

Henrik frowned. 'Why is that?'

'It would just be for the best,' she whispered.

Henrik sighed and leaned forward. 'What's his PA's name?'

'Lena Wikström. She's been his personal assistant for almost twenty years.'

'OK, we'll speak with her.'

Kerstin's shoulders sank and she clasped her hands.

'May I ask,' said Henrik, 'if you and your husband were close?'

'How do you mean? Of course we were close.'

'You didn't disagree about anything? Have a lot of arguments?'

'What are you getting at, Chief Inspector?' interjected Peter, leaning across the table.

'I just want to be sure we get the full picture for this investigation,' said Henrik.

'No, we rarely argued,' Kerstin said quietly.

'Apart from you, who else was close to him?'

'His parents have been dead a long time, unfortunately. Cancer, both of them. He didn't have any real friends, so you could say our social life was rather limited. But that was the way we liked it.'

'Sisters? Brothers?'

33

'He has a half-brother who lives in Finspång. But they haven't had much contact with each other in recent years. They are very different.'

'In what way?'

'They just are.'

'What's his name?'

'Lars Johansson. Everyone calls him Lasse.'

Mia Bolander had been sitting with her arms crossed, listening in silence. Now she asked straight out, 'Why don't you have children?'

Surprised by the question, Kerstin hastily pulled her legs under her chair. So hastily that one shoe came off.

Henrik turned to look at Mia. She could see he was irritated with her, but she was pleased she'd asked. Kerstin bent down and groaned as she stretched to reach her shoe under the table. Then she sat up straight again and put her hands on the table, one atop the other.

'We never had children,' she said.

'Why not?' demanded Mia. 'Couldn't you conceive?'

'I think we could have. But it somehow never happened. And we accepted that.'

Henrik cleared his throat and started talking to prevent Mia from continuing this line of questioning.

'OK. So you didn't socialize much, correct?'

'No, we didn't.'

'When did you last have visitors?'

'Oh, a long while ago. Hans was working all the time . . .'

'No visitors to the house? Repairmen, for example?'

'Around Christmas a man knocked on the door selling lottery tickets, but otherwise there haven't been—'

'What did he look like?'

Kerstin stared at Henrik, surprised.

'Tall . . . blond, as I remember. He seemed nice, presentable. But I didn't buy any tickets from him.'

'Did he have any children with him?'

'No. No, he didn't. He was alone.'

'Do you know anybody with children?'

'Well, yes, of course. Hans's half-brother. He has an eight-year-old son.'

'Has he been to your house recently?'

Kerstin frowned. 'I don't follow. Why . . . ? But, no, he hasn't been to our house for ages.'

Jana Berzelius drew a ring around the half-brother's name on her notepad: Lars Johansson.

'Do you have any idea who might have done this to your husband?' she asked.

Kerstin squirmed and her gaze shifted to the window as she answered, 'No.'

'Did your husband have any enemies?' said Henrik.

Kerstin looked down at the table and took a deep breath.

'No, he didn't.'

'Nobody he was angry with or had argued with or who was angry with him?'

Kerstin didn't seem to hear the question.

'Kerstin?'

'What?'

'Nobody who was angry with him?'

She shook her head 'no' so violently that the loose skin under her chin wobbled.

'Strange,' said Henrik as he laid out copies of the threatening letters on the table in front of her. 'Because, as you know, we found these at your house.'

'What are they?'

'The letters from your wardrobe. We're hoping you can tell us about them.'

'But I don't know – I've never seen them before.'

'They seem to be threats. So your husband must have had at least one enemy, if not more.'

'But, no . . .' Kerstin shook her head again.

'We're very anxious to find out more about who sent these – and why.'

'I have no idea.'

'You haven't?'

'No, I told you, I've never seen them before.'

Click-click could be heard from Peter Ramstedt's pen.

'As my client has said, twice, she does not recognize these letters. Would you be so kind and note that for the record? Then you won't have to waste time repeating the same question.'

'Mr Ramstedt, you are surely aware how we conduct interviews. Without extended questioning, we cannot get the information we need,' said Henrik.

'Then please stick to relevant questions. My client has clearly stated that she has *not* seen these papers previously.'

Peter looked straight at Henrik. CLICK-CLICK.

'So you don't know if your husband felt threatened in any way?' Henrik continued.

'No.'

'No strange phone calls?'

'I don't think so.'

'Don't think so or don't know?'

'No, no calls.'

'You can't think of anybody who wanted to warn him? Or get revenge?'

'No. But of course the nature of his work made him vulnerable.'

'Vulnerable in what way?'

'Well . . . my husband found the decision-making process for granting asylum very difficult. He never liked having to turn away asylum seekers, even though he wasn't personally responsible for having to tell them. He knew how desperate they could be when refused asylum here. But not everyone qualified. No one has threatened him, though. Or sought revenge, if that's what you're asking.'

Henrik wondered whether Kerstin was telling the truth. It was entirely possible that Hans Juhlén had kept the threatening letters hidden away from her. But it was hard to believe that in all his years in the job he'd never once felt frightened or talked to his wife about it.

'There must have been a pretty serious threat against Juhlén,' Henrik said to Jana when the interview was concluded. They both left the interrogation room with slow steps.

'Yes.'

'What do you make of the wife?'

Jana remained standing in the corridor while Henrik closed the door. 'There were no signs of a violent struggle in the house,' she said.

'Perhaps because the murder was well planned.'

'So you think she's guilty?'

'The spouse is always guilty, right?' Henrik smiled.

'Yes, almost always. But so far we have no evidence to link her to the murder.'

'She seemed nervous.'

'That isn't enough.'

'I know,' said Henrik. 'But I get the feeling she isn't telling the truth.'

'And she probably isn't, or at least not completely. But I'm going to need more than that if we're to arrest her. Unless she starts talking or we come up with some concrete evidence, I'll have to let her go. You've got three days.'

Henrik ran his fingers through his hair. 'And the PA?'

'See what she knows. Visit her as soon as you can – tomorrow at the latest. Unfortunately, I have four cases that require my attention, so I can't go with you. But I trust you,' she said, turning to make her way to the exit.

'Fine. Mia and I will talk to her,' Henrik called after her.

Jana was no stranger to the interrogation rooms and holding cells that lined these corridors. It was a requirement of the job that she attend the station to determine whether a suspect should be detained or released while police carried out their investigation. All too often, such decisions had to be made out of office hours; for this reason, the Public Prosecution Office operated an emergency duty rota to ensure someone was always available in the middle of the night or at weekends. Jana tried to remember when her next turn on the weekend rota would fall. It wasn't the coming weekend, of that she was certain. Perhaps the following weekend? She paused at a bench at the end of the corridor, took her diary out and flicked through the pages. Nothing on Saturday 28 April. Sunday 29 April was blank too. Frowning, she turned the pages until she came to an ON CALL entry in her neat handwriting. Tuesday, 1 May: a public holiday. The day she had agreed to have dinner with her mother and father. How could she have made such a stupid mistake? It was tempting fate to make plans when she was on call. She debated whether to call and cancel, but didn't want to disappoint her father.

I'll have to swap days with somebody, she thought as she tucked her diary back in her briefcase and set off again. Per Åström perhaps? During the five years they had worked together, she had come to respect him as a colleague – aside from being a successful prosecutor, he dedicated a lot of his time to working with troubled adolescents – but more than that, a friendship of sorts had grown between them.

Per was thirty-three years old and in good shape. He played tennis on Tuesdays and Thursdays. He had blond hair, a little dimple in his chin and eyes that were different colours. He smelled of aftershave. He had a tendency to go on a bit, but he seemed a genuinely nice guy. So she considered him a friend – but nothing more.

Jana hoped Per would swap with her. If necessary, she would try bribing him with wine. But red or white? She weighed the choices in time with the click of her heels on the floor: Red or white? Red or white?

When she entered the lobby and saw Peter Ramstedt waiting for the lift, she cursed herself for her laziness in not taking the stairs to the garage.

'Ah, it's you, Jana,' said Peter, rocking back and forth on the soles of his shoes. 'What's this I hear about you going along to the medical examiner's office to review the autopsy and see the victim's body?'

'Where did you hear that?' Jana made no effort to close the distance between them. Ramstedt was best kept at arm's length.

'One hears a thing or two.' He gave a smirk, exposing his whitened teeth. 'So you like corpses?'

'Not particularly. I'm just trying to lead an investigation.'

'I've been a lawyer for ten years and I've never heard of a prosecutor attending an autopsy.'

'Perhaps that says more about other prosecutors than about me?'

'Don't you like your colleagues?'

'I didn't say that.'

'Isn't it simpler in your position to let the police do the legwork?'

'I am not interested in what is simple.'

'You know, as a prosecutor, you can complicate an investigation.'

'In what way?'

'By calling attention to yourself.'

Hearing those words, Jana Berzelius decided she would take the stairs after all. And with every step, she cursed Peter Ramstedt.

THE ROCKING HAD STOPPED. THEY WERE TRAVELLING
in silence, shut inside the dark container.

'Are we there?' said the girl.

Her mama didn't answer her. Nor her papa. They seemed tense. Her mother told her to sit up. The girl did as she was told. The others also began to move. There was a feeling of unease, several of them were coughing and the girl felt the warm, stuffy air as it sought its way down into her lungs. Even her papa made a wheezing sound.

'Are we there now?' she said again. 'Mama? Mama!'

'Quiet!' said Papa. 'You must be completely quiet.'

Falling into a sulk, the girl pushed her knees up toward her chin.

Suddenly the floor shuddered under her. She fell to one side and stretched out an arm to brace herself. Her mother grabbed her and held her close. It was silent a long, long time. Then the container was lifted up.

They all hung on tight in the cramped space. The girl gripped her mama's waist. But even so, she hit her head when the container landed on the ground with a bump. At last they were in their new country. In their new life.

Mama got to her feet and pulled her daughter up. The girl looked at Danilo, who was still sitting with his back to the wall. His eyes were wide open; like the others, he was trying to hear what was going on outside. It was hard to hear anything through the walls, but if you really concentrated you could sometimes distinguish the faint sound of voices. Yes, there were people talking outside. The girl looked at her papa and he smiled at her. That smile was the last thing she saw before the container was opened and daylight poured in.

Outside the container stood three men. They had something in their hands, something big and silvery. The girl had seen such things before, in red plastic that sprayed water.

One man started to shout at the others. Something weird was on his face, an enormous scar. She couldn't help but stare at it.

The man with the scar came into the container and waved the silvery thing. He was shouting all the time. The girl didn't understand what he said. Neither did her parents. Nobody understood his words.

The man went up to Ester and pulled at her sweater. She was scared. Ester's mama was scared too, and didn't realize what was happening until it was too late. The man pulled Ester and held her in a firm grip around her neck as he backed away, all the time with the silvery thing pointed at Ester's mama and papa. They didn't dare do anything; they stood there, rooted to the spot.

The girl felt somebody take a firm hold of her arm. It was Papa; he pushed her behind his legs. Her mama spread out her skirt to cover the girl even more.

The girl kept as still as she possibly could. Behind the skirt she couldn't see what was happening. But she could hear. She could hear the grown-ups start to shout. They were shouting no, no, NO! And then she heard Danilo's desperate voice.

'Mama,' he shouted. 'Mama!'

The girl put her hands over her ears so she wouldn't have to hear the other children crying and shrieking. The voices of the grown-ups were worse. They were crying and shrieking too, but they were much louder.

The girl pressed her hands even harder against her ears. But then after a while, all was silent.

The girl took her hands away and listened. She tried to look out between her papa's legs, but when she moved he pressed her hard against the wall. It hurt.

The girl heard steps approach and felt her papa press her harder and harder against the steel wall. It was all she could do to breathe. She was about to open her mouth to complain when she heard a popping sound and her papa fell down on his face on the floor. He lay there unmoving in front of her. When she looked up, the man with the scar was standing in front of her. He smiled.

Her mama threw herself forward and held on to her as best she could. The man looked at them and shouted something again. Mama shouted back.

'You don't touch her!' she screamed.

Then he hit her with the silver thing he had in his hand.

The girl felt how her mama's hands slipped down her tummy and legs until she lay on the floor with staring eyes. She didn't blink, just stared.

'Mama!'

She felt a hand on her upper arm as the man yanked her up. He held her arm tightly, pushing her ahead of him out of the container.

And as she left she heard the dreadful sound when they fired the silver things. They didn't have water in them. Water didn't sound like that. They shot something hard, and they shot straight into the dark.

Straight at Mama and Papa.

CHAPTER
SEVEN

Tuesday, 17 April

JANA BERZELIUS WOKE UP AT FIVE IN THE MORNING.

She had had the same dream again; it never left her in peace. She sat up and wiped the sweat from her brow. Her mouth was dry from what she imagined was her shrieking. She straightened out her cramped fingers. Her fingernails had dug into the palms of her hands.

She had been dreaming the same dream for as long as she could remember. It never varied It irritated her that she didn't understand what it meant. No matter how much she analysed the images and events, she was still none the wiser.

Her pillow lay on the floor. Had she thrown it there? She must have done; it was too far from the bed to have fallen off.

She picked up the pillow and placed it against the headboard, then pulled the duvet back over herself. When she had lain there restless under the warm duvet for twenty minutes, she realized there was no hope of getting any more sleep. So she climbed out of bed, showered, dressed and ate a bowl of muesli.

With a mug of coffee in her hand, she gazed out of the window at the unsettled weather. They might be halfway through April, but winter was in no hurry to release its grip.

One day it was icy rain, the next it was snowfalls and freezing temperatures. From her flat in Knäppingsborg, Jana had a view of the river and the Louis de Geer Hall. From her living room she could also see shoppers out and about in the quaint streets below. Knäppingsborg had recently been renovated, but the urban planners on the council had managed to retain the feel of the original neighbourhood.

Jana had always wanted a flat with high ceilings, and when approval was granted for the renovation scheme to go ahead, her father had immediately invested in a housing association apartment for his then newly graduated daughter. As luck would have it, or thanks to a few phone calls, Karl Berzelius was given first pick. Of course he chose the apartment that was 40 square metres larger than the others, with a total floor area of 196 square metres.

Jana massaged her neck. Her scar was always irritated by cold weather. The pharmacist had recommended a new cream which was supposed to soothe and heal scarring, but she hadn't noticed any improvement.

She draped her long hair over her right shoulder, exposing her neck. With a careful touch, she gently rubbed the cream into the carved letters. Then she covered her neck with her hair again, removed her dark blue jacket from the wardrobe and put it on. Over that she buttoned up her beige Armani coat.

At half past eight she left the flat, walked to her car and drove through the icy drizzle to the courthouse. She was due in court at nine for a domestic violence case. Her fourth and final case probably wouldn't finish until half past five at the earliest.

It was going to be a long day.

★

It was shortly after 9 a.m. when Henrik Levin and Mia Bolander entered the Migration Agency offices. They checked in at reception and were assigned a temporary key card.

Lena Wikström, Juhlén's personal assistant, was in the middle of a telephone conversation when they stepped into her office on the second floor. She held up her finger to signal that she would be with them in a moment.

From Lena's desk, you could see straight into what had been Hans Juhlén's office. Henrik noted how tidy it was. The surface of the wide desk was empty, apart from a computer and a neat stack of folders next to it. Lena Wikström's space was quite the opposite. Papers were strewn everywhere, on the desk, on top of file folders, underneath ring binders, in trays, on the floor, in the paper-recycling box and in the wastebasket. It looked completely disorganized. Documents lay all around.

Henrik wondered how anyone could concentrate in such chaos.

Lena ended the call and invited Henrik and Mia to sit down. As soon as they were seated in the worn visitors' chairs next to her desk, she began:

'It's dreadful what happened. I still can't understand it. It's simply terrible. So terrible. Everybody's wondering who would do such a thing. I'm answering calls about Hans's murder non-stop at the moment. He *was* murdered, wasn't he? Oh my god, it's too awful.'

Henrik watched her picking at her peeling nail polish and tried to determine how old she was. Fifty-five plus, he reckoned. She had short dark hair and was wearing a light lilac blouse and earrings in a matching colour. The overall effect was one of elegance and affluence – or it would have been, if not for the flaking nail polish.

Mia took out her pen and notepad.

'I understand you've worked with Hans Juhlén for many years?' she said.

'Yes, more than twenty,' said Lena.

'Kerstin Juhlén said it was almost twenty.'

'Oh, she's never been good at keeping track of her husband. No, it's actually twenty-two. But I haven't been his assistant the whole time. I had another chief first, until he retired many years ago and handed over to Hans. Hans was in charge of the accounts department when I first knew him.'

'According to Kerstin, Hans had been rather stressed of late. Was that your impression too?' Henrik said.

'Stressed? No, I would hardly say that.'

'She was referring to recent criticism of the department in the media—'

'Oh? Yes, well, there was that. The newspapers accused us of making a complete shambles of finding accommodation for asylum seekers. But it's hard to know exactly how many will come. All you can do is make a projection, which is nothing more than an educated guess.'

Lena took a deep breath.

'Three weeks ago we received a large group of asylum seekers from Somalia. It meant a lot of extra work, coming in early and staying late day after day. Hans didn't want to risk more exposure in the local papers. He took the criticism seriously.'

'Did he have any enemies?' said Henrik.

'No, not as far as I know. But you always feel a bit vulnerable in this job. Emotions tend to run high, a lot of people behave threateningly when they're refused permission to remain in Sweden. So potentially he had a lot of enemies – which is why we have a security firm patrolling the premises,' said Lena. 'But I don't think Hans felt he had specific enemies.'

'Have you ever been threatened?'

'No, not personally. But the people we're dealing with can be completely mad – one man poured petrol over himself then ran into reception and threatened to set himself on fire if he didn't get a residence permit – so the agency can't afford to be complacent about security. Oh yes, we get all sorts in here.'

Henrik leaned back in his chair and glanced at Mia. She moved on to the next question.

'Is it possible to speak to the security officer who was on duty on Sunday?'

'This past Sunday? When Hans . . .'

'Yes.'

'I'll see what I can do.'

Lena picked up the phone, punched in a number and waited. By the time she hung up, the security firm had promised to send over Jens Cavenius, the guard who had been on last Sunday.

'So did Hans mention feeling threatened in any way?' said Henrik.

'No,' said Lena.

'No strange letters or phone calls?'

'Not that I saw, and I open all the mail . . . No, I haven't seen anything.'

'Do you know if he had any contact with a child?'

'No. Not specifically. Why do you ask?'

Henrik declined to answer.

'When he was here, late evenings and Sundays, do you know what he did?'

'I don't know exactly, but he was busy with paperwork and

48

reviewed lots of documents. He didn't like using the computer, so I had to print out all the documents and reports for him.'

'Were you usually here with him when he was working?' said Mia, pointing at Lena with her pen.

'No, not on Sundays. He wanted to be by himself. That was why he liked working evenings and weekends: there was no one to disturb him.'

Mia nodded and wrote in her notepad.

'Do you have a list of the names of all the asylum seekers that we can take with us?' said Henrik.

'Yes. Of course. For this year, or further back?'

'This year's list would suffice to start with.'

Lena's fingers rattled across the keyboard for a couple of minutes and then her laser printer sprang to life, delivering page after page of names listed in alphabetical order. Lena picked the sheets up as they came out. After twenty pages, a warning light began to flash.

'Typical! Useless thing's always going wrong,' she said, turning red in the face. She opened the paper tray which – to her surprise – was not empty.

'Oh, what's the matter now?' She pushed the tray back in. The printer made a noise but again the red light indicated something was amiss.

'Technology is a wonderful thing, but only when it works,' she said in an irritated voice.

Henrik and Mia sat watching in silence.

Lena opened the tray, checked there was still some paper left, and closed it again, this time with a bang. The printer started up, but no pages came out.

'Oh, why are you being so difficult!' Lena hit the start button with her fist and the printer whirred to life. Embarrassed, she ran her fingers through her hair until all the pages printed out. As she handed them over, the phone rang. Jens Cavenius had arrived.

Jens Cavenius was leaning against a pillar in reception. The nineteen-year-old looked as though he had just woken up. His eyes were red, and his hair was flattened on one side and untidy on the other. He was wearing a lined denim jacket and white Converse sneakers. When he caught sight of Henrik and Mia, he approached with his arm extended to shake hands.

'Shall we sit down?' Henrik asked, gesturing toward a sofa and armchairs surrounded by two-metre-high plastic yucca palms. Some brochures in Arabic were in a display on the white coffee table.

Jens flopped on to the sofa, leaned forward and despite his bloodshot eyes, looked expectantly at Henrik and Mia. They sat down opposite him.

'You worked here on Sunday?' Henrik said.

'Yeah, that's right,' said Jens, clapping the palms of his hands together.

'Was Hans Juhlén here then?'

'Yep. I chatted a bit with him. He was the boss, like.'

'What time was it?'

'Around half past six.'

Henrik nodded at Mia, giving her the go-ahead to take over.

'What did you talk about?' she said.

'Well, it was more like we said hello to each other,' said Jens. 'Or nodded. I nodded to him when I went past his office.'

'Was anybody else here?'

'No, no way. On Sundays it's dead here, like.'

'When you went past Hans Juhlén's office, did you see what he was doing?'

'No. But I could hear him using the computer keyboard. You know, you've got to have good hearing to be a security guard, so you can notice sounds that might be weird or something. And my night vision is pretty good too. Out of all the candidates for the job, I did best in the test. Not bad, eh?'

Less than impressed by Jens' stellar test results, Mia rolled her eyes and turned toward Henrik, who was staring at one of the yucca palms, apparently lost in thought. She thumped him on the arm.

'Hans Juhlén's computer?' she said.

'Yes?' said Henrik.

'Seems he did use it after all.'

'Yes, all the time,' said Jens and clapped his hands.

'Then I think we should take it with us,' said Henrik.

'So do I,' said Mia.

OFFICER GABRIEL MELLQVIST WAS SHIVERING. HIS
shoes were leaking and the cold rain trickled from his cap down
the back of his neck. He didn't know where his colleague Hanna
Hultman had got to. Last he saw, she was standing outside number
36 ringing the doorbell. Their door-to-door enquiries had taken
them to at least twenty houses this morning. None of the residents
had seen anything of use. Not one sighting of a strange man or
woman. Hardly surprising, given that most of the residents weren't
at home on Sunday. They preferred to spend weekends at their
summer cottages, on golf courses, at horse-jumping competitions
and god knows what else. A mother had seen a little girl go by,
probably a playmate heading home for the evening, and Gabriel
wondered why she had even bothered to mention it to him.

He swore to himself and looked at his watch. His mouth was
dry, and he was tired and thirsty – clear signals that his blood
sugar was too low. Nevertheless, he continued to the next house,
which was set back from the street behind a high stone wall.

Door-to-door canvassing was not his favourite occupation.
Especially not in the rain. But the order had come from the
very top of the criminal department, so he'd no choice but to
get on with it.

The gates were closed. Locked. Gabriel looked around. From here he could hardly see Östanvägen 204 where the murder had been committed. He pressed the intercom next to the gate and waited for an answer. Pressed again and added a 'Hello!' this time. Gave the locked gates a bit of a push and they rattled. Where the hell was Hannah? He scanned the street and could see no sign of her. She wouldn't have gone down one of the parallel streets, not without telling him first. She'd never do that. He sighed, took a step back and walked straight into a puddle. Cold water filled his right shoe. Oh great! Just great!

He looked up at the house again. He longed to give up and go off to the nearest lunch place and get some grub. But then he saw something. Something that moved. He screwed his eyes up a little in an effort to see what it was. A security camera! He pressed the intercom, shouted a few times to elicit an answer and managed in his enthusiasm to suppress the sensation of dizziness that was gradually creeping up on him.

Forty minutes and ninety-eight kronor later, Henrik Levin had eaten his fill. The Thai buffet had consisted of far too many tasty dishes. Mia Bolander had accompanied him, but chosen something lighter, a salad.

Henrik began to regret his choice of lunch as soon as he got in the car. He felt heavy and drowsy and let Mia drive to the police station.

'Next time, can you remind me to have a salad too?' he said.

Mia laughed.

'Please?'

'I'm not your bloody mother! But all right. Does Emma want you to lose weight or what?'

'Do you think I'm fat?'

'Not your face.'

'Thanks.'

'She won't let you fuck her, is that it?'

'What?'

'I mean, you seem to want to go easy on the carbs, which means you want to lose weight. I read online that the biggest motivation for men to lose weight is because they want to have more sex.'

'All I said was, I should eat a salad next time. What's wrong with that?'

'Nothing.'

'Do you think I'm fat?'

'No. You're not fat. You only weigh eighty kilos, Henrik.'

'Eighty-three.'

'Sorry, eighty-bloody-three kilos. Why would you want to weigh any less?' Mia winked provocatively.

Henrik remained silent and kept his real reason for a change of diet to himself.

Mia didn't need to know that seven weeks earlier he had embarked on a low-carb diet. He was also aiming to get more exercise on weekdays. But it was hard to keep to his new lifestyle choices, especially when Thai food tastes so much better with rice. After work it was simpler: home, eat, play, bathtime, tuck the kids into bed, TV, sleep. His time with his five- and six-year-old when he got home was pretty much routine. Admittedly, he hadn't actually asked his wife if she'd mind him spending an hour, once or twice a week, at the gym. Hopefully Emma would say yes. But deep down Henrik was afraid the answer would be a firm *no*. When he'd asked her permission to play football with the local club on a Saturday, he'd been turned down. 'Weekends are for family,' she'd said. They should be out in the garden, visiting the zoo, going to the cinema – anything, so long as they were spending family time together. She'd made it clear that she resented his spending too little time with them.

But surely, if he went to a gym and got in better shape, they would have better and more frequent sex. To him it was a win-win situation.

Emma disagreed. She thought they needed to nurture their relationship by spending more time cuddling together.

Henrik didn't particularly like cuddling. He liked having sex. To him, sex was the greatest proof that you loved your partner. It didn't matter when or where you did it, as long as you did it. But for Emma, it had to be pleasurable and relaxing, and you needed lots of time and the right setting. Their bed remained her preferred spot, and then only when the children weren't awake. Since Felix, who was afraid of ghosts, insisted on going to sleep every night between them in bed, their opportunities for sex were few.

Henrik had to settle for the hope that things would get better. This past month he had felt more desire. And Emma had gone along with it too. Once, at any rate. Exactly four weeks ago.

Henrik smothered a bit of heartburn. Next time he'd stick to the salad.

Henrik and Mia entered the conference room to be greeted by the news that Officer Mellqvist had fainted while knocking on doors in Lindö. He had been found by an elderly lady who had heard her doorbell ring a number of times. But since she was confined to a wheelchair, she couldn't hurry to the door. When she finally opened it, she saw the policeman lying on the ground.

'Luckily, Hanna Hultman came to his aid. She found a glucose syringe in Gabriel's pocket and jabbed it into his thigh,' said Gunnar. 'So now you've had the bad news. The good news is, we found a security camera outside the lady's house.' Gunnar drew an X on the map that was displayed beside the timeline on the wall. 'Best of all: the camera's directed towards the street.'

The whole team was in the room. All except Jana, which pleased Mia.

'If we're lucky, Sunday's footage will still be on a server somewhere. I want you, Ola, to check it out.'

'Now?' said Ola Söderström.

'Yes, now.'

He got up.

'Hang on,' said Henrik. 'I've got a job for you as well. We've confiscated Hans Juhlén's computer and need to go through it.'

'Did the interview with Lena Wikström lead to anything?'

'She doesn't share Kerstin Juhlén's view of Hans. According to Kerstin, Hans always worked on his computer. According to his PA, he never did. I think it's a little odd that they would have such different impressions.'

Ola, Gunnar and Anneli Lindgren agreed.

'What's more, Lena didn't think Hans Juhlén was as stressed as his wife claimed,' said Henrik.

'So she says. If you ask me, he was bloody worried. I would be too if there had been a lot of shit thrown at me in the newspapers and threatening notes addressed to me,' said Mia.

'Exactly,' said Ola.

'Lena said there was always a security concern over asylum seekers who were denied asylum. So we've asked for a list of all the people who have sought asylum so far this year,' said Henrik.

'Fine, anything else?' said Gunnar.

No one had anything to add. With the exception of the potential CCTV footage, door-to-door enquiries had drawn a blank.

'No witnesses?' said Mia.

'No. Not a one,' said Gunnar.

'That's crazy!' said Mia. 'So we've got fuck-all to go on.'

'For the time being we have no witnesses. Zero. Nada. So we'll have to hope the security camera will give us something. Ola, see if we can get hold of the images right away,' Gunnar said. 'Then you can go through Hans's computer. Meanwhile I'll see if the call logs from the mobile phone network are ready. If not, I'll phone and pester them till they are. Anneli, you go back to the crime scene and see if you can find anything new. Anything at all would do in the present situation.'

CHAPTER
NINE

AT FIRST THE GIRL HAD CRIED HYSTERICALLY. BUT *now she felt calm. She had never felt like this before. Everything happened as if in slow motion.*

She sat with her heavy head bent over her thighs, her arms hanging limply from her sides, almost numb. The engine in the van in which they were travelling growled weakly. Her thighs were stinging. She had wet herself when her captors had gripped her hard and pushed a needle into her arm.

She peered at her left upper arm, trying to focus on the little red mark. It was really tiny. She giggled. Really tiny. Teeny weeny. The syringe was also really tiny.

The van jerked and the asphalt turned to gravel. The girl leaned her head back and tried to balance its weight so she wouldn't bang herself against the van's hard interior. Or against somebody else. They were sitting tightly packed, all seven. Danilo, who was next to her, had cried too. The girl had never seen him cry before, only smile. The girl liked his smile and always smiled back at him. But now he couldn't smile. The silvery bit of tape was stuck hard over his mouth, and he breathed in what air he could through his nostrils.

A woman sat opposite them. She looked angry. Terribly, terribly angry. Grrrr. The girl laughed to herself. Then she sank down again with her head against her thighs. She was tired and most of all wanted to sleep in her own bed with the doll she had once found at a bus stop. The doll with only one arm and one leg. But it was the finest doll the girl had ever seen. The doll had dark curly hair and a pink dress. She missed her doll dreadfully. The doll was still back there with Mama and Papa. She would fetch her later, when she came back to the container.

Then everything would be all right again.

And they would go back.

Home.

THE CCTV FOOTAGE HAD JUST ARRIVED BY messenger from the security firm. Ola Söderström opened the package, inserted the disk into his computer and began scanning through the images. Judging by the angle, the camera must have been about two metres above the ground, perhaps three, and provided adequate coverage of what was going on in Östanvägen, but unfortunately the rotating lens didn't reach all the way to Hans Juhlén's house. Still, the quality was good and Ola was pleased with the sharpness. He fast-forwarded past Sunday morning. A woman with a dog walked by, a white Lexus left the street and then the woman with the dog came back again.

When the clock counter showed 17.30, he slowed down the speed. The empty street looked cold and windy. The overcast weather made it hard to detect any movement and the street lighting was of poor quality.

Ola was wondering whether it would be possible to adjust the brightness so he could see the scene more clearly, when he caught sight of a boy.

He froze the image. The counter showed 18.14.

Then he let the recording continue. The boy darted across the street and vanished out of view.

Ola reversed the footage and studied the sequence again. The boy was wearing a dark hooded sweater which hid his face. He walked with his head down and both hands rammed inside the big pocket on his stomach.

Letting out a sigh, Ola rubbed his hand over his face and through his hair. Just a child on his way somewhere. He let the footage continue and leaned back with his hands clasped behind his head. Before long, he saw Kerstin Juhlén coming home from the walk with the dog.

When the counter showed 20.00, he still hadn't seen anything. No movement. Not a single person. Not a car had passed during those two hours. Only the boy. It was then that Ola realized what he had seen. Only Kerstin returning home – and the boy.

He got up so fast that the chair fell backward with a crash.

'You seem to be in a good mood.'

Gunnar gave a start when he heard Anneli Lindgren's voice. She stood in the doorway with her arms folded over her chest. Her hair was tied back in a tight ponytail that accentuated her clear blue eyes and high cheekbones.

'Yes, I've just been promised the call logs,' he said. 'It helped when I kicked up a fuss.'

'Well now, is that all it takes to put you in a good mood?' said Anneli.

'It's certainly a start. Shouldn't you be on your way?' Gunnar said.

'I'm waiting for some support. It's a big house; I can't get through it all on my own.'

'I thought you liked working alone.'

'Sometimes. But you tire of it after a while. Then it's nice to have some company,' said Anneli.

'But you don't have to go through everything again. Just gather up anything of interest.'

'Well, I never would have thought of that!' Anneli shook her head. 'What do you take me for, huh?'

'Talking of going through things,' said Gunnar, 'I've been tidying the storeroom and I came across some stuff that belongs to you.'

'You've been tidying the storeroom?'

'Yes. What of it?' Gunnar said and shrugged his shoulders. 'I needed to get rid of some junk and I found a large cardboard box with ornaments in it. Perhaps you'd like them back?'

'I can fetch them later in the week.'

'No, better if I bring the box to work. Now, if you'll excuse me, I'll see if those lists have arrived as promised.'

Anneli turned to leave and almost collided with Ola Söderström in the doorway.

Gunnar looked up at the commotion. 'What is it?'

'I think I've found something. Come and see!'

Gunnar got up from his desk and followed his colleague into the computer room.

Ola, twenty years his junior, was tall and thin with a pointed nose. He was dressed in jeans, a red checked shirt and a cap. Regardless of the temperature on the thermometer, be it minus or plus thirty degrees Celsius, he always wore a cap. Sometimes it was red, sometimes white. Sometimes striped, sometimes with a check pattern. Today it was black.

Gunnar had told Ola countless times not to wear headgear during working hours, but in the end he'd given up. The cap might be irritating, but Ola's wizardry with computers had earned him the right to wear it.

'Look at this.' Ola pressed some keys and the footage began to play. Gunnar saw the little boy on the film.

'He turns up at exactly 18.14,' said Ola. 'He cuts across the street and seems to be on his way up toward Östanvägen, toward Hans Juhlén's house.'

Gunnar observed the boy's movements. Stiff. Almost mechanical.

'Play it again,' he said when the boy disappeared from view.

Ola did as he was told.

'Freeze it there!' said Gunnar, moving closer to the screen. 'Can you zoom in?'

Ola pressed Ctrl + Z and the boy's image grew larger.

'He's got his hands in that hoodie pocket. But the pocket is bulging too much. He must have something else in there,' said Gunnar.

'Anneli found a child's handprints,' said Ola. 'Could it be this boy?'

'How old?' said Gunnar.

Ola looked at the figure. Although he was dressed in a large hooded sweatshirt, you could still make out the size of his body under it. But it was his height that decided the matter.

'I'd guess eight, perhaps nine,' said Ola.

'Do you know who's got a child of that age?'

'No.'

'Hans Juhlén's half-brother.'

'Shit.'

'Zoom in closer.'

Ola zoomed in again.

Gunnar put his face right up to the screen so he could examine the bulging pocket better.

'Now I know what he's got in his pocket.'

'What?'

'A gun.'

Henrik Levin and Mia Bolander were driving toward Finspång. They sat in silence, deep in their own thoughts as they passed a road sign advising them they had five kilometres to go.

Henrik pulled over to the side of the road so he could look up the address on the sat nav. According to the digital map they were 150 metres from their final destination; the navigator's voice told him to keep driving straight ahead at the next roundabout. Henrik followed the directions and approached the address, which was in the Dunderbacken district.

Mia pointed to an empty parking space next to a recycling station overflowing with discarded paper and packages. Somebody had put an old radio in front of the green bins.

'So this is where he lives, the half-brother,' said Mia. She got out of the car, stretched and yawned out loud. Henrik got out and slammed the car door on his side.

A few people were standing chatting in the grassy area between the low-rise apartment buildings. Nearby a couple of children played with a bucket and spade in a sand pit next to a set of swings. The chilly April weather had made their cheeks rosy. A man, presumably the father, sat on a bench next to them, fully occupied with his mobile phone. A woman in an ankle-length winter coat appeared, carrying a shopping bag in each hand. She stopped and said hello to a long-haired man who was unlocking a yellow Monark bicycle from a bike stand.

Henrik and Mia walked across the grass and looked for the building number. They entered number 34. A man was standing in the entrance hall pacing back and forth impatiently as if he was waiting for somebody.

Mia scanned the list of residents next to the lift and read the name for the third floor: Lars Johansson. They walked up the stairs and rang the doorbell.

Lars opened immediately. He was wearing underpants and a pale football jersey adorned with the Norrköping team's emblem. He stood there in front of them, unshaven, dark rings under his eyes, massaging his neck as if uncertain what to do next.

'Are you Lars Johansson?' Henrik asked, showing his warrant card.

'Yes, what's this about?' said Lars. 'I thought for a moment there you were journalists from one of those tabloids. The place has been crawling with them the last few days. Come in, come in.' He stepped aside to let them pass. 'I haven't cleaned recently so keep your shoes on. Have a seat in the living room, I'll just go put some trousers on. I must go for a pee too. Are you willing to wait?'

As Lars backed away toward the bathroom, Henrik glanced at Mia. She was shaking her head in disbelief as she made her way along the hallway.

The bathroom was straight ahead and they could see Lars, picking out a pair of grey cotton trousers from the laundry basket. Then he closed the door and locked it.

'Shall we?' said Henrik, and gestured politely for Mia to go first.

The kitchen was to the left. The door was ajar, giving them a view of worktops littered with piles of dirty plates and pizza cartons. A tied-up bag of rubbish sat in the sink. The bedroom opposite was rather small and contained an unmade single bed. The Venetian blinds were closed and Lego pieces of various sizes cluttered the floor. To the left of the bathroom was the living room.

Henrik hesitated, peering dubiously at the brown leather sofa. There was a duvet in one corner, suggesting that the sofa doubled as a bed. It smelled stuffy.

A flushing sound could be heard and Lars came into the living room wearing trousers that were five centimetres too short.

'Sit down while I . . .' Lars tossed the pillow and duvet on to the apricot-coloured linoleum. 'There now, take a seat. Coffee?'

Henrik and Mia declined and sat down on the sofa, which made a hissing sound under their weight. The smell of sweat was pervasive and made Henrik feel queasy. Lars sat down on a green plastic stool and pulled his trousers up another two centimetres.

'Lars,' Henrik began.

'No, call me Lasse. Everyone does.'

'OK, Lasse. First and foremost, our condolences.'

'For my brother, yeah. Bloody awful, that.'

'Did it upset you?'

'No, not really. You know, we weren't exactly best buds, him and me. We were only half-brothers, on our mum's side. Just because you're related, doesn't mean you spend loads of time together. It doesn't necessarily mean you even like each other.'

'Didn't you get on?'

'Yeah, or perhaps . . . hell, I don't know.'

Lasse thought about it for a second or two. He lifted one leg, scratched his crotch and in doing so exposed a hole the size of a large coin. Then he started to talk about his relationship with his brother. How it wasn't that good. They'd had no contact whatsoever the past year. All because he used to be a gambler. But he didn't gamble now. He'd given it up for his son's sake.

'I could always borrow money from my brother when things were really bad. He didn't want Simon to go without food. It's tough living on welfare and, you know, you've got to pay the rent and so on.'

Lasse rubbed the palm of his hand against his right eye, then went on: 'But then things got strange. My brother went all stingy, claimed he didn't have any money. As if! You live in Lindö, you've got money.'

'Did you ever find out what was going on?' said Henrik.

'No, all I know is he said he couldn't lend me anything. His old lady had put a stop to it. I promised to pay him back, even though it wouldn't be for a while, but he still wouldn't give me any money. He was an idiot. A stingy idiot. He could have done without a steak dinner one evening and given me a hundred kronor, couldn't he?' Lasse thumped his chest. 'I would have, if I were him.'

'Did you argue with him about money?'

'Never.'

'So you've never threatened your half-brother or exchanged harsh words?'

'The odd curse word, perhaps, but I would never have threatened him.'

'You have a son, right?' Mia went on.

'Yes, Simon.' Lasse pointed to a framed photo of a smiling boy with freckles.

'Mind you, he's only five in that photo. Now he's eight.'

'Have you got a better picture of him, a recent one?' said Henrik.

'I'll have a look.'

Lasse reached into a white cupboard with glass doors and pulled out a little box crammed with odds and ends. Sheets of paper, batteries and electric cables, all tangled together. Henrik could see a smoke detector, a headless plastic dinosaur and some sweet wrappers.

'I don't know if I've got a recent one. The photos they take at school are so hellishly expensive. They charge four hundred kronor for twenty pictures. Who can order those? Bloody daylight robbery.'

Lasse let the sheets of paper fall on to the floor so he could get a better look at the contents of the box.

'No, I haven't got a good one. But come to think of it, I might have one in my mobile.'

Lasse disappeared into the kitchen and came back with an old-fashioned flip phone in his hand. He remained standing and pressed the buttons.

Henrik noticed that the arrow button was missing and Lasse had to use his little finger to browse through the picture folder.

'Here,' said Lasse, and held the mobile toward Henrik, who took it and looked at the photo on the screen.

A low-res image showed a short, stocky, still-freckled boy. Reddish cheeks. Friendly eyes.

Henrik complimented Lasse on his son's good looks, then asked him to send the picture via MMS to him. Within a minute he had saved it in his image archive.

'Is Simon at school?' said Henrik as he put his telephone back in his pocket.

'Yes, he is,' said Lasse, sitting down on the stool again.

'When does he come home?'

'He's with his mum this week.'

'Was he with you last Sunday?'

'Yes.'

'Where were you between five and seven in the evening?'

Lasse rubbed his hands up and down his shins.

'Simon played his video games.'

'So you were both here, at home?'

He rubbed again.

'No. Only Simon.'

'Where were you?'

'Er . . . an early poker evening, you know, down the block. You've got to join in when your mates ask you. But this was the last time. Absolutely the last time. Because I don't gamble. Not any more.'

ELEVEN

THE MAN WITH THE SCAR PACED BACK AND FORTH.
He glared at them with a wild look in his eyes as they stood there in a row, barefoot on the stone floor. The windows were covered but in one or two places a sliver of light shone in between the planks.

The girl's lips and cheeks ached from the glue of the silver tape they had slapped across her mouth. She had had difficulty breathing through her nose when they were in the van. Then, later, when they were pushed into the little boat, she had felt sick and been forced to swallow the vomit which had risen in her throat. The woman had ripped the tape off when they finally got to the big room, or hall, or whatever this place was.

The girl looked around without moving her head. Big beams supported the ceiling and she could see many spiders' webs. Was it a stable? No. It was much bigger than that. There were no rugs and no mattress to sleep on. It couldn't be someone's house. At least, it didn't look like one, except for the stone floor. The girl had a stone floor at home too. But there the stones were always warm. Here, they were icy cold.

The girl shuddered but immediately straightened up again. She tried to stand up as straight as she could. Danilo, too, had pushed out his chest and raised his chin. But not Ester. She just cried. She held her hands in front of her face and refused to stop.

The man went up to Ester and said something in a loud voice. She didn't understand what he said. Nor did any of the other children. So Ester cried even louder. Then the man raised his hand and hit her so hard she fell down. He waved to the other two grown-ups who stood by the wall. They got hold of Ester's arms and legs and carried her out. That was the last time she saw Ester.

The man walked slowly towards her, stopped, then leaned forward until his face was only a couple of centimetres away from hers. With eyes cold as ice, he said something in Swedish which she would never forget.

'Don't cry,' he said. 'Never cry. Never ever.'

CHAPTER
TWELVE

MIA BOLANDER SAT WITH THE OTHERS IN THE conference room for the last briefing of the day. They were reviewing the latest developments in the Hans Juhlén murder investigation. The most significant lead so far was the boy whose picture was now displayed on the large screen.

Tracing the as yet unnamed boy was their number one priority. He was either directly connected to the murder, or he was a key witness in the investigation. Regardless, he had to be found. That meant yet more door-to-door enquiries in the hope someone could identify the boy.

Relieved that she had left all that tedious drudgery behind when she was promoted, Mia helping herself to the biggest cinnamon bun on the dish in the middle of the table. She had always been competitive – she had her brothers to thank for that. Five and six years older than her, the boys had fought constantly to show who was best, who could do the most press-ups, who could race to the corner first, and who could stay awake the longest. They would never let her win but, desperate to impress them, she had never stopped trying.

At school, her competitive streak and volatile temper had got her into trouble. She frequently got into fights with her fellow pupils, and in her fifth year at school she hit a classmate so hard that she drew blood. She could still remember the boy; he used to tease her and throw gravel at her during PE lessons. He was also the only pupil who could beat her in the 100-metre dash. He hadn't gone unpunished. Mia kicked him so hard, he had to be taken to hospital to have the crack in his shin bone looked at. The headmaster had threatened to suspend her, but she claimed it was an accident and he let her off with a caution and a note on her record. Not that Mia cared; the important thing was that she had won the next 100-metre race.

Mia gobbled up the rest of the bun. The granulated sugar fell on to the table and she scooped it all into a tiny mound, then licked her fingertip and used it to pick up the sugar and put it in her mouth.

Mia had almost no friends during her school years. When she was thirteen, her eldest brother died in a gang fight. Growing up in a tough neighbourhood where teens did anything they could to stand out from the crowd – piercings, dyed hair, partly shaved hair, no hair, tattoos, tribal scars, open wounds (Mia pushed a needle through one eyebrow in an effort to fit in) – the thing that really set Mia apart from the rest was her attitude. Determined not to end up like her loser brother, she graduated with the qualifications she needed to make something of herself.

After helping herself to another cinnamon bun, she held the dish out to Henrik. He shook his head.

The projection screen showed a frozen image of the boy from the security camera file. He was slightly turned away, crossing the street. Ola tapped his keyboard and the next image in the sequence appeared. He continued to display the images one by one as the team sat around the conference table, following the boy's progress until the last thing to disappear was his hood.

Henrik picked up his mobile and compared the images on the screen with the shot of Lasse Johansson's son Simon.

'The nephew is short and muscular,' he said. 'The boy on the CCTV is thinner.'

'Let me see.' Ola reached out for Henrik's phone and studied the image.

'And Simon has reddish hair. I think our guy is darker. That's what it looks like, anyway,' said Henrik.

'OK, so we can forget Simon. Which means we're back where we started. Who is this boy? We must get hold of him,' said Gunnar.

Next on the agenda was the telephone log. Usually Ola would have checked out each of the calls listed in the phone company's records, but he'd been tied up with the CCTV footage so Gunnar had taken on the task. He passed copies of the log around the table.

Henrik took a gulp of coffee and looked at the first page.

'Hans Juhlén's last call was on Sunday at 18.15 to the Miami pizzeria.'

Ola got up and noted the call on the whiteboard timeline.

'The phone call has been confirmed by the pizzeria and they also confirmed that he picked up the pizza at 18.40. You can see the other calls on the next page,' said Gunnar.

They all turned to page two.

'There weren't many,' said Henrik.

'No, and most of them were to or from his wife. There was an outgoing call to a car service, but nothing remarkable about that,' said Gunnar.

'What about texts?' said Mia.

'Nothing of interest there either,' said Gunnar.

Mia folded up the pages and threw them on to the table. 'So what do we do now?'

'We find the boy,' said Gunnar.

'Do we know anything about the half-brother?' Anneli wondered aloud.

'Not much,' said Henrik. 'Mia and I interviewed him. He is single, on welfare, he says, with shared custody of his child. And he's addicted to gambling.'

'Does he have a criminal record?' said Mia.

'No,' said Gunnar.

'My gut tells me he isn't involved in the murder,' said Mia.

'What do we think about Hans Juhlén's wife?' said Gunnar.

'I don't think she did it,' said Mia.

'I'm not convinced either,' said Anneli. 'We don't have any witnesses or any decent technical evidence.'

'The half-brother said something interesting when we saw him. Hans claimed to be broke, told Lasse he couldn't even lend him a few kronor,' said Henrik. 'Since we know he had received some threatening letters, we can assume somebody had a hold on him. Perhaps that's where the money went.'

'Could Hans have had gambling debts, too?' said Mia.

'Possibly. It would explain why he seemed so stressed, at least to his wife. Maybe it wasn't just the criticism his department was getting, but the threatening letters too.'

'Right, we'll use that as a starting point. Ola, I want you to check his bank accounts first thing in the morning,' said Gunnar.

'What about the computer?' said Ola.

'Bank statements first, then the computer. OK, everyone, we're done for today,' said Gunnar.

Henrik looked at the clock and swore to himself when he saw

it was already half past seven. Overtime again. Emma would have finished dinner and the children would have gone to bed by the time he got home. Oh hell!

He sighed and drank the last of the coffee, which was now cold.

Henrik Levin unlocked the front door as quietly as he could. He opened it hurriedly, stepped into the hall and nipped into the bathroom.

When he had finished, he washed his hands, then looked at his face in the mirror. The stubble had grown over the last three days, and it needed trimming more than he had thought. He couldn't face shaving now though. A shower perhaps.

Henrik ran his fingers through his brown hair and noted a grey hair on his temple. He pulled it out and let it fall into the washbasin.

'Hi.'

Emma poked her head into the bathroom. Her hair was clumsily done up in a bun on the top of her head. She was wearing a red velour jumpsuit and black socks.

'Hi,' said Henrik.

'You snuck in very quietly,' said Emma.

'I didn't want to wake the children.'

'How's your day been?'

'OK. And yours?'

'Fine. I managed to paint the hall drawers.'

'That's great.'

'Yeah.'

'White?'

'White.'

'I thought I'd take a shower.'

Emma leaned her head against the doorpost. A strand of hair fell on to her brow and she pulled it back behind her ear.

'What's the matter?' said Henrik.

'What?'

'It looks as if you want to say something.'

'No.'

'Are you sure?'

'Yes, sure.'

'OK.'

'There's a film on TV, I'm going to watch it in the bedroom.'

'I'll come soon, once I've had my shower.'

'And shave?'

'OK, I'll shave.'

Emma smiled and closed the door behind her.

Oh well, Henrik thought, and dug out his razor from the drawer. He'd be having a shave after all.

Fifteen minutes later, Henrik came into the bedroom with the towel wrapped around his hips. Emma seemed lost in some Oscar-winning drama, which probably meant he'd be forced to watch the tearful ending. At least there was no five-year-old in the bed.

'Felix?' he said.

'Asleep in his room. He made a ghost drawing for you.'

'Another one?'

'Yes,' Emma answered without taking her eyes off the huge TV on the wall.

Henrik sat down on the edge of the bed and glanced at the couple entwined around each other on the TV. Felix was in his own bed. Now perhaps there might be a chance to . . .

He put the towel aside, slipped in under the warm duvet and snuggled up close to Emma. He put his hand on her naked tummy, but her eyes stayed glued to the film. He leaned his head against her shoulder and stroked her thigh. He felt her hand on top of his, and they played with each other's fingers under the duvet.

'Emma,' he said.

'Mm-hm.'

'Darling . . .'

'Yes?'

'There's something I wanted to ask you.'

Emma didn't answer. She studied the couple on the screen who were now united in a long, intense kiss.

'I've been thinking . . . I'd like to start back at the gym. So I thought . . . if it's OK, I . . . I might go twice a week. After work.'

For the first time Emma took her eyes off the film. She gave him a disappointed look.

Henrik supported himself on one elbow.

'Please, sweetie?'

Emma raised her eyebrows. Then she very deliberately lifted Henrik's hand off her tummy.

'No,' she said, and returned her attention to the tear-jerker.

Henrik was still leaning on his elbow. Then he moved over on to his back with his head on the pillow and cursed himself. He knew better. He should have phrased his request in such a way that she couldn't say no. He stared up at the ceiling, then plumped up the pillow and turned his back to Emma with a sigh. No sex today either. And it was his own damned fault.

It had just started snowing when Jana Berzelius and Per Åström decided to leave The Colander. Per had suggested a restaurant dinner out to celebrate their judicial successes in a dirty divorce case, and Jana had finally given in. Cooking a meal to eat alone was not exactly her favourite pastime, nor was it Per's.

'Thanks for this evening,' said Jana, getting up from the table.

'Happy to do it again soon. If you'd like to,' said Per and smiled.

'No, I wouldn't,' said Jana and refused to return his smile.

'That was a dishonest statement.'

'Not at all, dear Mr Prosecutor.'

'It wasn't?'

'No.'

'May I remind you that you appreciate my company?'

'Not one bit.'

'A drink before we go?'

'I don't think so.'

'I fancy something with gin. It'll have to be the usual. You?'

'No, thank you.'

'Then I'll get two.'

As Per headed off to the bar, Jana reluctantly sank back into her seat. Outside, snow was beginning to settle on the ground. She turned away from the window to watch Per, who was talking to the barman.

She caught his eye and he waved from the bar the way small children often do, by opening and closing his hand. She shook her head at him and then looked toward the window again.

She'd met Per shortly after she joined the Public Prosecution Office. Torsten Granath had introduced them and asked Per to give her a run-down on routine procedures. He had given her some tips about good restaurants too. Also about music.

And asked her questions about all kinds of other things that weren't work related. Jana had kept her answers brief – when she answered at all. Per, unfazed, had continued his questioning. Feeling as if she were being interrogated, Jana had told him to stop. When she informed him that she did not like small talk, Per had merely grinned at her in a dreadfully stupid way. Their friendly relationship had continued ever since.

The restaurant was fully booked. The dining room felt rather cramped with all the winter coats, and the brown chequered floor was wet from snow tracked in on the guests' shoes. The buzz of voices was loud and the clinking of glasses quiet. There were a few lamps and a lot of candles.

Jana's eyes left the window and were again drawn to the bar, past Per and to the mirror shelf behind the barman. She looked at the selection on offer and recognized the labels: Glenmorangie, Laphroaig, Ardbeg. She knew they were classics, distilled in Scotland. Her father was a whisky drinker; Jana's interest was limited, but she had been brought up not to say no to a glass when it was offered. She preferred a glass of white, from a well-chilled bottle of Sauvignon Blanc.

Per came back and Jana looked suspiciously at the large measures in the glasses he put down on the table.

'How strong?' she said.

'A single.'

Jana glared at her dining companion.

'OK, OK, a double. Sorry.'

Jana accepted his apology. She sipped her drink and made a face at the dry, smoky taste.

Somewhat later, when they had emptied the contents of the glasses, and Per had insisted on ordering two more, the conversation turned to a recent case in Stockholm where two adolescents had lodged an appeal after a lay magistrate fell asleep while the court was in session.

'I've said it before and I'll say it again, the lay-magistrate system should be radically changed. Instead of political nominees they should appoint people who care about law and justice,' said Per.

'I agree,' said Jana.

'You want people who are dedicated. After all, their votes on the magistrates' bench are decisive.'

'Absolutely.'

'It's totally unacceptable that we have to incur the expense of a retrial because some lay magistrate dozed off. He should be docked his pay. Unbelievable,' said Per.

He took a gulp of his drink, then leaned across the table and gave Jana a serious look. Jana met his eyes. Serious too.

'What?' she asked.

'How are you getting on with the Hans Juhlén murder?'

'You know I can't say anything about that.'

'I know. But how's it going?'

'It's not going.'

'What's happening?'

'You heard what I said.'

'Can't you tell me a little? Off the record?'

'Drop it.'

'Is there some dirt there?' Per smirked at Jana and his eyebrows went up and down. 'Bit of a dirty story there, right? There's usually some dirt when it's about bosses.'

She rolled her eyes and shook her head.

'I interpret your silence as a yes.'

'You can't—'

'Can't I? Cheers, by the way!'

CHAPTER THIRTEEN

Wednesday, 18 April

JOHN HERMANSSON FOUND THE BOY.

Seventy-eight years old and a widower for five years, John lived at Viddviken, a little village by the coast, five kilometres from Arkösund. The house was too large for a single man and required far too much upkeep. But what kept him there was his love of the natural surroundings. Troubled by sleepless nights since his wife died, he would get up at first light and go for a long walk, regardless of the weather. Even on a damp, chilly morning like this.

He'd stepped into his wellingtons, pulled on his anorak and set off just as the sun was starting to rise. As he passed through the gate and looked back at the garden shrouded in frost, he decided to skip the forest for once and go down to the sea instead. It was only a couple of hundred metres to the shore and the rocks facing Bråviken Bay. He followed the narrow lane, the gravel crunching under his feet, as it turned off to the right and after the two big pine trees he came to the sea. Usually the bay was anything but tranquil, with waves pounding the rocks, but today the sea was like a mirror in front of him. John took a deep breath and watched it form a cloud as he exhaled. He was about to turn back when he caught sight of something by the shore. Something silvery that glistened. He went closer to the ditch and bent down to look. It was a gun and it had blood on it.

John scratched his head. A bit further away, the grass was red. But his eyes fastened on what was lying under the fir tree. A boy. He lay on his side, his eyes wide open. His left arm was bent at an unnatural angle and his head was covered in blood.

Nausea overwhelmed him. Breathing heavily, John tried to turn away but his legs failed him and he had to sit down on a rock. Unable to get up again, he sat there with his hand over his mouth, staring at the dead boy.

In his heart he knew that this horrific scene would be etched in his memory for the rest of his days.

The call came through to Norrköping police at 05.02 a.m.

Thirty minutes later two patrol cars turned down the gravel lane at Viddviken. Five minutes after that, the ambulance came for John Hermansson, who was still sitting on the rock by the sea. A man delivering newspapers had noticed the old guy and asked him if everything was OK. He had pointed at the dead boy and then rocked back and forth and made a strange mumbling noise.

Just after 06.00 another police car turned down the lane.

Gunnar Öhrn hurried across to the ditch, closely followed by Henrik Levin and Mia Bolander. Anneli Lindgren, who had paused to retrieve her forensic examination kit from the boot, was last to arrive.

'Shot,' she said, slipping on her latex gloves.

The boy's lifeless eyes stared at her; his lips were dry and cracked. His hooded sweater was dirty and discoloured by the coagulated blood. She took in the scene, pulled out her mobile and speed-dialled the medical examiner.

Björn Ahlmann answered after the second ring.

'Yes?'

'We've got a job for you.'

It was inevitable that the media would seize upon the story. As soon as the TT national wire service reported that a young boy had been found murdered, the Norrköping police press officer found himself fielding calls from dozens of journalists eager for more details. Since it involved a minor shot to death, the entire nation was gripped, and on the morning TV shows various experts were invited to give their views. The presence of a weapon near the body led many to assume the boy was involved in criminal activity, which sparked discussions about the level of violence among today's youth, and the tragic consequences.

When the phone rang with the news, it woke Jana Berzelius from her sleep. She got out of bed and took a shower, hoping it would wake her up. Thanks to Per, she had a dreadful hangover. They'd ended up having three glasses of Scotch – more than she could handle. And before that they had shared a bottle of wine with their meal and ignored the advice about drinking one glass of water for every glass of something stronger.

Feeling a little better after her shower, she swallowed a painkiller for her headache and stretched out on the bed for a few moments, her hair still wet. She counted slowly to twenty, then got dressed, brushed her teeth and looked for a packet of peppermint-flavoured gum. Only then was she ready for the meeting at the police station.

'We are here to summarize what we've been able to discover

about the boy who was found dead out at Viddviken this morning.'

Gunnar used a magnet to put up the photo on the whiteboard before continuing.

'Anneli, who is still at the scene, says the boy had been shot. She estimates that he died between 19.00 and 23.00 on Sunday night, though we'll need to wait for the medical examiner to confirm that. According to Anneli, broken vegetation around the body indicates that the boy was in motion, and his injuries are consistent with having been shot from behind.'

Gunnar took a sip of water and cleared his throat.

'At present we don't know whether the victim has other injuries or if he'd been sexually assaulted. Again, we'll have to wait for the autopsy – the medical examiner has given his word the report will be with us as soon as possible, hopefully tomorrow. The boy's clothing has been sent to forensics.'

He got up and went to stand by the map on the whiteboard.

'We're still combing the area, but as yet we haven't found any footprints or trace evidence left at the murder scene by the perpetrator. The only thing we can be relatively certain about is that the dead boy at Viddviken is the same boy who was seen on CCTV footage from Östanvägen.'

'And the murder weapon?' said Henrik.

'We don't yet know whether the weapon found near the body was used to shoot him. All we can say for certain is that the weapon found near the boy was a Glock, and Hans Juhlén was killed . . .'

'. . . with a Glock.' Henrik completed the sentence.

'Exactly. The serial number is as yet unknown. The weapon's been sent to the national lab. They'll examine the bullets still in the gun and let us know whether they're a match for the ones that killed Hans Juhlén. If they are, it supports the theory that this boy was somehow involved in Juhlén's murder. We've taken his fingerprints too.'

'And?' said Mia.

'They matched. The handprints and fingerprints in Hans Juhlén's house match the boy's,' said Gunnar.

'So he was there,' said Mia.

'Yes. And my first guess says he . . .'

'. . . is the murderer.'

Jana mumbled the words and felt a creeping sensation along her backbone. She was surprised at her own reaction.

'. . . is the murderer, exactly,' said Gunnar.

'But, what the hell, kids don't murder people. Not like that. And especially not here in Norrköping, not in Lindö. I think it's extremely unlikely he could have done it – or rather, done it alone,' said Mia.

'Perhaps. But right now we don't have anything else to go on,' said Gunnar.

'What's the motive?' said Henrik. 'And why would a child send threatening letters to a head of department at the Migration Agency?'

'It's up to us to find out whether the boy is the murderer or not. And we must find out who killed the boy,' said Gunnar, breathing heavily.

'Who is this boy?' said Mia.

'We don't know that yet either. Nor do we know why he was in Viddviken or how he came to be there. At least he wasn't in the water. His body was found on the shore, with his back turned against the sea,' said Gunnar.

'He was running away from somebody,' said Henrik.

'It seems so,' said Gunnar.

'No tyre tracks?' said Henrik.

'So far, we haven't found any, no,' said Gunnar.

'He came by boat then. And the perpetrator must have been on board,' said Henrik.

'But we can't exclude the possibility that he arrived by car or some other means,' said Gunnar.

'Witnesses?' said Mia.

'None. But we are checking the entire coast from Viddviken to Arkösund.'

'Who is he, though?' said Henrik.

Gunnar took a deep breath. 'So far he doesn't show up on our databases. Mia, I want you to check through all cases of missing children – new ones as well as old. Even those where the statute of limitations has expired and prosecution is no longer possible. Get a photo of the boy and talk to social services, schools and youth clubs. We might have to ask the public for help,' said Gunnar.

'Via the media?' said Henrik.

'Yes, but I'd rather not go down that route if we can avoid it. There would be such a . . . how can I put it? . . . such a circus.'

Gunnar pointed at the map on the wall. 'This is where the body was found. So we're looking for some sort of a boat or vehicle that passed Viddviken on the water between 19.00 and 23.00 Sunday night.'

He moved his hand upwards across the map.

'We've put in a unit to go door-to-door there, and there's a dog patrol going over the crime scene area.'

'What shall we do about Kerstin?' said Jana. 'If you can't

get me more evidence, I'll have to release her early tomorrow morning.'

'Perhaps she knows who the boy is?' said Mia.

'We must also ask her about her husband's financial situation,' said Gunnar.

'Ola, make sure you've scoured his bank accounts. Private, savings account, investments – you name it. Check them all.'

Ola nodded in response.

'Henrik, interview Kerstin again. We haven't finished with her. Not by a long way,' said Gunnar.

CHAPTER
FOURTEEN

IT HAD HURT. SHE KNEW IT WOULD. SHE HAD HEARD
it through the walls. But she didn't know it would hurt so badly.

One of the grown-ups had told her to follow him into the dark storeroom. There he had tied her hands behind her back and forced her head forward. With a sharp piece of glass he carved her new name on her neck. It said KER. From now on that was what she would be called, that was who she would become and remain forever. While the man with the ugly scar gave her an injection, he had conveyed to her that she would never be hurt again, nothing would happen to her now. Even as the sense of calm spread through her body, a strength began to grow within her. She didn't feel fear any longer. She felt powerful. Undefeatable. Immortal.

The grown-ups made her stay in the storeroom with her hands tied so she wouldn't touch her wound until it had healed. When she was finally let out, she felt weak and cold and had no appetite.

The girl tried to see the carved letters in a mirror but she couldn't. She put her hand on the back of her neck. It stung; the skin was still sensitive. A scab had formed and the girl couldn't help fingering it, but then it started to bleed. She was angry with herself and tried to stop the bleeding by applying pressure with the sleeve of her sweater. But the red stains on the cloth grew larger each time she pressed it against her neck.

She looked at her arm in front of her. The stains were large and she turned on the tap and held her arm under it to try to get rid of the blood. But it didn't help, it only got worse. Now the sleeve was bloody and wet.

She leaned against the wall and looked up at the ceiling. The glow from the round lamp was weak and there were dead flies inside the glass globe. How would they punish her now? She wasn't meant to touch her neck. They had warned her. The wound had to heal completely. If you touched it, it would look much worse. Ugly.

She slid down to the floor with her back against the wall. The break was soon over; she couldn't stay much longer in the toilet. How long had she had been on the island? A month? Perhaps several months. The trees had lost all their leaves. She had thought the golden-brown leaves were so lovely. At home she had never seen a tree change colour like that. Every time she stood to attention in the yard, she wished she could cast herself into the piles of golden leaves. But she never could. She was only allowed to fight. All the time. Against the wiry boy Minos. And even against Danilo. He was bigger and stronger than she, so she hadn't been a match for him. He tried not to hit her too hard, but eventually he had to. If you didn't fight, you got beaten, beaten a lot, so Danilo hit her. At first he tried to be careful, a light thump and a slap. But then the man with the ugly scar had lifted him up so violently by his hair that he pulled clumps of it out.

She had tried to defend herself; she had attacked Danilo with kicks and blows, but nothing helped. In the end, Danilo had punched her so hard with his fist that he split her lip. It was swollen for three days. Then it was time for the next fight. This time she was pitted against another boy who was one year younger than her. When he deliberately aimed a blow at her painful lip, she became furious and slammed the boy on his ear so hard that he collapsed on to the floor. She kept on kicking and punching him until the man with the scar stopped her. Then he smiled. He pointed at his eyes, his throat and his crotch.

'Eye, throat, crotch,' he had said. Nothing else.

The girl heard the bell ring. It was time for the next lesson.

She wrung out her wet sleeve as tightly as she could. The water dripped on to the floor and formed a little puddle. She stretched out her hand to rip off some paper and wiped up the water. Then she got up and flushed the paper down the dirty toilet.

She rolled up her sleeve to hide the bloody stains, unlocked the door and went out.

FIFTEEN

PETER RAMSTEDT WAS IN A FOUL MOOD WHEN HE picked up the phone, refusing Levin's request that he attend a second interview with Kerstin Juhlén before he'd even finished speaking. When the detective persisted, he replied through gritted teeth that he was far too busy to call at the station this afternoon at the time the chief inspector proposed.

'Since my client is particularly anxious I be with her and I am at present in court, it would be more suitable if the interview take place this evening or tomorrow morning,' said Ramstedt.

'No,' said Henrik.

'I beg your pardon?'

'No,' said Henrik. 'This can't wait. You may not be aware of this, but we're in the middle of a murder investigation here – we need to talk to Kerstin Juhlén now.'

There was silence at the other end. Then the lawyer spoke slowly and precisely, as if addressing a complete imbecile.

'You may not be aware of this, but as her legal representative I must be present in order for the interview to take place.'

'Fine, in that case you'd both better be here at eleven this morning.'

And with that Henrik ended the call.

★

At two minutes to eleven the lawyer stormed into the interview room to join Kerstin and the others. His face was bright red. He set his briefcase on the floor with a deliberate thud and sat down next to Kerstin. He gave Henrik and Jana a condescending smile, putting his mobile phone in the pocket of his striped jacket. Then the interview began.

Henrik started by asking some direct simple questions about Hans Juhlén's finances, which Kerstin answered in a soft voice. But when he moved on to more specific details, she pleaded ignorance.

'Like I told you, I didn't have access to all of my husband's accounts and have no idea how much was in them.' But she did say that his salary was transferred to a joint current account which covered their mortgage payments and household bills.

'He was the one who took care of all our financial affairs,' said Kerstin. 'After all, it was his salary that paid for everything.'

'As a couple, would you say you were quite well off?' said Henrik.

'Yes, very.'

'But you said he wasn't one to waste money?'

'That's right.'

'Was that why he didn't help his brother with money?'

'What has Lasse been saying? Did he tell you he didn't get any money from Hans?' Kerstin's voice had risen in pitch.

Henrik didn't answer. He stared at her pink T-shirt. A loose thread was dangling from one sleeve. He had the urge to reach across the table and pull it out. How could she just leave it hanging there?

'He did get money from Hans,' said Kerstin. 'Far too much money. Hans did his best to help him, but Lasse gambled it all away. He didn't want Simon to suffer, so he transferred funds directly into an account in Simon's name. But Lasse was the boy's legal guardian, so he simply withdrew cash from the boy's account – and then lost it all on the horses. Of course my husband got angry and stopped sending money. Perhaps it was hard on the boy, but what else could he do?'

'According to Lasse, it was you who stopped the payments,' said Henrik.

'No, he's wrong.'

Kerstin put her thumb up to her mouth and started to gnaw on an already raw cuticle.

'He didn't receive any money recently?' said Henrik.

'No, not for the past year.'

Henrik pondered this, then looked at Kerstin again.

'We're going to look into your accounts,' he said.

'Why?' Kerstin met Henrik's gaze and continued biting her cuticle.

'To verify that what you've said is correct.'

'You need permission,' said Ramstedt, leaning across the table.

'It's already been arranged,' said Jana, and held out the signed search warrant.

Ramstedt snorted, leaned back and put his hand on Kerstin's shoulder. As she turned to look at him, Henrik noticed she'd developed a nervous twitch in her left eyelid.

'Well then,' said Henrik. 'I have one more question. This morning a boy was found dead. I have his photo here.'

He placed two high-resolution images, one from the crime scene and one from the security camera, in front of her.

She gave the pictures a cursory glance.

'So far we have only one suspect in the murder of your

husband, and that is you,' said Henrik. 'If you want us to release you and shift the focus of our investigation elsewhere, you must start cooperating. Please, look at these pictures again and think hard: have you ever seen this boy anywhere near your house?'

Kerstin studied the photos in silence.

'I have never seen him before,' she said. 'I swear, I've never seen him before. Never.'

'Certain?'

'Absolutely certain.'

Jana's headache had eased up, but she wasn't taking any chances, not with a mountain of paperwork to get through and three new cases that Yvonne had just dropped on her desk. Letting the tap run until the water was as cold as it would go, she filled a large glass and then took a second pill. When she was done, she rinsed the glass and put it away.

She was turning to leave when Torsten Granath came hurrying into the office kitchen. He went straight to the cupboard and took out a coffee mug.

'Busy?' said Jana.

'Always,' said Torsten, and swung around to place the mug on the tray of the coffee machine, but in his eagerness he lost his grip and the mug fell.

Instinctvely, Jana's right hand shot out and caught the mug before it hit the floor.

'Nice catch!'

Jana handed the cup to her boss, acknowledging the compliment with a slight nod.

'Did you play handball at that posh boarding school of yours?'

Jana remained silent. Accustomed to her taciturn ways, Torsten focused on making himself a cup of coffee without dropping or spilling anything.

'If I can't even manage a cup of coffee, perhaps I should retire!' he joked.

'Or at least take things a bit more slowly,' said Jana.

'No, I haven't time for that. How are you getting on with the Juhlén case, by the way?'

'I'll have to release his wife tomorrow,' she said. 'I've got nothing concrete to link her to the murder. Ramstedt's going to be delighted.'

'That man! For him the law is simply business.'

'And the women are his reward.'

Torsten gave Jana a broad smile. 'I trust you,' he said.

'I know.'

Jana knew he meant what he said. He had trusted her from the start. There had been stiff competition for the job, but he'd been impressed by her excellent grades and glowing references from her time as a trainee. And of course it didn't hurt that she was the daughter of former Prosecutor-General Karl Berzelius, who had influential contacts within the civil service in general, and Sweden's courts in particular. But nepotism had played no part in her graduating Uppsala University with the highest grades in her year. Her father would have felt proud when she was given her certificate. Or at least satisfied. She couldn't be certain because he wasn't there. Her mother had told her, 'Your father sends his greetings and congratulations,' as she handed over a bunch of carnations the colour of port wine, then gave her a pat on the shoulder and a smile that let Jana know she shouldn't expect more.

It had always been taken for granted that Jana would follow in her father's footsteps. To choose another career would have been unthinkable. So she'd secretly hoped Karl would come and congratulate her in person. But he didn't.

Jana scratched at her neck, then held her hands together over her chest. She looked at Torsten, who was still smiling, and wondered if he'd had a call from her father. Karl Berzelius had retired two years earlier, but it didn't stop him involving himself in Swedish jurisprudence. Especially cases his daughter was prosecuting. Twice a month he would phone Torsten to enquire how she was doing. This was something her boss couldn't possibly object to. And neither could Jana.

Karl was like that.

Forceful.

Controlling.

'Oh well, I must get on,' said Torsten, checking his watch. 'I have to be at the vet's at four – my wife is worried about Ludde. Thanks for catching the cup, you've saved us having to buy a new one.' He gave Jana a wink on the way out.

She remained standing beside the granite counter and watched him leave.

'You're welcome,' she said quietly.

The Juhlén bank account printouts ran to fifty-six pages. Ola Söderström started with the pages relating to Hans Juhlén's private account. On the twenty-fifth of each month the credit column showed a payment from the Migration Agency of seventy-four thousand kronor. Ola whistled at the impressive sum. It was a lot more than his salary of thirty-three thousand. Two days later, on the twenty-seventh, the debit column recorded a transfer of all but five hundred kronor. That had been the pattern over the past ten months.

It was when he started looking at the couple's joint account that he realized something was amiss. This was where the money from Hans Juhlén's account had been transferred to. Nothing strange about that; what was odd were the large withdrawals. Once a month, forty thousand kronor was withdrawn from the Juhléns' joint account.

Always on the twenty-eighth. Always at Swedbank. And always at Lidaleden 8.

The information about the large cash withdrawals reached Henrik Levin while he was in the police station lift. The reception on his mobile was poor, and so he had to concentrate to hear Ola's voice. He leaned against the lead-grey lift wall and held his head at an angle, keeping the phone as high as possible. When that didn't help, he stood as close to the doors as he could. The signal improved the moment he got out of the lift.

'So you're saying forty thousand kronor has been withdrawn from their joint account every month, on the same day and for the last ten months,' he said.

'Correct,' said Ola. 'The question is, what was the money for? To pay a blackmailer?'

'We'll have to find out.'

Henrik ended the call, and fast-dialled Mia.

'He paid out forty thousand a month?!' Mia said.

'I'm going to visit the branch in Hageby where the money was withdrawn. Do you want to come with me?'

'Can't, I'm only halfway done here,' said Mia. It was taking forever to go through all the reports of missing children and adolescents. She'd drawn a blank with social services, no one at the Migration Agency's refugee centres had recognized the boy, and so far she'd had no joy with teachers in the local junior secondary schools. If no one ID'd him by the end of the day, Mia would have to look further afield, starting with neighbouring municipalities.

'But it could be the case that this boy doesn't have any papers. He might be one of those illegal immigrants who's had no contact with the Migration Agency,' said Mia.

'It's possible, but he must have had some sort of contact – why else would he have shown up inside Juhlén's house?' said Henrik.

'True,' said Mia.

While they were talking, Henrik had exited the police building, unlocked his car, got in and started to drive. He was grateful that Sweden had yet to ban the use of mobile phones while driving.

'Perhaps it's simply a question of his parents not having noticed he's missing. Perhaps they don't read the papers, and think their son is staying with a friend or a relative or something,' Mia went on.

'If he were older, I'd say you're right. But a boy of eight or nine? I think most parents know where their children are at that age, and they'd soon contact the police if their kid didn't come home in time. Wouldn't you?' said Henrik, pulling up at a red light.

A mother with two small children crossed in front of him. Both children took big steps so as not to touch the black tarmac between the white pedestrian crossing lines. The blue bobbles on their caps bounced up and down with every step.

'Yes, I suppose I would, but not all parents react in the same way.'

'True.'

'Let's hope you're right though, and we do get a report of a missing boy. It would be good to find out who he is.'

'Either that or you strike it lucky at one of the schools you haven't checked yet.'

Henrik ended the call, put the phone down and gazed out at the street, his thoughts on the dead boy. It *was* strange that he still hadn't been reported missing. And stranger still that his finger- and hand-prints had been found in Juhlén's house. Could it be that Juhlén was a paedophile? Had the boy killed the man who abused him? The thought wasn't completely absurd, but it was unpleasant and he dismissed it.

Traffic was heavy on Kungsgatan and Henrik made slow progress past Skvallertorget and on toward the park. He took the third exit at the roundabout and continued down Södra Promenaden. It was a relief to reach the E22 and hit the accelerator, if only for a couple of kilometres until he took the exit for Mirum Galleria.

The big parking area was deserted, and when he got out of the car his steps echoed off the concrete slabs that surrounded him.

Ten minutes before closing, Henrik entered the brightly lit Swedbank branch office. Three customers were waiting with numbered tickets in their hands. A young cashier with back-combed hair was dealing with a customer at one window; the other counters were closed.

Henrik showed his warrant card and was asked if he could wait ten minutes until the bank closed. He took a seat in an egg-shaped armchair, and watched shoppers passing by to the tune of an advertising jingle which insisted everybody was welcome at H&M, which was located on the second floor of the mall.

'Thank you for waiting, Chief Inspector. Please, come with me.'

The cashier led Henrik to a small conference room. The bank manager, a shortish woman in her fifties with a flowery red blouse, joined them a moment later.

Henrik explained why he was there.

'I'm grateful that you came to us in person. As you know, we are bound by strict confidentiality rules. I spoke to your colleague earlier today,' said the woman.

'Ola?'

'Yes, Ola. We gave him all the details we could about the Juhlén account.'

'According to those details you supplied, Hans Juhlén withdrew forty thousand kronor every month here, at your bank. We need to find out why he withdrew such a large amount of money – it could have a bearing on our investigation.'

'We rarely ask what customers are going to use their money for, but when it comes to large cash withdrawals we insist on being given advance notice.'

'In which case, Hans Juhlén must have given you advance notice many times,' said Henrik.

'No, he wasn't the person who did it,' said the woman.

'Well, who then?'

'It was his wife, Kerstin Juhlén.'

CHAPTER SIXTEEN

GUNNAR ÖHRN WAS LISTENING TO THE CAR RADIO.
The DJ had just announced that the next track was the work
of a rock legend. When the first notes came out of the speaker,
Gunnar immediately recognized the voice of Bruce Springsteen
and began drumming on the steering wheel in time to the
music.

'The Boss! Oh yeah!' he yelled, turning up the volume.

He sneaked a glance at Anneli Lindgren in the passenger seat.
Unimpressed by his drum solo on the wheel, she'd closed her
eyes and was sitting with her head back against the neck-rest.

It was 15.30. She'd spent the last ten hours gathering evidence
at the murder scene in Viddviken. When Gunnar arrived, he'd
found her up to her waist in water. She walked back to the shore
to meet him.

'How are you getting on?' Gunnar had asked.

'I've taken some water samples,' Anneli replied, unfastening
the shoulder straps before pulling off her insulated waders. 'We've
combed the area. There's too much foot traffic to make it worth
even worth thinking about shoe prints.'

'Have you dragged the bay?'

'Twice, but we found no other weapons.'

'And the bullet? Did you find it?'

'Yes. We found something else too. Come, I'll show you.'

Gunnar had followed Anneli away from the bay and along the gravel road. After twenty metres, she stepped off the track and on to the grass verge, carefully bending back the undergrowth in front of her. Gunnar leaned forward to see what she wanted to show him. A smile spread across his face.

Tyre tracks were visible on the ground.

And they were deep.

Gunnar turned the volume down.

'Tired?' he said.

'Yes.'

'Can you manage a briefing? I've called everybody in for 4 p.m.'

'Sure.'

'I can give you a lift home afterwards.'

'Thanks, but I've got to get my car home – I'll be needing it later. Adam has his football practice at eight o'clock. Had you forgotten?'

'Oh Christ, yes! It's Wednesday.' Gunnar shook his head, annoyed with himself. 'But I can give him a lift too. I mean, if you want me to. We can all go together,' he said.

'Fine, if you'd like to . . . that'd be nice.'

Anneli rubbed under her eyes.

'Oh no,' said Gunnar, clapping his hand to his forehead.

'What's the matter?'

'I've forgotten it again – the big box in the attic.'

'That's OK.'

'But it's the last box with your things.'

'Well, if it's been up in the attic until now, surely it can stay there a bit longer.'

'This evening I'll put it right next to the front door. Then I'm certain to remember to bring it with me.'

'Good idea.'

There was silence for a few seconds.

'It's nice that you're coming along with us this evening. Adam will be happy,' Anneli said.

'I know,' said Gunnar.

'I'll be happy, too.'

'I know.'

'Won't you be happy?'

'Anneli, stop it. There's no point.'

'Why isn't there?'

'Because.'

'Have you met somebody?'

'No, I haven't. But we've decided to leave it like this now.'

'You've decided, yes. Not me.'

'OK, this time it was me. I really want it to be this way. I think things are OK between us. We keep it on a good level, I mean.'

'On your level.'

'What's that supposed to mean?'

'Nothing.'

'I was only trying to be friendly by giving you and Adam a ride.'

'You don't have to give us a ride. We can manage quite well without your help.'

'OK, let's skip it then.'

'Yes, let's do that.'

'Fine.'

'Fine.'

Gunnar muttered something, and turned up the volume on the radio just in time to hear Bruce Springsteen fading away.

Anneli walked a few steps behind Gunnar, glaring at his back, her lips pursed. She knew he could feel her eyes on him, so she glared a bit harder just for the sake of it.

Gunnar turned off when he came to his office.

Anneli spotted a fax from the National Forensics Lab, SKL, in his in-tray. Probably important. But she walked on without saying a word. He'd share the contents with her in his own time.

She carried on down the corridor until she came to the conference room. As she reached for the door handle she straightened up and tried to put on her 'work face', the mask of calm professionalism she wore when dealing with colleagues.

Since Anneli and Gunnar chose never to discuss their relationship with anybody, they never showed their feelings openly either. They had been a couple before she joined the criminal investigation unit in Norrköping. When the position of forensic technician was advertised on the police intranet, Anneli – who had all the necessary experience and qualifications – had sent in her application, addressed to the head of the relevant department, who just happened to be her lover. She couldn't see why it should be a problem, working alongside her life partner.

Gunnar, for his part, found himself in a dilemma. He considered setting Anneli's application aside because of a possible conflict of interest. But since her professional experience outshone that of all the other applicants, it would have been crazy not to employ her. His decision was made easier by the fact they'd kept their relationship secret. Anneli had agreed that they would continue to be as discreet as possible in their professional life.

But it wasn't long before the rumour of their relationship spread and allegations circulated that Anneli had landed the job because she was Gunnar's girlfriend. The gossip-mongers ignored her talent for discovering evidence that others missed, such as broken vegetation or a faint tyre track; in their eyes she'd got where she was by sleeping with the boss.

What most people didn't know was that Anneli and Gunnar had an on–off relationship. They shared a son, and for his sake they had tried to make a go of living together, but their commitment to one another just wasn't strong enough. In total, they had moved in together and then separated seven times. Their most recent stint of living together had lasted ten months, ending the previous month when their son celebrated his tenth birthday. This time around it had been Gunnar who told Anneli he wanted a break.

Anneli pushed aside all thoughts of Gunnar as she joined the others sitting around the conference table.

'A witness has seen a white van at Viddviken,' Mia told her, but she was prevented from going into more detail by Gunnar, who rushed in waving the fax from SKL.

'They've identified the fingerprints on the threatening letters,' he said. 'Where's Henrik?'

'He's interviewing Kerstin again. Evidently she's been lying about their financial affairs,' Ola replied.

'That's not the only thing she's lied about,' said Gunnar, turning to go back out the door. 'I need to get hold of Henrik right away!'

★

Peter Ramstedt's neck was bright red as he stepped into the interview room for the second time that day. The lawyer swung his briefcase up on to the table, grabbed a notepad and pen out of it and then dropped the case to the floor. He unbuttoned his jacket and swept the two sides back like a cape before settling down on the chair. Then he sat with his arms crossed, clicking his pen incessantly with his right thumb.

Henrik Levin smiled to himself, knowing he held the trump card. The statements from the bank staff had triggered the second interview, but it was only when Gunnar phoned him a moment ago that the last pieces of the puzzle had fallen into place.

'I'd like to ask you . . .' Henrik addressed Kerstin Juhlén, who was sitting with her shoulders hunched and yellow plastic slippers sticking out under the table, '. . . do you normally shop with cash or a bank card?'

Kerstin looked up at him.

'Card.'

'You never use cash?'

'No.'

'Never?'

'Well, on the odd occasion, perhaps.'

'How often would you say?'

'I don't know. Once a month, I should think.'

'Where do you withdraw your cash?'

Ramstedt continued to click his pen.

Henrik had an urge to grab the pen and squirt ink all over the lawyer's red tie.

Kerstin interrupted his thoughts. 'Well, when I need to, I use an ATM.'

'Which ATM?'

'The one in Ingelsta, next to the café.'

'Do you always go to the same one?'

'Yes.'

'How much money do you usually draw out?'

'Five hundred kronor.'

'You don't queue up in a bank to see a cashier?'

'No, never.'

Kerstin put her little finger to her lips and chewed at her nail.

'So you have never visited a bank?'

'Well, yes, of course I have.'

'When did you last visit a bank?'

'Perhaps a year ago.'

'What did you do when you went?'

'Perhaps it was even longer ago. I can't really remember.'

'So you haven't been in a bank since then?'

Silence.

Henrik repeated the question: 'So you haven't been in a bank since then?'

'No, I haven't.'

'Strange,' said Henrik. 'We have two witnesses who've given statements saying they've seen you in the bank in Hageby.'

Ramstedt stopped clicking.

In the silence that followed, Henrik could hear his own breathing.

'But I haven't been there,' said Kerstin anxiously.

Henrik got up and walked to one corner of the room. He stood underneath the camera fastened to the ceiling and pointed at it.

'Bank premises are fitted with cameras like this one which register all customers who come and go.'

'Hang on,' said Ramstedt, getting up too. 'I need to have a few words with my client.'

Henrik pretended not to hear him. He returned to the table and looked straight at Kerstin.

'So, I ask you again. Have you been to the bank at Hageby?'

Ramstedt put his hand on Kerstin's shoulder to stop her from answering.

But she answered anyway.

'Perhaps, I may have.'

Henrik returned to his seat. 'For what purpose were you there?'

'Withdrawing money.'

Ramstedt let go of Kerstin's shoulder, sighed and sat down again.

'How much money did you withdraw?'

'A few thousand. Two, perhaps.'

'Stop lying. You have withdrawn forty thousand kronor from your joint savings account every month for the past ten months.'

'Have I?'

'As I said, I have two witnesses, Kerstin.'

'Don't answer,' Ramstedt urged her, but again Kerstin ignored him.

'Well then, I must have, mustn't I,' she said quietly.

Ramstedt hurled his pen across the room in fury.

Henrik ducked even though the pen passed by him at a distance. It hit the door and fell to the floor. The detective looked at Ramstedt, then smiled to himself. He said nothing, which he knew would irritate the lawyer more than any verbal response. Then he calmly returned to the subject.

'What did you want the money for?'

'Clothes.'

'Clothes?'

'Yes.'

'You've spent forty thousand kronor a month on clothes?'

'Yes.'

'I don't mean to be offensive, but for that kind of money I think you can buy something better than a T-shirt and some plastic sandals.'

Kerstin hurriedly tucked her feet in under the table.

'For the last ten months either you or your husband have been received threatening letters,' he said.

'I don't know anything about that.'

'I think you do.'

'No, I don't. I swear. It was you who told me about the letters.'

'So you have never seen the letters? Never touched them?'

'No, no, no! I haven't. I haven't.'

'Once again, you are not telling the truth. We have analysed those letters and found fingerprints on them.'

'Oh?'

'Your fingerprints.'

Kerstin started looking around nervously.

'May I tell you what I think has been going on?' said Henrik. 'I don't believe you've bought clothes with that money. I think you have taken the money and given it to the person who sent the threatening letters. There were ten threatening letters and you have withdrawn a large sum of money ten times.'

'No . . . I haven't . . .'

'You disappoint me, Kerstin. It's time you told us the truth. What really happened?'

Ramstedt got up, adjusted his jacket and went to pick up his pen. Behind Henrik's back he tried, using body language, to warn Kerstin not to say another word.

But she swallowed. Drew a deep breath.

And started telling her story.

All of it.

Henrik lingered in the interview room and stared for a minute. The interview was over, but he was still thinking. He replayed the sequence in his head. When Kerstin's lip started to tremble. When she dried the tears on her cheeks. When she described what her husband had done.

'I don't think I ever really knew him. He was always absent in some way. He always has been . . . I knew something was wrong. I knew it when he wanted me to have a pillow or something over my face when we had sex. He insisted, otherwise he would feel sick to his stomach, he said.'

She stared down into her lap, tears dripping on to her hands.

'That was in the beginning, soon after we got married. He'd do such strange things. I'd wake up in the middle of the night and he'd be lying there, staring at my breasts. And when he saw I'd woken up, he'd shout at me that I was a stupid fucking cunt and then he'd ram in his . . . his . . .'

Kerstin couldn't get the words out. She wiped her nose on her sleeve, swiped the tears from her eyes, took a breath and continued:

'He'd ram his penis so far down my throat I couldn't breathe. I'd be choking, and then when he was finished, he'd tell me I was so disgusting he needed to go and wash himself after having been with his ugly wife.'

She was hugging herself tightly as if trying to contain the hurt, sobbing like a child. Henrik said nothing, waiting patiently until she calmed down. Then she went on:

'He never really wanted to sleep with me. I thought it would get better. I told myself someday everything would get better, that it was all too much for him – his work, I mean – and I should feel sorry for him. But then he started to have sex with other women . . . and girls. He started . . . they must have been afraid, they must have been afraid of him. I don't understand how he could, I . . .'

She shuddered as the memories came flooding back to her.

'He told me how one woman screamed when he raped her on the floor. How the panic in her eyes grew when he penetrated her. How he laughed when she started to bleed from her behind. And then . . . while she was bleeding . . . and he . . . down her throat . . .'

Kerstin covered her face with her hands and laid her head on the table.

'Oh, god . . .' she cried.

Henrik could still hear her crying, even though he was now alone in the room. He looked out of the window and stared at the pale grey light. Then he got up. In half an hour, he had to be in the conference room with the team. He needed to compose himself.

Henrik Levin slowly made his way up the stairs and along the deserted third-floor corridor where the conference room was. He kept his gaze directed at the floor in front of him, never once looking up or casting a glance through the open office doors on either side.

Alarmed by the expression on Henrik's face, Gunnar Öhrn

asked if he needed a break before debriefing the team. But Henrik insisted he would prefer to do it now. Gunnar pulled out a seat for him but he opted to remain standing.

'The threatening letters were directed at Hans Juhlén,' he began. 'Juhlén had sexually abused several female asylum seekers, and in return they were promised permanent residence permits. But the permits never materialized.

'When the first letter arrived, Kerstin realized immediately that it was written by someone connected to one of these women. She suspected it was the brother of a young girl who had been subjected to a particularly brutal rape by her husband. She knew about the rape because Hans Juhlén was in the habit of boasting about his so-called "conquests". How naive the girls were. How they cried when he degraded them and forced them to have sex.'

Anneli Lindgren felt so uncomfortable hearing this she was squirming by the time Henrik paused to draw breath. Then he continued:

'Kerstin made sure that Hans never saw the letters. Initially, she considered going to the police to bring an end to the rapes. But she was afraid he would divorce her, and she didn't know who she would be without her husband. Who would look after her? She didn't have any money of her own; no way to support herself. And if the story got out, it would be the end of her husband's career, he might even get sent to prison and then she wouldn't have any money to live on. Besides, everybody would scorn her for having been married to a rapist. So she decided to hide the letters and pay. For silence,' said Henrik.

'How can you protect somebody who treats you so badly?' said Mia.

'I don't know. Hans Juhlén was a nasty piece of work. According to Kerstin, he turned on her soon after their wedding when he found out that she could never have a child. He reminded her of her failings every single day. He crushed her.'

'And she let him do it?'

'Yes.'

'But didn't he notice all that money being withdrawn from the account?' said Gunnar.

'Oh yes, he asked her about the withdrawals, but Kerstin lied and said they were for purchases for their home or to pay a repair bill or something of that nature. He flew into a temper and hit her. But she stuck to her story. And after a while, even though her excuses never made sense, he lost interest in it – and in his wife. In any event, she says he stopped asking her about it,' said Henrik.

'Who did the threatening letters come from?' said Mia.

'Yusef Abrham. He's originally from Ethiopia but now lives in Hageby, where he shares a flat with his sister. That's why Kerstin always withdrew the money from that particular branch. We'll talk to Abrham straight after this meeting. Is it OK if I . . .' Henrik indicated an empty chair.

'Of course, of course – sit down,' said Gunnar. 'You don't need to ask permission.'

'No, you can just bloody well sit down,' said Mia.

Henrik sat down, opened a bottle of mineral water, poured half the contents into a glass and drank it.

Jana Berzelius had been sitting in silence, observing, at the far end of the table.

'Has Kerstin confessed to anything else?' she asked.

Henrik shook his head.

'Then there's nothing concrete to link her to the murder,' said Jana. 'So I have no choice but to let her go.'

'Kerstin did of course have every reason to want to see her husband dead, given how he had treated her,' said Mia. 'They might well have argued, and in the heat of the moment she pulled out a gun and shot him.'

'But how would she have got her hands on a gun? And after shooting him, then what? Did she give the gun to a child who climbed out through the window? And who was this child?' said Henrik.

'I don't know. Think of something yourself, then!' Mia hissed.

Henrik gave her a tired look.

'OK, now let's all calm down,' said Gunnar. 'Jana's right: we have to release Kerstin, at least for now.'

'What about Lasse Johansson?' said Jana.

'He's of no interest; his alibi has been confirmed by several people.'

'So all we have is the unnamed boy and this Yusef Abrham?'

'And whatever is on Hans Juhlén's computer,' said Gunnar.

'Right,' said Ola Söderström. He shifted his weight on the chair. 'It's a slow process, but I'm working on the hard drive. The strange, or perhaps the most revealing, thing is that someone tried to wipe it.'

'Wipe it?' said Mia. 'But you can retrieve deleted files, can't you?'

'Absolutely. Deleted documents and cookies remain on the hard drive and can be recovered . . . so long as the hard drive hasn't been bombarded with EMP.'

Seeing the puzzled looks exchanged by his colleagues, Ola added: 'Electromagnetic pulse. It knocks everything out.'

'There must have been something he wanted to hide,' said Henrik.

'Perhaps. We'll have to wait and see what I can salvage.'

SEVENTEEN

'I TOLD YOU IT WAS DIRTY.'

Per Åström gave Jana Berzelius a wide smile.

They'd bumped into each other outside the Public Prosecution Office, decided to skip the coffee machine upstairs and go to the bakery café. Jana had thought about going for a ham and cheddar on sourdough, but in the end they both ordered a cup of coffee and a scone with jam. They were now sitting at a table next to the window.

The interior was typical of modern Scandinavian design, and it felt a bit like sitting in a hotel lobby. Black leather chairs were squeezed around oval oak tables. Armchairs with high backs stood in pairs in the corners. Lightshades of different sizes in black-and-red cloth hung from the ceiling, and a pleasant aroma of newly baked bread permeated the room.

'I'm beginning to regret having told you anything about the investigation,' Jana said to Per.

She had told him in confidence about Hans Juhlén's darker side.

'Why? I find it rather fascinating. Can you imagine what the media will make of it when they find out the boss at the Migration Agency was abusing female asylum-seekers!' Per said.

'If you don't keep your voice down, the papers will find out extremely quickly.'

'Sorry.'

'It's a complicated investigation.'

'Tell me more!'

'Not a word to anyone about what I say.' Jana gave Per a piercing look. 'OK?'

'I promise.'

'So here's the thing: Hans Juhlén was shot. In his house the police found handprints and fingerprints from a child. The same child was later found shot to death – with the same type of gun that was used to kill Hans Juhlén. And then there's this business with the girls . . .'

'The dirty—'

'Call it what you like. But can you explain to me how it all fits together?'

'No.'

'Thanks.'

'You're welcome.'

Jana lifted the coffee cup to her lips. She looked at Per, at his stylish, beautifully tailored clothes. Per had been single for as long as she could remember. He'd had a couple of longish relationships but didn't seem to feel comfortable living with anyone.

'Better alone on your own, than alone in a relationship,' he had told her once.

Jana knew that his work as a prosecutor and his commitment to helping vulnerable adolescents took up all his time. It was not in her interest to try to interfere with anybody's life. Not even Per's.

There had been times when conditions seemed ripe for

something to develop, but there was no chemistry between them. As far as Jana was concerned, Per was a friend and a colleague. Nothing more.

'I need your help,' she said, setting her coffee cup on the table.

'But I don't know how everything fits together,' said Per.

'I don't mean with the investigation. I need to switch work days with you.'

'Why?'

'Dinner with Mother and Father on the first of May.'

Per angled his head to one side and whistled.

'Fine.'

'I'll buy you a nice bottle of wine as compensation. Red or white?'

'Neither. I'll do it for you gratis, but first you must tell me more about that filthy Hans. I'm thinking of selling the story myself. I'll make a fortune out of it!'

'You're impossible.'

Jana forced a smile and took a bite of her scone.

Makda Abrham saw them coming from the kitchen window. She knew right away it was about the man at the Migration Agency. She'd known this day would come when she would be forced to tell them all about the evil she'd been subjected to.

The worry grew in her tummy and when she opened the door the pressure was so hard on her diaphragm she had to support herself against the wall. She barely registered the names of the police officers and she didn't even look at the ID cards they showed.

'We're looking for Yusef Abrham,' said Henrik and put his ID away. He studied the woman in front of him. Young, perhaps twenty, dark eyes, slim face, long hair, a cloth bracelet and a sweater with a low neckline.

'Why?' she said.

'Is he at home?' said Henrik.

'Me . . . sister. Why?'

Makda found it hard to form the words. Why her brother? Weren't they going to talk to her? Why did they want to talk to Yusef?

She swept her dark hair behind her ear and revealed a long row of pearls on her earlobe.

'We want to talk to him about Hans Juhlén.'

The policeman said his name.

The name of the filth.

That revolting beast she hated above all else.

'Yusef? Police!' Makda called into the flat.

She stepped aside and let Henrik and Mia enter the ground-floor apartment, and then she moved to the left. She knocked carefully on a closed door.

Henrik and Mia waited in the hall.

There was a traditional Swedish woven mat on the hall floor and an empty yellow hat rack on the wall. On the floor were three pairs of shoes, two of them white and presumably newly purchased sneakers. They were a well-known brand and Henrik knew they were expensive. Otherwise there was nothing in the hall, no drawers, no pictures or anything to sit on.

Makda knocked again on the closed door and said something in a language Mia thought sounded like Tigrin.

She smiled at the police officers by way of apology, and knocked again.

Noticing that the sister appeared to be getting more and more anxious, Henrik and Mia decided to step in. They walked into the apartment and stood beside her at the bedroom door. From there they could look right into the kitchen, which had its own back door. A fan whirred above the oven and an ashtray on the table was overflowing with cigarette butts. In the other direction was a bathroom, a second bedroom and a living room. There was almost no furniture.

'Yusef, open the door. We just want to talk to you.'

Henrik banged on the bedroom door but there was no answer.

'Open the door now!'

He banged harder. Several times.

Then he heard a creaking sound from inside the room.

'What was that?' Mia wondered out loud.

'It sounded like a window—'

At that moment she caught sight through the kitchen window of a dark-skinned, barefoot man darting through the backyard.

'Damn!' Mia shouted and ran to the back door and into the yard.

Henrik came after her.

Mia saw the man force his way through some bushes, then he disappeared from view.

'Stop!'

Mia charged through the bushes and there he was, veering off into a playground. In a few strides he crossed the sandpit and jumped over the fence beside the swings. Mia was not far behind. She shouted again for the man to stop, then leapt over the fence and pursued him along a narrow cycle path, not too many metres behind. She would soon catch up. Nobody could beat her.

Nobody.

Muscles burning, she powered on, and as he reached the end

of the path she sprang forward, felling him with a well-directed tackle. They both rolled over in the snow. Mia grabbed hold of the man's left arm as he lay facedown on the ground beneath her and she bent it up on to his back. Then she crouched over him, trying to catch her breath.

Henrik came running up, pulled out a pair of handcuffs and locked the man's arms behind his back. He dragged him to his feet and showed his ID card before leading the man to the car.

Makda had set off after them but, unable to vault the fence, she'd remained in the playground. When she saw her brother in handcuffs, she slapped her hands over her mouth and shook her head. She went up to her brother and shouted at him in Tigrin, trying to grip his neck.

Mia pulled her away.

'We're only going to talk to him,' said Mia in a calming voice as she led her away to the swings. 'He needs to come with us to the station. Don't worry.'

Mia stopped, put both her hands on Makda's shoulders and looked her in the eye.

'Now listen to me. We will be talking to you, too, about what has happened. About what was done to you. I'll send a woman who knows your language and you can talk to her in private.'

Makda couldn't understand what the woman police officer had said. But she could see in the woman's eyes that it was something good. She nodded. Mia smiled and left the playground. Makda didn't know where she should go. So she just stayed there.

Anxious.

And completely lost.

As soon as they got to the station, Yusef Abrham had claimed, in broken English, that he didn't know a word of Swedish. Henrik Levin and Mia Bolander struggled for more than forty minutes to get hold of an interpreter. When the interpreter finally came, Yusef claimed he couldn't talk because he had a throat infection. That was when Mia lost her temper. She threw the threatening letters down on to the table and let fly a long stream of expletives which the interpreter then repeated in Tigrin but without the same anger. Yusef just glared at her sullenly.

After a few more expletives from Mia, he let out a sigh and finally started to talk about Hans Juhlén. About how Hans had abused his sister.

It had started one cold January evening. Juhlén had come to the apartment and asked to speak to Makda about her residence permit.

'She was alone at home, she didn't want to let him in, but he forced his way in and raped her in the hall,' said Yusef. 'When I came home, she was in her room sobbing. I wanted to help her, but she told me not to say anything to anybody about what had happened.'

He rolled his eyes. His sister's naive hope that she would be granted a residence permit had meant that she continued to open the door every time Hans Juhlén rang the bell.

Yusef had kept his word about keeping the sexual encounters secret, but his suspicion that Juhlén was lying about granting his sister a residence permit was gnawing at him.

'Juhlén seemed to be an idiot, and you shouldn't trust idiots.'

When three months had passed and Makda still hadn't received a positive answer from the Migration Agency, Yusef decided to use the same blackmail techniques as Juhlén. But instead of sex, he wanted to be paid in cash. So he hid in the apartment and documented Juhlén's visit with his mobile phone. Afterwards, he sat down and wrote the first threatening letter and posted it to Kerstin Juhlén. She immediately made contact, pleading with him to withdraw the threat, but Yusef refused.

'He'd abused my sister, now it was my turn to abuse him. I told his wife if they didn't pay, I would leak the photos to the media.'

Realizing he would carry out his threat, Kerstin delivered the money the following day.

'But I didn't say anything to Makda; I kept the money for myself. My sister knows nothing about it. If she wanted to fuck him for nothing, then she could just go ahead.'

'So you admit that you were the one who wrote the threatening letters?' Henrik asked.

'Yes.'

'Then you do know Swedish.'

Yusef smirked.

After that, he answered all the questions in fluent Swedish.

Yusef had been living in Sweden for a year and a half and had mastered the language fairly quickly. He was born in Eritrea and grew up there, but had left the country on account of the troubles with Ethiopia.

'We were lucky,' he said. 'Lucky that we could make our way here. That we survived the whole journey. That we didn't end up in a ghost container.'

'What do you mean, "ghost container"?' said Henrik.

'For refugees, it's one of the most common ways of travelling to a new country these days, and it isn't safe. Especially not for illegals. Many die on the way. Sometimes they all die. It's happened in Afghanistan, Ireland, Thailand. Even here.'

'Here?' said Henrik.

'Yes.'

'In Sweden?'

'Yes.'

The detectives exchanged puzzled glances. They'd heard stories of such things happening in other parts of the world, but not in Sweden. 'Surely we'd know about it, if that were the case?' said Mia.

'You don't see everything that happens. Anyway . . . my parents are going to come here too,' said Yusef.

'When?' said Henrik.

'Next year, I think. It's dangerous to stay in Eritrea.'

Henrik nodded. 'Let's go back to the threatening letters. Have you told anybody about them?'

Yusef shook his head no.

'You know you have committed a crime?' said Mia.

'It is only a letter, not a real threat.'

'Oh yes it is. And making threats against people is a very serious crime in this country. You will probably end up in prison for it,' said Mia.

'It was worth it,' he smirked.

Yusef didn't protest when the policemen took him away to a cell. If anything, he seemed quite relaxed, now that the truth was finally out about Hans Juhlén.

Ola Söderström stared at the computer screen, the only source of light in the room. He was going through the files he had found on Hans Juhlén's computer. The office was quiet apart from the muffled sound of the lift going from floor to floor, the hum of the ventilation system and the angry whirring the hard drive

126

made as he hunted down deleted files. But then the hard drive fell silent. Ola had gone through everything.

Now we'll see, he thought. There had to be something interesting hidden away, there always was. In every computer. But you had to look in the right place. Computers hid more than people knew, and often you had to search through the files several times to uncover all the little secrets.

He started by looking through Hans Juhlén's cookie folder to see which sites he had visited. Headlines from the national newspapers showed up, and Ola glanced through the articles about the Migration Agency. Most of them were about the agency's illegal contracts with landlords. One journalist had written a series of articles detailing his investigation into the agency's procurement processes, which were the responsibility of Juhlén's department. The agency was severely criticized for dragging its heels when it came to finding and paying for accommodation for asylum seekers. Hans was quoted in one article, attempting to defend his department's performance by saying 'there's a difference between buying a photocopier and buying accommodation'.

Ola continued his trawl through the cookie folder, turning up four sites connected with the transport of goods by sea, and another with details of shipping containers. Then he came upon a long list of sites with pornographic content, mainly featuring dark-skinned women.

Ole straightened his back and let the computer work its way through these hidden folders and files. He opened a document titled 'Statistics 2012' to reveal a chart comparing the number of refugees in 2011 and 2012. There was a league table showing the fifteen countries from which most of the refugees came. During the first months of the year, the largest number of residence permits had been granted to people from Somalia, with Afghanistan and Syria not far behind.

Ola opened a folder that seemed to be full of official reports and standard forms. He skimmed through documents that dealt with Athletics and Migration, the European Refugee Fund, and Labour Immigration. He found folders devoted to conferences and summits, government guidelines, official reports and fact sheets, legislation governing the agency's activities. And in the course of his searches he found three folders on the hard drive that were unnamed. It was in one of these that he found a document that had been deleted at 18.35 on the day Juhlén was murdered.

He clicked on the file to open it, blinking in surprise at the page that filled his screen. It was completely blank except for a series of capital letters and numbers.

There were ten lines in all:

VPXO410009
CPCU106130
BXCU820339
TCIU450648
GVTU800041
HELU200020
CCGU205644
DNCU080592
CTXU501102
CXUO241177

Ola Söderström had no idea what these letters and numbers could mean.

He copied the top line and pasted it into the search field, but it didn't match any document. He repeated the procedure with each of the other lines, but met with the same result each time. He tried writing just the letters: another dead end.

His first guess was it must be some form of code. But what could it mean? Names, perhaps? Or perhaps each entry was some form of personal ID, with the numbers representing birth dates? He quickly dismissed that idea too.

It was almost midnight, and still the mystery remained unsolved as he worked through the night.

CHAPTER EIGHTEEN

THE SWEAT DRIPPED FROM HER BROW.

The girl fought as hard as she could.

Right fist jab, duck, left fist jab, kick, kick, kick. The man with the ugly scar pointed at his eyes, his throat and his crotch.

'Eye, throat, crotch!' he shouted.

She shouted after him:

'Eye, throat, crotch!'

Right fist jab, duck, left fist jab, kick, kick, KICK!

'Attack alert!'

The girl froze. The man disappeared from her field of vision.

No, she thought. Not a surprise attack! She hated them. She had no problem with close combat; she was good at it now. The training had honed her instincts and developed her ability to react. Especially with a knife. She knew where to put her weight to get the blade as close to her attacker's throat as possible. It was a question of getting her challenger off balance and then down on the ground. Often all it took was a few well-directed kicks to the knees. If that didn't work, or if she met with tough opposition, she elbowed or kneed her challenger in the head several times.

Against Danilo – or Hades as she was now supposed to call him, the name carved on his neck – she'd clench her fist right before her hand reached his throat. When he doubled up in pain, she'd grab hold of his head and knee him in the face until he fell down. But all too often he'd outwit her, and she'd find herself on the ground with him sitting astride her chest, his hands around her throat. Sometimes she would black out, but it was all part of the training. She was meant to be hurt. How else would she learn never to give in, not even when it got dark?

She had become physically stronger, and she'd learned how to escape from a vulnerable position and regain the advantage. All it took was a knee driven into Hades' back or kidneys, then she could get loose. If she managed to land a kick to his face, she might even win the fight.

Kicks were important in close combat. She practised over and over, perfecting the movement of her hip so as to get more power in her leg. Rotating movements demanded balance, so she practised with particular attention to maintaining her centre of gravity in any given position. It was a matter of life and death that she master these techniques to perfection. Each night as she lay in bed she would rehearse the moves in her head – back leg forward, raise knee, rotate, kick – until she fell asleep.

The endurance exercises weren't so bad. She had learned to ignore the pain as she crawled naked across snow-covered ground. She could handle endurance running and interval training, even on hilly terrain. The one thing she hadn't mastered were the surprise attacks. It wasn't the attack that was the problem; she had trained to defend herself whether standing, sitting or lying down. She had trained in dazzling light and in total darkness, against armed opponents and multiple opponents, in confined spaces and in unfamiliar surroundings. But for all her training, she still struggled with the surprise element.

Now she focused her gaze at a point on the wall and listened for the slightest sound. She would probably have to stand there a long time. That too was part of the training. On one occasion she had been forced to stand at the ready for seven hours before she was attacked. Her arms and legs had been trembling from the effort and she had felt dehydrated, *but she had turned off all emotion and didn't feel the pain any longer. She was Ker after all. Goddess of Death. The one who never gave up.*

Suddenly she heard the sound of a stone crunching underfoot as somebody tried to creep up on her from behind.

She tensed her muscles and let out a roar of aggression as she spun round. The man with the ugly scar was close, and the girl saw the knife leave his hand at high speed. She watched it, lifted her hand and caught the knife by the handle in a swift movement. She squeezed the handle hard in her hand as she met the man's eye. He crouched and a second later he pounced. Quick as a flash, she shifted her weight and used all her strength to direct a kick at him. It hit the mark perfectly.

The man collapsed onto the floor and she was there in an instant. She put one foot on his chest and leaned over him with the knife against his brow. Her dark eyes burned. Then she raised the knife and threw it to the ground. It landed two centimetres from the man's head.

'Good,' he said, and gave her an encouraging look.

She knew what she had to say.

But she found it hard.

'Thank you, Papa!'

NINETEEN

Thursday, 19 April

HER RUNNING SHOES DRUMMED AGAINST THE asphalt as she set off along Järnbrogatan. Minutes later she exchanged the hard surface for the gravel footpath that ran alongside the river. She could feel the chill penetrating her black leggings. She hadn't bothered putting on extra layers; by the time she reached the first kilometre, she would be sweating.

Jana Berzelius enjoyed running outdoors. She trained regardless of the weather, through snow, sleet and icy winds, mostly following the same route: Sandgatan to the park, on to Himmelstalund and then back. She preferred an urban setting; anything else would involve getting in the car. It was a waste of time, driving. When she exercised, she wanted to get going the moment she left her apartment.

Joining a gym didn't appeal to her, and the thought of doing aerobics surrounded by others appalled her. She liked to be on her own, free of the need to interact with anyone. So she'd kitted out her apartment with fitness equipment that allowed her to finish her ten-kilometre run with a full workout. Push-ups, sit-ups, chin-ups – before showering she'd power her way through a series of lifts and stretches. Nothing could beat the feeling of having full control of her body.

Her daily regime complete, she lay on the floor, exhausted.

It was 06.57 – plenty of time before she had to set off. She checked her pulse. When it had returned to normal, she got up, stripped off her clothes and climbed into the shower. For twenty minutes she let the high-pressure jet of water massage her muscles, then she dried herself, picked out a matching set of underwear and a sheer blouse to go with her deep blue trousers and jacket.

She fried four slices of bacon and two eggs and ate her breakfast while watching the morning news on TV. She turned up the volume when an item about the dead boy who was found outside Norrköping came on. As the boy's face filled the screen, a reporter announced that the police had yet to identify him. The next picture showed a smiling Hans Juhlén, as the reporter raised the possibility of a link between the two victims. It was hoped that the police would provide answers at a press conference scheduled for 9 a.m. that morning.

Then it was time for the weather. A storm was on its way across the North Sea. The female presenter was beaming as she warned of the chaos that would ensue in central Sweden. The region had already seen record amounts of snow this April, and now more was expected.

Jana turned the TV off. She put on some make-up, brushed her teeth and combed her hair. When she checked herself in the mirror, she was not completely satisfied with what she saw and so put on another coat of mascara. Then with her jacket hanging over her arm she made her way to the garage.

Mist and icy roads meant that the journey to the forensics centre in Linköping took her fifty-five minutes rather than the usual forty. Traffic was crawling along and Jana had to concentrate to keep on the correct side of the divide. The mist began to clear as she approached Norsholm, and by the time she took the exit for Linköping North it had gone completely.

She arrived at the medical examiner's office fifteen minutes before the meeting was due to start. DCI Henrik Levin and DI Mia Bolander were already seated in the visitors' armchairs. Björn got up from his ergonomic office chair and greeted Jana with a firm handshake.

As a young medical student, Ahlmann had planned to specialize in neurology, but during the course of his studies he'd developed a fascination for forensic medicine. He enjoyed the puzzle element, the challenge of determining the sequence of events that led to an individual ending up on his autopsy table, but he never allowed enthusiasm to cloud his judgement. He'd earned his stellar reputation through meticulous attention to detail, considered analysis and informed judgements. Always mindful of the crucial importance of his testimony in court proceedings, he was never arrogantly dismissive of less qualified colleagues, encouraging them to ask questions and offer insights in the hope he himself might learn something new in the process.

'The report is ready,' he told Jana. 'Though we're still waiting for some of the lab results. I'd like you to come and look at the body; there's something interesting I want to show you.'

One of the ceiling lights flashed on and off as they stepped out of the lift into the basement corridor.

The two men had immediately fallen into conversation,

chatting happily about Henrik's children and Bjorn's grandchildren and their latest exploits.

Neither Jana nor Mia made any attempt to join in. They were fully occupied with avoiding each other's gaze.

Björn unlocked the fire door and turned on the lights in the autopsy suite.

Mia as usual took up a position as far as possible from the autopsy table, while Jana and Henrik stood right next to it.

Björn washed his hands thoroughly, put on latex gloves and folded back the white sheet. The naked body only filled about two-thirds of the bench. The boy's eyes were closed, his face white and stiff. His nose was narrow, his eyebrows dark. His head had been shaved and the exit hole in his forehead was visible. It was obvious he had been shot from behind.

Jana gasped when she saw all the bruises covering his arms and legs.

Henrik too.

'Are those bruises from when he fell? When he was shot?' said Henrik.

'Yes and no,' said Björn. 'These are from where he fell' – he indicated the large dark bruises on the boy's outer thigh and hip – 'and there are also wounds on the inside, bleeding at various depths of the muscles.'

Then he drew their attention to bruising on the boy's arms: 'Many of these bruises are from some time before he died. He has previously been subjected to brutal violence, especially to his head, his throat and around his genitals. And his legs, I might add. I would say these injuries were caused by kicks and blows, or he may have been beaten with a hard object.'

'Such as?' said Henrik.

'A piece of iron tubing, perhaps. Or whoever kicked him may have been wearing steel-toed boots. Not easy to say. I'll have to wait and see what the cell-tissue samples can tell us.'

'And regularly, you said?'

'Yes, he has several old scars and some internal bleeding which would indicate that his body had been abused over a lengthy period.'

Henrik nodded slowly.

'No sign of any sexual abuse,' Björn continued. 'No traces of sperm, no redness or tearing around his anus. No sign that he'd been restrained in a stranglehold either. He died from a shot to the back of his head. The bullet is still being analysed.'

'The weapon?'

'Not confirmed yet.'

'When will you get the results of the bullet and tissue sample analysis?'

'Tomorrow, or perhaps the day after.'

'The boy's age?'

'Nine or ten years. Difficult to be more precise.'

'OK, anything else?' said Henrik.

'I've found traces in his blood of drugs that depress the central nervous system. He was under the influence of narcotics. Heroin, to be precise. A rather large dose. There are puncture wounds consistent with repeated injections into the veins in his arm. Look here.'

Björn showed them the festering skin in the crook of the boy's arm, then twisted the arm to reveal a large inflamed area.

'On the underside here you can see the signs of advanced infection. Presumably whoever injected him missed the vein, so the solution ended up in the surrounding tissue and not in his blood.'

Henrik winced at the sight of the small wounds all over the surface of the child's arm.

'If you press here, it feels . . . how can I put it? It feels like clay. That's because the arm is full of pus. This sort of infection is not uncommon with intramuscular injections. I've seen horrific cases where parts of the body have simply rotted away with infection. Large holes straight into the skeletal bone are not unusual, nor is sepsis – blood poisoning. Eventually, veins collapse from all the injections, especially in the groin area. In the worst cases, amputation of an infected limb is the only treatment.'

'Are you saying that this nine- or ten-year-old was an addict?' said Henrik.

'Most definitely. Yes.'

'A dealer?'

'That I don't know. I'm not the right person to make that judgement.'

'A drug runner, perhaps?'

'Again, that's not something I can tell you from looking at the body.' Björn cleared his throat and moved to the end of the table, next to the boy's head. 'Now let's see . . . this is what I wanted to show you.'

He turned the boy's head to one side, then pointed to an area at the back of the neck that had been hidden until now.

Jana could see letters carved into his flesh. They were uneven and looked as if they had been cut with a blunt object. She saw that the letters spelled out a name, and the ground began to rock beneath her feet. She gripped the edge of the table with both hands so as not to fall.

'Are you all right?' said Henrik.

'I'm fine,' Jana lied, unable to tear her eyes away from the boy's neck.

She read the name again. And again. And again.

Thanatos.

God of death.

TWENTY

GUNNAR ÖHRN WAS BROWSING THE LOCAL PAPERS
online. He leaned his head back while he looked at the sports
pages. He always read the sports before the news. Always the
financial pages before politics. And always the arts pages before
the motoring section. Blogs and family pages – he never touched
those.

During the month since his most recent separation from
Anneli, Gunnar had fallen into a routine: he got up at six thirty,
ate breakfast and drove to the police station. He was often home
by six in the evening and would eat something then run a few
errands in town if his son was not with him. By eight o'clock
he'd be back home, reading or on his computer until midnight. If
the weather was good, he might consider going out for an hour's
walk, but not often. Anneli had always insisted he needed to
get more exercise and when they lived together she would drag
him off on walks all the time. Left to his own devices, he could
walk when he liked and stick to the leisurely pace he preferred.

Abandoning the sports pages, Gunnar clicked to the local
news. A fifteen-year-old trumpeter had been awarded a music
scholarship of two thousand kronor. The boy wore braces on his
teeth and reminded him of his son Adam.

Two days a week Adam would come to his place for dinner, if his sports schedule allowed. They would go out for pizza and sometimes a movie. Gunnar had thought about volunteering to be an assistant coach for his son's team, but he had already missed the first pre-season training session. Maybe next time, he thought as he saw his own image appear on the computer screen. The photograph had been taken at the morning press conference.

The media frenzy following the discovery of the boy's body was such that they'd had to move the press conference to the largest conference room in the police station, and even then it was standing room only. Gunnar Öhrn and County Police Commissioner Carin Radler had let the press officer, Sara Arvidsson, do most of the talking. She had played down the murder of the boy, focusing instead on the Hans Juhlén investigation, now in its fourth day. Most questions met with a brisk, 'No comment!' But when asked if it was true that the widow was being held in connection with the murder, she stated that Kerstin Juhlén had been released from custody but was still helping police with their inquiries.

Carin Radler was of the opinion that it was better to feed the media a few titbits than to have them indulge in wild specula-tion because of a lack of information, but Gunnar found press conferences an ordeal. Investigative journalists had a knack for asking questions that could trip you into revealing more than you'd intended. Others would use the media briefing as a forum to air bogus claims which would later be transformed into absolute truths by unscrupulous hacks. It was a pain having to keep saying 'No comment', but it was necessary. Especially in this case.

Gunnar could only hope that the letters and numbers Ola Söderström had shown him first thing this morning would lead to something.

The team were due to meet again at noon. Half an hour from now. He decided to grab some lunch from the cafeteria beforehand.

Jana's hands shook as she unlocked the door.

Once she was inside her apartment, she kicked off her shoes and sank to the floor with her back to the door. She remained sitting like that for a while. Getting her breath back.

She tried to replay the morning's events in her mind, but it was like everything was shrouded in fog. She had made her apologies and rushed out of the forensics centre claiming she had to attend an urgent meeting with a client. The journey home was a blur, apart from a near-collision with a motorist who had been travelling well below the speed limit. She could recall the shocked expression on the other driver's face as she sped by, but she had no recollection of anything after that, no memory of parking the car or making her way upstairs to her apartment.

She got to her feet and stumbled unsteadily to the bathroom, tripping over the threshold and only saving herself from falling by catching hold of the washbasin at the last minute. Her entire body was trembling as she searched for her hand mirror in the bathroom cupboard. Irritated when she couldn't locate it, she tipped the contents of a drawer on to the floor. A bottle of perfume smashed, spilling the contents over the floor tiles. She pulled out another drawer and rummaged through it, but still no mirror.

Jana stopped to think. Her handbag! There was a pocket

mirror in her handbag. She went back into the hall, found her handbag, and took out the little round mirror.

Back in the bathroom, she stood in front of the wall mirror and hesitated. Her heart was thumping, her body trembling. With shaking hands she pulled her hair to one side, angled the pocket mirror towards her neck and held her breath.

She didn't dare look. She shut her eyes and counted to ten. When she opened them again, she saw the reflected letters.

K-E-R.

KER.

'The god of death,' said Mia.

'What?' said Henrik.

'Thanatos. It means god of death.'

They had left Linköping and were on their way back to the police station in a hurry. The meeting with Björn Ahlmann had gone on longer than expected and now they would be hard pressed to make it to the noon briefing.

Mia zoomed in on the online encyclopedia and read aloud:

'"In Greek mythology, Thanatos was the god of death. He was extremely fast and strong. If you saw Thanatos with a torch pointing downward, it meant somebody would die. But if the torch was pointing upward, there was still hope."'

'Don't tell me you believe that stuff?' said Henrik.

'No, but the kid had the name on his neck. It must mean something.'

'Or perhaps it's what he was called,' said Henrik. 'One thing's for sure: he can't have carved it himself.'

'With the help of a mirror, maybe.'

'No, he'd never have got the letters so straight.'

'But who would cut the name of a god into a child's neck?'

'Don't know.'

'Some crazy bastard.'

'Perhaps he belongs to a gang?'

Mia deleted Thanatos and entered a new word in the search engine.

With ten kilometres to go till the exit for Norrköping and Mia in the passenger seat beside him absorbed in her internet searches, Henrik's thoughts wandered from the dead boy to Jana Berzelius. Her hurried departure from the autopsy this morning had been completely out of character. Whenever he'd worked with the prosecutor in the past, she'd invariably been the one who stayed longest, asked the most questions, even on occasion challenging Björn Ahlmann's conclusions. Today she hadn't asked a single question.

Henrik frowned. Cases involving children were always difficult, and the sight of a small body on the autopsy table was enough to make anyone feel queasy. But Jana had seemed fine initially; it was only when she saw the letters on the boy's neck that she turned pale. Or had he imagined it?

They made it to the conference room thirty seconds before the meeting was due to start. Jana was already seated, looking perfectly composed as she read through her notes. Next to her, Anneli was reading the local paper. Ola and Gunnar were sitting with their heads close together, conferring about something.

Mia flopped down on her usual chair and reached for the coffee thermos. Henrik took the empty seat next to Jana.

Gunnar, noting that the whole team was now present, got the meeting under way. 'OK, everybody, let's start. Henrik and Mia, you first. What did Bjorn have to say about the boy's injuries?'

'He confirmed that the boy was shot from behind,' said Henrik. 'He had older injuries on his body, consistent with being subjected to a vicious beating, though there were no signs of sexual assault. And there were traces of heroin in his blood.'

'How old was he?' Gunnar asked.

'Nine or ten, and already an addict. He had scores of puncture wounds from needles and infections on his arms.'

'That's very young to be an addict,' said Gunnar.

'Once you start, you're hooked – regardless of age. Heroin is an extremely addictive drug,' said Ola.

'But still, it's not often you come across a ten-year-old heroin addict,' said Gunnar.

'Maybe he was at Hans Juhlén's house to steal money for his addiction?' suggested Mia.

'Well, that's one theory,' said Gunnar. 'We need to get a better idea of who the boy was, whether he was a member of a gang, a dealer, a runner, who he bought the stuff from, sold to, and so on. That's going to mean reaching out to all the heroin addicts and dealers we know.'

'Selling often takes place in deprived areas,' said Mia.

'But drugs are a problem in all classes of society, aren't they?' said Henrik.

Mia looked at Jana and smiled. 'Only in rich areas they're better at hiding it.'

'But what would make children sell drugs?' said Henrik.

'Money, of course,' said Mia. 'If there were summer jobs for all teenagers, they wouldn't need to push drugs.'

'So you're saying they start selling drugs because the council doesn't give them summer jobs?' said Jana, breaking her silence.

She leaned across the table and glared at Mia. 'A job is something you find for yourself, it's not something you're given.'

Mia fought the urge to rise to the bait, suspecting the others would take Jana's side.

'But we're talking about a ten-year-old here, and ten-year-olds don't have summer jobs,' said Henrik.

Mia gave him an irritated look.

'But why would a ten-year-old be involved in drugs? Could he have been forced into it?' said Ola.

'That would be my guess,' said Henrik.

'Let's skip the guessing and move on,' said Gunnar. 'The tyre tracks at the Viddviken crime scene were Goodyear – Marathon 8. We don't know for certain whether the tracks were left by the white van a witness reported seeing. Incidentally, have we got any more on that sighting?'

'Yes. According to the witness, the vehicle was an Opel,' said Mia.

'Model?'

'He didn't know.'

'Then how did he know it was an Opel?'

'I suppose he recognized it.'

'The make but not the model?'

'That's right. He didn't know the model.'

'How big?'

'He described it as "a little van".'

'And what is the name of this witness?'

'Erik Nordlund.'

'Where does he live?'

'Jansberg. He was doing some forestry work out there and saw the van driving at high speed past his house. He lives close to Arkösund Road, a couple of kilometres before the turning for Viddviken.'

'Ask him to come in to the station as soon as possible. He must surely know what type of van he saw. Print out pictures of all the Opel models and put them in front of him. We must find that van. Even if it isn't connected with the murder, the driver might have seen something important.'

Gunnar paced back and forth in front of the map on the wall, trying not to vent his frustration on the team, then picked up a red marker and wrote on the whiteboard: *Opel.*

'You said the van was going fast,' Henrik said to Mia.

'Yes, according to the witness, it was,' said Mia.

'Are there any speed cameras on Arkösund Road?' said Henrik.

'Yep.'

'Perhaps it was caught on camera?'

'Good point, Henrik. Check with the department of transport up in Kiruna. They'll be able to tell us if their cameras registered any vans violating the speed limit that evening,' said Gunnar.

Ola raised a finger. 'I'll get on to it,' he said. 'But have you abandoned the theory about the boy arriving by boat?'

'No, but nobody we've spoken to so far saw or heard a boat in the area at that time. So we'll concentrate on the van first.'

Gunnar nodded to Ola. 'OK, over to you.'

Ola tapped on his keyboard and opened the document with the letters and numbers; he started the projector but the screen showed nothing.

'Now what's wrong?' he said and got up from his chair. 'Is it the light or what?'

Ola adjusted his cap and then climbed on to the conference table to reach the apparatus hanging from the ceiling.

Jana barely glanced at him. Somehow she'd managed to maintain an air of calm since arriving at the police station, but it was only superficial; inwardly, she was struggling to control her nerves and maintain focus.

Mia glared at the prosecutor as she reached out for the coffee thermos and pulled it across the table towards her.

Ola was still busy adjusting the projector, and the rest of the group seemed too deep in their own thoughts to notice what was going on around them.

Jana took a sip of coffee.

Ola broke the silence. 'Right. It should work now.'

He climbed down from the table and woke the computer from sleep mode. The screen showed the strange combinations of letters and numbers.

Jana looked up at the enlarged image. Her eyes opened wide, as her heart beat rapidly. She could hear a rushing sound in her ears; the room was rocking. She recognized the first line. She had seen it before. In her dream. The one that recurred night after night.

VPXO410009.

'Right, I found this list in Hans Juhlén's computer. I've gone through every single folder and file and document on his hard drive and this document is the only one that looks weird. Hans Juhlén used these combinations for something several times and saved the document with the same name over and over. But I've no idea why. Nor do I know what the numbers and letters mean. Does anyone here have any ideas?'

They all shook their heads. Except Jana.

'I've searched online, but so far I haven't come up with anything,' said Ola. 'Perhaps his PA might know? Or his wife?'

'Henrik, check with Lena. Mia, you can ask Kerstin. And check whether Yusef knows anything. We'll have to ask everybody. Right, Jana?' said Gunnar.

Jana was caught unawares.

'What?'

'What do you think?'

She forced herself to smile as she replied:

'I agree. We'll keep at it.'

CHAPTER
TWENTY-ONE

THE STEEL WAS COLD IN HER HAND.

The girl swallowed and looked up at the man with the ugly scar.

They were in a cellar. Usually it did service as an isolation cell. They were put there if they had failed some exercise or command, if they didn't finish their food, or hadn't shown enough endurance when running. Sometimes simply because the older ones felt like it.

She had been locked up in there twice before. The first time she had misunderstood the routines and had gone to the toilet without permission. She was locked up in the room with no light for three days and was forced to defecate on the floor. The stench was as bad as in the container. That seemed to be the only thing she still remembered from the journey with her mother and father. The memory of them faded with every passing day. But, using a stone, she had carved their faces on the wall next to her bed, hidden behind a small cupboard so no one else could see. Every evening she pushed the cupboard to one side and said goodnight to her parents.

The second time the girl had been forced down into the isolation cell was when she had picked at the carvings on her neck. The man with the ugly scar had found the bloodstains on her sleeve and pulled her by her hair across the yard. Five days, that was how long she'd had to stay there. The first day she slept almost the entire time. The second day she thought about trying to escape; and the third day she trained herself how to kick hard and attack with a knife. She had found a little piece of wood on the floor and used it as a knife. On the final two days she explored the room in all its darkness. She rarely left the rooms in which they trained, so being down in the cellar was both unpleasant and exciting. In her curiosity, she examined every object she could find. She particularly liked the old workbench which stretched along one wall, with its tin cans of paint and various plastic containers. The girl examined them all as best she could in the dim light. On the second wall were two shelves with cardboard boxes and newspapers. A rusty bicycle leaned against the wall under the stairs with a brown suitcase in front of it. An old door was propped up against the banisters, with a stool next to it. The girl noted that nobody had moved anything since she'd last been there.

'It's time,' said the man with the ugly scar and gave her a gun. 'Now is the time for you to prove to me that you deserve to be my daughter. The target is not the usual one.'

The man nodded to the woman who was standing against the wall on the top stair. She opened the door and let Minos in. He slowly walked down the steps and tried to accustom his eyes to the dark.

'This is your new target,' the man said to her.

When Minos heard those words, he stopped short on the stairs. In that instant, he forgot everything he had learned. Panic took over, and he tried to dart back up toward the door. But the woman who stood there pulled out her gun, pointed it at his head and forced him down the steps again.

Minos begged for mercy.

He threw himself at the man's feet and screamed.

The man kicked him away. 'You're a loser. If you had done as you'd been told, you would be standing here instead of Ker. It is only the strongest who survive, and she is one of them.'

Minos's eyes rolled with fright. He was kneeling now on his bare knees and shaking.

The man went up to the girl and grabbed her hair and forced her head back. He pulled hard to show that he was serious, and looked her straight in the eye.

'Soon you'll be in complete darkness. So you will have to make use of your other senses. Do you understand?'

She understood. Her heart started pounding.

'Make me proud!' the man whispered.

The stairs creaked as the man and the woman climbed back up and left the cellar. When the door was shut, the girl held the gun tightly and raised it.

The dark surrounded her. She didn't like it and her breathing grew rapid. She wanted to scream but knew an echo would be the only reply. An empty echo. Her heart was thumping and the darkness began to voluntarily release its hold.

Now she heard Minos as he bumped into the bicycle. She assumed he had crawled in under the stairs. She tried to calm herself. Breathe deeply. She could manage this; she would conquer the darkness. She gained control of her breathing, inhaling deeply and exhaling through her nose. She concentrated and listened. Silence. Numbing silence.

The girl took one step forward, stopped and listened. Then another step, and then one more. After three more steps she knew she would reach the staircase and would have to step to the side to get past them and reach the area where Minos was.

She stretched out her hand to feel the staircase railing and counted the steps in her head: One, two, three. Now she felt the cracked handrail beneath her fingers. After three more steps, she let go of the wooden rail and blindly felt for something with her hand in front of her. With her next step, she kicked the suitcase on the floor; the sound gave her a start. At the same time she heard Minos crawling up through the space near her. Pointing the gun in front of her, she followed his sound from right to left. But it disappeared as quietly as it had come. The movement had made her breathe faster, and she closed her mouth again so she could listen. Where was he now? She slowly turned her head so that she could hear her target. She searched her memory. Could he be sitting under the workbench?

Or next to the shelves?

She stayed where she was, silent and not moving. Waited for a signal, a breath or a sense of movement. But all she could hear was silence.

She knew there was a risk she would be ambushed.

Perhaps Minos was already standing behind her back?

The thought made her turn round. Her brow became sweaty and her damp hands warmed the steel. She must do something. Couldn't just stand there waiting for him.

The earth floor was uneven and she put one foot forward to keep her balance. Let the other foot follow.

Then she stood completely still again. Hesitating. One more step forward, then another. She turned to the right and the left, all the while with the gun pointing forward. Her other senses worked hard to compensate for her unseeing eyes.

She stretched out one hand in a sweeping movement and felt the hard surface of the bench. She knew it was two metres long and she felt her way along it with her hand. When she reached the end, she stopped.

Then she finally heard it.

A breath.

The signal.

She reacted instinctively and pointed the gun in the direction of the sound. And then she was hit by a hard blow across her arm. She lost her balance and concentration. A second blow was more painful, straight to her head, and she put up her arms to shield herself. She mustn't drop the gun.

Minos was close, dangerously close. His anger was dreadful. He hit out again. And again. The girl tried to keep her footing, to focus. When Minos tensed up for a final blow, she reacted. She threw a punch in the dark, and hit her mark. Minos grunted.

She hit out again. This time with the gun. The third time she hit his forehead and heard the heavy thud as he fell to the ground.

She put both hands on the gun and aimed it downward.

Minos was whining. His voice felt cold as metal and cut like a knife through the darkness.

A sense of calm settled over her. She felt strong, with a greater presence than ever. She was no longer afraid of the dark.

'Don't do it,' said Minos. 'Please, don't do it. I'm your friend.'

'But I'm not yours,' said the girl and fired the gun.

TWENTY-TWO

WHEN ERIK NORDLUND WENT IN THROUGH THE
main door to the police station, he hoped the meeting would
take about ten minutes at most.

The reception was crammed with people, most of whom
seemed to be applying for passports.

The uniformed woman behind the counter took down his
name and called Henrik Levin.

A minute later, Henrik appeared and escorted him to an office
on the third floor.

'Coffee?'

'Yes, please.'

'Milk? Sugar?'

'Sugar.'

'OK, take a seat, I'll be back shortly . . .'

Erik sat down and looked through the glass wall to a large
room where police officers were working away at their desks.
Telephones were ringing, conversations were going on and
keyboards were clicking. He suddenly felt a strong urge to get
back to his duties in the forest.

He wondered whether he should hang up his warmly lined

jacket, but decided not to, it would only be a short visit. Tell the policeman what he saw, and then leave.

In the distance he could see the chief inspector approaching with two cups of coffee. As he came into the room, a drawing taped to the wall fluttered in the draught. A green ghost, drawn by a child. Erik thought of his three grandchildren who sent him drawings every week, squeezing them into an envelope that was far too small. They mainly drew suns and trees, flowers and boats. Or cars. But never ghosts.

He took the cup that Henrik offered him, and sipped some coffee. The steaming liquid burned his throat.

The detective inspector sat down and pulled out a notepad. His first question was about Erik's profession, so he talked about felling trees.

'Most trees have a natural fall direction.' Erik put his cup down and gesticulated. 'And the direction of the fall is influenced by whether the tree leans to one side, the extent and form of its branches and the direction of the wind. A lot of snow and ice in the crown can easily weigh a ton, and that can make it tricky to judge which way the tree will fall. This winter has been bloody cold.'

Henrik nodded in agreement. It had been an exceptionally cold winter with record snowfalls in many parts of the country.

Erik went on, warming to his subject now: 'The basis of safe tree felling is the width of the holding wood, the bit between your front wedge and your back cut. This is the "hinge", and if your hinge is too wide it will be a heavy and clumsy fall. But if the hinge is too narrow that's even worse because it might give way and then the tree would fall out of control.

You can really hurt yourself if you don't do it properly. You can't mess around with nature. Bang!' Erik clapped his hands together. 'You can end up under a tree trunk with a broken leg or worse. One of my co-workers was knocked out by a birch that splintered. He was out cold for several minutes before we managed to revive him.'

Erik picked up the cup and took another sip of coffee.

Henrik then began to steer the conversation back toward the reason for Erik's visit.

'You saw a van?'

'Yes.'

'On Sunday?'

'Yes, at about eight in the evening.'

'You're sure about that? And the time too?'

'Yep.'

'According to the officers who visited you yesterday, you said it was an Opel. Is that correct?'

'Yep.'

'And you are quite certain it was an Opel?'

'Absolutely. I've owned one myself. See!'

Erik unhooked a bunch of keys from his belt and showed Henrik a metal key ring with a symbol.

'Opel. And I've got one of these too.' Erik picked out a Volvo symbol from the bunch.

Henrik nodded.

'Where did you see it? The Opel?'

'On the road outside my house. It was going very fast.'

'If I get a map, can you point out exactly where you saw the van and which direction it was travelling in?'

'Of course.'

Henrik Levin went off and came back with a map that he unfolded on the desk.

Erik took a marker, looked for his house on the map and put a red cross and arrow on the road.

'This is where I saw it. Right here. And it was heading for the coast.'

'Thank you. Did you catch a glimpse of the driver?'

'No. I was blinded by the headlights. I couldn't see anything except the colour of the van.'

'Licence plate?'

'I couldn't see that either.'

'Did you notice any other vehicles?'

'No. At that time of day the road is usually empty. Except for the occasional truck.'

Henrik fell silent. The man in front of him seemed credible. He was wearing red work clothes and an orange high-vis vest.

Henrik folded the map and picked up a pile of pictures of Opel vans.

'I know you can't remember which model of van it was, but I want you to look through these and see if there is anything that reminds you of the van you saw.'

'But I didn't see . . .'

'I know, but look at the pictures and take your time. Give it the time it needs.'

Erik sighed. He unzipped his jacket and hung it on the back of the chair.

This wasn't going to be a quick visit after all.

Jana Berzelius was still feeling nauseous. She rested her head in her hands and tried to gather her thoughts. The lettering on the boy's neck had affected her in a way she had never previously experienced. She knew what the name meant. But the fact he should have that particular name . . . it just wasn't possible.

It couldn't happen.

It wasn't allowed to happen.

She sat on the edge of her bed. The room suddenly felt small. Shrinking. Stifling.

Jana tried again to gather her thoughts but realized she was in a state of mental paralysis. Her brain refused to function. When she finally made her way to the kitchen, her hands shook. A glass of water made no difference. And nothing in the fridge could help; the nausea was too strong to allow her to eat. So she turned on the espresso machine.

With the cup in her hand, she went back into the bedroom and sat on the bed again. She put the cup on the bedside table, opened the cupboard and took out one of the black notebooks she kept there. She pored over her notes detailing the images and symbols she saw in her dreams. Arrows, circles and letters of the alphabet in neat rows. Here and there a drawing. Some of them were dated; the first date appeared under a sketch of a face: 22 September 1991. She was nine years old and for therapeutic reasons had been encouraged to keep notes about her recurring dreams. She had told her parents about her horribly realistic dreams, but Karl and Margaretha Berzelius had thought they were far too imaginative. Her brain was playing tricks on her. They had taken her to a psychologist to help her to get over this 'phase', as they put it.

But nothing helped. The dreams continued to trouble her so much that she tried everything she could to stay awake. The never-ending anxiety and sheer despair that she felt, combined with difficulty breathing, was more than she could bear. When her parents said goodnight and closed her bedroom door, she would sit up in bed and try to come up with ways to stay awake all night long. She liked games in the dark and she often passed the time by galloping with her fingers across the covers and bunching up feathers inside the duvet into small obstacles that her fingers could jump over.

She'd move around in her darkened bedroom, or sit in the bay window and look out over the garden. She'd stretch up as if she could reach the ceiling of the three-metre-high room, or crouch down to make herself as small as possible under the bed. The psychologist had told her she should let things take their course and in time her dreams would disappear.

But they didn't.

They only got worse.

And after two more weeks of disturbed nights, her father had taken her to the hospital and the doctor there had given him a bottle of sleeping pills.

The pills put her to sleep for a few hours at most, but the side effects lasted much longer. Jana lost her appetite as well as her concentration. Finally her teacher took Jana's mother aside and told her the child was falling asleep in class. She was so tired, it was all she could do to string a sentence together. When asked to solve a mathematical formula that she would have managed with ease in the past, now she simply mumbled incoherently. Given the high ambitions Karl and Margaretha had for their daughter, it was no surprise that they took immediate action.

Jana was delighted when they stopped the medication. Since she never wanted to visit a hospital again or talk to a psychologist, she lied to her parents and told them the dreams had disappeared.

Even the psychologist was fooled. Alone in her room of an evening, she sat in front of the mirror training herself how to smile. She masked her own personality by copying the gestures of others, their body language and their facial expressions. She learned the social game and its rules.

Pleased with the improvement, Karl Berzelius had patted her on the head. She knew that so long as she maintained the lie about everything being fine, she need never worry about having to visit another analyst.

But she dreamed.

Every night.

The keys clinked against the letterbox when Mia Bolander unlocked it. She took the pile of letters and browsed through them. All bills. Mia sighed and relocked the box, ran up the stairs to her second-floor flat. Her steps echoed in the stairwell. The door to her flat creaked. In the hall, she opened a drawer and put the post on top of the pile of unopened bills. She locked the door, pulled off her boots and threw her jacket on the floor.

It was seven o'clock. They would be getting together at Harry's in an hour.

Mia went straight into the bedroom and got undressed. She picked out a dress she had bought at the Christmas sales three winters ago.

It would have to do, she thought.

Then she went into the kitchen and opened the fridge. Her face fell when she realized there was no booze left. She checked her watch again. Too late to buy any; the shop would be closed now. Oh, fuck!

She couldn't face going to the supermarket to buy the low

alcohol beer they sold, so instead she set about going through all the cleaning materials in the cupboard under the sink, and then the cupboard where she kept her cups and saucers and vases. She even opened her microwave in the hope of finding something. In the end, to her relief, she found a single can of Carlsberg in the pantry, tucked behind a loaf of bread. It had passed its sell-by date, but only by a month or so and in the absence of anything else it would have to do. She opened the can and drank straight out of it with her mouth around the edge to stop the froth from dripping on to the floor. It tasted of sour cardboard.

Mia wrinkled her nose, wiped her mouth with her bare arm and went into the bathroom. She twisted her hair into a ponytail and took another gulp of the beer, then decided to put on some make-up. Two shades of blue eye shadow and black mascara. Then she applied a coat of blusher, building up a dark tone under her cheekbone. She liked the way it narrowed her face.

She picked up the can of beer and went into the living room to wait. Forty minutes to go.

Her thoughts turned to money. Today was the nineteenth; a week to go till payday. Yesterday she had seven hundred left in her account. But that was before she went out.

How much had she spent during the evening? Two hundred?

Entrance, a couple of beers, a kebab.

Perhaps three hundred?

She got up from the sofa, drank the last of the beer and set the empty can down. She grabbed her jacket and went out into the cold night air. The wind stung her bare legs as she walked. She could have taken the tram, but she saved over twenty kronor by walking. From where she lived at Sandbyhov, it was only a fifteen-minute walk to the centre.

Her stomach was rumbling as she passed the Golden Grillbar. She read the signs outside. Hamburger plate, sausage with bread, chips . . .

She cut across the tramlines. At the corner of Breda Vägen and Haga Gatan she found an ATM. She checked her balance and saw that she had only three hundred and fifty kronor. She must have spent more than she thought yesterday. She'd have to go easy this evening. Just one more beer. Perhaps two. Then she'd have some money left over for tomorrow. Otherwise I'll have to borrow from somebody, Mia thought. As usual.

She crumpled the ATM printout and threw it on the ground and continued to walk toward the centre.

The notebook had two hundred pages. But that was only the first. In her bedside table there were twenty-six more. One year of dreams in each. Jana turned to the final page, to a drawing she had done when she was young. It showed a knife with the edge of the blade coloured red.

Jana closed the book and stared out of the window. Then she opened the book again and turned to a page with a combination of letters and numbers. There it was: VPXO410009. The exact same combination Ola Söderström had shown her. Had shown the team.

Jana got up with the notebook in her hand, went into her study and unlocked a door that led to a little storeroom. She had transformed the storeroom into a place where she could archive anything that might help her to understand her background. Until now, she'd had only her dreams to guide her in the search for answers.

She turned on the ceiling light and stood there in the middle of the room. Her gaze was directed at the walls. The room was ten square metres. Two walls consisted of noticeboards, and these were completely filled with images, photos and sketches. On one wall there was a whiteboard covered with scribbled notes. Under it was a small desk and a chair. There was a safe next to that. There was no window in the room, but the LED spotlights in the ceiling illuminated every surface.

She had never shown this room to anybody; her parents would probably try to get her hospitalized if they found out. And she had never confided in Per about her research. She had never uttered a word about it to anyone, and she never would. This was her business, and hers alone. Everything in the room was about her life as a child.

The truth was – and she had realized this a long time ago – she liked digging into the past. She had done it for as long as she could remember. It gave her a kick, like solving a complicated puzzle, only the puzzle was her. But suddenly another player had joined the game, and it felt completely absurd, unreal.

Jana put the notebook down on the table, went up to one of the noticeboards and looked at the various scraps of paper attached to it. At the very top was a picture of a goddess. She had found it in a book she'd happened across in one of Uppsala's antique shops, and she had bought it for fifty kronor.

In that old university city she had used the public library as well as the university library. But the law department library became her natural refuge. She always sat in the same place in the Loccenius room, right in the corner with her back to a bookcase and with a high narrow window on her left side. From there she could see the entire reading room and all the students who came and went. There wasn't a lot of room on the desk and the green reading lamp wasn't very bright. Her law books didn't take much space, but the ones on Greek mythology were large and unwieldy.

At the main university library they had, over the centuries, acquired large and valuable collections. Jana had found tomes that described mythology in general and goddesses in particular. She had been especially interested in goddesses of death, and when she had come across texts of importance in her research, she copied them and later put them on a noticeboard in her student apartment. Titles such as *The Goddess, Imaginary Greece* and *Personification in Greek Mythology* were obvious choices for her private reading. She wrote down all the texts that interested her and made copies of key illustrations. She tried to understand all the links she could find.

The one thing all these hours of research had in common was a single name:

Ker.

Jana had devoted all her free time to trying to solve the mystery of the carving on her neck, but she got nowhere. The only fact she'd been able to establish was that Ker was the goddess of violent death.

She had eventually found the name in an old encyclopedia. It was among the other books, standing in the middle of a row of volumes neatly lined up in order of height. She pulled it out and opened it at the page with the yellow Post-it note. She ran her index finger along the lines that had been marked with a faint cross: *Ker. Greek mythology. The goddesses of death (or more correctly, of violent death) in Ancient Greece. Hesiodes however only mentions one Ker, daughter of Night and sister of Death (Thanatos) . . .*

Jana stopped reading.

Thanatos!

She sat down and put the book on the desk. She took a sheet of paper from one of the noticeboards; under the heading *Greek Mythology – Gods of Death* she'd written out a list of about thirty names. On the third line was the boy's name: *Thanatos*.

Feeling the nausea rise again, Jana leaned back and took a deep breath.

After a while she got up and went to the other noticeboard. On an otherwise empty sheet of paper there was a list of combinations. Letters of the alphabet and numbers in large print and next to this a picture of a shipping container. In her earliest memory she had recalled a name plate and at the same time she had seen a blue container in her mind's eye. But she didn't know how they were connected. She had assumed that the combination was associated with the container and had tried to find it on one of the millions of Internet pages out there, but her search had been in vain. She had then convinced herself it had all been a meaningless dream, and at that point her efforts to try to understand who she was had come to a dead end.

It had been a long time since she'd ventured into her secret room. She'd stuck to her resolution to leave things as they were, to abandon the search. But now she found herself wondering whether the time had come to get an answer. The boy was an important piece of the puzzle. Back in the autopsy room, when Björn showed her the name carved on the boy's neck, she had been frightened. Now, however, she was fast coming to the conclusion that the name could be her best chance yet of solving the riddle that had dominated her life. The combination was an important piece of the puzzle too. Would it be the name or the combination that would lead her to the truth? Or perhaps both together?

Jana's musings were cut short by the realization that the police now had the same list of letters and numbers in their possession. She had no idea how to deal with that. Should she be grateful to have help? Should she open up to her colleagues and tell them about her own investigations? Show them the drawings? The name on her neck? No. If she uttered so much as a word about having a personal interest in the investigation, she would be taken off the case.

Jana sat down again. Her thoughts were whirling around, leaving her utterly confused. On the one hand she knew she had to let the police take care of the investigation. But she couldn't just stand on the sidelines and passively watch, not when new pieces of the puzzle had fallen into her hands, placing the solution tantalizingly within reach.

How should she proceed? Which lead should she follow first? The boy or the combination? She had to make up her mind.

Jana got up from the chair, locked the storeroom and went into her bedroom.

Then she got undressed, climbed into bed and turned the light off. The decision had come to her and she was content with it.

Very content indeed.

TWENTY-THREE

Friday, 20 April

DURING THE WINDLESS AND CLEAR NIGHT, FROST had formed and created a pattern on the paving stones that looked like snowflakes. The ice crystals had gathered in clumps on windows and the bare tree branches were silvery white. Gunnar Öhrn was hurrying along the icy pavement, hoping to get an early start, when Mats Nylinder waylaid him outside the police station.

Nylinder was a general reporter with *Norrköpings Tidningar*. He was ambitious and tenacious, characteristics that Gunnar found worrying in a journalist. With his greasy hair tied back in a ponytail, his tatty brown leather waistcoat and baggy jeans, he looked like a member of a motorbike gang. Gunnar eyed the camera hanging around Nylinder's neck and quickened his pace.

'Gunnar Öhrn, wait! I have a few more questions. How exactly was the boy murdered?'

'I can't go into that,' Gunnar snapped.

'What weapon was used?'

'No comment.'

'Had the boy been sexually abused?'

'No comment.'

'Are there any witnesses?'

Gunnar pushed open the door in front of him, eager to leave his interrogator behind.

'Was Hans Juhlén killed because he'd been exploiting asylum seekers?'

Gunnar stopped, his hand on the door. He turned.

'What do you mean?'

'He forced female refugees to have sex with him. He demeaned them.'

'That is not something I'm prepared to comment on.'

'There'll be a massive scandal when the story gets out. You must have some comment?'

'My job is to investigate crime, not worry about scandals,' said Gunnar, and with that he slipped inside and closed the door behind him.

In desperate need of his morning dose of caffeine, he made straight for the kitchen area. He felt a lot better by the time he sat down at his desk with a steaming cup of coffee in his hand.

A new pile of documents had arrived from the National Forensics Lab. He was just about to open the package when he heard Anneli ask, 'Did you bring the box?'

She was leaning against the doorframe with one leg crossed in front of the other. She was wearing beige chinos, a white top and a white cardigan. On her wrist she had a twined gold bracelet that Gunnar had given her for her birthday.

'No, I forgot it again. Can you pick it up from the house?'

'When?'

Gunnar put his coffee down and started to flick through the documents on his desk.

'When can I fetch it?' Anneli repeated.

'The box?' he said, without taking his eyes off the papers.

'Yes. When can I fetch it?'

'Whenever it suits you. Any time.'

'Tomorrow?'

'No.'

'No? But you just said . . .'

'Well, OK . . . or . . . I don't know. Hey, do you know what this is?'

He waved the papers in front of Anneli's face.

'No.'

'This is progress. Finally we're getting somewhere in this investigation!'

'But can you tell me what they mean?' Mia Bolander gave Lena Wikström a pleading look.

'No, I've no idea. What are they?'

'That's what I want you to tell me.'

'But I haven't seen those numbers before.'

'And the letters?'

'No, nor those. Could it be some sort of code?'

Mia didn't answer. For more than twenty minutes she had tried to get Lena to explain the weird combinations they had found on Hans Juhlén's computer. She thanked Lena for her help, even though she hadn't offered any, and left the Migration Agency.

In her car she thought about how tired the PA was looking. Her face was pale, the area around her eyes was a purple–blue colour. With slow movements, she had pushed around the documents lying spread out on her desk. Mia had asked how things were, and Lena had told her she was depressed.

What a pathetic woman, Mia thought. And bloody useless with it!

Her temper wasn't improved by the slow-moving traffic that was delaying her return to the police station. But the thing that really made her angry was the fact that she was broke. Yesterday's evening out had cost more than she had intended. She'd wasted two beers on some bloke she didn't even know. Somebody who, on top of it all, turned out to be married.

It was all so annoying. So. Bloody. Annoying.

Her mobile made a shrill noise to alert her to an incoming call from Ola Söderström.

'How did it go?' he said.

'It didn't. She didn't know anything about the list.'

'Oh, great.'

'Yes, isn't it just!'

Mia pinched her upper lip with her index finger and thumb.

'Ola,' she said, 'have you tried turning the numbers around?'

'No. But I have tried combinations with the numbers first and the letters afterwards.'

'But what if you were to reverse them?'

'You mean I should search on 900014 instead of 410009?'

'I don't have the combinations in front of me, but it sounds like you get what I mean.'

'Hang on . . .'

Mia listened to Ola's fingers rattling across the keyboard. She turned her head to see if she could change lanes, but the cars in the next lane were going just as slowly. She was midway through an exasperated sigh when Ola's voice came back on the line.

'All I get is pages with ISO 900014 – that's international standards. And a report from Harvard about X-rays.'

'But what about the other combinations?' said Mia.

'Let's see, 106130 becomes 031601. No, that's a hex code. The next one, 933028, is a hex code too. I don't think he was interested in colours on the Internet.'

'No, nor am I.'

Mia tried to get a glimpse of how many cars there were in front. The queue was hopelessly long.

'How did you get on with the department of transport and their cameras?' she said.

'Still waiting. It all depends on whether the driver exceeded the speed limit or not. If he did, there will presumably be an image. And then we can run a facial-recognition check against photos on passports and driving licences. If it can be matched, then we can track him down. And even if there's no match, at least we'll get a licence plate that will give us the name of the owner of the van. With luck it'll be the same person who was driving,' said Ola.

'So everything depends on whether he or she was driving too fast,' said Mia.

She straightened her back in the driving seat and put her hand on the wheel. The traffic had started to move.

''Fraid so. The cameras only react to speed violations. The department of transport are checking their—'

'Jesus, what now!'

'What's the matter?'

'Bloody traffic! Get a move on, you idiot!'

Mia banged her hand against the steering wheel and gesticulated at the driver in front who had stalled his engine.

'What's put you in such a good mood today?' said Ola.

'None of your fucking business.'

Mia immediately regretted her harsh words.

'OK,' said Ola. 'It's none of my fucking business. But you might be interested to know that we've got an answer from the National Forensics Lab.'

Ola was in a bad mood, too, she could tell. She waited for him to continue.

'The boy was shot with a .22 Sig Sauer. The gun has not been used in any criminal activity in Sweden. But the only fingerprints found on the Glock recovered next to the body were the boy's. All the forensic evidence so far points to him being the person who fired the gun that killed Hans Juhlén.'

CHAPTER
TWENTY-FOUR

THERE WERE SEVEN OF THEM IN THE BEGINNING.
_Now she and Hades were the only two left. She had shot Minos, and
Hades had killed his opponent in the cellar. One boy had got a deep
knife wound between his ribs during an exercise and he died some days
later from his injuries. One girl had tried to escape and then been locked
up in the cellar, and when they opened it again she had starved to death._

A weakling, that's what Papa had called her.

_Then there was Ester who disappeared when they got to the farm.
But it was her own fault. If only she had listened to Papa and done as
he had said, then she would certainly have still been with them. Alive._

_The girl stroked her head with her hand. She had no hair. The trainers
had shaved her. It was so that she would create a stronger identity of her
own, they had said. Hades, too, had a shaved head and he rubbed the
bare top of his scalp. They were sitting opposite each other in the middle of
the stone floor and staring at one another. Neither of them said anything,
but Hades smiled at her when her eyes met his._

_Spring had come and the rays of the sun sought their way in through
the cracks between the wall planks. They had been given a new set of
clothes but the girl wasn't interested in that. She was longing to get her
hands on the weapons that lay in front of them. The sharp blade glistened
now and then, reflecting the light. Next to the knife lay a gun, and the_

girl had never seen it so well polished. Hades had done a good job. He must have polished it for hours.

Hades had once been extremely fond of technology. On the garbage heap he had found lots of broken machines and tried to repair them. He had dreamed of finding a telephone. But he never did.

She knew this, because she had helped him with his scavenging.

The girl's thoughts were interrupted by the door being opened. In came Papa, closely followed by the lady trainer and another man whom they didn't know. Papa stopped in front of them, bent down and examined their shaved heads. With something that resembled a look of satisfaction, he stood up and ordered the girl and the boy to do the same.

'Well,' he said. 'It's time. You're going on a mission in Stockholm.'

CHAPTER

TWENTY-FIVE

JANA BERZELIUS SAT IN HER CAR WITH THE ENGINE running. After several hours spent weighing up and dismissing strategies, she had finally come to a decision.

The name carved on the boy's neck had the same connotation as hers: death. This could not be dismissed as coincidence. She needed to find out if there were other links between them – without involving the police. If it came out that she was conducting a parallel investigation, she'd be suspended and her own name, Ker, would be the object of an inquiry that would spell the end of her career. So she would have to proceed with extreme caution. She couldn't afford to leave a trail that would lead back to her; she'd seen how Ola could track his way through telephone logs and emails and browser history to implicate a suspect. And there could be no acting on impulse; at every stage of her investigation she would have to analyse the risks, consider each possible scenario and prepare herself to deal with it.

Her most promising lead so far was the list of number and letter combinations Ola Söderström had found in Hans Juhlén's computer, so her investigation would start there. In her dreams, she had seen that combination, together with a shipping container.

Could this be significant? The best way to find out would be to pay a visit to the docks.

Which was why Jana was now parked across the road from the port authority's headquarters. The building was in darkness and the doors were locked. According to the sign displaying operating hours, the office had closed an hour earlier.

At this hour, there weren't many people about. Even so, there was a chance that some passer-by might notice her, maybe even recognize her, and wonder why she was parked there. If called upon to explain herself, she would have to say she was acting on a hunch, trying to stay a step ahead in the investigation. As the prosecutor in charge, she had every right to try to hurry things along.

Jana took out the list of combinations. She hadn't yet settled on how she was going to present her interest in them. Much would depend on who she found herself dealing with. She'd have to weigh her words carefully. Not reveal too much.

She folded the piece of paper and put it back in her pocket, then stepped out of the car.

The door to the port authority office was, as she'd surmised, locked. She took a step back and peered up at the office windows; they looked like empty black holes in the yellow building. A cold wind made her shiver and she pulled her leather gloves out of her pockets.

As she made her way towards the terminal she realized that they had stopped working there too. In the darkness she could hear waves lapping against the concrete below. Two huge cranes towered over a freighter berthed by the quay. Further along she could see two more ships. Trucks were parked in a fenced-off area, and large batches of timber had been stacked beside the wall of a hangar. Spotlights cast long shadows on the warehouse and the asphalt parking area.

Jana was about to return to her car when she spotted light coming from a shed at the end of the dock area. Inside her gloves, her hands were freezing; she pushed them into the pockets of her trench coat. The clicking of her heels on the concrete surface merged into the noise from the traffic crossing the port bridge behind her. She glanced at the warehouses where the light from the spotlights didn't reach. The area appeared to be deserted.

The shed was close now, and she slowed her pace. She hoped somebody would be there. Anybody at all, somebody to ask. With only a couple of steps to go, the sound of music reached her ears. The door was ajar and a sliver of light shone out through the narrow opening.

Jana raised her hand and knocked. Her glove dulled the sound so she knocked again, only firmer this time. Nobody opened. She stood on tiptoe and looked in through the window but couldn't see any movement in the shed. She pulled the door open and looked inside.

A coffee machine was bubbling away on a cabinet. Two folding chairs stood next to a table. An old mat covered the floor, and a bright lightbulb hung from the ceiling. But nobody was there.

A loud noise startled her. She turned round and tried to locate it. Then she saw that the big doors to the closest hangar were open.

'Hello?' she called out.

No answer.

'Hello?'

She closed the shed door and approached the entrance to the hangar. It was bitterly cold. At the far end she could make out a number of machines and smaller cranes. Tools were strewn on the floor, and the shelves running along the walls held a variety of spare parts, tyres and truck batteries. Cables hung down from the ceiling and there was a lifting mechanism, presumably to repair vehicles. To her right was a long narrow room leading to a grey steel door.

A man was crouched with his back to her, working on a truck. She knocked on the metal wall next to the entrance, but he didn't react.

'Excuse me!' she said in a loud voice.

The man lost his balance and had to put out a hand to save himself.

'Bloody hell, you gave me a scare!' he said.

'Sorry. But I need to talk to whoever's in charge.'

'The boss has gone home.'

Jana stepped into the hall and extended her hand. 'I'm Jana Berzelius.'

'Thomas Rydberg. But I don't think you want to shake hands with me.'

He got up and showed her his greasy hands.

Jana put her hand back in her pocket. Thomas was well built, with dark eyes and a wide chin. A knitted grey cap covered the top of his head, and under his jacket she could see his trousers were held up by old-fashioned braces. She guessed that he must be approaching retirement. A dirty rag stuck out of one trouser pocket and he was trying to clean his fingers on it.

'I wonder if you can help me?' she said.

'With what?'

'I'm investigating a murder.'

'Shouldn't the police be doing that? You don't look like a police officer.'

She sighed. Her plan of not revealing too much was already going wrong. She had to rewind the tape a little.

'I'm the prosecutor investigating the murder of Hans Juhlén.'

Thomas stopped cleaning his hands.

Jana went on: 'We've found a list of combinations of numbers and letters that we know are significant but we can't fully understand. We have reason to believe they could be some sort of code for shipping containers,' she said, and unfolded the sheet of paper with the combinations on it.

Thomas took the paper out of her hand.

'What've you got—'

His expression changed. He hurriedly refolded the sheet and handed it back to Jana.

'I've no idea what these mean.'

'Are you certain?'

'Yes.'

Thomas took a step back. And another.

'I need to know what the combinations stand for,' said Jana.

'No idea. I can't help you.'

Thomas looked at the steel door and then looked back at Jana.

'Do you know anybody who can?'

He shook his head. Took another step back, two, three . . .

Jana realized what he was going to do.

'Wait,' she said, but Thomas had already turned and started to run towards the steel door.

'Wait,' she shouted again, and ran after him.

When Thomas saw that Jana was following him, he started grabbing at tools as he passed, throwing them at her. Either his aim was poor or he intended it as a warning, because nothing hit her and she continued the chase. He finally reached the door and tugged at the handle, only to discover it was locked. Panicking, he pulled harder on the handle and threw his weight against the door – but it was pointless. He couldn't get out.

Jana came up behind him and stopped about three metres away. He was standing still now, breathing heavily. His head swung from side to side as he tried to find another escape route. But he was trapped.

He spotted a large adjustable wrench on the floor, bent down and picked it up. He turned and held it up threateningly. She didn't budge.

'I don't know anything!' he shouted. 'Get out of here!'

He waved the wrench to show that he meant it. That he would hurt her. Badly.

She realized that she ought to do as he said. This had gone too far. She took a step back, and saw Thomas smile. She took a few more steps back, tripped and was caught by the wall.

The next thing she knew, he was standing in front of her.

Close. Too close.

Now she was the one who was trapped.

'Wait,' she said.

'Too late,' said Thomas. 'Sorry.'

In that moment, Jana felt as if she had been transformed. A sense of calm took over. She stared right into his eyes. Focused. Stretched out the fingers of her right hand.

Thomas let out a roar and swung the heavy tool at her. She ducked and he missed. He swung again but she jumped to one side. He renewed his grip on the wrench and tensed his muscles. Then Jana took a step forward, raised her hand and hit him.

Eye, throat, crotch.

Bang, bang, bang.

And then a kick. Back leg forward, rotate, kick. Hard.

She landed a kick in the centre of his forehead.

Thomas collapsed at her feet.

Lifeless.

When she realized what she had done, the adrenaline high vanished and she was overcome with horror. She clasped her hands over her mouth and took a step back. *What have I done?* She lowered her hands, held them in front of her and saw that she was shaking. *How did I . . . ?* Now she became aware of her surroundings. What if somebody had seen her? Twice she looked round to make sure she was safe. There was no one in sight. The hangar was deserted. But what should she do now?

A vibrating sound came from the lifeless man's clothes. It developed into a ringing sound that got louder.

Jana bent down and patted his pocket: nothing. She rolled him over to expose the other pocket, and there she found his mobile. *Missed call*, it said on the screen. *Number withheld*.

She decided to take the phone with her. She threw a quick glance at the lifeless body, took off her gloves, turned and walked out.

The dark shadows hid her as she made her way back to her car. The docks were just as desolate as before.

As soon as she was safely in her car she opened Thomas Rydberg's phone and went through the list of calls received. There were several *number withheld* entries and a few telephone numbers which she wrote down on a parking receipt. In the list of outgoing calls, there were numbers connected to names, and Jana made a note of these too. Nothing seemed out of the ordinary.

It wasn't until she checked the list of outgoing text messages that she found something strange. One of them read: Del. Tues. 1.

She stared at the message, wrote it down, along with the date it was received. Then she slid out the SIM card so the mobile couldn't be traced and put both phone and card in the glovebox.

She took a deep breath, leaned her head against the neck-rest and felt calm again.

It shouldn't be like this, she thought. I ought to be hysterical: screaming, crying, shaking. I just killed a man!

But she didn't feel anything.

And that worried her.

CHAPTER
TWENTY-SIX

Saturday, 21 April

AS USUAL, THE CHILDREN WOKE UP AT SIX.

Henrik Levin stretched and yawned, then glanced across at Emma. She was still asleep. He checked his mobile but no new messages had come during the night.

His pyjamas were comfortably warm as he went up the stairs to the children's room. Felix had tipped the whole box of Lego over the floor and smiled happily when he saw his dad in the doorway. Vilma was sitting on her bed and rubbing the sleep out of one eye.

'Well now, what do you think, guys? Time for breakfast?'

With whoops of joy Felix and Vilma ran down the stairs and into the kitchen. Henrik followed after them. He closed the door to keep the sound down and laid the table with bread, butter, ham slices, juice, milk and yogurt. Vilma opened the pantry cupboard and got out a box of cereal.

While he waited for his own breakfast – two boiled eggs – to be ready, Henrik buttered bread for the children, adding spread or ham to each slice according to their wishes. Felix managed to turn the cereal box upside down and transformed the kitchen table into a buffet with the colourful fruity rings.

Henrik sighed. There was no point getting out the vacuum cleaner. That would wake Emma and she deserved to sleep in for a change. But he couldn't leave the kitchen looking like a battlefield. So while his eggs were cooling he set about picking up all the cereal. Inevitably, some pieces got trodden on and the crumbs fell into the gaps in the rush matting. He hated crumbs. He considered it a cardinal sin to leave a table with crumbs on it. It must be left clean. Wiped down, and preferably sparkling clean.

He looked out through the window. Today he would try to find time for a run. If he got the children fed and dressed and saw to it that they brushed their teeth, Emma would surely let him take half an hour to get some proper exercise. Especially when he'd let her sleep in.

Felix pushed some cereal off the edge of the table. Vilma's joyful laughter encouraged him to do it again. He pushed off a green ring, then an orange one. With his index finger he flicked one that landed in the flower pot. Vilma laughed out loud and Felix flicked off yet another, and another.

'Stop it. That's enough,' Henrik said.

'All right then,' said Vilma.

'All right then,' said Felix.

'Stop copying me,' said Vilma.

'Stop copying,' said Felix.

'You're stupid.'

'Stupid is stupid.'

'Stop it now,' said Henrik.

'It was him,' said Vilma.

'It was her,' said Felix.

'I said, stop it!'

'Stop it yourself.'

'All right, now we're finished.'

Henrik was about to start on his boiled eggs when he heard his mobile ringing.

'Good morning! Sorry to call so early,' said Gunnar Öhrn.

'That's all right,' Henrik lied.

'We've had a call from a witness who saw Hans Juhlén a few days before his death. We ought to check it out. Can you come?'

'Can't Mia take it?'

'I can't get hold of her. She's not answering.'

Henrik looked at Felix and Vilma.

He sighed.

'I'll come.'

The bread had gone mouldy. Mia looked at the green fungus spreading its tentacles across the slice, threw it back in the bag with the rest of the loaf and tossed it in the bin. Then she busied herself finding an alternative breakfast. She heard her mobile ring, but didn't bother to answer. She wasn't in the mood to talk to anybody. She wanted to eat. The fridge didn't have much to offer her, nor the freezer compartment. The pantry had long since been emptied of everything edible, except for a packet of fusilli. She pulled out a saucepan, measured a litre of water and threw in a couple of handfuls of the twisted pasta. Boil for twelve minutes, it said on the packet. Far too long, Mia thought, and turned the timer to ten minutes.

She went into the living room and flopped down on the sofa. With the remote in her hand she surfed channels, trying to choose between repeats of *Garden Wednesday*, *Wilderness Year*, *Spin City* and *Border Guards*.

Bored with the selection, Mia sighed and threw the remote aside. What she needed was a good film channel. But then she'd need a new TV too. With a really good picture. Plasma. Or LCD. With 3D. Henrik had bought one, a 50-inch high-definition model, and Mia had been green with envy. A friend of hers had also bought a huge flat-screen. These days, everybody had one. Except her.

The grey weather outside the window meant you could hardly tell it was daylight, even though dawn was hours ago. She hadn't come home until four in the morning and she had fallen asleep with her clothes on. When she woke up she had her phone in her hand and the battery was dead.

In other words, she'd had a good night out – the best for a long time. She'd got talking to a guy who was nice as well as generous. Even so, Mia had declined his invitation to go home with him. Now she regretted it. If she'd been at his place, she would certainly have been given a decent breakfast with freshly squeezed juice. Then they would have been able to lie entwined in front of his big flat-screen TV. She assumed he had one. It would have been so much better than sitting alone staring at her old TV.

She considered dropping by the Ingelsta shopping mall to check the price of a new one.

She had two kronor left in her account. At least she was in the black. And it wasn't as if she was going to buy one today. She'd see what was available, that's all.

The timer buzzed in the kitchen. Mia went in and took the pasta off the hotplate. I'll just have a look, she thought.

Just looking.

Not buying.

Jana Berzelius took an extra long shower and let the hot water ease away the tension from the night before. She had hardly slept; at dawn she had given up on sleep altogether, put on her jogging gear and run fifteen kilometres. Too far, too fast. It was as if she was trying to run away from what had happened. But she couldn't. The image of the dead man came back to her. For the last kilometre she had run so fast that her nose started bleeding. Despite the blood dripping on to her windcheater, she had sprinted the last hundred metres. Back in her flat, she had felt strangely empowered. She managed to do twenty-three chin-ups on her bar, something she'd never managed before.

Now she stood in the shower and thought about Thomas Rydberg. What was it about that list of combinations that had made him so desperate? What had caused him to panic?

Her thoughts moved on to the way she'd responded to his attack. She'd reacted coldly and instinctively, and that perplexed her. She'd hit back fast, without thinking. And her blows had struck home, each one finding its target. But the thing that troubled her most was that the violence had made her feel good.

Who am I? she wondered.

Karl Berzelius stood by his study window, telephone in hand. The display had long since turned itself off. The voice at the other end was silent. His white shirt was buttoned up to his neck and tucked into the neatly pressed trousers. His hair was grey, thick and combed back.

Outside, the sun's rays had begun to pierce the heavy clouds.

Like spotlights on a stage, all the light fell on a single point: a tree with buds.

But Karl didn't see the sun. He didn't see the tree. He had his eyes closed. When he opened them, the light was gone. Only greyness was left.

He wanted to move, but was unable to do so. It was as if the parquet floor was ice and his feet had frozen to it. He was a prisoner of his own thoughts. He thought about the conversation he had just had with Chief Public Prosecutor Torsten Granath.

'It's a difficult investigation,' Torsten had said, the sound of his car engine in the background.

'I understand,' Karl had answered.

'She'll manage it.'

'Why shouldn't she?'

'It's taken a turn.'

'Yes?'

'The boy . . .'

'I've read about him, yes. Go on.'

'Has Jana told you about him?'

'She never tells me anything, you know that.'

'I know.'

Torsten had then told him in detail where the boy's body had been found. He described the position of the body, the gun discovered close by, and everything else that was recorded in the police report. Then the background noise began to get worse and Karl had to concentrate to make out what he was saying:

'The strange thing is, everything points to him.'

Karl scratched his forehead and pressed the phone even harder against his ear.

'It seems he's the perpetrator. He was the one who killed Hans

Juhlén.' After a thirty-second pause, Torsten spoke again, his voice troubled. 'Even more disturbing, this boy has something carved on his neck – a name, the name of some Greek god, the god of death.'

Karl's heart began to race. He found it hard to breathe. The floor rocked. Torsten's words reverberated in his mind like shockwaves after an explosion.

A name.

On his neck.

Karl opened his mouth but couldn't recognize his own voice. It was alien, distant and cold.

'On his neck . . .'

Then he fell silent. Before Torsten could say anything else, he ended the call. The shock had left him feeling winded, unable to breathe.

I must get some air, he thought now, and pulled open the top button on his shirt. The cloth seemed to cling to him as he struggled with the next button. He tugged so hard that it came loose and fell to the floor. He inhaled deeply, as if he had been holding his breath.

Thoughts whirled around inside his head. He saw a neck, downy black hair against light skin. He saw letters, pinkish-red deformed letters. But it wasn't the neck of a boy.

It was a girl's neck.

It was his daughter's neck.

She was nine years old and quite a handful. She slept poorly and at breakfast she'd describe dreams that seemed to him pure fabrication and the product of a warped imagination. One morning, unable to stand it any longer, he'd grabbed her by the arms and ordered her to be quiet. She did fall quiet, but he was so incensed he took a firm hold of her neck to steer her into her room. It was then he became aware of the uneven skin. He pushed her hair aside to see the scarring, exposing those three letters carved into her skin. It was a sight he would never forget. He'd had to fight the urge to be sick.

Just as he was fighting the nausea that threatened to overwhelm him now.

Karl shut his eyes.

His first thought had been to get the scars removed. He had visited dermatologists and even tattoo parlours, but they'd all said the same thing. It would be difficult to remove the three letters. They couldn't say in advance how many treatments would be necessary. And all of them wanted to see the scars first. Karl couldn't bring himself to admit that the three letters carved into his daughter's skin spelled out a name. How could he expose that to anybody? What would people think?

He opened his eyes.

In the end he'd decided the carved letters would have to stay. He had warned her in no uncertain terms never to show her scars to anybody, and he ordered Margaretha to see that they were covered with plasters and polo-neck sweaters. Her hair was to be allowed to grow and it must be worn long, not put up in a bun or a ponytail. After that they never spoke about it again. It had been dealt with. The subject was closed.

Now there was a boy with a name carved on his neck.

Should he say anything to Jana? But what could he say? They had already dealt with this issue. Filed it away. There was nothing more to add. She was an adult now. It was her own private business. Not his.

Karl's heart beat fast.

The telephone vibrated in his hand and Torsten's name appeared again in the display. He didn't answer.

Just squeezed the telephone and let it go on ringing.

Nils Storhed stood on the port bridge walkway holding his little dog in his arms. To Henrik Levin, who was walking towards him, he looked like a Scot with his tartan beret, lace-up shoes and dark green overcoat.

'He looks like he comes from Scotland,' said Gunnar.

'My thought exactly,' said Henrik and smiled.

The port bridge was a heavy concrete construction which linked Jungfrugatan to Östra Promenaden across the water. Even on a Saturday it was clogged with motorists impatient to escape the congestion. The seagulls had to shriek to make themselves heard above the noise of the traffic.

Storhed was leaning against the railing with the rowing club and city behind him, the docks in front of him, and power station towering up against the grey sky to his left.

The little dog in his arms was panting. Up close they could see that it was shedding; Nils's coat was covered in little white hairs.

'Is your dog tired?' said Gunnar.

'No, she's freezing. She doesn't like the cold,' said Nils.

Neither Henrik nor Gunnar had time to say anything before Nils went on: 'Yes, well, I'm sorry. I know I ought to have called you sooner. I didn't think it was important at the time, but now I realize it is, and yes, my wife's been nagging me all week saying I should phone, but I've had lodge meetings here and dinners there, so it wasn't until this morning I pulled myself together. Anything to put an end to the nagging, if you know what I mean,' said Nils and gave them a wink.

'Yes, I—' said Gunnar.

'Anyway, so I called in and said how it was.'

'You saw Hans Juhlén?' said Gunnar.

'The very same.'

'Where did you see him?' said Henrik.

'Over there.'

Nils pointed towards the docks.

'In the docks?'

'Yes. I saw him there the Thursday before last.'

'And you're quite certain it was him?' said Gunnar.

'Oh yes, I'm certain it was him. I knew his parents. His dad and I were in the same class and we always said those were the days.'

'I see. Can you point out the exact place where you saw him?' said Gunnar.

'Of course. Come with me, boys.'

Nils let his dog down and brushed the hairs off his overcoat. Gunnar and Henrik followed Nils across the bridge towards the docks.

'It's hard to believe he's dead. I mean, who could do something so evil?' said Nils.

'We're trying to find out,' said Gunnar.

'Good. Yes, I hope I can be of some help.'

He led them across the car park and up to the yellow building that housed the port authority offices. They stopped outside the main entrance.

'He was walking along here. He was on his own. And he seemed angry.'

'Angry?'

'Yes, he looked very angry. But he acted as if he knew where he was headed.'

Gunnar and Henrik looked at each other.

'You didn't see anyone else nearby?'

'No.'

'Did you hear any voices or other sounds?'

'No, not that I remember.'

'Did he have anything in his hands?'

'I don't think so, no.'

Henrik looked up at the main building and the dark office windows. He tried the door handle: locked.

'What time was it?' he asked.

'Yes, well it was in the middle of the afternoon, around three, I think. That's usually when we take our walk.' Nils looked at his dog and smiled. 'That's what we usually do, isn't it, old girl? Oh yes. We usually do that. We do, don't we?'

Gunnar pushed his hands into his pockets.

'Do you know if his car was parked here?'

'No idea.'

'We've got to try to get hold of somebody in the office.'

Henrik phoned the police communication centre and asked the operator to contact the managing director of the port authority.

'Shall we look around for the time being?' Gunnar wondered aloud, looking in the direction of the big warehouses.

Henrik nodded. He started to thank Nils for his cooperation and tell him they'd take it from here, but the old man had other ideas.

'I don't suppose you gentlemen would have anything against my coming along with you? I know a lot about the port here.'

Without waiting for an answer, he began telling them the history of the port and what it looked like on the quay in the old days. For a while the two detectives walked in silence while he rambled on about construction materials, the flexibility of the cranes, the old goods wagons that used to carry freight from the ships. Then Gunnar interrupted.

'Hans Juhlén came walking along here, you say?'

'Yes, he came from here.'

Nils pointed in the direction of the warehouses they were now approaching.

'So perhaps he hadn't been in the office building?'

'I don't know. I said I saw him outside, not that he'd been in there.'

Henrik's mobile rang. It was the police operator; the managing director of the harbour authority wasn't answering his phone – should they try the person on call instead? Henrik said yes.

Gunnar took the lead as they crossed the asphalt, peering between the warehouses as they went.

Henrik was not far behind, and after him came Nils with his dog straining at the leash.

Gunnar saw a shed a bit further along and went towards it. He opened the door and looked in. Tables, folding chairs, a coffee machine, some cupboards and an old mat on the floor. The ceiling light was on, as was the radio.

Henrik, still standing on the quay, looked around. His gaze fell on some containers lined up next to a couple of tall gantries equipped with cranes to lift them on to ships.

'Would you believe those metal things are transported around the world?' said Nils, who had now come up beside Henrik. 'They carry anything you want . . . Iron, gravel, garbage, toys.'

Gunnar closed the door to the shed and noticed that the sliding door to a warehouse was open. He motioned to Henrik, trying to attract his attention. But it was futile. Henrik was focused on Nils, who was still listing items that might be transported in containers: '. . . machines, timber, cars, clothes . . .'

Gunnar slid the door to one side and went inside. He cast a glance at the large space. The ceiling lights were on, and he could see that the steel-clad walls were lined with storage shelves and cupboards. Forklifts and trucks were parked on one side, and on the floor lay . . . a man.

Henrik was still standing on the quay with Nils, who wouldn't stop talking.

Then, as if his prayers had been answered, Henrik's phone started to ring. The operator had got hold of an emergency number and was now putting the call through. While he waited for someone to pick up, Henrik excused himself and walked toward the area where Gunnar had been standing.

He peered into the shed, but it was empty. Then he heard Gunnar shout: 'Henrik! Come here!'

Henrik ran into the warehouse and found his boss leaning over the body of a man.

Dead.

'Phone forensics!'

Henrik was already dialling the station.

Jana Berzelius felt clean again.

She brewed a cup of coffee, made a bowl of oatmeal and squeezed some oranges for juice. It took her fifteen minutes to eat her breakfast. She thumbed through the morning paper without much interest before going into her study. She started up her computer and then unlocked the secret storeroom. She had placed Thomas Rydberg's telephone and SIM card in a box. She knew she must get rid of both right away. The box also contained the parking receipt on which she had written all the numbers stored in the mobile phone. She took the receipt to the computer and keyed the first number into the search engine. The number belonged to a company that sold spare parts.

The next number turned out to be a restaurant. The next two were a private individual and an inspector at Norrköping docks. One after another she checked all the numbers Rydberg had called, but there was nothing of interest.

Jana fingered the parking receipt and wondered about that mysterious text message: Del. Tues. 1.

You only wrote as cryptically as that if you had something to hide.

The message had been sent on 4 April. Presumably it meant Delivery Tuesday 1. But what did the 1 stand for? Was it the number of items to be delivered? Or the date?

Jana glanced down at the right-hand corner of the computer screen. Today was 21 April. Ten days to the first of May. She entered the telephone number that the text message had been sent to into the search engine. In less than a second she had an answer. The result surprised her. Could it really be correct?

She read the name again.

The Migration Agency.

THEY SAT IN SILENCE IN THE BACK OF THE VAN. THE
vehicle jolted over rough terrain and it was very noisy inside the cramped space. The girl tried to brace herself against the movement.

Hades sat next to her with a dogged look on his face. His gaze was locked on a point straight in front of him.

The girl was falling asleep when the van finally stopped. The driver told them to do it quickly. Not to waste any time, just complete the mission and then come back out again.

The woman sat opposite them and fidgeted with her necklace. A thin gold chain, with a name engraved on a small ornament that hung from it. The girl couldn't stop staring at the chain. The woman twirled it between her fingers, stroked and fingered the shimmering ornament. The girl tried to read the name but it was hard to see the letters between the woman's fingers. She saw M . . . A . . . M.

The van jerked to a stop. That same moment she saw the last letter and she put them all together in her head to form a word: Mama.

The woman gave the girl an irritated look. She didn't say anything but the girl understood that the time had come.

Now they would leave the van.

And carry out their mission.

CHAPTER TWENTY-EIGHT

THE POLICE CRIME-SCENE TAPE VIBRATED IN THE wind. The docks had been cordoned off and a lot of people had gathered, curious to catch a glimpse of what was happening on the other side of the police tape.

Anneli Lindgren was collecting evidence in the chilly hall. Gunnar Öhrn had called in two additional forensic experts, one of whom had come from Linköping, and they were crouched beside the dead man. They had been examining the body for two hours.

Gunnar and Henrik stood outside, freezing. It hadn't occurred to them to put their hats on – they'd thought they were only going to talk to a witness. But when they discovered a body, their mission at the docks had changed.

'I'm finished,' Anneli called out, waving for them to come back in. 'As far as I can see, he died here. He suffered blows to the head and throat. Björn Ahlmann will be able to tell you more.'

She pulled off her gloves and looked directly at Gunnar. 'That's number three,' she said.

'I know. I KNOW. Do you think they're connected? Any similarities?' he said.

'There may be connections, but no similarities as to the

manner of death. Hans Juhlén and the boy were both shot, but with different weapons. This man has been beaten to death. A heavy blow to the head. Traces of bruising around his neck.'

'The boy had bruising too.'

'True, but apart from that there are no similarities. Unfortunately.'

Anneli pulled out her camera.

'I need to take some pictures of the area,' she said.

Henrik nodded and looked at the man on the floor. 'Looks about sixty,' he said to Gunnar.

'We've asked the manager to come to the station and identify him,' said Gunnar.

'Now?' said Henrik.

'At four. And then we'll have a briefing. First, I must get hold of Ola. And Mia. She never answers.'

Henrik's shoulders sagged.

His Saturday was wrecked.

The price was 12,990 kronor. In instalments. No interest. No charges the first six months. Perfect.

Mia Bolander folded the receipt and smiled at the shop assistant, then manoeuvred her fifty-inch TV out of the store. It even came with 3-D and a special digital-TV package. That alone was worth 99 kronor a month. The contract was for twenty-four months. It was worth it. Now at last she had a state-of-the-art flat screen and all the movie channels. It was a squeeze, but she managed to fit the box into her wine-red Fiat Punto, driving off with the hatch open. On her way home, Mia wondered whether she might invite a couple of friends over for the evening to celebrate. If she provided the venue, perhaps they could be persuaded to bring along booze and nosh. She felt in her pocket for her phone but the pocket was empty. The other one was as well.

Back in her flat she found her mobile with no charge under one of the pillows in her unmade bed. She dug out her charger and plugged it in. Before she could phone her friend, the telephone vibrated in her hand.

It was Gunnar Öhrn.

'Mia's on her way,' said Gunnar, looking at the people seated around the conference table in front of him.

Henrik Levin had a grim expression. Anneli Lindgren looked tired. Ola Söderström, however, looked alert, almost upbeat as he drummed lightly on the table.

Only Jana Berzelius seemed her regular self. She sat ready with her notepad and pen, her long hair hanging down her back as usual.

'As you all know, at 8.30 this morning we found the body of a man, now identified as Thomas Rydberg, at a warehouse in the docks.'

He paused. Nobody asked any questions.

'This is the third murder in a week.'

Gunnar went up to the whiteboard where photos of all three victims had been posted, and he pointed to one of them.

'Here we have Hans Juhlén, shot in his home during the evening of Sunday the fifteenth of April. No sign of a break-in. No witnesses. But on a security camera we saw this boy . . .'

Gunnar moved his finger from the portrait to an enlarged still from the CCTV footage.

'. . . who, on the morning of Wednesday the eighteenth of April, was discovered dead at Viddviken, also shot, but with a different weapon. All the evidence points to this boy having murdered Hans Juhlén. But why? That we don't know.'

Gunnar put his finger on the third photo. 'And today we found another body: Thomas Rydberg. Sixty-one, married, two grown-up children who live on their own. He's worked in the docks all his life, and lives in Svärtinge.

'Apparently, he used to have a bit of a temper. Bad enough that he picked up a couple of convictions for assault and threatening behaviour. He's behaved himself the last few years, though, since he gave up the booze. The forensic team reckon he was beaten to death and that his body had been in the warehouse a number of hours. Which means the murder probably took place yesterday afternoon or evening.'

'How do we know this murder is connected to the other two?' Ola wondered out loud.

'We don't,' said Gunnar. 'Right now, we know very little. But the murder has landed in our laps. And the one connection we do have is that Hans Juhlén was seen in the docks area a few days before he was murdered.'

Gunnar looked gravely at the team.

'We've got a lot to do, to put it mildly. The boy is still unidentified, and nobody has reported him missing. We've had the Migration Agency check asylum seekers' centres throughout the country, and his photograph has been circulated to every single school in Sweden, but no one knows who he is. Our next step is to approach Interpol.'

Anneli stared up at the photos on the wall. 'Two of the victims were shot,' she said, 'but so far all the evidence suggests we are looking for more than one perpetrator.'

'So even if the boy did kill Hans Juhlén, we still have at least one, if not two, perpetrators running loose,' said Gunnar.

Jana swallowed and looked down at the table.

'We need to take another look at Yusef Abrham,' said Gunnar. 'We haven't ruled out the possibility that Hans Juhlén's murder was connected with the blackmail letters – or the rapes, for that matter. There could be a connection between Yusef and this "Thanatos" kid.'

'Are you suggesting the boy might have carried out the murder on Yusef's orders?' said Henrik.

'It's a theory. Another possibility is that both the boy and Thomas Rydberg were part of some drug ring. The drug angle is a weak link, I know, but—'

'We did find narcotics at the docks. Five bags of white powder on a shelf under a storage cupboard,' said Anneli.

'Heroin?' said Ola.

'Looks that way. We've sent the bags to the lab for analysis,' said Gunnar.

'The boy was doped with heroin,' said Ola.

'But where does Hans Juhlén fit into all this? Could he have been selling drugs?' said Anneli.

This met with frowns and shrugs from around the table. Sensing that it was time to rally his team, Gunnar cut in:

'Look, I know it's been a long hard day after a long hard week for most of you, but there's still a lot to be done. I know what you're capable of. I have every confidence that if there's a link between these victims, you will find it.'

He turned to the whiteboard and wrote *LINKS*.

'OK, so let's take Hans Juhlén and Thomas Rydberg. Were

they born in the same town? Did they go to the same school? Cross-check their relatives, friends, everything.'

Next, he wrote *HEROIN* on the board.

'We need to check out all known heroin dealers, big or small. Talk to every addict in town. Contact every informant, see if anyone knows anything.'

Gunnar turned back to the whiteboard wrote *CALL LOGS*, then underlined the words.

'Here's the number of Thomas Rydberg's mobile,' he said, handing a piece of paper to Ola. Across the table, Jana froze; she thought about the phone and SIM card sitting in a box in her apartment.

'The phone's missing,' Gunnar went on, 'so we'll need a list of all incoming and outgoing calls from the phone company. Find out if he had a computer, if he did, get it and examine it.'

'Did you find anything at the docks crime scene?' Jana said.

'No, nothing besides the heroin,' Anneli answered.

'Nothing else? No tracks, no prints.'

'None.'

'Security cameras?'

'No, there weren't any.'

Internally, Jana heaved a sigh of relief.

'The narcotics unit should be able to analyse the heroin and trace it back to whoever supplied it. Henrik, will you follow up on this?' said Gunnar.

'Sure,' said Henrik.

The meeting lasted thirty minutes. When it was over, Jana pulled out her diary and thumbed through it as her colleagues filed out of the conference room. As soon as she was alone, she went and stood in front of the photos of the victims. She studied each one in detail. Her gaze fastened on the boy. His throat was blue. A mark of violence.

She found herself instinctively putting her hand on her own throat. It was as if she could feel the pressure there . . . as if there was something familiar about it.

'Did you find something?'

She gave a start at the sound of Ola Söderström's voice.

He went to the table and retrieved a pile of papers. 'I forgot my notes,' he said. Then he came and stood beside her.

'Feels a bit panicky all of a sudden.' He pointed toward the photographs. 'That we still have so little to go on, I mean. Feels a bit desperate, this narcotics angle.'

Jana nodded.

Ola looked down at his notes.

'And these letters and numbers,' he said. 'I still can't get my head round them.'

Jana didn't answer.

'Have you any thoughts about what they could mean?' he asked, holding the list of the combinations in front of her.

She glanced at them, screwed her eyes and pretended to be thinking.

'No,' she lied.

'But they must mean something,' said Ola.

'Yes, I agree.'

'They must have a purpose.'

'Yes.'

'But I can't figure it out.'

'No.'

'Or I'm interpreting them wrongly.'

'Perhaps.'

'Frustrating.'

'Yes, I realize it is.'

Jana went to the table, picked up her briefcase and her diary and took a couple of steps toward the door.

'Better to be a prosecutor, right?' Ola said. 'And avoid this sort of riddle?'

'Be seeing you,' she said, as she left the room.

In the corridor she broke into a half run, desperate to get away from the police building as quickly as possible. She'd felt extremely uncomfortable lying to Ola, but what choice did she have?

Her phone started ringing the minute she got into her car. When she saw her parents' home number, she felt like ignoring the call. But at the sixth ring she lifted the phone to her ear.

'Jana,' she answered.

'Jana, how are things with you?'

Margaretha Berzelius's voice sounded uneasy.

'Fine, Mother.'

She started the car.

'Are you coming for dinner a week on Tuesday?'

'Yes.'

'It's at seven.'

'I know.'

She looked in the side mirrors and started reversing out of the parking space.

'I'm making a roast.'

'Lovely.'

'Your father likes it.'

'Yes.'

'He wants to talk to you.'

Jana was surprised. This was unusual. She stopped the car and heard her father clearing his throat at the other end of the phone.

'Any progress?' he said. His voice was deep, dark.

'It's a complex investigation,' said Jana.

He remained silent on his end.

She didn't say anything either. Her eyes were wide with anxiety. Something about this case seemed to have caught his attention.

'Well then,' he said finally.

'Well then,' she repeated.

And there the conversation ended.

Afterwards, Jana sat with the phone pressed to her chin, thinking about what he might have wanted to say. That she wasn't doing a proper job? That she wasn't clever enough? That she would fail?

She sighed and put the phone down on the passenger seat. She didn't see the little wine-red car coming into the garage and pulling up behind her until there was a screech of tyres and the long angry beep of a car horn. She pressed the button on the car door to lower the window, looked behind her and saw Mia Bolander behind the wheel of her Fiat.

Mia rolled down her window furiously.

'Can't you see anything when you're in a car like that?' she hissed.

'Oh yes, the vision is good,' said Jana.

'But didn't you see me?'

'Yes,' Jana lied, and smiled to herself.

Mia's face turned darker.

'A pity you didn't back out quicker – you could have crashed into me.'

Jana didn't answer.

'Quite a fancy car you got there. Comes with the job, does it?'

'No. It's my personal one.'

'You must earn plenty.'

'I earn the same as other prosecutors.'

'Evidently pretty good.'

'The car says nothing about my salary. It might have been a gift.'

Mia Bolander laughed.

'Oh yeah, right!'

'By the way,' said Jana. 'You're late, the meeting is already over.'

Mia swore out loud, pressed the accelerator hard and shot off with her tyres screeching.

TWENTY-NINE

THE MAN WAS LYING THERE ASLEEP WHEN THEY
climbed in through the window. Hades first, then the girl after him.
They moved nimbly and silently. Like shadows. As they had been taught
to do. They crept up on either side of the wide bed. At first they moved
slowly, listening for sounds, but the silence of the night was complete.

The girl carefully loosened the knife that was fastened to her back
and held it in a firm grip. Not shaking. Not hesitating. She looked at
Hades. His pupils had dilated, his nostrils too. He was ready. And at
the agreed signal the girl took a quick step forward, climbed up on to the
bed and cut the man's throat. The man gave a start, then he made a
choking noise as he struggled for breath.

Hades stood still, studying the jerky movements. He waited a moment
to let the man feel mortal dread and panic. The man opened his mouth
as if screaming, his eyes wide open. He stretched out one hand in a
desperate plea for help.

Hades smirked. Then he raised his gun and peppered the man with
all the bullets in the magazine. He shouldn't have done that. That
wasn't the order. He was supposed to keep guard. Protect her. But he
fired the gun anyway.

The girl looked at the man who lay lifeless between them. Blood was *pooling across the white sheet. Blood from the slash in his throat, the holes in his chest, stomach and brow.*

Hades was breathing heavily, a dark look in his eyes.

The girl knew that what he had done was wrong, he had broken the rules, but still she smiled at him. Because it felt good. When they stood there in the half-dark bedroom and looked at each other they were both filled with a euphoric feeling of being part of something bigger. They were the tools that they had so long been trained to be.

At last.

Together they climbed out through the window and made their way back to the van. The woman was waiting for them. Her face showed nothing. There was no sign of pride. She impatiently herded them into the back of the van without a word. The girl immediately sank to the floor. Hades sat down too. He sat directly opposite her, with long outstretched legs, and his gaze fixed on the ceiling.

The woman closed the doors and ordered the driver to take them away.

The girl leaned forward and took the bloody knife from the holder on her back. She pulled her legs up to her chin and looked closely at the blade. With her index finger she pushed the red blotches back and forth across the shiny surface. She had managed it; the first mission had been accomplished. Now they would return. Home.

And be rewarded with the white powder.

CHAPTER
THIRTY

HENRIK LEVIN AND MIA BOLANDER PARKED OUTSIDE
the pizzeria. On the assumption they would be working all
evening, they'd decided to grab a bite to eat. Henrik ordered a
salad and Mia asked for a calzone.

'So it could be a settling of accounts?' Mia said.

'Could be,' said Henrik. 'Remember those two people who
got shot last year in Klinga – that was drug-related.'

'But where does Hans Juhlén fit in? Can you see him as some
sort of gang leader?' said Mia. She didn't give Henrik time to
answer, but went on: 'I think it's more likely to be a contract
killing ordered by someone who wanted to be rid of Juhlén,
someone who hired the kid to carry out the murder.'

Mia took a large bite of her calzone.

'I'm still not convinced he was murdered by a nine-year-old
boy,' said Henrik.

'What more would it take to convince you? *Everything* points
to it being the boy who killed Juhlén. Absolutely everything,' said
Mia. 'The murders might be some kind of retribution ordered
by gangs, but carried out by children.'

She looked at Henrik.

'You're sick in the head,' said Henrik. 'Children, killing . . . It's not . . .'

He fell silent.

Mia stared at him. 'But it does happen. And now if you'll excuse me, I'm going to finish my calzone.'

Henrik leaned across the table. 'What I mean is, *how* do you get a child to kill somebody? And who turns a child into a murderer?'

'Good questions,' said Mia.

They ate in silence for a while.

'Perhaps it's all a coincidence. I mean, the murders might not be connected at all,' said Henrik and wiped his mouth with a serviette.

'Drop it, can't you?' Mia ate the last of the calzone, then pushed the plate to one side. 'Shall we be off?' she said.

'Yes. We just have to pay first.'

'Oh yeah. Shit, I've left my wallet at home. Can you cover me?' said Mia with a big ingratiating smile.

'Of course,' said Henrik, and got up from the table.

It was ten o'clock on Saturday evening and Gunnar had completely run out of steam. He sat in his office, coming at the case from every possible angle, and still he couldn't make sense of it. What motive could there be for killing Juhlén, the unidentified boy and Thomas Rydberg? Where did the blackmail letters fit in, the deleted documents, the number and letter combinations? The heroin? The letters carved into the boy's flesh?

Gunnar sighed.

Door-to-door enquiries in the area near the docks had

produced a witness who'd seen a dark-coloured car in the car park at around five o'clock on Friday.

At first he said it was a black BMW, one of the bigger models. Gunnar had immediately ordered a check of all black X-model BMWs in the town. Then the witness changed his mind and said it could have been a Mercedes, so Gunnar stopped the check. When the witness changed his mind again and said the car wasn't dark at all and it could have been a Land Rover, he dismissed the information completely.

Henrik, meanwhile, had been reaching out to all the known heroin addicts in town. So far, he had nothing to show for it.

The officers who'd spoken to Thomas Rydberg's wife hadn't found anything that could help them in the investigation.

When he last looked, Gunnar had forty-two unanswered emails and nine voicemails on his mobile, all from journalists. The media had questions – and expected answers – about the investigation. But Gunnar had no answers to give them.

He got up from the chair, turned off the office light and walked across to the lift. He thought about phoning Anneli. What he needed more than anything right now was to stretch out on the sofa with a cold beer in his hand, and it would taste so much better if he had some company.

When the doors opened again on the ground floor, he was standing with his mobile in one hand. If he called Anneli, she might get the wrong idea. And then it would start over again.

No, no, no, he wasn't going to phone.

He put the mobile back in his pocket, then pressed the button for the third floor again. No point in going home; he might as well go back to the office and carry on working.

Back at his desk, he started to write an urgent appeal for assistance.

It was addressed to Interpol.

THIRTY-ONE

Sunday, 22 April

JANA BERZELIUS WOKE UP LYING ON HER BACK, HER right hand tightly clenched. She flexed her fingers, closed her eyes and consciously tried to relax. There had been something different about her dream last night. A picture of something she had never seen before. But she couldn't quite pinpoint it.

She dragged herself out of bed and went to the bathroom. Once up, she felt a shudder go through her body.

The wind was roaring outside and the rain was beating against the window. She wondered what time it was. Because of the dark she couldn't tell whether it was still night or early morning.

She went back into the bedroom and sat down on the edge of the bed. The covers lay in a pile on the floor, as usual. When she reached down to pick them up, she tried again to remember what had been new in her dream last night.

She lay down and shut her eyes. The images came flooding back. The face. The scarred face and the voice that shouted at her. He held her in a firm grip. Hit her. Kicked her. Shouted at her again. He had a tight grasp of her neck, she couldn't breathe. She fought to come out of his grip, to get some air, to survive.

He merely laughed at her. But she didn't give up. She had a single thought. To never give up. And just as everything started to black out, she saw the detail that hadn't been there before.

A necklace.

A shining, glimmering necklace lay by her side. She reached out for it. Something was written on it. A name. Mama. Then everything went black.

Jana sat up and pulled all the notebooks out of the cupboard under the bedside table. She spread them out across the bed. Then she flicked through them, back and forth, back and forth, from notebook to notebook, trying to find anything she had written about a necklace or an image of a necklace. But she searched in vain. Then she did something she hadn't done for ages.

She turned to an empty page, picked up a pen and started to draw.

For the greater part of the night, Henrik Levin had lain awake. When the clock struck six, he got up, made coffee and ate a bowl of yogurt with some sliced banana. He wiped the draining board and the kitchen table down twice, then brushed his teeth before waking Emma to tell her he must work yet another Sunday. When he opened the front door, he heard the children waking up and hurried out so he wouldn't have to see their disappointed faces.

One of the leads he was following, and which he had been thinking about during the sleepless night, concerned the drugs the forensic team had found in the docks. He thought a larger search of the dock area was needed, and that they ought to start interviewing the staff.

The steering wheel was cold to the touch when he placed his

bare hands on it. As soon as he turned the key in the ignition, the CD player started at full volume. Markoolio's voice sang joyfully about Phuket, summer all year round, and then 'Thai, Thai, Thai.' Henrik turned the CD off and backed out of the drive.

In the silence he thought about the previous evening. After dinner at the pizzeria, and before they called it a day, he and Mia had called on a few more heroin addicts. They had also spoken to an informant who'd helped them in the past with information about underage dealers. Henrik had hoped that the man would be more willing to talk than the addicts, but he turned out to be as taciturn as the rest.

Mia had pushed the man against a wall, moved in until her face was three centimetres from his, and yelled, 'Now just you listen to me, you're going to tell me everything you know.' Then she had threatened him with all sorts of retribution if he didn't give them information.

Henrik had been forced to intervene and drag her back to the car. She had calmed down eventually. There was no point trying to frighten people into giving information. Most of them were far more scared of the people they'd be informing on than they were of anything the police might do to them.

While waiting at a red light, Henrik found himself thinking he ought to put more emphasis on the weapons in the investigation, a Glock and a .22 Sig Sauer. And then he needed to chase the transport department for details of any vehicles caught by the speed cameras in the area where the boy's body was found.

By the time he arrived at the office, he was feeling much more positive about the day ahead.

Gunnar was already sitting in front of his computer, fingers tapping away on the keyboard.

'Did you have trouble sleeping, too?' said Henrik.

'No, though it was a bit awkward trying to fit on the sofa in here,' Gunnar answered without taking his eyes off the screen.

Henrik grinned. 'I thought I'd go through the files again, see if anything leaps out at me,' he said.

Gunnar whirled around on his chair. 'Do that. I'm just forwarding a few emails from curious reporters to the press officer. Only twenty-two to go!'

Gunnar whirled back and carried on typing.

Henrik went to the conference room, turned on the lights and looked down from the window at the empty roundabout. Norrköping had not woken up yet. One by one he laid out the files with all the information they had on Hans Juhlén, the unknown boy they'd taken to calling 'Thanatos' after the carving on his neck, and Thomas Rydberg. When the big table was completely covered, he sat down to look through them all.

The file on Thomas Rydberg consisted mainly of thirty or so pictures that Anneli had taken at the scene the day before. The last four pictures had been taken outside in the docks. Henrik looked at them absentmindedly and felt a tiredness creep up on him. He closed the ring binder noisily and wandered off to the kitchen where he drank a large glass of water. As he did, it occurred to him that he had seen something in the photos.

He banged the glass down, hurried back into the conference room and opened the Rydberg file again. Once more he looked through the photographs, page by page, photo after photo. He was close to giving up when he got to the very last photo. It was an overview of the crime scene, and Anneli had probably been kneeling when she took the photo. The wide-angle showed Forensics busy working. In the background, through the open doors of the hangar, you could see the container depot. Several different-coloured containers were standing there.

He tried to see what was written on them. But the writing was too small to make out. He hurried down the corridor to Gunnar's room.

'Have you got a magnifying glass?'

'No, look in Anneli's room.'

Anneli's office was in perfect order and every item had its place. Henrik opened the desk drawers one after the other. In the bottom one he found what he was looking for and hurried back to the conference room. Now he could see the details he needed on the photo. The picture had been taken from too far away for him to be absolutely certain, but on one container there were some letters and numbers.

Henrik opened the Juhlén file and got out the list with the ten combinations. He started to compare them and gave a start. The combination had the same format: four letters and six numbers.

At a quarter to eleven Henrik Levin and Gunnar Öhrn got in the car to drive to the docks. They had arranged to meet the port authority director, who was going to show them round the container depot.

When they turned in to the parking area a man of short stature with reddish hair and black glasses was standing there waiting for them. He was wearing a blue checked shirt and light jeans. He gave them a friendly smile and introduced himself as Rainer Gustavsson. Henrik declined his offer of coffee and asked to be taken directly to the container area.

A large ship was in the process of being loaded. Container after container was being lifted up by the cranes on the dockside gantries. Metal clanged against metal, cranes winched and low-ered and trucks passed by in an endless line. Several dockers in blue overalls with company logos were standing on the deck. They were all wearing safety helmets. Two men checked that everything was safely stowed and fastened. They knocked on the steel wires, occasionally pulling out a spanner to tighten them.

Henrik looked up at the hull where the containers towered five high.

'It takes a lot of man-hours to load a ship,' said Rainer. 'And it must all be done quickly. If something goes wrong and delays the ship, everyone starts losing money. Efficiency is everything in the freight world.'

'How many containers can you load on a single ship?' Henrik asked.

'The largest ships that come to us can take six thousand six hundred containers. But there are ships in other parts of the world capable of carrying more than eighteen thousand containers. If you lose one minute for every container, that would mean more than three hundred hours' delay. Which is why, in recent years, we'e made wide-ranging investments in the docks to improve the logistics. Now we have a complete system to deal with everything from notification, in-delivery, examination, estimates, repairs and out-delivery. Thanks to our two new ship-to-shore gantry cranes, we can also handle larger and larger container ships,' said Rainer.

'What sort of goods do you handle?' said Gunnar.

'Every kind imaginable.' Rainer stiffened with pride.

'How do you check the contents?' said Gunnar.

'That's down to customs. But sometimes it's hard to determine who's responsible for the freight.'

Rainer stopped and looked at the two men.

'We've had quite a few investigations here over the years, carried out by authorities ranging from the local council to the Environmental Protection Agency.' He lowered his voice a little. 'Not long ago we had three people from Nigeria who had filled a container with scrap from old cars. They wanted to send it from here to Nigeria because they thought the scrap was valuable. What we regard as scrap here, can be useful there. But they didn't know about documentation. So the council stepped in and insisted that the entire container be emptied so they could evaluate its contents. Some car parts were confiscated as hazardous waste. I don't know what happened to the container after that.'

Rainer started walking again.

Henrik and Gunnar came up on either side of him.

'But how often does that happen? That you have to empty a container?' said Henrik.

'Not so often. Freight is governed by customs formalities. The seller is obliged to declare the goods for export and the buyer must declare for import. There's a whole set of regulations for sea freight. Sometimes the parties to an agreement don't even know the delivery conditions in the other party's home market. That's when things can go wrong.'

'How so?' said Gunnar.

'Confusion can arise as to who will pay for insurance, when the risk is transferred from the seller to the buyer and so on. There are international regulations, but legal responsibility can still be a bit of a grey area.' Rainer threw out both hands. 'Here we are!'

The containers were piled like enormous metal building blocks. On the right stood three orange-coloured ones on top of each other. After them another three were stacked in the same way. Grey, rusty and with the name Hapag-Lloyd on the sides. Fifty metres further on there were another forty-six containers: blue, brown and grey, mixed together.

The wind found its way through the narrow space between them, making a weak howling sound. The ground was damp and the clouds looked threateningly dark.

'Where do the goods come from?' asked Henrik.

'Mainly from Stockholm and the Mälardal region. But also from Finland, Norway and the Baltic states. And of course Hamburg. Most of the goods from abroad are reloaded there and then they come to us,' said Rainer.

'We found narcotics in the place where Thomas Rydberg was murdered. What would you know about that?'

'Nothing.'

'So you have no idea whether there is any trading in drugs going on in the docks?'

'No.' Rainer looked down at his shoes, stamped on the ground. 'Of course, I can't be certain it doesn't happen. But if that sort of illegal trade were taking place on a large scale, then I think I would have noticed it.'

'Has there been any other illegal trade? Liquor, for example?'

'Not any longer. Nowadays a lot of ships have forbidden consumption of alcohol onboard.'

'But before that?'

There was a delay before he answered.

'We've had problems with ships from the Baltic states. They were selling bootleg liquor and we caught youths buying vodka directly from the ships.'

'Have you discovered any trading recently?'

'No. But it's hard to prevent. We have six thousand metres of quays to keep an eye on, and we can't have staff just patrolling the docks. We don't have the resources.'

'So there could be drug trading going on here?'

'Yes, you can't categorically say that there isn't any.'

Henrik walked up to a blue container and studied the length of it. Drops of water were running down its corrugated metal side. He then went round to the doors. There were four galvanized lock mechanisms from the top down, and in the middle was a box covering a sturdy padlock. On the right-hand door there were numbers and letters.

It was a combination he was now familiar with.

'It's been confirmed that Hans Juhlén, head of the Migration Agency's asylum department, was here in the docks a few days before he died,' said Gunnar.

'Oh?' said Rainer.

'Do you know what he might have been doing here?'

'No, I don't. No idea.'

'Do you know if he met anyone?'

'You mean like a relationship?'

'I don't mean anything. I'm just trying to find out what he was doing here. I wondered if perhaps he was acquainted with someone employed here?'

'Not that I know of, but it's possible.'

'In Hans Juhlén's computer we found ten different combinations of numbers and letters.' Henrik pulled the list from his pocket. 'Can you tell me what they mean?'

Rainer took the list and pushed his spectacles up his nose.

'Yes, these are numbers for containers. That's how we identify them.'

*

Jana Berzelius thoroughly wiped Thomas Rydberg's mobile with a cloth and some degreasing cleaner and then put it inside a 3-litre freezer bag that she placed on the table. She worried about how she was going to get rid of the phone. Her first thought was to burn it. But where? In the flat it would set off the fire alarm, and even if she took the battery out, it would probably smell of smoke and burned plastic out in the hallway and stairwell. Another idea was to throw it into the Motala Ström River and let it sink to the bottom. That seemed to be the best option, but she'd have to throw it in from a place where she couldn't be seen. She thought about places where you could access the river, places you could rely upon to be deserted.

In the end, she decided the only thing to do was to go out and look for such a place.

She put the bag with the mobile in her handbag and left the apartment.

Gunnar Öhrn and Henrik Levin sat in the dock office and watched as Rainer Gustavsson typed at his computer.

'OK, shoot!' said Rainer. His reddish eyebrows rose above his glasses and his brow became furrowed.

Henrik unfolded the sheet of paper in front of him and read out the first combination on the list.

'VPXO.'

'And then?'

'410009.'

Rainer punched the keyboard.

There was a slight buzzing sound as the computer searched the web-based international register of shipping containers. It barely took a minute, but to Henrik it felt like an eternity.

'Ah, right. This container is no longer in the system. It must have been scrapped. Shall we check the next one?' said Rainer.

Henrik was squirming on his chair.

'CPCU106130,' he read out.

Rainer entered that.

'Nope, that's not there either. Next one?'

'BXCU820339,' Henrik read out.

'No, the system says it isn't in use. They've probably all been scrapped.'

Henrik felt a stab of dejection. A moment ago they had a decisive lead, and now they were back to square one.

Gunnar rubbed his nose in evident irritation.

'Can you see where the containers came from?' he asked.

'We can look. This one came from Chile. I'll see where the other two . . . yes, they were from Chile too,' said Rainer.

'Who scraps them?' said Gunnar.

'The company that owns the container. In this case it's Sea and Air Logistics, SAL.'

'Can you check where the other containers came from? And who owns them?'

Henrik put the list down on the table. Rainer entered the fourth combination and made a note. The same with the fifth. And the sixth.

When the tenth and final combination had been checked, the pattern was clear.

All the containers came from Chile.

CHAPTER
THIRTY-TWO

'STOP!' THE WOMAN SHOUTED.

'Now?' asked the driver.

'Yes, now! Stop!' she shouted.

'But we've got a long way to go. This isn't where—'

'Shut up.' The woman cut him off. 'I'm going to do it, and I decide where. Not you and not him.'

The man braked and the van came to a halt.

The girl immediately understood that something was wrong. Hades reacted too and straightened his back.

The woman glared at the girl.

'Give me the knife!'

The girl obediently handed it over.

'And the gun. Give it to me!'

Hades looked at her when he handed the gun over. The woman grabbed it from his hand and checked the magazine.

It was empty.

'You weren't supposed to shoot,' said the woman in a hard voice.

Hades lowered his head.

The woman opened a box in the corner of the driver's cab and pulled out a full magazine which she loaded the gun with. Then she pulled the *firing mechanism as far back as she could, let go and pointed the weapon at the girl.*

'Out,' she said.

They stepped out of the car and into the forest. The silence was like a lid. The night was turning into day and the first rays of the sun were appearing between the fir trees. The woman pushed her along with the gun pressing against her back. Hades went first. He was hanging his head as if he had done something wrong and was ashamed.

The path they were walking along was narrow. Now and then she stumbled on the roots which stuck up from the soft ground. The branches scratched her arms and wet the thin cotton of her sweater. The further they went into the forest, the weaker the glow of the van's headlights.

One hundred and fifty-two steps, she counted silently and continued counting as they approached a dip in the terrain.

The dense forest opened up in front of them.

'Keep on walking!' said the woman, shoving her hard between her shoulders with the muzzle of the weapon. 'Move on!'

They went down into the dip using their hands to push away the thick branches.

'Stop there!' said the woman, grabbing her by the arm.

She pushed the girl towards Hades and positioned them next to each other. She gave them a last glance before walking round them and disappearing behind them.

'You thought you were immortal, didn't you?' she said.

She hissed the words.

'You couldn't have been more wrong. You are nothing, just so you know. You are completely worthless little insects that nobody wants! Nobody wants anything to do with you! Do you hear me? Not even Papa cares about you. He needed you to kill, nothing else. Didn't you know that?'

The girl looked at Hades and his eyes met her panic-stricken look.

Please smile, she thought. Smile and say it's only a dream. Let that little dimple on your cheek become even deeper. Smile. Just smile!

But Hades didn't smile. He blinked.

One, two, three, he indicated with his eyelids. One, two, three.

She understood what he meant and blinked back, in confirmation.

'Of course you didn't grasp that. You're brain-dead, the pair of you. Programmed. But now it's over.'

The woman spat out the words.

'Now it's over, you damned monsters!'

Hades blinked again. Harder this time. One, two, three. And then again. The last time. One. Two. THREE.

They threw themselves backward. Hades got a firm hold of the woman's arm and twisted it to make her drop the gun. The woman was caught unawares and instinctively pulled the trigger. A shot went off. The sound echoed between the trees.

But then she couldn't resist the pressure from Hades any longer and shrieked with pain when he forced her arm back.

The girl got hold of the gun and pointed it at the woman. Then she saw Hades sink down on the grass. He had been hit.

'Give me the gun,' snarled the woman.

The girl's hands shook. She stared at Hades lying still in the grass. His throat was bare and his breathing was laboured.

'Hades!'

He turned his head towards the girl and they looked into each other's eyes.

'Run,' he whispered.

'I said, give me the gun,' shouted the woman.

'Run, Ker,' Hades whispered again and coughed violently.

'Run!'

The girl backed away a couple of steps.

'Hades . . .'

She didn't understand. She couldn't just run off. Couldn't leave him.

'Run!'

Then she saw it.

His smile.

It spread right across his face. And that very same moment she understood.

Then she turned and ran.

CHAPTER THIRTY-THREE

JANA BERZELIUS DROVE ALONGSIDE THE MOTALA Ström River for more than thirty minutes without finding a single place that suited her purpose. People were present at every potential site and it would presumably have been regarded as odd if she had gone to the water's edge and thrown a mobile phone straight into the river.

She manoeuvred the car into a parking space on Leonardsbergsvägen and turned the engine off. How was she going to get rid of the phone? Finally the frustration that had been building up inside her erupted. She hit the steering wheel. And again. With both hands.

Hard.

Harder.

Then she leaned her head back and caught her breath. She put her elbow against the car door and the fist of her right hand against her mouth. She sat like that for a long while, gazing out across the barren landscape. Everything was grey. Depressing. The trees had no leaves, the ground was brown from the dirty snow that had recently melted. The sky was the same dark grey as the asphalt on the road.

Then an idea started to take form inside her head. Jana opened her handbag and pulled out the plastic bag with the mobile in it. Why hadn't she thought of this before!

She sat up in the driver's seat and put the phone next to her bag. The number the text message had been sent to belonged to the Migration Agency. That much was clear. But she hadn't bothered trying to phone the number – yet.

She started the car, absolutely certain she would make the call. But first she had to buy a prepaid card.

She pulled out of the parking space and set off to find the nearest petrol station.

Mia Bolander sat rocking on the chair in Henrik Levin's office. She was biting her thumbnail while reading the list with the combination numbers.

Gunnar stood in the middle of the room, Henrik sat at his desk.

'SAL manufactures containers in Shanghai, China,' said Henrik, adjusting the desk pad so it lined up with the edge of the table. 'They own, or rather they owned, the first three containers on Juhlén's list. They've all been scrapped.'

'What about the others?' said Mia.

'Four of the others were owned by SPL Freight and the rest by Onboardex. The strange thing is, every single one of those containers has been scrapped. So we must find out what the containers were filled with. Henrik, you take SAL. Mia, you take SPL. I'll take Onboardex. I know it's Sunday, but surely we can get hold of somebody. We must get an answer to why Juhlén had identification codes for scrapped containers in his computer.'

Gunnar strode out of Henrik's office like a man on a mission.

Mia got up and left the room, dragging her feet. Henrik sighed and suppressed the urge to tell her to get a move on.

He put the landline phone in front of him, and dialled the number to SAL in Stockholm. He was automatically connected to an exchange abroad where a digitally recorded voice announced in English that the telephone wait time was five minutes. Eventually he heard a male operator answer in English with a German accent.

Henrik explained what he wanted in rather limited English and was connected to a female administrator in Stockholm with a drawling voice.

After introducing himself, Henrik got to the point.

'I want to check a couple of shipping containers that you owned in the past.'

'Have you got their identifying numbers?'

Henrik read out the numbers and heard the woman keying them into her computer.

Silence followed.

'Hello?'

'Hello, yes?'

'I thought you had hung up.'

'No, I'm waiting for an answer from the system.'

'I know that the containers were scrapped, but I want to know what sort of goods they contained.'

'Well, as far as I can see, they weren't scrapped.'

'They weren't?'

'No, they aren't in the system at all.'

'What do you mean?'

'They're missing.'

'All three of them?'

'Yes, all three. They've disappeared.'

Henrik stood up, thoughts whirling in his heard. He stuttered his thanks and ended the call.

In five quick strides he was in Mia's office.

She was just putting the phone down.

'That's odd,' she said. 'According to SPL, those containers were never delivered. They've vanished without trace.'

Henrik went straight into Gunnar's room and almost bumped into him in the doorway.

'You won't believe—' Gunnar started.

'Don't tell me,' said Henrik. 'The containers are missing, aren't they?'

'Yes, how did you know?'

The pay-as-you-go SIM card cost fifty kronor. Jana Berzelius paid in cash and refused the offer of a receipt. She left the little kiosk, edging out sideways so as not to bump into the display shelf loaded with sweets and chewing gum.

She had opted to purchase the card at the kiosk after realizing that petrol stations were equipped with security cameras. Here, there was no chance of the transaction being recorded.

Once she was back in her car, she pulled off her gloves, opened the envelope with the SIM card and slotted it inside Thomas Rydberg's mobile phone. Then she turned the phone on and remained sitting with it in her hand for quite a while before dialling the number that the text message had come from. She waited to see if the call would go through. She had expected that the person she was ringing wouldn't answer, that the phone would have been turned off, or the number was no longer in use.

When she heard the first ring she was genuinely surprised. Her heart started to beat faster. She put one hand on the steering wheel and squeezed it hard. Then she heard a voice announcing a name.

The name astounded her.

The temperature in Henrik Levin's office had gone up a couple of degrees. Gunnar Öhrn sat with a sheet of paper in front of him. Mia Bolander was leaning against the wall, and Henrik sat on a chair, one leg crossed over the other.

'So not one of the three companies received their containers. They're all missing?' said Mia.

'Yes,' said Henrik. 'But that isn't so unusual. Shipping freight containers can fall overboard in heavy seas and the risk is greater if the crew haven't secured them properly. Or if they've been loaded wrongly.'

'Evidently a lot of containers are lost every year. It's hard to get any exact figures, but I heard it can be between two thousand and ten thousand,' said Gunnar.

'That's one hell of a wide range,' said Mia.

'And the companies didn't seem especially concerned,' said Gunnar.

'No, apparently it's quite normal,' said Henrik.

'They'll be well insured,' said Mia.

There was silence in the room while they considered their next move.

'OK, so if these containers, the ones we've been looking for, are somewhere on the seabed, then that isn't particularly strange. The odd thing is: why would Hans Juhlén have these identification numbers in his computer?' said Henrik.

'What did they contain? I mean, they're containers, they must have contained something,' said Mia.

'Nobody can tell us. All they know is that they came from Chile, they arrived in Hamburg, were reloaded here in Norrköping and then supposedly shipped back to Chile again. But they never arrived; they disappeared during the return journey across the Atlantic,' said Henrik.

'So there's a whole lot of valuable goods lying on the seabed, in other words? I ought to become a diver,' said Mia.

'The first container on the list was recorded as missing in 1989,' said Henrik. 'Another two went missing in 1990 and 1992. The last one disappeared a year ago. In between, the others went missing. So why did Hans Juhlén have these ten container identification numbers, all of them missing, in his computer?' Henrik recrossed his legs and sighed.

Mia Bolander shrugged her shoulders in a gesture of helplessness.

Ola Söderström came in, brushing against the wall with the ghost drawing on it. The drawing fell to the floor. 'Sorry,' said Ola.

'Doesn't matter,' said Henrik, as Ola picked up the drawing and handed it to him.

'Nice ghost,' Ola said.

'My boy is in a difficult period right now. Everything is about ghosts.'

Henrik put the drawing on his desk and went back to his musings.

'Ghosts?' said Mia.

'Yes, he dreams about ghosts, draws ghosts, watches films about ghosts,' said Henrik.

'No, I mean . . . ghosts! When we questioned Yusef Abrham, he said something about ghost containers, didn't he?' said Mia.

'Yes,' said Henrik.

'He was talking about refugees dying en route.'

'But these containers were on their way *from* Sweden, not to Sweden.'

'Yes, you're right,' said Mia.

'Have you found out what was inside them?' said Ola.

'It's almost impossible to get any information about that,' said Henrik.

'Perhaps they were empty?' said Ola.

'Doesn't seem likely. If that were the case, why would Juhlén bother keeping the numbers? Most of these containers disappeared years ago.'

Henrik got up from the chair and went on: 'The document was deleted Sunday evening, correct? Ola?'

'Yes, at 18.35,' said Ola.

'Hang on a moment . . . What time did he pick up the pizza?'

'At 18.40, if I remember right,' said Ola.

'How far is it between the Migration Agency and the pizzeria that we're talking about?'

Mia pulled out her phone and entered the addresses in a map app.

'Eight minutes by car.'

'But that assumes one is already sitting in the car, doesn't it?'

'Yes . . .'

'Then it would have been impossible for Hans to leave his office, get into his car, drive to the pizzeria and pick up his order in five minutes, wouldn't it?'

'Yes . . .'

'So somebody else in his office must have deleted the document,' said Henrik.

★

'I don't know how we could have missed this. But it is now clear Hans Juhlén could not have deleted the document from his computer,' said Henrik into the phone.

Jana wished she hadn't answered the call. Henrik just went on and on.

'He died sometime between seven and eight in the evening. The document was deleted at six thirty-five. So somebody else must have done it.'

'Yes.'

'We need to find out who.'

'Yes.'

Jana was silent for a moment or two, then she said, 'The young security guard who worked at the Migration Agency that Sunday . . . why don't you phone him again? Ask him if he saw anybody else in the building. And now I'm afraid you'll have to excuse me. I'm busy.'

'OK,' said Henrik. 'I only wanted to let you know.'

Jana Berzelius ended the conversation and stepped out of her car. She had parked in an out-of-the-way spot, but she could see the terraced house she was going to in the distance.

She crossed the street with quick strides and kept away from the street lamps as best she could. Now and then she looked over her shoulder to check there was no one else in sight.

She checked the windows but there was no movement from the curtains. She was grateful for the darkness when she passed through a gate in the white-painted fence and went up to the front door. The letterbox outside had the number 21 on it. And a name: Lena Wikström.

*

Mia Bolander took a noisy bite of the pear she had found in the fruit bowl in the staff kitchen.

Henrik had tasked her with phoning the security company that patrolled the Migration Agency. She took another big bite while she punched in the number. A receptionist answered.

'Mia Bolander, Norrköping CID.'

But the words were hard to distinguish with a piece of pear still in her mouth. Mia swallowed and started again.

'Hello, this is Detective Inspector Mia Bolander. I need to get hold of . . .'

She reached for the carelessly scribbled name on the notepad and read it out loud.

'. . . Jens Cavenius. It's urgent.'

'One moment please.'

Mia waited thirty seconds and managed to eat the rest of the pear.

'Unfortunately, Jens Cavenius is not working today,' said the receptionist.

'I must get hold of him as a matter of urgency. Make sure he phones me, otherwise I'll trace his number myself. OK?' said Mia.

'Yes, right.'

She gave the receptionist her number and thanked her for her help.

Within five minutes, Jens Cavenius returned her call.

Mia got straight to the point.

'I need to know exactly what you saw that Sunday Hans Juhlén died, so think carefully. Did you actually see him?'

'I went past his office.'

'Yes, but did you *see* him?'

'No, not exactly, but the lights were on in the room.'

'And?'

'I heard him typing on the computer.'

'But you didn't see him?'

'No . . . I . . .'

'So somebody else could have been there?'

'But . . .'

'Think a bit *more* now: did you see anybody else in the office, did you notice any items of clothing or anything else?'

'I'm trying to think.'

'And I'm trying to get you to think quicker.'

'I believe I saw an arm through the crack in the door. A lilac arm.'

'And if you think a bit more, who might have a lilac arm at the office?'

'I don't know . . . but perhaps . . .'

'Yes?'

'Perhaps it could have been his PA, Lena.'

Lena Wikström was feeling uneasy. She fingered her gold necklace and bit her lip. She felt sick when she thought about Thomas Rydberg not being there. That he had been murdered. In the docks. By whom?

She felt even more sick when she looked at her mobile which still lay on the bed, on top of the blanket. Two lamps on the dresser were turned on, and light fell on the three frames which were placed between them. Happy children's faces with midsummer garlands, a reminder of last summer. Small imitation crystals hung from a white enamel ceiling light.

Who had phoned?

She let go of the necklace and opened one of the wardrobe

doors, pulled out a suitcase and put it next to the phone on the bed.

She had never before been called on that number. She was the only one who initiated the communication. Nobody else. That was the arrangement. The others were only allowed to text messages which were memorized by the recipient and deleted forever. Nobody ever phoned. That was how it worked. Now the rule had been broken.

By whom?

She hadn't recognized the number. Now she didn't dare touch the phone. Just let it lie there on the bed.

Lena unzipped the suitcase. Her instinct was to run away. Of course it could have been a wrong number. A mistake. But she wasn't convinced. The worry of being exposed was simply too great for her to let the call pass.

She opened another wardrobe door and picked out three cardigans, a blouse and four tops. She didn't bother about underclothes, just packed what was on top in the drawer.

She could buy some new clothes wherever she went. She had often thought this day would come; she had *known* it would come. Even so, she had no idea where to go. Where she could run to.

Then the doorbell rang.

Her hands froze on the suitcase. She wasn't expecting a visitor.

Lena looked out through the bedroom window which faced the front door. But she couldn't see anybody.

With a growing sense of unease, she tiptoed out of the bedroom, through the living room, past the bathroom and into the hall. She looked through the peephole in the door but her eye only met with darkness.

With both hands she unlocked the door, then the two extra locks and looked out through the narrow chink.

A woman was standing there.

'Hello, Lena,' said the woman, and put her foot in the door.

'What have we got on Lena?' said Gunnar Öhrn.

They were all standing around the conference table. Everybody felt the tension in the room.

'She is fifty-eight years old, unmarried, two adult children, her son lives in Skövde and her daughter in Stockholm. No criminal record,' Ola Söderström read out.

'So what do we do now?' said Mia.

'We must bring her in for questioning,' said Henrik.

'But so far all we have is a scatterbrained teenager who thinks he might have seen her in Juhlén's office that Sunday,' said Mia.

'I know, but it's the most promising lead we've got,' said Henrik.

'Henrik's right. It's important that we follow up on this. Right away!' Gunnar pointed a finger at himself. 'I'm going there. Henrik and Mia, you're coming with me.'

He left the room with Henrik and Mia close behind him.

Ola was left on his own.

He knocked on the tabletop, absorbed the news that the investigation had at last gained some momentum, and went into his room to start up the computer. Then he took his lunchbox into the staff kitchen and put it in the fridge.

On his way back, he happened to notice a bundle of papers in Gunnar Öhrn's inbox. He picked up the bundle to see what they were. They were conversation logs from a mobile operator. The number belonged to Thomas Rydberg.

Ola had a quick look at the lists. When he came to the page with outgoing text messages, he was astounded. Then he suddenly found himself in a hurry, ran across to the lift and frantically pressed the button to catch up with his colleagues.

Lena Wikström didn't have time to react when Jana Berzelius pushed her way in and closed the door behind her. It wasn't very light in the hall, but Jana could see some china figures and an embroidered cloth above a sideboard. A mirror with an ornamental frame. A frosted shade on the ceiling light.

Jana stood absolutely still on the mat in the hall. There was something familiar about the woman in front of her. She didn't know what.

'Who are you?' Lena said, her eyes riveted on Jana.

'My name is Jana Berzelius. I'm investigating the murder of Hans Juhlén.'

'Indeed? But what are you doing in my home at this time of day?'

'I need answers.'

Lena stared uncomprehendingly at the woman in high-heeled shoes and a dark trench coat.

'I can't help you.'

'Oh yes, you can,' said Jana and went straight into the kitchen.

'You can't just barge in here like this,' said Lena, watching her from the hallway.

'Yes I can, and if you object, I'll issue a search warrant. Then I'll have every right to be here.'

Lena sighed. 'OK, what do you want to know?'

'Hans Juhlén was murdered in his home,' Jana said.

'That's not a question.'

'No.'

Lena walked up to the front door and locked it. She carefully opened a drawer and took out a gun which she tucked inside the waistband of her trousers. Then she pulled her sweater over it to hide the bulge. When she was done, she went into the kitchen with a forced smile on her lips.

'So, what's the question?' Lena said.

'Hans Juhlén was murdered at approximately seven o'clock. When the police went through his computer they found some identification numbers for shipping containers. The combinations were deleted from the computer at half past six. So he couldn't have done that himself. Was it you?'

Lena was at a loss for what to say. She could feel pressure building in her chest.

Jana went on: 'I have an important reason to find out what was in those containers.'

'I'm sorry, but I must ask you to leave.'

'I just want to know.'

'You will leave my home.'

Jana remained standing by the table while Lena's hand inched behind her back, towards the gun.

'I'll stay until I get an answer,' said Jana. She had seen Lena's hand start to move behind her back and made herself ready for what might come next.

The moment Lena pulled the gun from her waistband, Jana threw herself forward, struck Lena in the kidneys with the side of her hand, then kneed her in the stomach. Lena lost her grip on the gun and groaned from shock as well as the crippling pain.

Jana checked the gun, which was loaded, cocked the trigger

and crouched down in front of Lena. She could see something glimmer around Lena's neck.

Something goldish.

The floor rocked when she saw what it was. Everything started swimming before her eyes, and she heard a roaring in her ears. Her temples ached and her pulse was racing so much, it hurt.

A necklace.

With a name.

Mama.

The lift descended extremely slowly. At least, it felt like it did.

Ola Söderström stared at the display as the lift passed each floor. When the lift stopped and the doors opened, he ran out as fast as he could into the garage to find his colleagues. He heard a car door slam and walked rapidly towards the sound. He heard another door and stretched to see over the tops of the parked cars.

Then he saw Gunnar Öhrn's silhouette disappear into a car and the sound of yet another car door echoed in the garage.

'Stop!' shouted Ola.

The red brake lights lit up in front of him.

Gunnar opened the door and stuck his head out.

'What's the matter?'

Ola caught up with the car, rested one arm on the door and tried to get his breath back.

'We've . . . got . . . hold . . . of the call logs,' he said.

He gave Gunnar the lists.

Mia and Henrik looked at each other.

'Thomas Rydberg's . . . mobile. Check page eight. His . . . texts.'

Ola leaned against the door and took three deep breaths while

Gunnar found the right page. On line two there was a text that caught his attention: Del.Tues.1.

'Thomas sent this?' he said.

Ola nodded briefly.

'To whom?'

'The phone is registered with the Migration Agency.'

'Hans Juhlén?'

'Yes, or perhaps his PA, Lena?' said Ola.

Gunnar nodded, then closed his car door and drove off in a great hurry.

THIRTY-FOUR

IT SEEMED THAT LENA WIKSTRÖM WAS STILL IN GREAT pain. She pressed her right hand against her kidney and glared at Jana Berzelius, who was standing in front of her with the loaded gun. She had stood there a long time, staring fixedly.

'The necklace,' Jana whispered.

She was blindsided by a memory. A girl, a boy and a woman. *The woman had a gun and she and the boy threw themselves backward. He got a firm hold of the woman's arm and twisted it to make her drop the gun. A shot was fired. The sound echoed between the trees.*

The woman shrieked with pain when the boy forced her arm back.

The girl got hold of the gun and pointed it at the woman. Then she saw the boy sink down on the grass. He had been hit.

And the girl . . . was me.

It was me!

Jana felt dizzy and had to hold on to the kitchen table to support herself.

'Hades,' she said.

Lena gasped.

'You! You killed him!' said Jana. 'I saw it. You killed him right in front of my eyes!'

Lena was silent. Her eyes turned into narrow slits and she examined Jana from top to toe.

'Who are you?' she said.

Jana's hands started to shake. The gun was vibrating. She held it in both hands to keep it still, to keep her aim on Lena.

'Who are you?' Lena repeated. 'You can't be the person I think you are.'

'Who do you think I am?'

'Ker?'

Jana nodded.

'It can't be true . . .' said Lena. 'It can't be.'

'You killed him!'

'He isn't dead. Who has said he's dead?'

'But I saw it—'

'Don't believe everything you see,' Lena cut her off.

'You know what's inside those containers, don't you?' Jana said.

'Yes. You ought to know too,' said Lena.

'Tell me!' said Jana.

'You don't know? Can't you remember?'

'Tell me what was in them!' Jana insisted.

Lena got up from the floor with some effort, sighed heavily and sat with her back against the kitchen cupboards.

'Nothing remarkable . . .' Wincing with the pain, Lena pulled up her sweater and looked at the red mark that Jana's blow had left.

'Go on!' Jana said.

'About what?'

'What was in them? Narcotics?'

'Narcotics?' said Lena. She looked with surprise at Jana and smiled.

'Yes, exactly,' she said and nodded. 'That's right, narcotics. We—'

'Who is this "we"? Tell me!'

'Pah, there isn't so much to tell . . . it started mainly by chance, one could say, but then it got more . . . organized.'

'Do you know why I have a name carved on my neck?'

Lena didn't answer.

'Tell me!'

Jana took a step forward and pointed the gun right at Lena's head. Lena played it cool and shrugged her shoulders. 'It was his idea. Not mine. I had nothing to do with it. I just . . . helped a little.'

'Who is *he*? Tell me!' screamed Jana.

'Never,' said Lena.

'Tell me!'

'No! Never, never, never!'

Jana gripped the gun more firmly. 'And Thomas Rydberg, what did he do?' she said.

'He knew when the containers were on their way. Then he informed me. First by calling, later by sending me a message. Stupid really.'

Lena took a deep breath.

'But he paid well,' she said.

'Who? Thomas? Who paid well?'

Jana heard the sound of a car braking.

'Are you expecting anybody?'

Lena shook her head.

'Get up. Be quick! Up!' Jana ordered when she heard car doors slamming. She held the gun against the back of Lena's head and pushed her towards the window.

'Who is it?'

'The police!'

'The police?' Jana thought. *What are they doing here? What do they know?*

She bit her lip. They had to leave the house immediately. But what should she do with Lena? She smothered a vengeful impulse to kill her. Killing Lena was out of the question. Lena was an important source and for the moment she was the only one who could say who was responsible for everything that had happened and why. But what should she do? Tie her up? Leave her be? Knock her unconscious?

Jana swore to herself. She put her hand into her pocket and pulled out Thomas Rydberg's phone and placed it in front of Lena.

'Using texts these days isn't stupid at all,' she said. 'In fact, it was extremely well done. Do you know what this is? It's Thomas Rydberg's mobile.'

'Why have you got it?'

'That doesn't matter, but now I know how to get rid of it.'

Jana nodded to Lena.

'Move!'

Footsteps could be heard outside the door.

Jana held the gun pointed at the back of Lena's head and pushed her towards the bedroom.

When she saw the open suitcase on the bed, she told Lena to sit down next to it. She wiped the mobile and pressed Lena's fingers on it.

'What are you doing? What do you think you're doing!?'

She put the mobile in the suitcase.

'The police are here. You will confess everything to them. That you were the one behind the murder of Hans Juhlén and Thomas Rydberg.'

'You're crazy. Never!'

'I see you've got children. Grandchildren too. I shall kill them, one for each day that passes, until you confess.'

'You can't do this!'

'Oh yes I can. And you know I can.'

'It won't end here. It will never end. Never!'

'Yes, it will.'

'You'll get caught for this! I'll make sure you're caught, Jana, just so you know!'

'You know what? I don't think anybody will suspect a prosecutor. In fact, you and I will meet in court. In about two weeks I'll charge you with murder. Murder carries the highest penalty in Sweden. So, yes, it will end here. It's over. For you, *Lena*.'

When there was a ring at the door, Jana left the bedroom.

She silently unlocked the back door. The garden was enveloped in a darkness that embraced her when she stepped out.

CHAPTER
THIRTY-FIVE

SHE TASTED BLOOD IN HER MOUTH. SHE WAS *completely exhausted.*

The girl threw herself to the ground and crept up to a rock. The pine needles pricked her skin through her trousers and here and there you could see small red stains of blood. The branches had cut her legs when she ran.

She tried to hold her breath so that she could hear any sound. But it was hard. She was completely out of breath. Her heart was thumping from the effort and her head throbbed.

A strand of hair had stuck to her sweaty forehead; she pushed it away. Tried to straighten her fingers, which had a clamplike hold on the gun. There were seven bullets left in the magazine. She put the gun down on her lap.

She sat there for two hours. Against the rock.

Then she started to run again.

Monday, 23 April

LENA WIKSTRÖM HAD BEEN ARRESTED ON SUSPICION of murdering Thomas Rydberg. Jana Berzelius had asked the court to detain her in custody and there would be a hearing later the same day. Lena would be interrogated, and Gunnar was looking forward to that.

He whistled as he stood waiting in the stairwell. The lift was in use and the button with the upward-pointing arrow lit up. Even so, he pressed the button a second and third time. As if the lift would come faster.

He felt happy and somewhat relieved at having achieved a breakthrough in the investigation. They had visited Lena Wikström on routine business and quite unexpectedly found they now had a major suspect for the murder of Thomas Rydberg – at any rate, she was involved in his death. Finding Rydberg's mobile in Lena's house was a circumstance they couldn't ignore.

The news about the phone had leaked to the media during the morning and it was a quarter to two in the afternoon before Gunnar managed to leave the press conference.

The police press officer had tried to offer short answers to general questions about Lena Wikström while refusing to touch upon the matter of her involvement in the murders of Juhlén and the unidentified boy. Gunnar had hoped the press release they'd drafted would give the impression that the investigation was moving forward all the time and, thanks to the breakthrough with Lena, it would all soon be over. But when press officer Sara Arvidsson concluded her short announcement, keen hands shot up into the air, followed by a barrage of questions: *Is she guilty of the murder of Hans Juhlén? Did she kill the boy too? Can you confirm that she sold drugs?* Arvidsson gave the vaguest answers she could, and mentioned that the investigation was at a sensitive stage, then thanked those present and left.

Gunnar dropped by the cafeteria on his way back to his office to grab something to eat. It would be a while before they started questioning Lena. He was so hungry, he went straight to the vending machines and selected a chocolate bar, then gobbled it down where he stood. Out of the lift came Peter Ramstedt in a shiny suit, orange shirt and spotted tie. His hair was backcombed and surprisingly blond. He must be Lena's lawyer too, Gunnar thought.

'Eating on the sly, Gunnar? Doesn't Anneli keep track of you?'

'No,' said Gunnar.

'Are you still a couple these days or what? One hears so many rumours.'

'You shouldn't believe rumours.'

Peter smirked.

'No, no, of course not,' he said and pulled up his jacket sleeve to see what time it was. 'We start in ten minutes. Who's the prosecutor?'

At that moment the lift doors opened again and Jana Berzelius stepped out. Today she was wearing a knee-length skirt with a high waist, a white blouse and coloured bracelets. Her hair was dead straight and her lips a pale pink.

'Speak of the devil,' said Ramstedt loudly. 'Shall we?'

Gunnar led the way down the corridor.

Peter Ramstedt walked side-by-side with Jana Berzelius.

He glanced at her.

'Yes, well, you haven't got much of a case,' he said.

'No?'

'No technical evidence.'

'We've got the phone.'

'That doesn't tie my client to the crime.'

'Oh yes it does.'

'She isn't going to confess.'

'Oh yes, she is,' said Jana and walked into the interview room. 'Believe me.'

Mia Bolander stood with her legs apart and her arms folded. Behind the mirror window she had a good view of the interview room.

Lena Wikström sat huddled up, her eyes fixed on the table and her hands folded on her lap. The lawyer sat down, whispered something to her, and she nodded in answer without looking at him.

Opposite them sat Henrik Levin. Then Jana Berzelius walked in, put her briefcase down on the floor, pulled out a chair and settled down. She looked her usual alert self. Elegant. Smug. Bitch.

The door opened behind Mia, and Gunnar Öhrn came in. He checked that all the technical equipment was working. It was controlled from a few switches and the system allowed them to record on several different media at the same time. It had a function for two cameras that recorded simultaneously, so Mia and Gunnar could follow Lena and Henrik on the same screen.

Gunnar went and stood by the window.

At exactly two o'clock, Henrik started the tape recorder and began questioning Lena. Her eyes didn't leave the table when Henrik asked the first questions. She just mumbled her answers.

'We understand you deleted a list of number and letter combinations from Hans Juhlén's computer on Sunday the fifteenth of April. Why?' said Henrik.

'I was told to do so,' said Lena.

'By whom?'

'I can't say.'

'Did you know someone named Thomas Rydberg?'

'No.'

'Strange. Because he sent a text message to you.'

'Did he?'

'Don't play stupid. We know he did.'

'Well, then I suppose he did.'

'Good, so now you can explain what "Tues.1" means?'

'No.'

'You don't know, or you won't tell?'

Lena didn't answer.

Henrik fidgeted.

'But you do admit that you deleted the file containing the list of combinations?' he said.

'Yes.'

'Do you know what the combinations mean?'

'No.'

'I think you do.'

'No.'

'According to our information, you deleted identity numbers. For containers.'

Lena huddled slightly more.

'We need your help to find these containers,' said Henrik.

Lena remained silent.

'It's important that you tell us where those containers are.'

'It won't be possible to find them.'

'Why not? Why won't it—'

'It won't,' she cut him off. 'Because I don't know where they are.'

'I'm convinced you're not telling the truth.'

'Perhaps my client is simply saying what she knows, nothing more,' said Peter Ramstedt.

'I don't think so,' said Henrik.

And nor do I, thought Mia behind the mirror. She scratched under her nose with her index finger and then folded her arms again.

'We'll be sitting in this room until you tell us where the containers are,' said Henrik. 'So tell us now.'

'But I can't.'

'Why not?'

'You don't understand.'

'What is it we don't understand?'

'It isn't so simple.'

'We've got all the time in the world to listen. Tell us now what—'

'No,' she cut him off again. 'Even if I tell you, you won't be able to get at them.'

The room fell silent.

Mia looked at Jana, whose eyes were locked on Lena.

Henrik leaned back in his chair and sighed.

'OK, then we'll talk about something else,' he said. 'Tell me—'

Now it was Jana who cut him off. She had leaned forward slightly. Her dark eyes met Lena's uncooperative look.

'How many children do you have?' she said.

Oh, right, she's going to ask the questions now too, thought Mia, irritated. She looked at Gunnar, who stood next to her. He was deeply engrossed in the interview and didn't notice her eyes on him.

'Two,' whispered Lena, and looked down at the table. She swallowed.

'And what about grandchildren? How many grandchildren do you have?'

'But—' was heard from Peter Ramstedt.

'Let her answer,' said Jana.

Mia rolled her eyes and gave a bit of a grunt. She looked at Gunnar yet again. But he didn't notice her body language. He was too busy staring at Jana. Of course he thought she was pretty with her long dark hair and everything. If dark hair could be called pretty. Which in fact it wasn't. It was bloody ugly. And long – no style to it at all.

Mia touched her own blonde hair and watched Jana, who still sat there and waited for an answer from Lena.

'The prosecutor asked how many grandchildren you have,' said Henrik.

What the hell? thought Mia, and took a step back from the window. It looks as if . . . yes, it looks as if she . . .

Lena's lips quivered. She nervously clasped her fingers

together. Then she raised her head and looked at Jana, at Henrik, then Jana again.

A tear rolled down her cheek.

'The containers are on Brandö Island,' she said.

Two hours later, Gunnar Öhrn and Henrik Levin had a long and heated discussion with the county police commissioner, Carin Radler. The commissioner had listened patiently while they recounted the interview with Lena Wikström.

'You could say it is of utmost importance that we salvage those containers,' concluded Gunnar.

'How many people know about her involvement?' said Carin.

'So far, only the team. We must work quickly before the media get wind of all this.'

'And how will you explain the salvage operation?'

'We'll cover it.'

'But I consider a salvage operation to be irrelevant. The containers you talk of might not even exist.'

'I believe they do, and we must find out what they contain.'

'But I'm the one who makes the decision in this case.'

'I know.'

'Putting resources into such an operation is very costly.'

'But necessary,' said Gunnar. 'Three people, one of them a child, have been murdered. Now we must find out why.'

Carin thought for a while.

'What do you want?' Gunnar had asked.

'I want a solution.'

'Good. We do too.'

Carin nodded. 'OK. I'll rely on your judgement. The salvage operation can start tomorrow. Phone the docks.'

CHAPTER THIRTY-SEVEN

IT WAS EARLY MORNING WHEN SHE GOT BACK TO
Stockholm.

The girl stumbled along on the cobbled street, supporting herself with one hand against the rough façade of the buildings. The shop windows reflected her image but she did not care. Her little hand touched the locked doors as she passed by. She was looking for a place to hide. Somewhere she could rest. The gun rubbed uncomfortably against her tummy; she had to stop it falling out from her waistband so she used her other hand to keep it in place.

A pedestrian tunnel appeared in front of her. She staggered down the stairs and when she was on the bottom step she met an elderly couple. They stopped and stared at her. But she just kept on going.

The girl felt dizzy. Suddenly her legs gave way and she thrust out her arms to break the fall when she landed on the hard concrete floor. She got up again. Took one step at a time. Supported herself with one hand on the tiled walls. She looked straight ahead and counted every time she put one foot down in front of the other. She had to keep focused. At the end of the tunnel she saw a barrier; she tried to get through but the doors wouldn't budge. So she sank down on the floor and crawled under it. Then she heard a female voice behind her.

'Hey there! You have to pay!'

But the girl didn't listen. Kept on going.

The voice got louder.

'Hey, you! You have to pay if you want to travel through here!'

She stopped, turned round and whipped the gun out from her trousers. A woman in uniform behind her immediately held up her hands and took a step back. The girl balanced the gun's weight in her hands; it felt dreadfully heavy. She could hardly hold it up.

The woman looked frightened. So did the other people who passed by. They all stopped in their tracks and stood completely still.

She waved the gun in front of her and backed toward the stairs. When she reached the top step she turned round and ran down as fast as she could. Her arms shook. She had trouble holding the gun up. She counted as she walked straight ahead: thirty-two steps, and then she lost her footing on the last one. She twisted her ankle in the fall; the pain was intense. Still she didn't show any emotion.

She got up again and limped across to a rubbish bin. A metallic sound could be heard when the gun landed on the bottom. She shuffled on, relieved that she no longer had to carry the heavy weapon. Now she felt all right. And she would feel even better if she could only get some sleep. Just a little.

Exhausted, she hid in a space behind a bench, flopping down with her back against a concrete wall. The hard surface pressed against her backbone. Her ankle was throbbing but she didn't care. She found herself in a dream-like state between dream and reality.

Then she fell asleep. Sitting in the underground station.

THIRTY-EIGHT

Tuesday, 24 April

HENRIK LEVIN WRAPPED HIS ARMS AROUND HIMSELF against the cold. His down jacket wasn't much help. The merciless Baltic wind seemed to find its way through the zipper of his coat. He had hoped a couple of extra layers would help, but three hours out in the bitter cold had taken its toll. He looked around to see if there was anywhere he could seek shelter. Ahead of him lay the open sea, and the waves washed against the slippery rocks.

Brandö Island was as far out as you could go in Arkösund. The tourist boats flanked the idyllic spot in the summer and the archipelago line passed close by. Now those summer months felt a long way off.

His scarf fluttered in the wind and Henrik wound it round his neck once more to keep out the draught. He contemplated sitting in the car and looked across to the cordoning tape where a total of fifteen police cars were parked.

The cordoned-off area was all of 500 square metres, and the harbour staff worked methodically so that they could start the salvage process.

It had taken a long time to locate the containers. They had to map the sea floor in the specified area with echo sounding. Every response was followed up by divers. The process had taken time; they'd been out here for more than two hours.

They had cordoned off a safety zone and forbidden other boat traffic to enter the area. A floating crane had been moved into place, along with a freight barge for the containers.

Henrik looked at his watch. Ten minutes, they'd said. Then the lifting would start.

Jana Berzelius listened to the radio. As in all complex operations, somebody always revealed more than necessary. Who leaked? The salvage work had attracted an enormous amount of attention and been the top news item all morning.

Jana turned down the volume and looked out through the windscreen. She didn't feel like getting out of the car and joining the shivering police officers who were standing next to the cordon.

Farther away stood Henrik Levin, and he too looked frozen. His shoulders were hunched and his scarf was tightly wound round his collar. Now and then he wrapped his arms around himself, trying to get warm.

She turned up the heat in the car – to 23 Celsius – then pulled out her mobile and downloaded the last hour's emails. There were eight of them, most about additional material for one case or another. One question asked about protecting a witness; another was about a future trial that would take place on 2 May. The charge was arson, and the victim was a young woman who fortunately had escaped with her life, but suffered severe burns to her face.

Jana put the phone down in her lap and felt it vibrate. She

saw her parents' number on the display. She wondered why they were phoning. Again. Three times in just over a week was out of the ordinary.

At the same time, someone knocked on her windscreen.

Mia Bolander waved lazily. Her nose and cheeks were red from the biting wind.

'We're about to start,' she mimed through the glass and headed off toward Henrik.

Jana nodded and hung up.

The dock workers started moving. Someone waved his arm, another one half ran towards the rocks. A bearded man spoke into a walkie-talkie and pointed out to sea.

Jana stretched up in the front seat to try and see what was happening. But she still couldn't. She would have to get out of the car. She put her mobile in her pocket, undid the top button on her parka, turned up her collar and left the car. Her checked cap and long matching scarf kept her warm as she made her way into the cordoned area.

Henrik noted her presence when she came and stood beside him.

The bearded man received a message on his radio and answered.

'You can go ahead now,' he said, before turning to Henrik and Gunnar. 'Here comes the first one.'

Jana looked out across the sea and the safety zone. She screwed up her eyes as she watched the floating crane work. Slowly, slowly, a steel cable was winched up. The waves crashed against the barge. The wind howled. Then a dark grey object broke the surface and a container became visible. Water poured down the sides. The container rotated half a turn and was then lowered cautiously on to the barge.

The second container was blue. When that one broke the surface, Jana went rigid. She saw the combination code. And recognized it. Paralysed, she watched the container's rocking movements before it landed on the barge. When the third container came up, she felt impatient. She wanted to see what was in them. Now!

The salvage operation took an hour and a half. One by one, the containers were lifted from the barge on to land.

Jana shifted her weight to her other leg, trying to release the tension.

Mia Bolander jumped up and down and windmilled her arms to keep warm.

Anneli Lindgren and Gunnar Öhrn stood next to Ola Söderström and chatted.

Henrik helped to direct the crane operators until all ten containers were lifted into place.

'We'll start with this one,' Gunnar shouted, and pointed at an orange container that had emerged from the water as number four.

They gathered together outside the steel, moon-shaped doors. The bearded dock-worker stood in the middle, in front of the locking mechanism.

'When we open it, we've got to be very careful. I want you all to move to a safe distance. These containers hold a lot of water,' he said.

'I thought they were watertight,' said Henrik.

'Oh no, believe me, they're not.'

Henrik's spirits sank drastically. Water could eliminate important evidence – often very quickly.

'Go back!' the dock-worker shouted.

Jana took several steps backward.

Gunnar got hold of Anneli's arm and pulled her along, as if he wanted to protect her.

Henrik and Mia came after them. From twenty metres, Henrik looked questioningly at the dock-worker.

'Go further back!' he shouted.

At fifty metres they stopped. The dock-worker gave a thumbs-up sign and then looked closely at the doors. He felt the locking rods and checked the locking mechanism. With the help of a hefty tool, he forced open the lock and set it down. He thought for a few moments about how he could avoid getting caught by any water that might be inside. He steadied himself, put his hand on the metal handle and pulled. His hand slipped. It was like holding a cake of soap. He tried again. Took a firm grip with both hands, tensed his muscles and pulled as hard as he could. The doors opened and water gushed out with enormous power. The dock-worker, caught by the flow, landed hard on his back. The water washed over him and he spat and hissed. He tried to wipe his face with his wet jacket, but it didn't help, so he tried to sit up.

But something else came gushing out of the container.

He tried to dry his eyes again so he could see what it was that had landed next to him. Something round and covered with algae. He gave it a slight poke and felt something stick on his hands. He poked again and then rolled the object to one side. When his vision cleared and he saw what it was, he let out a scream and recoiled in horror.

It was a decomposed head.

Jana stood stock-still. Her face revealed nothing as she looked across the wet ground. Body parts were strewn everywhere. Rotting arms and legs. Clumps of hair. The stench was awful.

Henrik Levin held his nose as his stomach cramped. He struggled not to vomit.

Anneli Lindgren was very cautious when she documented the head. The face had dissolved, the eye sockets seemed to have grown bigger and what was left of the eyes hung out.

'One year,' said Anneli, and got up. 'I'd say they've been in the water roughly one year. We can thank our cold climate for the bodies being so well preserved.'

Henrik nodded and felt queasy and swallowed several times.

Mia Bolander's face had turned white. She had already used up a whole year's supply of expletives.

Jana Berzelius remained standing at a safe distance. Immobile.

Anneli went up to one of the rotting bones, bent down and took a series of photographs. The skin hung down off the bone. When she touched it, the skin came off and stuck on her latex gloves. The bone had penetrated the skin in several places. Anneli got in close with her camera to catch all the details.

'Shall we open the next container?'

Henrik nodded, but he could no longer keep the contents of his stomach down.

It took longer to open the second container than the first. Given the macabre contents of the first one, they had to take rigorous safety precautions. Anneli Lindgren had discussed various methods with the dock manager, Rainer Gustavsson. They decided they would pump out the water before the doors were opened. But so as not to risk the contents of the container being sucked out, they needed a mechanical filter and the necessary equipment was only available in Linköping. Bringing it to their location further delayed the process. It took two hours before three technicians arrived with the special pump. They set up the filter unit, fit in the filters then inserted a large valve to regulate the flow of water.

Henrik Levin left all this to the specialists. Even though the outdoor temperature had fallen during the afternoon, he was no longer freezing. He just wanted not to vomit again. He had emptied his stomach three times, and that was three times too many. He wasn't the only one. Even Mia Bolander got sick. She was standing next to him now, looking ghostly pale.

'OK, start the pump!' called one of the technicians.

The water poured out from the container into a large tank. The emptying took place in silence. The rotted bodies had left everyone shocked and stunned. Henrik thanked the gods above that the cordoning had kept the journalists and their cameras at a distance. Anneli had called in reinforcements, and five police officers were now following her instructions and gathering together the body parts for transport to forensics. Henrik tried to focus on the rust that climbed the blue steel wall of the container.

Jana Berzelius stood behind him. She didn't see the rust. She saw the numbers. And letters. The combination.

Exactly as they had looked in her dream.

'I think we're going to find more bodies inside this one,' said Mia.

'Do you think so?' said Henrik.

'Yes, I fucking bet there'll be corpses in all of them,' said Mia.

'I hope not,' said Henrik dejectedly.

'Ready!' one of the pump technicians called out.

'Who's going to open it?' Henrik called back.

'None of my workers will touch it. The last one is at the clinic, getting his stomach pumped. He swallowed a bit too much water. And other stuff.' He shuddered. 'You open it.'

'Me?' said Henrik, surprised.

'Yes? Go ahead – open it now.'

Henrik went up to the doors and felt them. They were slimy. He pulled one rod toward him but the door didn't budge. He took a deep breath. He shifted his position to give himself leverage, then got a firmer grip on the rod and gave a sudden pull. The door creaked as it slowly opened.

The interior was dark. So dark it was impossible to see inside. Dripping water echoed as it hit the hard floor. The space sounded empty.

'Lights!' he said.

Mia Bolander rushed off to a car and got a large torch from the trunk. She hurried back to Henrik.

'Can someone see that we get some more lights!' she shouted. 'We need to be able to see!'

Henrik took the torch and turned it on. The torchbeam worked its way over the dark floor. He took one hesitant step forward, and then another. The light travelled across the floor from one side to the other, up to the ceiling and across it and finally back down into one of the far corners.

He caught sight of something in there. He lifted the flashlight and held it as steadily as he could while pointing it there. Then over to the other corner. Something was there too. A heap of some sort. Two more steps and he was inside the container. He made his way slowly forward, inch by inch so as not to risk treading on anything. He kept the torch pointing just in front of his feet on the floor to make sure nothing was in the way. Then up again and into the corners. Now he was halfway inside the container. And he saw the heap.

Of skulls.

That same moment the whole interior was lit up by car headlights. Henrik blinked in the strong beam, turned and saw Mia give him a thumbs-up sign. He responded with a thumbs-down.

'You were right, Mia. There are more here.'

Mia Bolander walked quickly up to the opening and peered in. Jana Berzelius was right behind her.

Side by side they stood and looked into the corner where Henrik Levin was pointing.

'Here,' he said.

'But what's that?' said Mia, nodding into the container. In the middle lay a rusty object with a pink frame.

'That's a mirror,' said Jana.

She recognized it. It was familiar. As if she had had one like it. And she had too. Of course she had. With a crack in it. Like this one. *But . . . if this was mine, what was it doing here?*

Jana held her breath. The hairs stood up on her neck. On her arms. Slowly she looked toward the heaps of bones that lay in both corners. She understood what they were.

They were all that was left of some people she once knew.

'Damn and blast! Right, from now on I want a twenty-four-hour watch on the docks!'

Gunnar Öhrn slammed his fist on the plastic table. He was bright red in the face and looked at the group of tired people sitting round the table.

Henrik had dark rings under his eyes.

Mia wore a vacant stare and Ola was yawning widely.

The only one missing from this briefing was Anneli – she was still documenting the remains of the bodies from the first container. She was being helped by five forensics experts from Linköping and Stockholm. A team from Örebro was on its way.

Because of the advanced state of decomposition, the work was very arduous. It was almost impossible to lift body parts with your hands. They had to use special lifting gear and soft bases so the skin wouldn't fall off during the move. They had opened all ten containers and found human remains in every single one. There were only bones left, except in the first container, which had only been on the seabed about a year.

It was now almost 9 p.m. The team had been on Brandö for eleven hours. What had at first been a technical salvage operation had been transformed into a high-pressure workplace for a small army of police officers, cadets and forensic personnel. The work would go on all night. Perhaps for several days.

Gunnar got even redder in the face thinking about it.

'Not a single container must be emptied without supervision. Is that clear? We must check everything that comes into the docks. And I do mean everything.'

They all nodded.

On the table was some takeaway food in aluminium dishes. Nobody had touched it. The stench from the decomposed body parts still hung over the area and they had all lost their appetites.

'The identifying numbers on the containers are the same as those Juhlén had in his computer,' said Ola.

'The document Lena Wikström deleted,' said Mia.

'Why did she do that?' said Ola.

'She had been given orders by somebody,' said Henrik.

'And we're going to find out who. We'll make her tell us,' said Gunnar.

'We're talking about loads of corpses here. There's, like, ten mass graves . . .' said Mia. 'Who are these people? Or rather, who were they?'

'Hans Juhlén must presumably have known,' said Henrik.

'And Lena Wikström must know his role in it all; they were working in the same department.'

They all nodded again.

'Are there any similarities between the containers?' said Gunnar.

'Well, all the containers were from Chile,' said Henrik.

'Yes, but apart from that. In which city were they loaded? Who loaded them?' said Gunnar.

'We'll find out,' said Henrik.

'According to the call log for Thomas Rydberg's mobile, it would seem another load is to be expected. In a text he sent to Lena, he wrote: "Del.Tues.1",' said Gunnar.

'She won't say what it means, but I'd guess it's about a delivery due on Tuesday the first. Next Tuesday is the first of May, so we need to check every nook and cranny on every freight ship that docks here in Norrköping,' said Henrik.

'But the message could mean there's a delivery to a house which is number one, or that it's a delivery to a person, or that the ship is number one, or . . .' said Mia.

'We get your point,' said Gunnar.

'All I'm saying is, perhaps we ought to widen the approach a little,' said Mia.

'Yes!'

'Were there any more texts? Similar ones I mean,' said Henrik.

'No, not from Rydberg, and nobody else either,' said Ola.

'Right then,' said Gunnar. 'We'll interview Lena again. Get her to talk. Find out in what way the Migration Agency is involved. Check all the employees.'

He rubbed his face and went on. 'And check Lena's mobile. Texts, conversations – everything! Then I want you to look for all the people who have ever had any contact with her. Classmates, boyfriends, aunties, uncles – every last one of them,' said Gunnar. 'And ask Rainer to write down the ships that are going to dock there. Talk to every captain and ask them to start to open the containers onboard.'

'But it's impossible to open the containers onboard, a ship can carry more than six thousand,' said Henrik.

'And out at sea there can be high winds or storms,' said Mia.

Gunnar rubbed his hand over his face again.

'Well then, we'll simply have to open them all when they reach the port. The most important thing is to nail the people who've done this. And nobody, NOBODY, can let up until we've found the bastards!'

PHOBOS DREW THE GUN FROM HIS HIP. HE GOT A good grip on the weapon. As always. With an accustomed hand he put the gun back into his waistband and covered it with his jacket. Then he drew it again. And again.

It was important to quickly switch from normal to emergency. Especially when he was on guard. Anything could happen, he had learned that. And it wasn't only darkly dressed men who were difficult. Even a lightly dressed woman could be a big problem.

On the roof he had a good view of the back street. He was only on the second floor and stood leaning against the concrete façade of the next-door building.

The premises under him were locked up, hidden behind a curtain of metal. A vertical advertising sign spread its flickering light over the cobbles. The fabric from a torn awning fluttered in the wind. An empty tin can rolled along the pavement edge. Phobos had his gaze directed towards a steel door. The windows next to it had bars on. Nobody could imagine that there was trade going on behind them. But there was. And it had been going on for four hours. That was how long he had been standing there. In the dark.

As soon as the business was finished he would make sure that what he was protecting would be safely conveyed. But it would probably be at least another hour. Hopefully it would be quicker than that.

Phobos sincerely hoped so.

Because he was freezing.

So he drew his gun to keep himself warm.

He had been thinking of her all day.

Karl Berzelius sighed, turned off the television and went across to the window. Tried to look out over the garden. But out there it was as dark as down a deep well.

Karl met his mirror image in the mullioned window. He was in a sombre mood and wondered why she hadn't answered.

It was silent in the house. Margaretha had gone to bed early. He had silenced her at dinner, hadn't been able to talk. Even less able to eat. Margaretha had looked at him in astonishment. Her short and sinewy body had squirmed. She had fiddled about with her steel-rimmed spectacles. Taken small bites of food.

There was nothing that Margaretha needed to know. Absolutely nothing, he said to himself.

He looked down at his hands and felt deep remorse.

Why hadn't he dealt with those carved letters? Why had he let the child keep them on her neck? He knew why – it had been too hard to explain to somebody why she might have had them or where they came from. If it had come out that she had marks carved on the flesh of her neck, she might have been called a freak. There would have been gossip. *Berzelius has adopted a freak.* She would probably have been classified as one of those people who cut themselves. Perhaps there would even have been talk of an institution for people with destructive behaviour.

Karl felt how his anguish turned into anger. It was as if history was about to repeat itself. Again she would risk not only his good reputation, but also her own. Accursed child, he thought. It was all her fault!

He was relieved now that she hadn't answered the phone. He no longer wanted to talk to her. From this moment on he would make no attempt to initiate contact with her.

He nodded to himself, satisfied he'd made the right decision.

Karl remained standing by the window for some time. Then he turned off the table lamps in the living room, went into the bedroom and lay down beside Margaretha to sleep. An hour later, he was still awake. He got up and put on his dark blue dressing gown and slippers. He shuffled across to the sofa, sat down with difficulty and started watching TV again.

The little fridge held twelve bottles of wine.

Jana Berzelius grasped one of them, pressed the electric corkscrew and filled a crystal glass to the brim. She took a gulp and felt how the light yellow liquid ran down her throat.

In the end she'd had to leave the salvage site. She had stood there as long as she could bear it, looking into the container, then she had told Henrik she had to go.

Now that she was home, she couldn't stand still. Needing something to occupy herself, she opened the fridge and pulled out some tomatoes on the vine. With a knife in her hand, she started to cut them up, slicing through the thin skin, putting the slices in a bowl. She swallowed another gulp of wine. Took out a cucumber, rinsed it and put that under the knife too. She thought about the container. Deep down inside, she had known its contents would be important for her. The dream had shown the numbers, letters, the combination. She had seen it and known. But she had had no idea that she would find the mirror in there. She cut slice after slice of cucumber. *How could she know it was her mirror?* The knife worked faster with the cucumber. *Had she been inside it? She must have been inside it.* The slices were coming faster now. *She had been inside it!* Suddenly she was violently hacking away at the cucumber. Then she raised the knife and stabbed it right into the chopping board. The blade sank deep into the wood.

Jana thought about it from different angles. Started thinking about the carved name on her neck. *Why did she have a name carved there? Why had she been marked in that way?* She longed for answers to all her questions. But there was nobody to ask. Except Lena. Jana immediately dismissed the idea of visiting Lena at the detention centre. Someone might overhear the questions she would ask. Perhaps they'd start to suspect something, or even find out that Jana was still carrying out her own investigation on the side. She didn't want to risk anything, not unnecessarily. She took a deep breath. There really was nobody else to turn to. Nobody at all. Unless . . . Jana looked up and saw the knife sticking straight up from the chopping board. No . . . there was nobody. Or was there? Well, perhaps there was one person. A single person, but he wasn't alive. If he had been alive, he would certainly have been able to tell her everything. But he wasn't alive. *Or was he? Could he . . . ? No . . .*

Jana grabbed the wine glass and went to her computer. She emptied the glass in one gulp, sat down in front of the computer and went to a site where you could search for companies and people throughout the country. She hesitated, then typed in the name *Hades* and pressed Enter.

Lots of company names showed up, but not a single person. She opened another search engine and wrote the same name. The search gave 31,000,000 results.

She sighed. It was hopeless. He wouldn't still be alive. He couldn't be. It was simply impossible. But why had Lena implied that he was?

She changed her search to 'Hades as a name' but that too resulted in far too many pages. She tried every possible combination of the name in the hope of finding something that would lead to him.

She was close to giving up when it struck her. If you really wanted to find somebody, then you ought to look in the police computers.

She needed to get into those databases.

And she needed to get into them without being found out.

FORTY

FREDERIC 'FREDDY' OLSSON DRUMMED ON THE garbage trolley. *The music pumped away in his earphones. A rasping voice at high volume.*

Billy Idol.

'Hey, little sister, what have you done?'

Freddy nodded in time and sang along with the lyrics.

'Hey, little sister, who's your only one?'

It was just before midnight and there was nobody on the platform.

Freddy parked his trolley routinely in front of a waste bin, opened the lid and lifted out the bag of rubbish. He had to exert himself, the bag was heavy.

Goddamn, so much rubbish, he thought before he tied the bag and let it join the others on the trolley.

He got out a new bag, turned up the volume on his Walkman and sang: 'It's a nice day to start again.'

Then he stopped, drummed on the trolley and bellowed out: 'It's a nice day for a white wedding.'

He smiled to himself, lined the bin with the new bag and locked the lid with a click.

When he steered the garbage trolley towards the next rubbish bin he caught sight of a leg sticking out from the space behind a bench. He went up to it and saw a little girl sitting there, leaning against the wall. She was fast asleep.

Freddy looked around as if he was looking for her parents. But the platform was empty. He slowly took off his earphones, went up to the girl and prodded her.

'Hey,' he said. 'Hey, you!'

She didn't move.

'Hey, little girl, wake up!'

With his fingers he prodded her cheek. Once again, a bit harder. Her dark eyes stared straight into his, and in a fraction of a second she was on her feet. She shouted and waved her arms, trying to get away from him.

'Easy,' said Freddy.

But she didn't listen. She backed away from him.

'Hey, stop there,' he said when he saw where she was going.

'Stop! Oh hell! Watch out!'

The girl continued to back away.

'Stop! Watch out!' he shouted and threw himself forward to catch her.

But it was too late. The girl stepped right over the edge on to the track. The last thing she saw was Freddy's terrified look.

Then everything went black.

CHAPTER
FORTY-ONE

ANNELI LINDGREN TOOK OFF HER GLOVES. SHE WAS
feeling faint with exhaustion. It had been an incredibly demanding day and she hadn't eaten anything all those hours she'd been working. She longed to get home to her flat and get some sleep. But first she'd have to pick up her son from her mother's; when she realized how much work she had ahead of her, Anneli had called her mother and asked her to look after him.

It was 11 p.m. Her camera contained over a thousand photos and the battery was almost dead. The team had left the salvage site, there were only a few uniformed police officers left, and Gunnar Öhrn.

He came up to her. 'Time to call it a day?'

'Yes.'

'Can I give you a lift?'

She looked at him with suspicion.

'You look tired,' said Gunnar.

'Thanks.'

'No, I didn't mean it like that . . .'

'I know. I'm tired and I want to get home, but I've got to go to the station first and leave the camera there and some other stuff.'

'Then we'll drop in there on the way.'

'Are you sure?'

'Positive. Come on.'

Jana Berzelius stood close to the wall with her briefcase in her hand and looked out over the open office landscape. Aside from one lone woman sitting at her desk typing away with her eyes fixed on the screen in front of her, the office was empty. It was 11 p.m. and presumably the rest of the night shift was out on calls. Or they had been sent to the salvage site.

Perfect, Jana thought.

Thanks to the lie about having to visit the detention cells, it had been easy to get into the police building. She walked determinedly toward the woman, who looked up from her work when she heard Jana approaching. She was young, twenty-something. Blue eyes, pearl earrings.

'Hello, I'm Jana Berzelius. Prosecutor.'

'Hi, I'm Matilda.'

'I'm working with Gunnar and his team and we usually meet in here,' said Jana, and pointed toward the conference room.

'Oh yes?'

'And I need your help. During our last meeting, I must have left my notebook in the conference room and I wonder if you could open it for me.'

Matilda looked at the clock and then at Jana, hesitant.

'I'm going to the arrest unit,' Jana explained. 'And I've got to have something to write my notes on if somebody is arrested tonight.'

Matilda swallowed the lie, smiled and got up from her chair.

'Of course I can open it for you.'

Matilda got up.

Jana glanced at her computer screen and saw that the police register was open. So Matilda was logged in.

She followed her down the corridor to the conference room. Matilda opened the door with her key card and held it open for Jana.

'Here you are.'

'Thank you,' said Jana. 'Now I'll manage.'

'Close the door after you when you've found your notebook.'

'Yes, of course. It must be here somewhere,' said Jana and stepped into the room.

She heard Matilda returning to her desk and computer, and walked round the conference table to make the search more credible. Then she opened her briefcase, took out her notebook and closed the door behind her.

'Here it is,' she said when she went past Matilda. 'Thanks for your help.'

'You're welcome. No trouble,' answered Matilda and waved absentmindedly to the prosecutor when she left the office.

It was silent again around Matilda. Now the hard drive sounded loud and the ceiling fan buzzed.

She liked working on her own, especially at night when you didn't have to worry about being disturbed by telephones ringing and people wanting answers.

There was a ping from the lobby and the sound of the lift doors closing.

She picked up her mobile and was about to phone her boyfriend when she heard something. It sounded like metal, and it came from the kitchen. She listened carefully to see if she could hear it again. Had she imagined it? No, there it was again.

She got up to go and see what it was. With her phone in her

hand she walked towards the kitchen, turned on the light and glanced around at the sink and the dining table. It was cold in there and she wrapped her arms around herself and shivered. The sound returned. She turned her head towards the windows and saw that one of them was open. She relaxed and went across to close it. But as she shut the window, she heard a loud noise behind her. She was scared and it gave her a start. The kitchen door had slammed shut.

'Oh, it's only the door, from the draught,' she mumbled to herself when she felt how fast her heart was beating.

She pressed the handle on the window frame to the locked position. She glanced at the well-filled fruit basket on the sideboard but decided she'd rather have something sweet. In a striped tin she found what she was looking for and popped a round biscuit into her mouth. With another one in her hand, she closed the lid and turned to go back to work. She took hold of the door handle but . . . nothing happened. It wouldn't budge. The door was locked! Damn!

She felt the door handle again. How could it lock itself? She couldn't understand it. She knocked lightly on the door before it registered she was wasting her time.

She was the only person in the department.

Jana Berzelius heard Matilda knock on the door as she sat down on the office chair and pulled the keyboard towards her.

Now she would have to work fast.

Gunnar Öhrn opened the door for Anneli Lindgren, who yawned widely. She had dozed off during the drive from the salvage site to the police building.

'Are we already there?' she said.

'Yes. Shall I take it all up for you?'

'No. I'll come with you.'

Gunnar opened the boot, lifted out a large, heavy bag and grasped the camera bag too, which he handed over to Anneli.

She hung it over her shoulder and yawned widely again. Then they walked side-by-side to the lifts, pressed the button and waited to go up to the third floor.

Matilda didn't know what on earth she should do. She pounded on the door. Felt the handle again and tried to push against the door with all her weight. But it didn't help. She banged on the door, once, twice and a third time.

'Hello!' she called out. 'Hello!'

Yet again she reminded herself that there wasn't a single person in the department apart from her. Then she realized she had her mobile in her pocket. But who could she phone? Her first thought was to ring her boyfriend. But he wasn't authorized to get into the police building. Reception? They could send somebody up, a maintenance man or something. But then she remembered that she only had her private mobile. And she didn't have any direct numbers or internal numbers for the various departments.

'Oh Christ, this is so stupid,' she said out loud and kicked the door.

Jana heard the lift start up. And Matilda, hitting the door. Although it sounded more like a kick.

She had done the search but . . . nothing. No results when she tried 'Hades'. What else could she try? She thought frantically. Think of something! Think! Think! Think!

The lift had stopped. Probably on the floor below, but as she sighed with relief she heard it starting again. On the way up.

Jana was still thinking. What could he be called besides Hades? What? She bit her lip, her thoughts all over the place. Then a name floated up from her memory. Something beginning with Dan . . .

She wrote 'Dan' and got lots of entries for people with that name. But it didn't feel right. Dano . . . Daniel . . . Danilo . . . Danilo! She entered the name.

The lift was close now.

Come on! Give me something!

Jana looked up over the screen then quickly down again. Then she saw the result. There were several Danilos. But her eye fell on Danilo Peña. In Södertälje.

Jana pulled out her mobile, took a picture of the screen and then exited from the register. She grabbed her things, took off her shoes and ran in her stockinged feet with them in her hand toward the lift. She pressed the button to call it. She sneaked up to the staff kitchen, carefully pulled the chair away from under the door handle, before rushing back to the now open lift, and pressing the button for the garage.

The doors closed slowly and as they did so she heard the neighbouring lift give a ping as the doors opened and somebody stepped out.

The heavy bag rubbed against his hip, and Gunnar changed his hold on it when he exited the lift.

Anneli was right behind him.

The department was empty and silent, as it usually was at night. They both went along to Anneli's room, turned on the light and left the two bags inside.

★

'Hello!' Matilda called out. 'Is someone there? Hello?'

She banged on the door and felt the handle, which . . . easily went down. She pushed open the door and almost bumped into an astonished Gunnar.

'Oh, God!' said Matilda. 'Good thing you're here. I've been locked in.'

'What did you say? Locked in?' said Anneli, who had just come out of her room.

'Yes, in the kitchen! The door locked itself. I couldn't get out.'

Gunnar went up to the door and felt the handle. Up and down, no problem at all.

'Strange. This door can't lock itself. You can't lock it at all,' he said.

'But . . . I couldn't get out,' said Matilda.

'Well, how did you open the door now?'

'Well, I . . . opened . . .'

'So it was unlocked?'

'No, it was locked. I couldn't open it.'

'But then you could.'

'Yes.'

Matilda felt like an idiot. How could she explain to them? She *had* been locked in! But now she couldn't face having to explain the whole thing.

'Well, I couldn't get out,' she mumbled to herself and walked back to her desk.

FORTY-TWO

Wednesday, 25 April

HENRIK LEVIN WOKE UP. DIDN'T KNOW WHERE HE was, but realized after a few seconds that he'd fallen asleep on the sofa in the living room. It was pitch-black in the room. He picked up his mobile; the display said it was 02.30, so he had only slept a couple of hours. The display turned off and the blackness engulfed him again.

At seven o'clock he woke up to the sound of a smothered ringtone. He had dropped the phone in his sleep and now he had to look on the floor to find it. It was under the sofa, and when he reached it he turned the alarm off, stretched out and felt that he had had far too little sleep.

After a quick breakfast with Emma and the children, he drove to the station. Gunnar Öhrn was the first to meet him and they made their way together to the conference room.

'It seems as if everyone in the containers was shot. There are marks on the skeletons to indicate that,' said Gunnar.

'So they were killed and then dumped into the sea,' said Henrik.

'Yes.'

'But why were they killed? Was it about money? Drugs? Were they refugees who didn't pay? Did somebody betray them? Were they smugglers?'

'I don't know, but I'm thinking along the same lines. The thing is, I can't see what Hans Juhlén's role was in all this. Why was he murdered?'

'Ought we to bring in his wife for questioning again?'

'Perhaps, but I think we can get some more out of Lena. To be honest, Henrik . . .'

Gunnar stopped and looked in both directions. Then he looked at Henrik. Sighed.

'This has turned into an extremely complicated series of events. I don't know any longer what we should concentrate on. First Hans Juhlén, then the boy and then Thomas Rydberg. And now this mass grave at sea – it's pretty hard to digest. And not something we can make public. But Carin is on me like a polecat.'

'She wants a press conference?'

'Yes.'

'But we've got nothing concrete to give them.'

'I know, and we need to play it all down. It already feels as if this is getting too much for us. I might have to ask the National Crime Squad for help, and you know how I feel about that.'

A shadow fell across Gunnar's face.

Henrik pondered. 'Wait until we've questioned Lena again,' he said.

Gunnar looked at Henrik. His eyes were red, shiny. He threw out his hand.

'OK, I'll wait until we know some more.'

★

At a quarter to seven, Jana Berzelius drove down the slip road to the E4, the motorway to Stockholm.

The sun was up and it dazzled her. The music on the radio was interrupted for news and weather reports and the meteorologists warned about black ice on the roads.

The traffic got heavier after Nyköping and the sun disappeared. The sky turned dark grey and the temperature went down to zero. The hard rain beat against the asphalt. She stared straight ahead on the wet road. Listened to the noise inside the car. The forest dashed past on both sides of her. The fencing was rubbed out in the periphery. Taillights turned into red streaks.

At Järna the lines started. While she waited for the traffic to start flowing again, she opened an app on her mobile and entered the address for Danilo Peña. She couldn't use the car's own GPS – it would have been extremely risky as her journey could easily be tracked, should anyone do a check.

The app presented a clear route and she could see that she was only ten minutes from her destination. The rain stopped but the heavy grey clouds remained. She turned off the motorway and drove toward the centre. A right turn and she was in Ronna. Here were blocks of flats with green, blue and bright yellow balconies. On the streets there were lots of neon-coloured signs with handwritten texts in languages other than Swedish.

A gang of five youths sat in a smashed bus shelter, an elderly lady stood some distance away supporting herself with a brown stick. A car with a flat tyre, a bicycle with the front wheel missing and an overflowing rubbish bin.

She looked for number 36 and found it at the far end of Smedvägen. She parked on the street and considered putting money in the parking meter, which was covered with graffiti, but it was out of order. On her way to the high-rise building, she passed several cars, all with crosses or icons hanging from the rear-view mirror. By taking small steps she avoided the pools of water that had formed on the ground.

In the entrance hall sat three ladies with shawls, chatting to each other. They stared quite openly and disapprovingly at Jana when she came in through the door. A child's scream, loud voices and the banging of doors echoed in the stairwell. It was cold and damp. Smelled of cooking.

The list of tenants showed that she would have to go to the eighth floor, so she took the lift. When the lift doors opened again she looked out cautiously. On the door closest to the stairs it said D. Peña.

She stepped out of the lift and raised her hand to knock on the door but that same instant discovered that it wasn't properly shut. She gave it a push and the door swung open.

'Hello?' she called out and stepped into the hall.

No furniture, just an old mat on the floor and yellowy-brown wallpaper.

She called out again and got an echo in reply.

For a moment she hesitated, but then felt bolder and stepped straight into the living room. A ripped-open sofa, a little table in front of it, a television, a mattress without any sheets, a pillow and a checked blanket. The wind howled through a crack in a window.

She went through the living room towards the kitchen. Stopped, held her breath and listened for any sound.

She stood like that for a few seconds, then stepped through the doorway into the kitchen. That same moment she saw a fist coming at her and the blow knocked her to the floor. She saw the fist again and raised her forearm to shield herself. The other forearm came up, the blow hit her wrist and the pain was intense.

Up, she thought.

I must get up!

She twisted her body to the left, put her right hand in under her chest and pushed herself up.

Then she saw the man and what he had in his hand.

'Don't move,' he said. 'If you want to live.'

CHAPTER
FORTY-THREE

THE GIRL TRIED TO SWALLOW BUT HER TONGUE FELT
numb. She tried to open her eyes but couldn't. As if in a tunnel, she heard a voice talk to her but she couldn't grasp the words. Somebody touched her and she tried to hit the hand away.

'Calm down,' said the voice.

When she lifted her hand to hit out again she felt an intense pain in her head which forced her to remain still. In the end she opened her eyes and met with a strong light.

She blinked several times until a stranger appeared in front of her. A man dressed in white was leaning over the bed she lay in.

'What's your name?' he said.

The girl didn't answer.

She screwed up her eyes to accustom them to the light. The man had blond hair, spectacles and a beard.

'I'm Doctor Mikael Andersson. You are in hospital. You've been in an accident. Do you know your name?'

She swallowed again, searched her memory for an answer.

'Do you remember what happened?'

She turned her head and looked at the doctor. The pain pulsated in her bandaged head. She shut her eyes for a few moments, and then opened them again. She didn't know how she should answer. Because she couldn't remember.

She couldn't remember anything at all.

FORTY-FOUR

PHOBOS FIDGETED WITH HIS GUN. HE KNEW THAT he had carried out the mission most satisfactorily. And it was a simple task to shoot the man who hadn't paid on time.

A single shot sufficed. In the back of his head. One hole. Blood on the floor.

It was better to sneak up on victims and shoot them from behind, then they didn't have time to react and there was less risk of opposition. They simply fell forwards. Most of them died instantly. Others shook. Made a noise.

The water broke against the boat and it rocked heavily. Even so, he felt relaxed and satisfied. Because he knew he would get his reward.

At last he would get the dose he deserved.

The gun was two centimetres from Jana Berzelius's cheek.

The man in front of her swiped a drop of saliva from the corner of his mouth. He had long dark hair, brown eyes and an angular face.

Who was he? Was it Hades?

'Who the hell are you?' said the man and pushed the gun even closer to her cheek.

'I'm a prosecutor,' she said, her mind racing through potential escape routes.

They stood in the kitchen; the living room was behind her, the hall in front. Two escape routes, one of which required more time. She could knock him out but he had the advantage with the gun.

She looked across at the kitchen table. No knives.

'Don't try,' said the man. 'Tell me what brings a prosecutor to my place.'

'I need your help.'

The man laughed.

'Oh really? You don't say. How interesting. And what can I help you with?'

'You can help me find out something.'

'Something? And what is this *something*?'

'My background.'

'Your background? How could I help you with that when I don't even know who you are?'

'But I know who you are.'

'Really? Who am I then?'

'You are Danilo.'

'Brilliant. Did you work that out all by yourself, or did you perhaps read my name on the door?'

'You are someone else too.'

'You mean I'm a schizo?'

'Show me your neck.'

The man fell completely silent.

'You've got another name written there,' said Jana. 'I know what it says. If I guess right then you must tell me how you got it. If I guess wrong, then you can let me go.'

'Let's change the agreement a little. If you guess right, then I'll tell you. Sure, that's no problem. If you guess wrong, or if I don't have a name on my neck, I'll shoot you.'

He cocked the gun, took a couple of steps away from her and stood with his legs apart, ready to shoot.

'I can report you for attempted murder,' said Jana.

'And I can report you for breaking in. Now guess!'

Jana swallowed.

She was pretty sure it was him.

But would she dare say the name?

She shut her eyes.

'Hades,' she whispered and heard the gun go off.

FORTY-FIVE

THE GIRL SAT BEFORE HER ON THE HARD CHAIR WITH *her eyes on the floor. Her shoulders were hunched up and her hands were hidden under her thighs.*

She just sat there.

Silent.

Welfare officer Beatrice Alm looked up over her reading glasses and delicately shut the folder lying on the desk.

'Well now,' she said and leaned forward and folded her hands. 'You are one lucky girl. You are going to get a mummy and a daddy.'

FORTY-SIX

JANA OPENED HER EYES.

The man was still standing in front of her with the gun lowered. For a second she felt her body to see if she had been hit. She hadn't. The bullet had gone right past her and left a hole in the wall behind.

She fixed her eyes on the man. He was breathing heavily.

'How do you know?' he asked, his jaws clamped together. 'How the fuck do you know? Tell me!'

He went up to her and stood with his face against hers.

'How the fuck did you know that? Tell me now!'

He grabbed her hair and forced her head back. Brutally. Then he hit her on her forehead with the gun and pressed it against her temple.

'I'll shoot again. And this time I promise it'll go right in here. So tell me. Spit it out!'

Jana made a face.

'I've got a name too,' she said roughly.

He thrust her head to one side. Pulled at her hair, scratching the skin. She felt her neck exposed to him and began to panic. She struggled to release herself from his grip. She backed away a few steps and looked up at him.

He shook his head.

'It can't be true, it can't be true. It can't be you.'

'Yes, it is me. And now you'll explain to me who I am.'

It took Jana Berzelius ten minutes to tell the brief story of her life. She sat next to Danilo on the thin mattress in the spartan living room. Both with their knees drawn up and with their heads bent down.

'So you were adopted?' he said.

'Yes, I was adopted. Jana is my first name now. Berzelius my surname. My father was the prosecutor general, but now he's retired. What he wanted most of all was a son who would follow in his footsteps. He had to make do with me.'

They studied each other. Both uncertain how to react.

'I remember nothing from before the accident. I've been told that I fell on to the tracks at an underground station and hit my head so hard I lost my memory. Nobody could tell me how I came to be there at the station or who I was. I was alone. There was nobody who asked about me, or who came looking for me after the accident.'

Jana stopped speaking.

'You can't remember anything at all?' Danilo said.

'Sometimes fragments or images come to me in dreams, but I don't know if they're real memories or just my imagination.'

'Do you remember your real parents?'

'Did I have any?'

Danilo didn't answer.

The wind howled through the crack in the window. The room suddenly felt cold. Jana wrapped her arms around her knees.

'Can't you tell me something about your life?' she said.

'There's nothing to tell.'

'I dreamed that you were murdered.'

Danilo squirmed uneasily.

'I escaped. OK? I got a bullet in my shoulder,' he said, and pulled down his sweater to reveal a large scar on his right shoulder. 'When you ran away, I lay there completely still, played dead. When Mama ran after you, I got up and ran off too. And here I am. End of story.'

'But didn't they find you?'

'No.'

Jana pondered.

'Is that what she was called?'

'Who?'

'Mama. Was she called that?'

'Yes.'

'Did I say it too?'

'Yes.'

Danilo's shoulders sagged. 'Why are you here? Why are you raking up the past?'

'I want to know who I am.' Jana bit her lip. 'Can I trust you?'

'How so?'

'Can I tell you secrets without you spreading them?'

'Hang on. Who sent you?'

'Nobody. I'm here on my own, for purely personal reasons.'

'So what do you want me to do?'

'I've got to a point where I need answers. And I need to find out things without involving the police.'

'But you're a prosecutor. Surely it's the police you should talk to?'

'No.'

'OK, OK. I need to know what you have in mind before I decide if I want to help you or not.'

Jana hesitated.

'I promise I'll keep quiet about everything you tell me.'

He sounded convincing and for the time being Jana didn't have anyone else to turn to. She had to trust him.

So she told him.

It took more than an hour to describe all the complex details of the investigation. She told him about Hans Juhlén, about the boy with the name carved on his neck who had been found dead out by the coast at Viddviken. She told him about Thomas Rydberg, but left out the detail that she was the one who had killed him.

When it came to telling him about the operation to salvage the containers, Danilo's face turned white.

'Oh, fuck,' he said.

'In one of the containers I found a mirror. I think it belonged to me. Now you must tell me – was I in there?'

'I don't know.'

'Please, tell me if I was in there.'

'I don't know, OK!'

'I just want to know who I am. You're the only person who can help me. Tell me who I am!'

Danilo got up. His face had become dark. 'No.'

'No?'

'You're welcome to dig into the past, but I don't want to know about it.'

'I never ask for favours, but please, help me.'

'No. NO!'

Danilo looked out through the window.

'Please!'

'No!' Danilo spun to face Jana. 'Never. I'm not going to do it. Get out of here now!'

He pulled her up from the mattress. She fought her way free.

'Don't touch me!'

'Never come here again!'

'I won't. I can promise you that.'

'Good. Get out!'

She remained standing where she was. Looked at Danilo one last time before leaving the flat. She cursed herself. For having told him everything. Having opened up. She should never have done it.

Never.

Henrik Levin looked at the clock: 15.55. Five minutes to go before the interview with Lena Wikström.

Jana Berzelius was late. She had never been late before.

Henrik scratched his head and wondered how he should handle the questioning without her by his side.

Mia Bolander noticed his concern.

'She's bound to turn up,' she said.

As she was speaking, Peter Ramstedt walked in.

'Oh I see,' he said. 'So the prosecutor doesn't want to join the interview? That is rather problematic.' He let out a fake laugh.

Henrik sighed and looked at the clock again. One minute to go. He was about to close the door when he heard hurried footsteps in the corridor.

Jana Berzelius was running across the stone floor. She had a large plaster on her brow.

'You're late,' said Mia triumphantly when Jana reached them.

'No, I don't think so. You can't be late to something that hasn't even started,' said Jana and slammed the door in Mia's face.

The interview had gone on for two hours.

Now Henrik Levin knocked lightly on Gunnar Öhrn's office door.

'Nothing,' he said.

'Nothing?' Gunnar repeated.

'She refuses to say who gave her the order to delete the file with the list of container ID numbers, or what the text she got from Thomas Rydberg means.'

'And what does she say about the containers?'

'She claims she doesn't know anything about them.'

'Well that's a lie. I mean, she told us where we could find them.'

'I know.'

'So what do we have?'

'She won't admit to anything and I can't see what we can actually prove.'

Gunnar sighed loudly and breathed in through his nose. 'Time to go home,' he said.

'I intend to. What about you?'

'I'll be done soon, then I'm off too.'

'Plans for the evening?'

'I'm having company. Female company.'

Henrik whistled.

'No, not that sort. It's only Anneli. She's going to drop by with a takeaway. And you?'

'Thought I'd surprise the family with dinner.'

'Exciting.'

'I don't know that McDonald's is what I'd call exciting.'

Gunnar laughed.

'See you tomorrow,' said Henrik, and set off towards the lift with light steps.

By the time Jana Berzelius sat down at the table for two at The Colander, she was already irritated by Per Åström. For more than twenty minutes he had talked nonstop about the tennis tournament he'd participated in the previous weekend. His chatter had never bothered her in the past, but now it was all she could do not to open her mouth and tell him to shut his.

Jana had long since realized that she didn't feel comfortable in social situations and she had made a life for herself as a hermit. She was satisfied with that. Of course, her work demanded social interaction with people, but the contact was always superficial and formal, which suited her down to the ground. She found the process of getting to know people arduous and time-consuming. And she hated it when people wanted to stick their noses into her private life, asking questions that she didn't want to answer. Per Åström often got on her nerves with his questions, but for some strange reason he hadn't given up like all the others when Jana had told him she wanted to be left in peace. On the contrary, he seemed to enjoy her frosty rebukes and over the years had learned to interpret her vague looks.

Per fidgeted with his wine glass.

'What's the matter?'

'What do you mean?'

'What's the matter? I can see there's something.'

'It's nothing.'

'Has something happened?'

'No.'

'Are you sure?'

'Yes, I feel fine.'

She met his gaze. It felt strange to lie to him. She had nobody else she could have a conversation with, and she would very much have liked to tell him everything. But how would he react if she told him she had murdered Thomas Rydberg? What would he say when she admitted to having sought out an old friend whom she thought was dead but who'd turned out to be very much alive? And how could he even begin to understand when she told him she was prepared to do anything to find out about her background? Her hidden background?

No, there was no point in saying anything. Not to anybody.

'Is it something you need help with?'

Jana didn't know what she should say. So she got up and left the restaurant without a word.

She walked down Kvarngatan, cut across Holmen Square and then the market square at Knäppingsborg. Inside her apartment, she took off her coat, pulled off her high-heeled boots and went into the bedroom. She'd stripped off her trousers, and her sweater was halfway over her head when she heard her mobile ringing. She went into the hall wearing only her silk underwear and looked at the display.

Hidden number.

It must be Per. He had blocked caller ID to prevent clients from getting his private number.

She answered.

'I don't want to know how tasty the food was,' she said.

There was silence at the other end.

'Hello?'

She was about to hang up when she heard a voice say: 'I'll help you.'

The hairs on her neck stood up.

She recognized the voice.

It belonged to Danilo.

'Meet me tomorrow, Norrköping Folkpark. Two o'clock,' he said.

Gunnar Öhrn freed himself from Anneli Lindgren's arm.

They were sitting on the dark brown leather sofa in the living room, each with a glass of wine. A three-way lamp in the corner gave off a soft glow. One wall had bookcases and a drinks cabinet. A few paintings waiting to be hung were leaning against another wall. Two wine bottles stood on a glass table. Both were empty.

'This isn't a good idea,' said Gunnar.

'What?' said Anneli.

'What you're trying to do.'

'You were the one who said I should come over.'

'To share a takeaway, not . . .'

'What?'

Anneli put a hand on Gunnar's leg.

'Don't do that.'

She moved closer and gave him a light kiss on his throat.

'That's better.'

Anneli slowly unbuttoned her blouse.

'That's actually rather nice.'

'And this?'

She took her blouse off, and climbed astride him.

'That is really nice,' said Gunnar, pulling Anneli towards him.

FORTY-SEVEN

Thursday, 26 April

FOLLOWING THE DIRECTIONS SHE HAD BEEN GIVEN, Jana Berzelius set off along the wide gravel path. Daffodils and lilac crocuses lined the path on either side. There was a smell of damp soil in the air. She turned off beside a large rock and continued for a hundred metres. When she saw the hot-dog stall she slowed down, checked her watch and saw she was on time.

She ordered a hot dog, paid twenty kronor and then continued along the gravel path until she came to the green park bench which had seating facing both ways. She sat down on the right, next to an anarchist symbol that had been carved on the seat.

Jana took a bite of her hot dog and looked out across the park. Two benches away sat four vagrants with a bag of beer cans, apparently without a care in the world. Their laughter mingled with the chatter of families passing by on their way to the playground. Two girls were competing to see who could swing the highest, and a little boy was sitting at the top of the slide hesitating as to whether he dared go down.

She had just taken another bite of her hot dog when she heard a voice behind her.

'Don't turn round. Pick up your phone.'

She felt his presence.

His back was against hers.

She put the mobile to her ear.

'Hold the phone all the time so it looks as if you're talking on it.'

'Why did you want to meet in Norrköping?' said Jana.

'I had some business here.'

'What made you change your mind? Why do you want to help me?'

'That's not important. Do you still want to do this?'

'Yes.'

'You'll have to do the heavy work yourself.'

'OK.'

'I can't give you everything.'

'Well, what can you give me?'

'Anders Paulsson. You'll find him in Jonsberg. Ask him about the transports.'

'What transports?'

'That's all I can give you.'

'But what sort of transports are they?'

'Ask him.'

'Is he the man behind it all?'

'No, but he's well placed.'

'How do you know that?'

'I just know. Believe me. See you.'

'But—'

She turned round.

Danilo had gone.

*

Danilo hurried from the park. He knew Jana would seek out Anders Paulsson. He smiled to himself. He knew she would go straight to Anders, knew too that it would be the last thing she would do in her life.

He picked up his phone and texted:

Expect company.

Gunnar Öhrn stepped out of the shower and wrapped a towel around his hips.

In the bedroom, Anneli had just finished fastening her bra and was talking to the babysitter on the phone. She ended the conversation and threw the phone on to the bed.

Gunnar looked at the clock. He was late for the press conference, which had been scheduled for one o'clock.

'How am I going to explain this?' he said to Anneli.

'Say you were out on a call or something. You're a policeman, damn it!'

Gunnar threw himself on to the bed and moved across to Anneli, supporting himself on his elbows.

'If we've just separated, we shouldn't be having sex with each other. Especially after a month.'

'You're right.'

'This mustn't become a habit.'

'No.'

Anneli got up, pulled on her jeans and blouse and buttoned it.

Gunnar followed her to the hall. He picked up the big cardboard box that stood next to the front door.

'Don't forget this,' he said. 'Do you need help getting it to the car?'

'I'll take it this evening,' Anneli answered and closed the door behind her.

Gunnar was left alone with the box in his arms.

He smiled.

Anders Paulsson drove home a lot faster than the speed limit allowed. He cut corners and let the van go well over the middle of the road into the opposite lane.

When he reached Jonsberg, he turned off and saw a black BMW parked at the side of the road. He pressed the clutch down hard and struggled to engage third gear.

Four hundred metres further on, he braked and skidded to a halt outside his house. The blinds were down in all the windows. Not to stop people from looking in – the nearest neighbours were quite some distance away – but because he didn't like daylight. There was rubbish everywhere in the house. Cardboard boxes piled high. Old newspapers in heaps, old paper plates with the remains of food on them, bottles, beer cans and cartons from various fast-food outlets. There was a rancid smell, shut-in and rotten, but that didn't bother Anders. He didn't much care about anything. Not about his home, not about himself. He had cared once about a woman, but she died a long time ago from cancer. After it happened, he gave up on housework and maintenance. The years passed and it got harder and harder to deal with one thing and the other. It was simpler to give up. Not to care at all.

Anders unlocked the door and went straight into the kitchen with his shoes on, managing to avoid the hardened lumps of excrement one of his cats had deposited a week or so ago. It had driven him to such a rage that instead of cleaning up the shit, he'd decided to clean up what caused it. He didn't know which cat was guilty, so he punished them all. The damned creatures protested and clawed him, spitting and hissing, but he nevertheless managed to get them all into the big freezer in the cellar.

Now he stood and looked quizzically at the knife block. It was empty. Strange. He pulled out a kitchen drawer. No knife there either. Unease crept up on him. He opened a kitchen cupboard and felt with his hand on the top shelf.

Empty!

Then he put his hand on his hip and felt the sheath in his waistband. At least I've got that, he thought.

'Are you looking for something?'

The voice came from somewhere behind him. Anders froze, his eyes like saucers.

Jana Berzelius stood in the doorway. She had a gun in her hand.

'Is this what you're looking for?' She flipped the safety catch, holding the gun in a firm grip with her gloved hands.

'Don't turn round!'

Anders started to laugh. A hollow, fake laugh. He shook his head and looked down at the kitchen worktop, still with his hand on his hip.

'How did you know where it was?' he said.

'I had time to check the house before you came home.'

'How did you get in?'

'I like windows.'

'Who are you?'

'I don't like questions.'

'So I can't even ask you what you're after?'

'I'm after details of your container transports,' she said.

'What container transports? I don't know what you mean.'

311

'I think you do.'

Anders sighed. He looked up at the pine-panelled ceiling and then down again.

'Tell me,' she said.

He straightened his back.

Jana noticed the slow tensing of the muscles in his forearm and had just enough time to lean her head to one side before she felt the whoosh of the sharp blade. Quick as a flash, he had turned and the knife was now embedded in the wall a couple of centimetres from her head.

She pointed the gun at him.

'You missed,' she said.

Anders looked around him, trying to find an object to defend himself with. He glanced at the black toaster.

'Please. Don't kill me,' he pleaded.

'I'm going to ask you again: what's in the containers?'

He glanced at the toaster again and in a fraction of a second grabbed it and hurled it at Jana with such force that she dropped the gun. It landed on the floor.

She looked at him.

He looked at her.

They both had the same idea.

They both threw themselves to the floor, but she was a fraction quicker and managed to get her hand on the magazine. He tried to pull it out of her grip. He elbowed her in the side to make her release the gun. But her fingers remained clamped tight. He hit her again, but she gritted her teeth and put all her force behind a single blow. The muscles in her back were tensed, her shoulders too, and she hit back as hard as she could. The blade of her hand found its way between his ribs, and he gasped for breath.

She held the gun to his head. He looked down at the floor. His panting turned to sobbing. It took her a moment to realize he was crying.

'Don't kill me,' he said. 'Don't kill me. Nobody was to know . . . I should never have done it.'

He looked up at her.

'I should never have done it.' He lowered his head again and sniffled loudly. 'Please, don't kill me. It wasn't me that hurt them. I just drove them to where they were going. They were ordinary transports. To their missions.'

Jana furrowed her brow.

'Who did you transport?'

'The children.'

Anders hid his face in his hands. He sobbed loudly.

She lowered the pistol.

'Which children?'

'The children . . . I fetched them when they were . . . ready. And when they had carried out their missions, I . . . took them back again. Then I saw the grave. I saw . . . they stood there . . .'

She stared at him, thought she had misheard.

'I didn't do anything. I only transported them to where they were going. To the training and then back from there. It wasn't me who killed them.'

Jana was speechless. She looked at the man kneeling in front of her. They stared at each other. His eyes were red, Saliva was dripping from the corners of his mouth on to his bleached sweater.

'I didn't kill them. Not me. It wasn't me, I didn't do anything. I promise, all I did was drive the van. Nothing happened, I just drove, and they didn't know anything anyway.'

'I don't understand,' she said.

'They must die. All of them. Him too . . .'

'Who? You mean . . . ?'

'They've got their own names . . . Thanatos . . .' Anders whispered. 'He was really special. He was . . .'

Anders started to shake.

'It wasn't meant to be like that. I didn't know. He ran.'

'Was it you who killed the boy, was it you who killed Thanatos?'

'I had no choice. He tried to escape from the boat.'

'The boat?'

Anders fell silent.

He looked at a point far in front of him. Blinking.

'The boat . . .'

'Which boat?'

'The boat! He tried to escape! I had to stop him. He had to go back to the island, but he ran.'

'What's the island called?'

'He didn't want to die.'

'Tell me, what is the island called?'

'It hasn't got a name.'

'Where is it? Tell me where it is!'

Anders went quiet, as if he had suddenly become aware of the situation he was in.

'Near Gränsö Island.'

'Are there children out there now?'

He shook his head.

'Who are you working for?'

He looked up at Jana again.

'I've told you too much,' he said.

'Who are you working for? Give me a name!'

Anders opened his eyes wide.

Tensed himself.

And then he launched himself at Jana. Tried to knock the pistol out of her hands.

She was caught by surprise but kept hold of the gun.

He put his hand on the pistol and pulled hard, put all his weight on to her arms and roared.

Jana's index finger was pressed hard against the trigger guard. The pain was intense. She concentrated all her strength on keeping it there; she mustn't lose her grip. Her arm trembled. The adrenaline was surging through her. She struggled as hard as she could. But she couldn't keep it up. Her finger was stuck. It felt as if it would break off.

He pushed up again and her index finger was forced up in a U-shaped arch.

She had to let go.

When the bone cracked she let go.

Anders grabbed hold of the pistol and pointed it at her. He took small, short steps backward. 'It's all over now. I know it is.'

He was sweating, his hands trembled, his eyes were darting here and there.

'I'm already dead. It's over. He's going to come. I know he will. It's over.'

Anders raised the pistol.

Jana realized what was about to happen.

'It isn't over. Wait!' she said.

'It's over now. Just as well,' said Anders, and he put the barrel into his mouth and pulled the trigger.

★

315

Torsten Granath was lying on a leather sofa outside his office. He looked up when Jana Berzelius appeared.

'What happened to you?' he said, indicating the plaster on her forehead.

'It's nothing. Just a graze. I fell when I was out running,' she lied.

'You sprained your finger too?'

She nodded and looked at her bandaged index finger. It wasn't very painful but it had swelled a lot.

'It's still very slippery in some places,' said Torsten, and stretched out at full length again.

'Yes.'

'Ice can be treacherous. You've got to think about your hip joints, especially at my age. I'm thinking about buying those studs you put on the soles of your shoes. You ought to get some. For when you're out running, I mean.'

'No.'

'No, you're right. They're actually rather silly.'

'Why are you lying here?'

'My back's hurting. Old men, eh? It's one problem after another. Time to take it easy.'

'That's what you always say.'

'I know.' Torsten pushed himself up into a sitting position. He gave Jana a serious look. 'How are you getting on with the investigation? I've got a feeling I was wrong to leave you to take care of all this on your own,' he said.

'It's going fine,' she said.

'Have you charged anybody?'

'Yes. For the death of Thomas Rydberg. But our suspicions about Lena Wikström are based on assumptions and a few witness statements. She hasn't confessed to murdering Rydberg yet. I'm starting to be concerned about whether I can make the charges stick.'

'And then you've got Juhlén, the mystery boy and the containers. How many murders are we actually dealing with here?'

'It's unclear. We haven't counted all the victims in the containers yet. The state of decomposition is making it difficult.'

'So I should expect dreadful statistics, in other words?'

'Yes.'

'Oh lord. A complex murder case to unravel, multiple victims, perhaps the largest in this country's history . . .' Torsten got up and rolled his shoulders to release the tension. 'Gunnar Öhrn isn't entirely convinced you're on the right track as far as Lena is concerned.'

'He isn't?'

'No, he thinks she's keeping back important information, but he doesn't believe she's the brains behind this awful business.'

'Has he said that?'

Torsten nodded. 'And he thinks you're a bit too . . . taciturn to be the investigating prosecutor,' he said.

'Oh, does he?'

'Yes, it might be a good idea to take the lead a bit more.'

Jana gritted her teeth. 'OK.'

'Don't take it personally.'

'I won't.'

'Good.'

He patted her on the shoulder before heading into his office on stiff legs.

She carried on into her own office and closed the door behind her. She was going to have to have a talk with Gunnar.

★

Gunnar Öhrn leaned back on his office chair and rubbed his eyes. The press conference was over and the media had bombarded them with questions about the salvage work. Press officer Sara Arvidsson had insisted that the police could not comment on anything specific at this stage, but she'd only succeeded in stalling them. It was only a matter of time before the media fathomed the extent of the crimes and someone leaked pictures of all the dead bodies found in the containers. Then there'd be no evading the hard questions.

Sensing that he was being observed, he twisted round on his chair.

Jana Berzelius was standing in the doorway.

'Oh, you gave me a fright,' he said.

'I have been informed that you think I am too weak to continue as the investigating prosecutor,' she said.

'I—'

She held up her hand and cut him off.

'It would be helpful if in future you made your constructive criticisms known to me directly, rather than going to my boss,' she said.

'Torsten and me, we're old colleagues.'

'I know. But if you have a concern about me, you should discuss it with me first. Not with him. So, do you think I'm doing a bad job as the prosecutor in this investigation?'

'No. You're not a bad prosecutor. It's just that you ought to be more active than you are. You seem to be absent and . . . I don't know . . . perhaps not fully committed.'

'Thank you for your opinion. Was there anything else?'

'No.'

'In that case I'll say what I really came in for.'

'Which is?'

'I want to check out an island.'

'Why?'

'I have received information that something is going on there that has to do with the investigation.'

'Such as?'

'That's what we need to find out.'

'What's the island called?'

'I don't know. It's somewhere off Gränsö Island.'

'How do you know something's going on there?'

'I received a tip-off.'

'Hang on – you got a tip-off about an island you don't know the name of. From whom?'

'Anonymous.'

'So you've had an anonymous tip-off about an island?'

'Correct.'

'When did you get it?'

'An hour ago.'

'How?'

Jana swallowed.

'It doesn't matter,' she said.

'Was that when you got the cut on your forehead?'

'No, that happened when I was out running,' she said, hiding her throbbing index finger behind her back.

'And you've no idea who this tip-off came from?'

'No, it was anonymous, like I said.'

Gunnar studied her intently, then asked, 'Did it come from a man or a woman?'

'The voice was deep, so presumably a man.'

'And how come this man contacted you and not the police?

How did he know you were involved? How did he get your number?'

'No idea, all I know is that we ought to check out this island.'

'But I want to know why. And what can we expect out there? How do I know it's not a trap? Some criminal out to sabotage the investigation? We're on the trail of something very nasty here, and—'

'Listen,' she said. 'This is the first time I've received an anonymous tip-off and I take it very seriously. You should too.'

He nodded and gave a weary sigh.

'OK,' he said. 'I'll send Henrik and Mia.'

'I'll go with them. Then I'll be a more active prosecutor,' said Jana, and marched out.

CHAPTER
FORTY-EIGHT

Friday, 27 April

HENRIK LEVIN, MIA BOLANDER AND JANA BERZELIUS
drove out to the archipelago in silence. Jana stared at the barren landscape. The closer they drew to the coast, the more the rocky scenery dominated the view outside the car windows. She was looking forward to getting out of the car and breathing in the fresh sea air.

Arkösund was a small coastal resort which attracted tourists who came by car and boat. There was a general store, a petrol station and several boat-building firms. A hotel had recently opened and there were a couple of pubs and restaurants. A town noticeboard announced the upcoming First of May celebrations: a bonfire and a traditional torchlight procession from one of the marinas for visiting boats. A firework display and a speech by a local dignitary would end the evening. The noticeboard also had a poster with a picture of a musician and the details of when he would be performing at the local outdoor theatre. The lines from the flagpoles chattered in the wind. Though the season wasn't in full swing yet, three plastic boats were lined up by the jetty.

Jana looked across the marina and could see a short man walking towards them with one hand on his cap to keep it from blowing away. The man introduced himself as Ove Lundgren and said he was the harbourmaster. It was his job to keep an eye on all the moorings and carry out routine maintenance work for the four small marinas. He had on rubber boots and a wind jacket. His face was tanned and weather-beaten. He helped the three of them aboard a Nimbus boat he had borrowed for the day.

'There are lots of islands out here,' he said as he manoeuvred the boat between the choppy waves. 'I'm not sure, but I think your Gränsö Island is a couple of nautical miles off the Kopparholm Islands. For fifty years it was forbidden to visit the islands – it was a restricted area and only the army was there. But we're going even further out.'

'Are we?' Mia squeaked, taking a firm grip on the railing to stop herself sliding back and forth on the seat.

The boat sped past several islands, some of them with gigantic summerhouses that belonged to various business leaders and wealthy local families. Ove knew the names of all the owners.

Gradually islands became more spread out and there were no more grand buildings.

Mia was feeling seasick and doing her best to suppress the impulse to retch. Her skin was pale and clammy. She gulped in the sea air and looked straight out over the railing at the horizon.

They passed islands big and small. Some were deserted and barren. Others were inhabited and full of birds.

A series of dry heaves racked her body. She closed her eyes for a moment, hoping that would quell the nausea, and when she opened them, she saw Jana. She wasn't the least fucking bothered by the rough sea. Mia muttered to herself and turned her head away. She wasn't going to let Jana see her discomfort. Hell no!

★

After following the charts for a couple of hours they reached the open sea. At last Ove pointed out a relatively large and tree-covered island called Grimsö. He steered the boat towards it, and when they got close to the rocks he slowed down.

Mia lifted her head to see the island better, but because of all the vegetation and especially the fir trees it was impossible to say whether there were any buildings.

Ove spotted a rock jetty and expressed his surprise that anybody had bothered to build one this far out in the archipelago. He manoeuvred the boat to the side of the jetty and helped Henrik and then Jana and Mia to climb out.

Mia was clutching her hand over her mouth and as soon as she got off the boat she vomited.

'Let's go,' said Henrik.

Mia waved in an attempt to say, *You go ahead.*

'You two go on – I'll look after her,' said Ove.

'Shall we?' said Henrik, and Jana nodded. They climbed up the rocks.

'So you got a tip-off?' he said when they were alone.

'Yes,' said Jana.

'Anonymous?'

'Yes.'

'Weird.'

'Mmm.'

'And you've no idea who it was?'

'No idea.'

Henrik took the lead along a narrow path and they walked in silence through a grove of trees and thick brushwood. The path opened up a little and then divided into two. They chose the path that looked the most used, and turned to the right.

Henrik kept his hand on his holster, constantly looking around and pausing occasionally to listen for any signs of life. The trees thinned out as they went down the path, and when they went round a large rock they caught sight of a house.

Jana stopped and took a step back. She was terrified.

Henrik stopped too with a surprised look on his face. He looked at her, then at the house, then back at her again.

'What's the matter?' he said.

'It's OK,' she said, and her face assumed its usual calm expression.

She passed Henrik, ignoring his look of surprise. As she strode resolutely towards the house she could sense him watching her.

She had a weird feeling, as if she were enclosed behind thick glass, observing herself walking along the gravel path . . . as if her body was reacting but not her being.

Her legs were taking her in the direction of the house as if they had a mind of their own.

Suddenly she had an urge to rush forward and yank open the door. Something about the house was familiar to her. It was . . . what was it?

She came to a halt.

Henrik stopped too, right behind her.

She looked up at the house and felt an equally strong urge to turn around and run back to the boat. But she couldn't do that. She had to control herself now. She looked down at the gravel and picked up a few of the small stones. Vague images flashed through her mind: she saw herself as a little girl, her small feet struggling to gain traction in the gravel. And she remembered how painful it had been when she fell on it. She held the gravel in her open hand, looked down at it and then squeezed it tightly with her fingers. She clenched her hand so hard that her knuckles went white.

Henrik cleared his throat.

'I'll go ahead,' he said, and walked past her. 'Stay here. I'll make sure it's safe first.'

He moved quickly across the grassy area and stopped a few metres from the front steps. He could see no movement inside the house. Cautiously he climbed the rotting wooden steps, pulled out his gun and knocked on the door with its peeling paint. He waited but there was no reply.

At the side of the house, rainwater dripped into an overflowing barrel from a crooked and rusty drainpipe.

He walked all around the house, stopping at every window, but couldn't see a living soul. Then he spotted a barn a bit further away.

He signalled to Jana as he disappeared behind the corner, heading in the direction of the red barn.

She stayed where she was for a few moments, still clutching the gravel in her hand. Silence surrounded her. Her muscles relaxed, the blood came back into her hand and she let the gravel fall to the ground. Slowly she approached the house, coming to a halt in front of the steps. Then she moved to the side, going right up to the cracked wood-panelled façade, and crouched down by the base of the building to peer in through a dirty, narrow cellar window. She saw a small room. The ceiling was low. There was a workbench along one side, two shelves with cardboard boxes and newspapers. Some stairs, a handrail and a little stool.

Like a pressure wave, the memories came flooding back to her. She realized that she had been inside that cellar. In the dark. And somebody had been inside there with her.

Who was it?

Minos . . .

'Have you found anything?'

Mia Bolander had made her way along the gravel path. Her face, so pale before, was bright red with exertion. She must have had to run to catch up.

Jana stepped away from the cellar window.

'Where's Henrik? Has he checked the area? Is he inside the house?' Mia said.

Jana had no desire to talk to Mia. And she certainly didn't want to explore the area with her or anyone else. Another unsettling feeling welled up inside her. In some inexplicable way, she felt an enormous need to protect the place. To drive Mia and Henrik away. They had no right to be here. It was her house. Nobody else should go inside. Nobody should nose around here. Nobody. Only her.

Mia came closer.

Jana tensed her muscles and lowered her head. Prepared to defend the house.

To fight.

Then Henrik came running. His eyes were like saucers and his mouth was hanging open in panic.

When he saw Mia, he shouted as loud as he could: 'Call for backup! Get everybody here – everybody!'

Phobos was barely nine years old, but even so he was an old hand.

He washed the bend of his arm with soap and water. Then he used gravity to get the blood to the right place. He swung his arm and clenched his fist. Sat down on the floor and tied the tourniquet hard.

The needle hit his vein with the angular filed edge downwards.

326

It was the same vein, the same procedure, in the same room, in the same building. As usual. Everything was as usual.

He drew the syringe handle back and saw the thick dark-red blood flow into the syringe. He released the tie around his arm and slowly injected the rest of the drug.

When there was one unit left in the syringe, he started to feel it. It wasn't the same feeling. He pulled the needle out of his arm. Two drops of blood ended up on his trousers.

The last thing he remembered was that he shouted out with an unrecognizable voice. His heart rushed. His head spun round. Suddenly he couldn't see, couldn't hear, couldn't feel. The pressure over his chest was enormous. He gasped for air. Tried desperately to stay awake.

Gradually he came back.

And when his vision returned, he saw Papa in front of him.

'What the hell are you doing?' Papa said and hit him hard on the cheek.

'I . . .'

'What?'

Yet another slap.

'I wanted to sleep,' Phobos mumbled. 'Sorry . . . Papa.'

The grave was oblong and looked like a ditch. The children had been cast down there like animals. They lay there in several layers, tightly packed together and covered with what remained of their clothes.

'There are about thirty skeletons,' said Anneli. 'But there are also bodies that have only been underground for about a year.'

From the bottom of the ditch she looked more like an archaeologist than a forensics expert. She had come by helicopter, as had most of the police officers and forensic technicians who were now on the island.

The house was being examined in minute detail.

'What do we do?' said Gunnar, from the edge of the ditch. There was despair in his voice.

'Every skeleton must be taken up one at a time, examined, photographed, weighed and described,' said Anneli. 'The bodies must be taken to the pathology lab.'

'And how long will that take?'

'Four days. At least.'

'You've got one day.'

'But that's imposs—'

'No buts. Make sure you get help and just do it. We need to act fast.'

'Gunnar? Can you come here?' Henrik Levin emerged from the barn waving at his boss with both hands.

'And call Björn Ahlmann right away. Tell him to get the lab prepared!' Gunnar said over his shoulder to Anneli as he strode off towards the barn.

It was damp inside and it took a while for his eyes to adjust. He blinked a few times before he could look around.

What he saw confounded him.

A gym. About 100 square metres.

Gunnar let his gaze sweep the premises. A rubber mat on the floor, a banister along one side and a punch bag hanging from the ceiling. In one corner was a stack of ten-kilo weights with a thick rope lying alongside. On the left he could make out a shabby storeroom full of old furniture, and next to that a door which looked as if it hid a lavatory. At the far end was yet another door with a lever tumbler lock. Here and there, rainwater had seeped in and mingled with the dirt on the floor to form brown pools. It smelled of mould.

'What the hell is this place?' he said.

Jana Berzelius stood at the foot of the interior staircase. She felt nauseous, uncertain. Should she go up or not?

'Whatever you do, don't touch anything,' said Officer Gabriel Mellqvist, who was standing by the entrance.

Something in his facial expression seemed to question her actions, but Jana pretended not to notice.

The house was deserted and would soon be examined by the forensic team. She knew that. She also knew that she shouldn't be in here. Nevertheless she set off up the stairs.

She had the impression that somebody had been in the house recently; there was hardly any dust on the banisters and no spider webs between the rails. She shivered as she turned to the left at the top of the stairs and entered a large room. The planks of the wooden floor were damp and warped. Four single beds with steel frames were lined up next to each other. The mattresses had holes with stuffing coming out and there were rat droppings everywhere. A broken lamp hung from the ceiling; the walls were a dreary grey colour.

Jana's gaze fastened on a chest of drawers next to one of the beds. She went up and pulled out the top drawer. It was empty. Then she pulled out all the others, and they were empty too. Then she used both hands to pull the chest away from the wall as quietly as she could. She leaned down and looked at the wall. Two faces were scratched on the wallpaper; they showed a man and a woman. A mama and a papa. Carved by a child's hand.

Carved by her.

Saturday, 28 April

SHE COULD REMEMBER IT SO CLEARLY NOW, COULD
see everything before her every time she closed her eyes. It was
as if somebody had given her a good shake. She remembered
the container, remembered how she was dragged out of it, how
she was taken away in a van, trained hard and how she'd fled
from it all.

From Papa.

At the same time, she realized that every single detail, every
note and every image in her notebooks came from the same
reality. They hadn't been dreams; they had been memories. And
nobody had believed her. Her father and mother had tried to
silence her with medication and psychologists.

Sitting in her car, Jana slammed her hand on to the steering
wheel.

She shut her eyes and roared. Then she sat quietly. Taking
deep breaths. And suddenly, behind her closed eyes, she saw
Papa before her.

★

He stood over her, watched how she tensed up. The terror had grown in her eyes. The hate in his.

And when he gave her the knife, she realized what she was being forced to do. She was being forced to kill so as not to be killed. So she turned and let the knife in her hand sink between the ribs of the boy lying beside her.

He, too, had tape over his mouth, and panic in his eyes.

It had been beautiful, in a horrible, dreadful way.

When Jana opened her eyes again, for a moment she experienced the feeling of carrying out one of Papa's orders. But then she slowly returned to the awful reality.

She started the car and drove out on to the motorway. When she passed the sign welcoming her to Linköping, she put her foot down on the accelerator and felt the adrenaline course through her. Outside the forensics centre she adjusted her jacket and ran her fingers through her hair.

She was back in her role as prosecutor.

Medical examiner Björn Ahlmann was leaning over the little girl who lay on his autopsy table. Her body was partly decomposed from lying in the grave. Her eye sockets were holes.

Björn gently held the girl's hand in his as he took her fingerprints. Hearing somebody in the doorway, he looked up and saw Jana Berzelius.

'Can you identify them?' she said.

'Let's hope so. For their parents' sake,' said Björn.

'They're not alive.'

'The parents?' said Björn, frowning.

Jana nodded. 'They're dead too.'

'How can you know that?'

'I assume it.'

'An assumption is only a guess. As prosecutor, you need to be certain.'

'I am.'

'Certain?'

'Yes. I believe the children's parents were in those containers that were salvaged.'

'To believe is also a guess.'

'Match their DNA with the children's and you'll see.'

'That's going to involve a lot of work.'

'Yes, and the possibility of identifying them.'

Björn Ahlmann was about to open his mouth to reply when Henrik Levin and Mia Bolander entered the room. Mia furrowed her brow when she saw the corpse on the bench and stopped a few metres away.

'She's not very old, is she?'

'About eight years old,' said Björn.

'What do we know?' said Henrik.

'Shot,' said Björn. 'They were all shot.'

'All of them?' said Henrik.

'Yes, but the entry holes are different,' said Björn.

'Did the children die where they were found?' said Henrik.

'In the ditch, yes. It seems so. Presumably they were forced to stand naked on the edge and then shot.'

'Presumably is only a guess,' said Jana and winked.

Björn cleared his throat.

'There is reason to believe the children belong to the people who were found in the containers,' Henrik said.

'Yes, and the prosecutor has requested that we attempt to match DNA,' said Björn.

Henrik ran his fingers through his hair. 'Fine. See if you can match them – as soon as possible,' he said.

Björn nodded.

'Anything else?' said Henrik.

'Yes, I found something interesting on the girl's neck,' said Björn.

He turned her head to one side and exposed her neck.

The letters E–R–I–D–A were carved in the skin below her hairline.

Mia pulled her mobile out of her pocket and typed Erida into the browser.

'It must be the same person who carved the name on the boy we found out at Viddviken,' said Henrik.

'Yes,' said Mia, without taking her eyes off her phone.

'So it's the same murderer,' said Henrik.

'The goddess of hate,' said Mia. 'Erida was the goddess of hate. It's Greek mythology, same as Thanatos.'

The room fell silent.

The only sound was the whirring of the ventilation system.

'One more thing,' Björn said. 'The girl's head was shaved, but I found several strands of long hair on her body. They are dark and thick and definitely not hers.'

'Send them to the National Forensics Lab,' said Henrik.

'Already done,' Björn answered.

The team sat in the conference room, waiting for the briefing to begin. Gunnar Öhrn thumbed through a pile of papers. Anneli Lindgren was fidgeting with her hair; Henrik Levin leaned back in his chair with his arms folded over his chest. Mia Bolander also leaned back, balancing her chair on its rear legs. Jana Berzelius was leaning over the table with her notepad in front of her.

'First,' said Gunnar, 'I've just spoken to Björn Ahlmann. He confirms that several of the murdered children have the same DNA profile as the remains of those adults who were found in the salvaged containers. Which means they are related.'

'Presumably, the parents,' said Henrik.

'Yes, it seems so,' said Gunnar. 'It's reasonable to assume that the children must have been in the containers, then they were taken out and brought to the island. The parents were shot and dumped in the sea.'

'The containers came from Chile, right? Could this have been human trafficking?' said Henrik.

'That would be my guess,' said Gunnar.

An oppressive silence spread around the table.

Gunnar went on, 'The children Björn Ahlmann has examined so far have all had names carved on their necks. Names from Greek mythology. Marking children is like imposing an identity on them. Carving into their flesh is beyond barbaric.'

'Marking is common among gangs. Think tattoos, gang insignia . . .' said Mia.

'But these children have been systematically kidnapped—'

'Why would anyone do that, it's crazy,' said Anneli.

'Toxicology results show that some of the children had drugs in their blood,' said Gunnar. 'Our boy, Thanatos, was drugged. My guess is that the children were used as couriers or runners in the drugs trade.'

'So we should look for a drug dealer,' Henrik noted.

'Or several, with a shared interest in Greek mythology,' said Mia.

'OK, it sounds far-fetched. But until we find out how this all fits together, we need to consider all possibilities,' said Gunnar. 'I think we need to talk to Lena again. She still hasn't told us how she knew about the containers or who gave her the order to delete the file on Juhlén's computer. And this makes me wonder: why delete a file? You do it to hide something. Hans Juhlén didn't delete it himself. So it must be Lena who has something to hide.'

'But did Juhlén know about the containers?' said Henrik.

'He had the list and he went to the docks, so he knew something. But he may not have known the whole story.'

'You mean about the children and the drug connection?' said Anneli.

'Exactly.'

'So the containers may also have contained drugs?' said Henrik.

'I don't think they'd smuggle drugs as well as refugees, but we can't rule it out.'

'If they got rid of the adults,' said Anneli, 'why keep the children?'

'Because they're under the age of criminal responsibility,' said Mia triumphantly. 'And they tend to be loyal to their task-masters . . .'

'On the island, a sort of training centre with quite a lot of weapons had been set up,' said Henrik. 'Do you think the children were trained to . . .'

The room fell silent. Henrik went on. 'I believe Hans Juhlén found out about all this. That's why he was in the docks with Thomas Rydberg. And Rydberg was scared he would be discovered, and he told Lena, who then deleted the file in the computer. She also gave somebody the order to kill Juhlén and then Rydberg.'

'We do actually have another name to add to the investigation,' said Gunnar. 'Björn Ahlmann found a few strands of hair on one of the children, and DNA analysis shows the hair came from this man.'

He picked up the remote and switched on the projector. An image filled the screen opposite: a dark-haired man with a broad nose and a large scar across half of his face.

'Christ, would you look at him!' said Mia.

Jana opened her mouth to shout out: 'That's him!'

But she stopped herself in time and sat rigid in her chair, not trusting herself to move.

'Gavril Bolanaki. Evidently, he's known as Papa,' said Gunnar. 'Ola, I want you to check for links between this man, Thomas Rydberg and Lena Wikström. See if their lives have overlapped at any point. Work? School? Known associates – anything.'

'What do we know about this Gavril?' said Henrik.

'Not much. Born 1953 on the island of Tilos in Greece. Swedish citizen since 1960. Did his military service in Södertälje. Some military equipment was stolen in the mid-seventies and he came under suspicion, but was subsequently found not guilty on what were described as dubious grounds,' said Gunnar.

'Do we know what weapons disappeared?' said Henrik.

'No,' said Gunnar.

'Where is he?' said Jana in an exaggeratedly soft voice.

'Whereabouts unknown. We've put him on the national Wanted List, and informed all police authorities. Let's hope we can bring him in quickly,' said Gunnar. 'I think we're finally on the right track.'

So do I, Jana thought to herself.

'In the first search of the island they found some food, which leads us to believe someone has been there recently. We don't know yet whether that would be Gavril or someone else. I've asked for a dog handler to go over the area. Anneli and I are heading back there now and I want you, Henrik and Mia, to come with us. We leave in ten minutes.'

Mia Bolander was seasick again.

She tried to fix her gaze on a point in the distance while the coastguard launch bobbed up and down on the waves. Having persuaded a trainee to treat her to a sandwich in the station cafeteria, she had eaten only half an hour earlier. Now she wished she'd gone hungry.

Today was the twenty-eighth. Only three days since she had received her salary and already she was broke. A whole month until the next pay cheque. And today was Saturday too, and that always meant going out somewhere. Mia wondered how she'd be able to afford a beer.

She pulled her hand away from her mouth, leaned over the railing and vomited.

The police dog had found an underground concrete bunker quite close to the barn. The entrance was well hidden by bushes.

Gunnar went in first. It wasn't very big and he stopped after about three metres. The ceiling was low and he had to keep his head down as he looked around. There were two empty bags on the floor. A large number of guns hung on the walls: AK-47s, Sig Sauers and Glocks. There was plenty of ammunition too, stored in various plastic containers. Five smallish knives and several silencers were laid out on a shelf.

Gunner turned round and went out to where Henrik and Mia were waiting.

'It's a weapons stash. The biggest I've ever seen.'

'Could they be from Södertälje?' said Henrik.

'Very likely. There are some older weapons there, but quite a few newer ones too.'

'So it could be that this Gavril smuggled weapons out of Södertälje and set up a weapons store here,' said Henrik.

'There are several Glock pistols in there, and that's one of the most common weapons in the army,' said Gunnar.

'It's also the weapon that was used to murder Hans Juhlén,' said Henrik.

Gabriel Mellqvist had only one hour left before he'd be relieved of sentry duty on the jetty. He couldn't wait to get indoors. In the meantime, all he could do was stamp his feet to try to keep them warm. As he stamped, he scanned the horizon – and spotted a boat heading towards the island. He looked through his binoculars to see if any of his colleagues were on board.

The boat slowed down, seemed to almost come to a stop and then suddenly turned sharply and sped off.

Gabriel grabbed his radio.

No time to lose.

Henrik Levin was on his way down into the bunker when Officer Hanna Hultman came running.

'An unknown boat has been sighted – it was coming towards the island but then veered off suddenly.'

Henrik Levin ran as fast as he could to the jetty and jumped on to the coastguard launch.

Mia Bolander was right behind him.

'After it!' he shouted. 'Don't wait for Gunnar. Go!'

Coastguard Rolf Vikman expertly steered them out of the jetty. Before the boat disappeared from sight, Mellqvist had pointed it out to him, so Ralf revved the engine and headed in that direction at full speed. He'd already radioed coordinates to the county communication centre, who were scrambling to deploy other vessels to the scene.

The launch threw up cascades of water as they hit 30 knots. Everyone on board was scanning the horizon for the other boat, but there was no sign of it. When the boat came to an island, they slowed down. Henrik looked in all directions. Mia too. They listened for the sound of an engine but couldn't hear anything except the noise of the launch they were sitting in.

When they reached the next island, Rolf slowed down again and Henrik's gaze swept over the jagged rocks. The wind whistled in his ears. Two seagulls circled high above them, with a shrill squawking.

Mia stood on her toes to look over the railing. They slowed down a bit more, and Rolf zigzagged among the waves to stop them from drifting into land.

'Go on,' said Henrik, as they rounded the island. Rolf increased the speed again and the wind caught Henrik's jacket. Doubt was beginning to set in. No boat to be seen.

'There!' shouted Mia and pointed with her hand. 'There! There! I can see it!'

Rolf immediately steered in the direction she pointed.

'A Chaparral,' he shouted. 'A faster vessel than us, I'm afraid.'

The Chaparral took off at speed, as if aware of the coastguard launch moving in. Henrik drew his gun and Mia did the same. Rolf kept the launch at full throttle, gradually closing the gap.

'Police!' Henrik shouted and showed his weapon. 'Stop!'

His words were drowned out by the noise from the engines.

The Chaparral put on a burst of speed and increased the distance between them.

'He's trying to get away,' Rolf shouted, attempting to keep up.

The chase continued, both vessels bouncing over the waves. Henrik's jacket flapped wildly in the wind. The cold bit into his cheeks and his hair kept getting in his eyes.

'Police!' he shouted again when they got closer to the boat.

He got his first good look at the man at the helm of the Chaparral as he steered right in front of them. He was an older man, his dark hair just visible under a rough cap.

'Damn!' shouted Rolf, and sheered too.

They clipped the waves. The spray got higher and higher.

Then the Chaparral slowed down unexpectedly.

Henrik raised his pistol without letting go of the railing.

'Stop!' he shouted to the driver.

But the boat sheered again and raced off.

'After him, Rolf! After him!'

Rolf opened the throttle and followed. The boat in front of them slowed down yet again, then sheered and pulled away at high speed.

Jana Berzelius knew that she shouldn't do it. Nevertheless, she tapped at her mobile phone, composing a text message to Danilo, doing her best to keep it as cryptic as possible. She had bought a new telephone and a prepaid SIM card and was confident neither could be traced back to her, but she didn't want to take any chances.

So she wrote:

A gave me the place. Papa soon home.

She was about to hit send when her own mobile started ringing in her pocket. She picked it up and saw *Number withheld*. Hoping it would be Danilo, and she answered immediately.

It was Henrik Levin.

'We've got him,' he said in a calm and controlled voice.

Jana held her breath.

'We got him, after a one-and-a-half-hour boat chase,' said Henrik.

'At last,' whispered Jana.

'We need a hearing. Right away.'

'I'll arrange it. And the interrogation?'

'That will start tomorrow morning.'

Jana ended the conversation with a brisk, 'Well done!' She was trembling. With shaking hands she again picked up the new pay-as-you-go phone and deleted the last part of the message. Instead she wrote:

A gave me the place. Papa is home.

Then she pressed the button and sent the message.

Danilo stared at his mobile.

'Hell,' he shouted as loud as he could. 'Fucking hell!'

He banged his fist against the wall with all his strength.

'Fuck, fuck, fuck, FUCK!'

He was in a rage. Absolutely incandescent. How could he have let it go so wrong? Anders should have killed her! Anders was an idiot, a useless fucking idiot who never did a single fucking thing right in the whole fucking world. First he fails to take the boy to the island, and then he fails to deal with Jana.

Danilo sighed. Now he would be forced to deal with it himself. As usual. It was always him who had to sort everything out. And everything was a fucking mess now.

'Fuck!' he shouted out yet again.

He ran through ways of dealing with Jana. Forever. Or was there a chance she could be useful? Could he make use of her?

A smile spread across Danilo's face.

The more he thought about the possibility of using Jana, the clearer his strategy became.

After ten minutes he knew exactly what he would do. She had only herself to blame. She was the one who'd started stirring the shit, and once you did that, you had to accept the consequences.

Whatever they might be.

Sunday, 29 April

CUP OF COFFEE IN HAND, GUNNAR ÖHRN WAS glued to the special news bulletin on TV. Gavril Bolanaki's arrest was headline news on every channel and in every paper.

'Does it feel OK?'

Anneli Lindgren lay on one side of the bed with a sheet wrapped around her naked body.

She too had been following the news bulletin.

'Yes, it feels good that we caught him. He's going to be interrogated tomorrow. Will there be time to search the whole island before then?'

Anneli stretched out on the mattress.

'Yes, we've got a forensics crew working there today, and the media frenzy should mean we'll be given top priority and our choice of labs for DNA testing. At least, I hope so.'

'Me too,' said Gunnar. He was about to take another gulp of coffee when the telephone rang.

It was Ola Söderström.

'Listen to this – we've finally got an answer,' he said. 'The department of transport has identified the owner of the van Erik

Nordlund saw on Arkösund Road. It's registered to an Anders Paulsson, fifty-five. He worked as a loader for DHL for twenty years. Now he's got his own firm, in the transport sector too. And guess what: he was married to Thomas Rydberg's sister, until she died of cancer ten years ago.'

'Where does he live?'

'Jonsberg, Arkösund,' said Ola.

'Excellent. I'll put Henrik and Mia on it right away,' said Gunnar and put the phone down.

Mia Bolander was leaning towards the visor, inspecting her face in the vanity mirror. During the night, her mascara had left tiny black dots all around her eyes.

'Oh, fuck!' she swore out loud.

'Hard night?' said Henrik.

'As if you'd know what that means.'

'I know quite a lot about parties.'

'Children's parties, or what?'

'No.'

'When was the last time you boozed so much your head exploded?'

'So that's what you've been up to, is it?'

'Yep. I have. And fucking, too. And it was out of this world!'

'Well, thank you, but that was more information than I needed.'

'Don't ask then!'

He sighed and concentrated on driving while Mia went back to trying to rub the mascara from around her eyes.

Fifteen minutes later they arrived outside the red detached house where Anders Paulsson lived. In the yard outside stood a white van, an Opel. The garden was neglected and overgrown, and the blinds were pulled down inside. The white paintwork on the window frames was now discoloured and grey.

Henrik drove slowly past, parked out of sight of the house, turned off the engine and got out. Mia downed the last drops of her coffee. As she put the mug in the holder between the seats, she saw Henrik's wallet lying there. She reached across, opened it and took out a one-hundred-kronor bill, shoved it into her trouser pocket, then put the wallet back. A broad smile formed on her face as she opened the car door and stepped out.

Henrik had snuck up to the house and was crouching down next to the back wheel of a parked van. His eyes glistened with enthusiasm when Mia approached.

Together they went up to the house and stood on either side of the front door. Mia placed a foot against the door to prevent anyone from knocking it open.

Henrik rang the doorbell. The sound echoed from inside. They waited thirty seconds. He rang again. Still nothing. They exchanged looks and he rang the bell once more. Still nothing.

Mia went around the side of the house and saw every window blind had been pulled down. The house was quiet. At the back she discovered an open window. She called to Henrik to come, took a firm grip on the window frame and hoisted herself up on to the sill. With a less than elegant jump, she disappeared inside the house.

The overpowering stench of excrement hit her immediately. She pulled up her jacket collar so that it covered her nose and breathed through the cloth as she surveyed the room. The floor was littered with piles of shit and dried-up stains that looked to be urine. There was rubbish everywhere. Cardboard boxes piled on top of each other. Old newspapers in heaps, mouldy remains of food on paper plates, empty bottles, beer cans and fast-food cartons. The carpet had been rolled up. The table had a big crack in it, and the wallpaper was ripped.

Henrik looked in through the open window and got a whiff of the acrid smell of faeces. He pulled his head back and retched.

Mia took a couple of cautious steps forward with her drawn weapon, and began picking her way through the piles of shit and rubbish.

'Police!' she called out, then clamped her mouth shut to avoid breathing in any more of the rancid air.

She entered the hall and saw a door that presumably led into the kitchen. The hall too was in a mess; there was so much rubbish piled up she could barely see the walls. She went into the kitchen and was met by an even worse odour. It came from a man who lay spread-eagled on the floor. His mouth was open wide, his eyes staring blankly, and Mia could immediately see that he was dead.

Monday, 30 April

JANA BERZELIUS WOULD HAVE LIKED TO DELAY THE
trial that had been scheduled for that morning, but she had no
legal grounds to do so. For the first time in her career she found
herself hoping that the judge would announce a postponement
due to one of the participants being taken ill or incapacitated in
some way. Unfortunately, to Jana's dismay, all parties were present
and so the trial would start at the designated time.

She sighed and opened the red folder that held details of the
evidence she was going to present in court. The charge was arson.
She looked at the clock. In five minutes the trial would start. And
in five minutes they would start questioning Gavril Bolanaki
at the police station. She had been in touch with Henrik Levin
by phone and told him to start the interview without her. She
hoped the trial would be over within an hour and then she would
hurry to the detention centre to confront him – confront Papa.

She tidied her hair. Let her hand stop on her neck. Felt the
carved letters.

The time has come, she thought.

At last.

★

Henrik Levin looked impassively at the man across the table. Black shirt with rolled-up sleeves. Dark hair, longish, combed back. A wide nose and dark eyes, framed by bushy eyebrows. The scar on his face went from his forehead down to his chin; it was hard to stop staring at it. Henrik fixed his gaze on the other half of the man's face and started to speak: 'What were you doing out at sea?'

Silence.

'Why did you flee from us?'

Silence.

'Do you live on the island?'

Still silent.

'Have you seen this boy before?'

Henrik showed him a photo of Thanatos.

The man raised one corner of his mouth in what resembled an arrogant smile.

'I want a lawyer,' he said.

Henrik sighed.

He had no choice but to comply.

After two hours, the trial showed no sign of ending anytime soon. Jana was frustrated. The injured party and the accused had both given their testimony, and after the break the witnesses and the written evidence would be dealt with. She got up from the prosecutor's bench and left the courtroom. After a quick visit to the restroom, she pulled her phone out of her pocket and saw that she had missed a call from a withheld number. A recorded message announced that Henrik Levin had tried to get hold of her.

'How are things going?' she said when Henrik answered.

'Nothing yet,' he said.

'Nothing at all?' said Jana.

'No. He's demanding a lawyer.'

'Then he'll get one. But I want to talk to him first.'

'It's pointless.'

'But I want to try.' She glanced at the clock. 'In three hours the trial here ought to be over. Then we can start questioning him again.'

'OK. The interview room at two o'clock,' said Henrik.

'Without a lawyer.'

'We can't do that.'

'Yes, we can. I'm the prosecutor and he's my client and I want to talk with him.'

Jana savoured the words: *my client.*

'I'll see what I can do.'

'Five minutes. That's all I ask.'

'OK.'

When the conversation ended, she remained standing there with the phone pressed to her chest. She felt exhilarated in some way.

Almost happy.

Mia sat back in the chair with her arms crossed over her chest. Henrik had left the interview room in a hurry to answer a call from Jana Berzelius, leaving her to keep an eye on the suspect. He sat with his head lowered and the lamp casting shadows over the scar on his face. His lips seemed to be twisted in a permanent half-smile.

'Do you believe in God?' said Mia.

The man didn't answer.

'Your name. Gavril. It means God is . . .'

'My strength,' he filled in. 'Thank you, I know what it means.'

'So you believe in God?'

'No, I am God.'

'Oh yeah? That's nice.'

He smirked at her. She felt uncomfortable. Squirmed. Gavril mimicked the movement.

'A god doesn't kill,' said Mia.

'God gives and takes.'

'But he doesn't kill children.'

'Oh yes he does.'

'So you've killed children?'

Gavril smirked again.

'What the fuck are you smirking at?'

She leaned back in the chair. Gavril did the same.

'I haven't killed any children,' he said. 'I've got a son myself; why would I want to kill such small creatures?'

'But we fucking well found your hairs on a little girl who lay in a mass grave on an island which you were on your way to!'

'That doesn't mean I killed her, though, does it?'

Mia glared at Gavril. He glared back. She refused to look away.

'But I wonder,' he said slowly. Still glaring at her. 'If I know who has killed them and if I tell you, what would you do for me?'

'Yes, what would we do for you?'

Gavril heard her sarcasm. He clenched his teeth, hissed.

'I don't think you understand what I'm saying. If I tell you who did it, what do I get in return?'

'This isn't a fucking negotiation. Don't you—'

'I want you to listen very carefully.'

Gavril leaned forward. Brought his face close to Mia's. Unpleasantly close.

She didn't look away. She couldn't lose.

'If you lock me up, I want you to remember my face for the day I get out. Do you get what I mean?' he hissed.

Then he calmly leaned back in his chair and said: 'You'll be making a big mistake if you lock me up. That's why I'm making you an offer. I can name several key players who run the Swedish drug trade. I can give you locations as well as names. But I think you are most interested in the children's role in all this. I'm right, aren't I?'

Mia refused to answer.

'So if I tell you how it all fits together, what will you do for me? I'm not going to confess to anything, but I can tell you everything I know about the others. If that is of interest, I mean. And I think it is.'

Mia bit her lip.

'I have a suggestion,' said Gavril. 'If I tell you everything, you must protect me and my son. If you lock me up now, you won't get to know anything and I can guarantee that more children will die. I am the only one who can put a stop to it. I want to have the best possible protection too. Otherwise I won't say anything. So – how do you want to play it?'

Mia lost. Her gaze left his. She looked down at the table, then straight into the mirror in the window. She knew that Gunnar stood there behind it, and she knew that he was just as uncertain as she was.

What the fuck should they do now?

It was 13.42. The trial was over and Jana Berzelius gathered up her papers and left the courtroom in a hurry. As usual, she went straight to the emergency exit and pressed the white fire door open with her hip. With quick steps she ran down the stairs to the underground car park. And while she manoeuvred her car out of the parking space, she phoned Henrik Levin to persuade him to prepare the second interview with Gavril. But the number was busy.

She drove out of the garage and made another attempt to reach Henrik, but even though she heard it ringing this time, he didn't answer. Every traffic light seemed to change to red as she approached. The pedestrians took an exaggeratedly long time to cross and the motorists in front of her crawled along at a snail's pace. When she finally made it to the police station, all the parking spaces were occupied and she had to drive round three times before she found a gap so narrow she had to suck in her stomach and hold her breath to get out of the car.

She ran to the stairwell and jabbed the button to summon the lift. She waited and waited but, according to the display, the lift was only going up and down between the higher floors. In the end she took the stairs.

Out of breath and struggling to compose herself, she opened the door and stepped into the corridor leading to the interview rooms. Her first impression was one of frantic activity, but before she could take it all in, someone stepped in front of her, holding up a hand to bar her from going any further. It was Officer Gabriel Mellqvist.

'This is a prohibited area.'

'I have a meeting with my client and I'm a bit late,' said Jana.

'What is your client's name?'

'Gavril Bolanaki.'

'I'm sorry, you can't come in.'

'Why not?'

'The case is closed.'

'Closed? How can it be closed?'

'I'm sorry, Jana, you must leave.'

Gabriel pushed her through the door she'd just entered and closed it in her face. She remained standing on the other side, surprised and angry.

She pulled out her phone and rang Henrik again. No answer. Rang Gunnar. No answer.

She swore out loud and then ran downstairs to the garage.

Lena Wikström sat in her cell and banged her head against the concrete wall. The only soft thing in the cell was a mattress with a plastic cover and yellowish faded sheets, and she was crouched at one end of the mattress with her arms clasped around her legs. On the wall was an oval-shaped white lamp and next to that somebody who obviously couldn't spell had used a black object to write *Fukc*. Weak light filtered in between the bars in the window. The cell was eight square metres and the only furniture apart from the bed was a wooden desk with a built-in and very solidly anchored chair, also of wood.

Lena had now spent seven days in the detention cell. So far she had coped because, deep down, she believed she would get out. But today her hopes had been dashed. As she queued for lunch, she'd heard the news that Gavril had been arrested and was also in the detention centre. She left her food untouched on the tray. She hadn't even been able to drink the milk she had been served. She'd been counting on him to get her out. Now he too was locked up, in a cell close to hers.

It's over, she thought and banged her head harder against

the wall. Everything is over, and I'm finished too. I just have to accept that.

Now only one thing remains for me to do.

Torsten Granath had his coat on and was just putting a folder in his briefcase when Jana Berzelius stormed into his office.

'What's happening?' she demanded.

Torsten looked up at her, his face a question mark.

'I must go home. My wife phoned – there are problems with Ludde. He's been eating his own excrement the last twenty-four hours. We must take him to the vet.'

'I mean Gavril Bolanaki. What's happening?'

'Ah yes, that. We were going to inform you: the case is closed. The security service has taken over. Nobody can talk to him. Not even you.'

'But he's my client. Why can't I talk to him?'

'He's going to be an informer.'

'What do you mean? Inform on what?'

'He's going to help the police in their mapping of the drug trade in Sweden. Because of the danger this will place him in, both he and his son are now in the care of the Security Service. They will be moved from the detention centre tomorrow morning at nine.'

'He has a son?'

'Evidently.'

'Where are they going to move him to?'

'That's confidential, Jana. You know how these things work.'

'But—'

'Drop it now.'

'But we've got—'

'Being a prosecutor isn't just about convicting people, it's about finding out the truth.'

'I know.'

'And now the police will have the best possible insight into the drug trade. That's the only good thing to come from this dreadful affair.'

No, it wasn't, Jana thought. And turned on her heel and stormed out again.

Jana felt like killing somebody . . . ideally the person who had decided to grant Gavril Bolanaki protection. Gavril had manipulated the police, she knew that. He had led them to believe he was only a minor figure in the operation, with good insight into what had gone on. Now he would avoid everything – the hearing, the trial and conviction. He was going to get off scot-free!

She drove into the garage, tyres screeching. Parked in her reserved place and slammed the car door behind her. She took the stairs two at a time up to her apartment. With a firm grip she put the key into the lock, opened the door and stepped into the hallway. She was about to close the door when she saw a hand grasp it from the outside. She didn't have time to react before he pushed his way in behind her.

His face was hidden by a large hood. Then he held up both hands, showing his empty palms.

'No fighting, Jana,' he said, and she immediately recognized the voice.

Danilo pulled off the hood, exposing his face.

'You ought to be more careful,' he said.

Jana snorted and turned on the ceiling light.

'Sending a text wasn't the smartest thing to do,' he went on.

'Why not? Are you hiding from somebody?' said Jana.

'No, but you are.'

'The police can't trace a prepaid SIM.'

'You never know.'

They both fell silent and stood staring at each other. It was Danilo who broke the silence.

'So he's been caught?'

'Yes. Or perhaps . . .'

'What do you mean?'

'Come in and I'll tell you.'

HENRIK LEVIN WOKE WITH A START. HE MUST HAVE dozed off. It was hardly surprising, given the day's events. He was exhausted mentally and physically.

On his stomach lay a book about a teddy bear. Vilma was fast asleep on his arm. Felix was curled up on his other arm, breathing deeply. Henrik tried as carefully as he could to get his arm out from under Vilma, but she pushed herself even closer. Henrik looked at his daughter's sleeping face. He pressed his nose against hers and then freed his arm. Felix didn't stir when Henrik eased the other arm free; in his sleep, he opened his mouth wide like a baby bird. Henrik stroked the boy's cheek. Then he delicately started to manoeuvre himself out from the narrow bed and after a couple of attempts he had to clamber over the high edge of the frame. The heat from the children's bodies had made him sweaty. He pulled the sticky shirt away from his skin and decided the children could stay on in the same bed for the night.

He turned off the moon-shaped bedside light and quietly closed the door to Felix's room.

It took him fifteen minutes to brush his teeth, floss and then rinse with exactly the recommended amount of mouthwash. He studied his face in the mirror and noticed that another couple of hairs on his left temple had turned grey. But he didn't bother to remove them. He was too tired for that. He turned off the bathroom light and went into the bedroom.

Emma was lying in bed in a pink T-shirt with the covers up to her waist, engrossed in a book. Henrik got undressed, folded his clothes and put them on the chair next to his side of the bed. With a yawn, he sunk down with his head on the pillow, put one arm under his head and looked up at the ceiling. The other arm was under the covers and his hand felt its way into his underpants.

Emma put her book down and looked at him. He felt her gaze. It hit him like an electric prod.

'What is it?' he said.

She didn't answer.

He pulled his hand out from his pants and lay on his side next to her.

'Well, we haven't . . .' she started.

'What haven't we?'

'Had sex so much lately.'

'No.'

'And it isn't because of you.'

'Oh?'

'It's because of me.'

'It doesn't matter,' said Henrik and immediately wondered why on earth he had said that. It certainly did matter. It mattered an awful lot. In fact, it was everything.

She leaned forward and gave him a long kiss. He responded likewise. They kissed again. A bit predictable, one might say. His hand on her breast. Her hands on his back. She scratched him a little. Then harder, and Henrik got the feeling this was an invitation. At last, he thought, and pulled Emma closer to him. But then he remembered what she had said, about there being something that had made her not want to as much as before. With a gentle hand he pushed her away. She looked at him with her big blue eyes and her gaze was full of desire.

'I'm wondering what the reason was,' said Henrik. 'You said it was because of you.'

Emma smiled and the laughter lines around her eyes showed up. He loved every one of them.

Then she bit her lip, still with the smile there. She had a mischievous look. Her fingers played over the sheet and drew an invisible heart.

Afterwards he had wanted to freeze that moment. He would have given anything for time to have stood still, right there and then. Because she looked so happy.

Then she said it.

'I'm pregnant.'

He wished he hadn't asked. Why couldn't he have given his desire free rein, so they could have got on with it? Why did he have to bloody go and ask?

'Isn't it wonderful?' gushed Emma.

'Yes.'

'It is, isn't it?'

'Yes, really.'

'Are you pleased?'

'Well, yes. I'm pleased.'

'I hadn't wanted to say anything. You've been so busy at work and there simply wasn't a good occasion. Until now.'

Henrik didn't move. He lay there under Emma, as if he had turned into stone. She moved slowly, rubbing her body against his. His thoughts spun around and around: pregnant? Pregnant! Now there would be no more sex at all. Not for nine months. That's what it had been like when she was pregnant with Felix and Vilma. Then he hadn't wanted to at all. It hadn't felt right to do it with Emma when she had a baby in her tummy. And now she had one again.

A baby.

In her tummy.

Yet again, he pushed her away.

'What's the matter,' she said. 'Don't you want to?'

'No,' he said, and held up his arm against her. 'Come on, lie down here.'

She looked at him with surprise.

'Come on,' he said. 'I just want to hold you a while.'

She lay her head on his chest. He let his arm sink down on to her shoulders.

'So you're pregnant.' He looked up at the ceiling. 'Great. Really great.'

Emma didn't answer.

Henrik knew she was disappointed that they weren't having sex. Now she could presumably feel what he had felt every time she hadn't wanted to. Now the roles were reversed, he thought, before he closed his eyes. He wasn't going to fall asleep, he knew that. And he was right.

He didn't get any sleep at all that night.

'So he's going to be moved tomorrow,' Danilo repeated. He stood in the middle of Jana's living room with his arms folded and his eyes fixed on a point far away outside the window.

She sat on the couch, her hands cupping a glass of water. It had taken her twenty minutes to tell Danilo what had happened. The whole time, he had stood in the same position.

'Where is he going to be moved to?' he said. 'Do you know?'

'No, I've no idea,' said Jana.

Danilo paced back and forth. 'What a fucking mess,' he said. 'What should we do?'

Danilo ignored the question, pacing all the faster. Then he stopped and looked at her.

'So you've no idea where they're going to put him?' he said.

'No, like I said, it's classified.'

'Then there's only one way to find out.'

'How?'

'With a tracking device.'

She looked at him, incredulous.

'I'm serious. A GPS tracker is the only option.'

'Why not simply follow the car transporting him? What do you think about that? A bit simpler perhaps?'

'And risk being seen? I don't think so. With a tracker we can follow them at a distance.'

'But we still risk being discovered.'

'Not if we do it right.'

'How do we get hold of a tracker?'

'I'll fix it.'

'How?'

'Trust me.'

'But haven't you forgotten an important detail? Gavril is locked up. In the detention centre. How do you think you're going to plant a tracker on him?'

Danilo sat down beside Jana.

'I'm not going to do it,' he said.

'You're not?'

'There's only one person who can fasten it on him. One who can always get inside the detention centre. One who the police will never suspect.'

'Who's that?'

'You.'

Tuesday, 1 May

THE CORRIDOR SEEMED TO GO ON FOREVER. HER heels echoed off the walls. To maintain her focus, she counted her steps. She had been counting ever since she stepped out of the lift on the floor for the detention centre, and now she was up to fifty-seven. She looked at her Rolex: 08.40.

She fixed her gaze on the door and squeezed the handle of her briefcase. Seventy-two steps in all, she thought as she put her briefcase down on the floor. She rang the bell to be let in and then heard a voice asking her to speak her name into the microphone on the wall.

'Jana Berzelius, the prosecutor's office. I'm going to talk to my client, Lena Wikström,' she said.

The door opened and Jana picked up her briefcase and went inside. A warder with a name tag that said Bengt Dansson and with a neck that was barely visible and earlobes big as wings smirked a stupid smile of recognition when she approached him.

Bengt looked at her identity card and smiled even wider when he handed it back to her, which made his chin pour out over his collar.

'A quick search too,' he said.

Jana stretched out her arms and felt Bengt's hands move from her armpits down over her ribs and hips.

He panted when he crouched down in front of her and she rolled her eyes in irritation when he continued to search her from her hips down her legs.

'Which do you prefer? Metal detector or a body search?' he said, and looked up at her with a lustful gaze.

'What do you mean?' said Jana.

'You can choose. Detector or naked.'

'You're joking, aren't you?'

'You can't be too careful when it comes to security.'

Jana was speechless.

Bengt broke out into such loud laughter that his cheeks bobbed up and down. He put one hand on his knee and pushed himself up but couldn't stop laughing.

'Ha, ha, ha, haaa! You should have seen your face!'

'Very funny,' she said and clutched her briefcase.

'You just . . . errr . . .' he said and pulled a face that looked like a cross-eyed seal.

She had an urge to thump him right in his face but reminded herself that the detention centre was not the best place to indulge in that sort of thing.

Bengt dried his tears. He shook his head and laughed some more.

'If you'll excuse me, I'm in a bit of a hurry. You see, I have a job to do. Some of us don't have time to play silly games.'

Bengt cleared his throat and opened the door for her.

'You can enter,' he said.

She stepped into the detention centre corridor and nodded

to the warder in the security office. He nodded back and then turned his attention to one of the three computer screens on the desk in front of him. Two warders were talking in a low voice next to the office. She couldn't help wondering if they were the ones who had been entrusted with fetching Gavril from his cell. She looked at her watch again: 08.45.

Fifteen minutes to go before he was to be moved. Her heart started beating a bit faster.

Bengt locked the door and led the way down the corridor, which was lit by strong fluorescent ceiling lights. A bunch of keys rattled noisily with every step he took. The walls were painted a light apricot colour and the linoleum floor was a weak mint-green. They passed a couple of detention cells, the doors white and reinforced with a wide band of steel at the bottom. They were all numbered.

At door number eight, Bengt stopped and lifted up the bunch of keys on the chain hanging from his belt. He looked for the right key, then he looked up at Jana, laughed quietly and shook his head again. At last he unlocked the door and let her in. Before she went inside, she saw the two warders shake hands with two uniformed policemen and she realized that the move would take place shortly.

'Stay outside,' she said to Bengt. 'This won't take long.'

Then she stepped into the cell and heard the door shut behind her.

'What are you doing here?'

Jana gave a start when she heard Lena Wikström's rasping voice. She was sitting on the bunk bed with her legs pulled up to her chin. The sheet hung over the edge, trailing down to the floor. She was dressed in dark green trousers and a dark green shirt. Barefoot. Her eyes were tired. The rings under them were wide and dark. Her hair was uncombed.

'I said, what are you doing here?' she hissed. 'Are you here to threaten me again?'

'No,' said Jana. 'I am not here to threaten you. I am here for a totally different purpose and I need your help.'

'I'm not going to help with anything.'

'You already have. By being here.'

Lena didn't understand. And she couldn't be bothered to try to understand either.

'How much longer will it be?'

'What do you mean?'

Jana put her briefcase down on the floor.

'Until you lock me up?'

'I might remind you that you already are imprisoned.'

'But this isn't for real. This is only a stage, a stop on the way.'

'Two more days before the trial,' Jana answered, and looked at her watch again: 08.52.

She crouched down in front of her briefcase, opened it and stuck her hands inside to hide them. She pulled off her Rolex and opened the back of the watch case. With her long nails she loosened a little tracking device that was in there, and then put the casing back on again. She put the watch back on her wrist and with the tracker in one hand she closed the briefcase with the other.

'So in two days it will come to an end,' said Lena almost inaudibly.

But Jana heard the faint words. Lena has capitulated, she thought. She has given up.

'Yes, then it will come to an end.'

Lena's face turned white.

'Then it will be over,' Jana went on.

'I want it to be over,' said Lena, and looked down at her hands. She suddenly looked very small and grey.

'I don't think I can take any more of this. I want to get away from here.'

'You are here to stay.'

'I don't want to be stuck in prison. I'd rather die. Please kill me! I know you can. Kill me!'

'Shut up!'

'I can't live like this. I must get away.'

Jana stood up and looked at her watch: 08.59.

It was time. Now she would do it. She raised her hand to knock on the door but stopped when she heard Lena's voice.

'Please,' she squeaked. 'Help me . . .'

Jana sighed. She thought a few seconds before walking across to where Lena was sitting. She got hold of the sheet, bit a hole in the cloth and then tore off a long strip. She put it into Lena's hand.

'You can help yourself,' she said.

Then she knocked hard on the door, which was opened by Bengt. She remained standing in the doorway a few moments. Waiting for the right opportunity.

Out of the corner of her eye she saw them approaching: the wardens, the policemen and then Gavril between them. As they passed her, she took a step forward and pretended to slip. She swung the briefcase, let one leg give way and affected to cry out. When she fell on to the floor her hand grasped Gavril's leg and quick as a flash she pressed the tracker on his trouser pocket.

Bengt rushed up to help her up.

'Oh, sorry,' she mumbled. 'It's my heels. They're new.'

The warders looked at her in surprise. The policemen almost disapprovingly. And Gavril, he smiled.

Jana couldn't help look at him. However much she tried to persuade herself to stop staring, she couldn't help it. Her heart pounded. She was so close to him but still so far away. Her hatred grew with every breath she took. Most of all she would have liked to have killed him there and then. Most of all she wanted to stick a knife into his body, time and time again. He should die.

Die.

Die.

Die.

'You ought to be careful, little miss,' he said with a smirk before he was taken along the corridor between the warders and the policemen.

You too, Jana thought.

You ought to be very, very careful.

'You do know what you're getting yourself into?' Danilo said from the passenger seat. In his hand he held a phone that showed Gavril's position on a map. On the floor of the car, between his legs, he had put a backpack.

Jana had her eyes glued to the road. She had one hand on the steering wheel and the other resting on the armrest. The seat was soft and upholstered. Danilo had either borrowed the black Volvo S60 from a friend or rented at short notice from a local firm. She didn't care which. The main thing was that she didn't have to arrange a car and thereby risk it being traced back to her should there be a search later.

There was a pungent smell of disinfectant inside the car. They were outside the small town of Trosa. There wasn't much traffic and they were going quite fast.

'I know very well what I'm getting myself into,' Jana answered. 'And for your information, Lena Wikström is dead. That's all you need to know right now.'

Never in her life had she been so certain of anything. Her entire body burned with desire to put Gavril against the wall – confront him. Then she would repay the wrong he had done to her. She would retaliate for his having killed her parents. And other parents. And their children. She would avenge their deaths if it was the last thing she did. There was no way she could just move on with her life, knowing he was going to get away with the things he'd done.

'You're risking everything. What if you get caught?'

She didn't answer.

She was well aware that this act of revenge could mean losing her career, everything she'd worked for, possibly even her life. Despite that, she was determined to proceed.

'Are you afraid?'

'I stopped being afraid when I was seven years old,' she said.

Danilo didn't ask any more questions and silence enveloped them. All that could be heard was the sound of the tyres on the asphalt.

They sat next to each other without uttering a word for the rest of the drive. The tracker showed them the way. After twenty minutes, Danilo straightened up.

'They've stopped,' he said.

She slowed down. There was forest on all sides.

'How far away are they from here?'

'Two, perhaps three hundred metres,' Danilo answered. 'We'll go by foot the last bit so that they don't hear us.'

'Where have they taken him?'

'We'll have to find out.'

Fifty metres down a gravel road they found a discreet place to park the car. Jana turned off the engine and looked at Danilo. He was holding the backpack.

'Perhaps it would be right to thank you,' she said. 'For helping me.'

'Thank me later,' he answered, and climbed out of the car.

The tall gates opened.

A uniformed police officer waved with one arm and a police car slowly rolled on to the gravel drive. Behind it came a black minibus with tinted windows and then another police car.

Phobos had butterflies in his tummy. He would get a new home. He looked up at Papa, who sat next to him on the back seat, and then turned his head towards the large white house ahead of them. A wall ran all the way round it with bushes along the side. There were several scraggly trees and a fountain in the form of a mermaid; over the years, the rippling water had formed brown lines on the light ceramic surface. Now the fountain was turned off. And ugly.

The house was like a mansion – it had two storeys and large windows. The front door was red, and it was well lit by strong spotlights as well as weaker wall lamps. And there were pillars too. With cameras.

Wow, what a place.

Phobos squeezed the brown teddy bear he had in his lap. He was pleased with it. This was the first time Papa had given him a present. But he was absolutely not allowed to show he was pleased, that's what Papa had said. No smile or anything silly. He wasn't allowed to talk about the teddy bear either, only hug it. The way ordinary little boys did.

Now the house was close and the car drove up to the front door and stopped. Two uniformed policemen came forward and opened the car doors. Phobos climbed out on one side, Papa on the other.

'Shall we check the son too?' one of the policemen called to the other, who was busy frisking Papa.

'No, he's only a kid,' came the answer.

'Come along,' said the policeman to Phobos, and led him towards the front door.

The chilly air pinched his cheeks. He walked with small steps beside the policeman, the whole time looking expectantly at what was to be his new home.

Phobos had butterflies again. He squeezed the teddy bear hard, and even though the teddy was well padded he could feel the hard steel inside it.

Jana leaned against the high wall that ran around the house. The grass under her was damp. The cold found its way through her tight black sweater and her black leggings. She was wearing a pair of lightweight running shoes that offered no insulation against the icy ground.

Danilo was also wearing dark clothes and he had his hood up. He crouched down and dug out a Sig Sauer from his backpack. He checked it carefully, then pulled out a silencer and screwed it on to the pipe with a practised hand.

'You've still got the technique,' said Jana.

Danilo didn't answer. He handed the gun to her.

'I don't need a pistol,' she said.

'What are you going to kill him with? Your hands?'

'I prefer a knife.'

'Believe me, you're going to need this. If nothing else, to get inside the house.'

'Where did you get it from?'

'Contacts,' Danilo answered briefly.

He put his hand into his backpack again and pulled out a second pistol, this time a Glock. It, too, was fitted with a silencer.

Finally he pulled the mask over his head.

'We'll wait until the police cars have left the area. Then we must work fast. In, shoot, out. Do you remember?' he said and smiled.

It was the first time she had seen that smile in years.

The police cars started and proceeded slowly across the gravel towards the gates. Four plainclothes but well-equipped policemen remained by the house. As soon as the gates had been closed, they moved to prearranged positions.

'You two on the sides, you in front of the house, and me at the back,' said one of the policemen to his colleagues. 'Understood?'

'Yes,' they answered in chorus.

'Right, to your posts. Report back exactly two hours from now.'

And exactly two hours later, the wardens discovered her. The braided strips of cloth had tightened round her neck, cutting off the respiratory passages. Her first thought was a feeling of relief.

Then came the panic, but it was too late. You couldn't change your mind.

She had taken her final decision and there was no going back. It was impossible to get out of the noose. She knew that. Even so, she struggled. She kicked out, stretched her naked toes, put her hands against the strip of sheeting and pulled. She struggled to the very end.

When the wardens pushed into the cell they just stood there and stared.

Lena Wikström hung from the bars of the window and stared back at them, lifeless.

CHAPTER FIFTY-FOUR

'OK,' SAID DANILO, AND LET GO OF THE TOP OF THE wall. The cars had left the area.

He landed in front of Jana and pushed the backpack under a bush.

'You first. Here.' He cupped his hands. 'I'll lift you up.'

She put her pistol inside her waistband at the base of her spine. She put her right foot in Danilo's hands and her hands on his shoulders.

'Ready?' he said.

She nodded in answer.

'OK, one, two, THREE.'

Danilo pushed up her foot and she got hold of the top of the wall with both hands and swung herself over. It was a long way down to the ground, and she made a hard landing. She crouched down beside a couple of almost bare bushes and made herself as invisible as she could, trying to get an overview of the area, listening for sounds and watching for any movement.

Danilo landed with a thud. He crouched down beside her and drew his pistol.

'Can you see the camera?' he whispered and pointed at a surveillance camera up on a pole opposite the entrance to the house. 'It's an IP camera which can see at a very long distance, like a telescope. Never show your face to one of those, it registers details and facial characteristics at more than one hundred metres. So you must always knock out the cameras first. We never used to have to think about that, but technology has moved on since we were kids.'

Then he pointed at the policemen who surrounded the house.

'There's one in front, one behind, two on the sides. Watch out for them. If they see you, you've had it, understand?'

She nodded.

'When I shoot at the camera, run to the house. Keep in the shadows.'

'I know what to do.'

'OK, OK.'

Danilo got up and pulled the hood further down over his face. He took a deep breath and then stepped out on to the lawn with the gun aimed at the surveillance camera, and fired.

When Jana heard the shot, she took off across the grass to the house. Hardly out of breath, she stood up against the façade and with a couple of steps disappeared into the shadows. Then she heard yet another muffled shot, followed by another two, then there was silence. She listened to her own breathing, looked right and left. Peered towards the front and the back of the house. Listened again. Crouching down, she took a few steps forward, stopped at the corner of the house and looked out.

As she did, a policeman came running. He was evidently reacting to the shots, heading towards the front of the house with his pistol drawn. After he turned the corner, she heard a pistol being fired again. And again. Then silence.

Jana peeped out a second time and spotted a rotating

surveillance camera at the back. In her head, she counted how long the camera was pointed in her direction. Far too long. It wouldn't be possible to get inside from here. Not without being seen.

She released the safety catch on her pistol and lay down in the grass. She was about to pull the trigger when the glass on the camera was shattered by another shot. It came from behind her and hit the lens spot on. She got up into a kneeling position as Danilo appeared by her side. Under his hood she could see his lips were pressed together in grim determination.

'Is the coast clear now?' he asked.

'Yes,' said Jana, and got up. 'Did you kill the policemen?'

'I had no choice.'

Danilo looked out at the rear and then ran across to the back door. He bent down under every window he passed. With a steady hand he felt the locked glass door and then waved to her.

'Listen,' he said to her when she reached him. 'Act fast. Don't think. Just complete your task. OK?'

'OK,' said Jana.

'I'll stay here. If you're not out in ten minutes, I'm coming in.' He pulled out a lock-pick and inserted it into the lock. Ten seconds later there was a click and he slipped the pick back in his pocket.

'Are you certain about this now?' he said.

'Yes,' answered Jana. 'I have never been more certain.'

She held up the pistol in front of her face and squeezed it with one hand. Then she took a deep breath and opened the door.

She was inside.

The room was about five by ten metres. It was a large living room with a sofa, armchair and a glass table. Landscapes hung on the walls. A side table stood on one side, a flowery standard lamp next to it. No plants. No rugs. She sneaked across the floor and stopped in front of an archway. She peered into the adjoining room, which was lit by a round table lamp, and noted that it was a dining room. Ten chairs were placed around an oval table. She scanned the area and then moved on to the next room, the door of which stood ajar. She peeped in through the crack. It was a hall. She saw a bench and a hat rail. The staircase was wide and there was a wine-red stair carpet. There were lights on upstairs.

Unable to resist the temptation to go up, Jana pushed open the door with her foot. As she did so, she heard a click behind her. Her heart missed a beat. She turned her head and saw a little boy in the half darkness. His eyes were afire. In his hand he had a pistol which he was pointing straight at her.

She didn't move a muscle. The boy was close, far too close. At that distance he couldn't miss. He edged closer.

'Take it easy,' she said.

'Throw down your weapon,' said the boy. 'Otherwise I'll shoot you.'

'I know you will,' she said, and lowered her pistol. Held out her other hand in a gesture of surrender.

'What's your name?' she said.

'Fuck that.'

'I just want to know what you're called.'

The boy hesitated, then said his name: 'Phobos.'

'Does it say that on your neck? Does it say Phobos there?'

Phobos looked astounded. Instinctively he put one hand up to his neck.

She went on:

'If you are what I think you are, then I want you to listen to me. I have also been like you,' she said, hoping to gain his confidence.

'Throw away the gun,' he said again.

'What you've got in your neck, that carved name. I've got one too,' she said. 'Shall I show you?'

For a fraction of a second he looked confounded. Then he said, 'No.'

'Can't I show you?' she said. 'Please, let me show you. I want to help you. I can help you get away from here, you don't need to be here any longer.'

But the boy was not listening.

'Throw down the gun!'

'As you wish.'

And then she threw it. The gun went high over Phobos and he followed it with his gaze. When it was right over his head she took a quick step forward, grabbed his pistol with her left hand, grabbed his arm with her right hand, and forced him round. She put the pistol against his head.

'I'm sorry,' she whispered. 'But I had to do that. I know what you can do, and this is the only way to protect both you and me.'

Phobos pulled with his arm to try to get loose.

She then took hold of his neck and pressed so hard that he gasped for air.

'Calm down,' she said. 'I'll help you. But you must do as I say. If you don't, it's going to hurt.'

He became still. There was a gurgling in his throat when he tried to get some air into his lungs. Jana released her hold a little.

'Promise you'll do as I say,' she said. 'Do you promise?'

He tried to move his head in a nod. She loosened her grip a

little more, and then looked around for the gun she had thrown. In the middle of the floor she saw a reflection of matte metal. But that wasn't the only thing she saw. There was a man staring straight at her. Despite the half-darkness, she saw who it was.

It was him.

Gavril.

'Bravo!' he said, and clapped his hands. 'It isn't easy to disarm him, I can tell you that, so you did well!'

His voice was calm and almost friendly from the darkness.

'I saw you come in.'

'Give me your weapon,' she said.

'I don't have a weapon.'

'Your son has a weapon. So you must have one too.'

'Yes, he does, but not me. Do you think the agents would let me bring a weapon into the house?'

'If your son could manage it, I presume you could too.'

'No, it wasn't possible.'

'How did he do it?'

'Magic,' he hissed, and threw out his hand towards the light from the lamp.

A quick gesture, then the hand drowned in the darkness again.

'So you don't have a weapon?'

'No, little miss. I don't.'

Jana scrutinized Gavril's clothes, trying to see if he was lying to her.

'Show me your hands!' she said.

Gavril raised his hands into the light and shrugged his shoulders.

'Hold your hands so that I can see them all the time. If you try anything I'll blow your son's brains out!'

'Sure, sure,' he said, and smiled a not particularly convincing smile. 'But if I may ask, what are you doing here?'

'I had to come here. There are so many questions.'

'Oh really? Are you a journalist?'

'No. I just want to know why.'

'Why what?'

'Why you do this.'

Jana nodded toward Phobos, who made a gurgling sound with each breath he took.

He still had his hands on Jana's arm and he was holding on hard.

'Why is a good word. Why, for example, should I tell you?'

'Because you owe me that.'

'I have debts to a lot of people.'

'Above all to me.'

'And what have I done to you?'

Jana felt the fury grow inside her, but forced herself to be calm.

'You used to call me Ker,' she said.

'What did you say?'

'You gave me the name Ker.'

Gavril took a step forward. The light from the lamp fell on his face and revealed the scar.

He stared at her with his mouth agape. She stared back. When she saw his look, she felt calm. Her shoulders sagged.

'Well now, Ker. So you survived after all. Don't I get a hug?'

'Go to hell.'

'Oh dear, we are angry, aren't we!'

'You stole my childhood, murdered my parents and carved a fucking name into me. Why? I want to know why. Answer me! Why do you do this?'

Gavril smiled.

Leaned his head back, exposed his teeth and hissed.

'Because it is so easy. After all, nobody misses people like you. Illegal kids, no papers – you don't exist.'

'And that makes it acceptable to kidnap and torture—'

'I don't torture!' Gavril cut her off. 'I train. I give them all a second chance in life. A chance to become something. To become a part of something greater.'

'Greater than what?'

'I don't think you understand how divine it is to govern a person's life and death.'

'This is about children,' Jana reminded him.

'Exactly. Innocent children. The perfect murderers.'

Phobos stretched a little and Jana tightened her grip around his throat. He responded by digging his fingernails deeper into her arm.

'Why do you train them to do that? To murder?'

'What do you think? I have to defend myself. It's fucking tough in the market today. I have the best suppliers, middlemen and pushers. There are lots of buyers and it's a matter of ensuring I keep my income. Money is everything. Whatever people say, that's what everybody is after. What everybody wants. And when money is involved, there's a lot of dirty work too. If drugs are involved, there is even more. So I surround myself with little soldiers who want to protect me. Who want to please me by making my problems disappear – problems like snitches, people who can't pay, who don't fulfil their obligations. Adults are nothing but trouble. They cost too much, they get greedy and try to cheat you, or they get cocky and try to take over.'

Gavril went on: 'From a crushed child you can carve out a

381

deadly weapon. A soldier with no feelings, with nothing to lose, is the most dangerous there is.'

'Is that why you kill—'

'The parents? Yes. Orphans are easier to deal with. More devoted. Aren't they? That's true, isn't it? You do agree with me?'

She didn't answer, but she had to clench her jaw to keep from responding.

Gavril threw his hands out again.

'I make Sweden a better country. People might think that my activities are unacceptable, but I contribute to a better world by weeding out the weak. You could say I'm doing society a service by reducing the number of illegal offspring. I let the migrant kids themselves clean up the dregs of society. Like Darwin said, only the strongest survive.'

'But then you kill your "little soldiers".'

'Children have always been murdered. All through history. The Bible is full of stories about the killing of children. Don't you remember the Gospel according to Matthew, where King Herod orders all the Jewish boys under two years of age to be killed because he has heard that a future king has been born and he doesn't want that infant to grow into a rival.'

'So you see yourself as the Herod of our time?'

'Let's just say I share his view of rivals.'

Gavril looked to the right and his scar wrinkled up in the movement and hung over his eye.

'Stand still,' Jana shouted.

Gavril turned his head and the reddish-pink skin smoothed out again.

'I am still,' he said.

'And the drugs? Why all the drugs?'

'You must reward your troops with something. And what could be better than to make them dependent? Not only on drugs, but on me too. Then they are less likely to run away. You see, children do as you tell them. They look up to you. If you give them a dose of the right stuff, you can be a father figure to them.'

'Like a god?'

'More like the opposite. A devilish god, you could say.'

'Why carve names into their flesh?'

'So that everybody will feel they belong. A community. Part of a family. All with unique names. But with the same meaning.'

'Gods of death.'

'Exactly. And I carve the name so that you won't forget who you are. I gave you your real name.'

'My name is Jana. That's my real name.'

'But you are Ker.'

'No.'

'Yes, you are! Deep inside you are exactly what I trained you to be.'

Jana didn't answer.

'What I do isn't anything new. In many countries there are young people who are conscripted, trained and used in the armed forces. I do the same here, but I've taken it a step further. Anyone can shoot with a pistol, but not anyone can be an assassin.'

'How many?'

'How many have we trained?'

'If you want to put it like that.'

'Seventy.'

Gavril's answer hit her like a blow from a fist. She loosened her hold on Phobos's neck slightly. Seventy! His fingers stopped digging so hard into her arm.

383

'But we only chose the strongest from every batch.'

'Batch? You mean from each container?'

'Yes.'

'So you took seven children from each one?'

'Sometimes more, sometimes less. Then we selected the two best. Or just one. The rest were surplus to requirements. You surely remember how we went about it?'

Gavril shaped his hand like a pistol and pointed it at Jana.

'Stand still!' she shouted.

The boy moved too. She tightened her grip around his neck and lifted him a couple of centimetres off the floor. He kicked with his legs until she lowered him again.

'It might be of interest to you that until recently I had a pupil on the island.'

'Thanatos?'

'Quite right. He was unique.'

'He killed Hans Juhlén. Why?'

'Goodness me, you *are* well informed. What should I say? Hans Juhlén interfered just a bit too much. He turned into a bit of a problem for us.'

'By "us" you mean you, Lena Wikström, Thomas Rydberg, and Anders Paulsson?'

'Precisely!'

Gavril waved his hand and Jana reacted by raising the pistol. He smirked and threw out his hand even further. As if to frighten her.

'Keep still!' she shouted. Her mouth was dry and she swallowed. 'Go on, explain!'

'You've already worked it out.'

'Go on!'

Gavril became serious.

His bottom teeth were exposed in a weird grimace.

'Hans Juhlén managed to dig out a list of all the containers. He put pressure on Thomas Rydberg for information. He threatened to reveal everything, so we had to get rid of him. Thanatos carried out the mission to our great satisfaction. But Anders messed things up. When he was taking Thanatos back to the island, something went wrong. Thanatos tried to escape and Anders shot him, a mistake that was very costly for us.'

'The container that I came in . . .'

'That was the first one; it required a lot of planning. Mind you, it still does.'

'You're expecting a new one?'

Gavril made a grimace again. He raised his chin and hissed between his teeth.

'It is better to renew everything all the time. Then they won't have a chance to understand anything. When they have carried out their task, when we don't need them any longer, we can let them disappear. They're easily replaced: there are new children coming along all the time. Thousands cross Sweden's borders every year. And nobody misses them. Nobody is looking for them. That's right, isn't it, there hasn't been anybody looking for you? Nobody, that's right, isn't it?'

'Shut up!'

'Nobody . . . who . . . looked . . .'

Gavril held up both hands toward her and waved them while he hissed. Like a snake.

'Ssssssssssss!'

'Keep still! I'll shoot!' she shouted and pointed her pistol at him.

Gavril calmed down. He lowered his head a little.

She felt her heart pounding.

'I know that you'll do it. I know exactly how you think. After all, I'm the one who trained you,' said Gavril.

'Not just you . . .'

'No, it wasn't just me,' said Gavril loudly and took a step towards the gun on the floor. 'You must have people around you that you can trust. But the others are long since dead.'

Jana swallowed. She squeezed the pistol hard.

'It's over now,' she said in a resolute voice.

'It will never be over. Children are our future.'

Gavril took another step forward.

She noticed his movement.

'Stand still! Stand still!'

He didn't listen, took another step.

'Stand still! Don't move! Otherwise . . .'

'Otherwise what?'

He took yet another step.

'Otherwise I'll shoot him,' she shouted, and pointed the pistol at Phobos.

Gavril stopped and smiled.

'Do it. He's worthless anyway.'

'He's your son,' Jana shouted. She pressed the pistol hard against Phobos's forehead, forcing his head to the left.

His face was taut, he whined.

'He isn't my son, he's one of those worthless kids. Just as worthless as all the others. A nobody.'

She looked at Gavril, unable to fully grasp his meaning. Then at Phobos, who was whining louder now. She stopped pressing the gun so hard and saw the red mark from the muzzle on his thin skin.

'Go ahead, shoot him. I'll do it anyway, later. He knows that. Nevertheless, he does everything I tell him. Don't you, Phobos? You do everything I tell you, don't you?'

Gavril blinked at Phobos who immediately understood the signal and started to kick at Jana's legs. He hit her on the lower part of her shin and she gave a start from the pain. Gavril seized the opportunity to pick up the pistol from the floor.

Jana took a firmer grip of Phobos's neck and forced him up on his toes to keep him still. When she looked back at Gavril again, she saw the gun in his hand. She turned and Gavril pressed the trigger . . . but the weapon just clicked.

He pressed the trigger again and again. Click. Click. The magazine was empty!

Gavril started to laugh.

Jana stared at the pistol he held in his hand. That's my pistol, she thought. Why is the magazine empty?

Suddenly a voice could be heard from the other side of the room.

'You're out of luck today.'

Danilo came out of the shadows and stood a couple of metres from Gavril with a gun pointed at him.

'What the fuck are you doing here?' said Gavril.

There was something about Gavril's tone that confused Jana. And why was Danilo just standing there, as if they were friends? Then she realized: they were friends.

'Allow me,' said Danilo, and pointed his Glock at her.

'You see,' Gavril said. 'You have to surround yourself with people you can rely on.'

'Yes, you're right about that,' said Danilo. 'But I'm not the reliable sort.'

He swung the pistol and aimed it at Gavril again.

'What the fuck are you doing?' said Gavril.

Those were his last words.

When he fell forward and hit the stone floor, he was already dead.

Danilo went behind Gavril and shot him again. In the back of the head.

Phobos stood absolutely still. His breathing was short. His eyes like saucers. Jana moved the muzzle of her pistol from his head and pointed it at Danilo. He took off his hood and looked at her. His eyes were black. His gaze cold as ice.

'Jana,' he said. 'Little, sweet, lovely Jana. Why did you have to go and dig into the past? I said that you ought to let things be.'

He walked towards her with the pistol hanging from his finger.

'I know what you're thinking. How could Papa recognize me? That's what you're thinking, isn't it?'

Jana nodded.

'Do you remember when I said that I pretended to be dead there in the forest, when Mama ran after me? And I said that I ran the other way? Do you remember?'

Jana nodded. 'You lied to me?'

'No, it was true. All of it. I ran but I couldn't run very far. Anders found me in a ditch. He pulled me into the van. I thought I would die. It's thanks to him I'm still alive. He took care of me. He's always been an old woman, soft as anything. But he knew his stuff. That's why I thought he'd shoot you when you showed up at his house.'

Danilo moved in a crescent around Jana. The pistol in her hand followed the same course.

'That's why you gave me his name,' she stated quietly.

'Exactly,' said Danilo.

'You're a part of it all.'

'Right again.'

Danilo was behind her now.

'But how . . .'

'How could I survive? I grew up on the island. Learned everything I needed. I was clever and got more missions. Not just one, like all the others.'

With dragging steps he was in front of her again.

'When I was seventeen, I took over as trainer. Papa got rid of the other trainers. And all the other idiots too.'

'I can't believe you call him that.'

'What? Papa? You did too.'

'But no longer.'

Danilo was to her left now. He kept on walking the same path around her.

'He is my papa. Oh no, I beg your pardon – he *was* my papa. And it was him, me, Lena, Thomas and Anders who took care of everything. Now they're all gone. Except me. It worked. Admittedly, a bit earlier than I was expecting, but it bloody well worked.'

Jana had heard every word he said, but she struggled to make sense of it.

'What do you mean? You planned this?'

'Planned? Well, sort of. I hadn't planned to kill Thomas Rydberg. Somebody else did that.'

She looked down. Danilo was silent for a moment before going on: 'When Thomas was out of the game, I saw that as a sign. It was time.'

'For what?'

'To step forward.'

Then she understood.

'You made use of me to kill Gavril,' she said.

'And you swallowed it.'

'I trusted you.'

'I know. That made it so easy. All I had to do was help you to help me.'

Jana stretched her back. The gun in her hand felt heavy.

She looked at Danilo, his ice-cold gaze. Then he took three steps and kicked Gavril's dead body several times.

'I wanted you dead. You didn't think that, did you? You had no idea I wanted to kill you!' He kicked as hard as he could. The blood vessels on his forehead became distinct. His nostrils were dilated, the tendons in his neck were tensed like violin strings, and his teeth were bared in a grimace.

And then he calmed down.

Jana didn't say a word.

Nor did Phobos.

Danilo sat down on a chair, flicked his hair off his forehead and looked at her.

'I'm sorry,' he said. 'But you do realize that you're going to die here?'

She didn't know what to say, so she nodded instead. Her hand was shaking and it took an effort to hold it steady.

'To think that you didn't suspect!'

'I ought to have done,' she said and met his gaze. 'I ought to have understood long ago. But it's only now that I see how it all fits together. You gave me a Sig Sauer. Thanatos was killed with a Sig Sauer. The gun you gave me was the murder weapon. But you emptied the magazine first, so that I would die here.'

Danilo laughed in reply.

'You wanted to leave me here so nobody would suspect you,' she said.

The laugh became loud and nasty.

'Exactly!' He jumped up from the chair, and moved to within a few steps of Jana.

'When the police come, they'll find your body and they'll realize you were the one who killed all my dear ones, my pretty prosecutor. Just think what a scandal there will be!'

Jana bit her lip. How was she going to get out of this? Her hand was shaking more than ever. The pistol was heavy now.

'And when they do an autopsy on your body, they'll find the name on your neck. Then they will understand: you were one of those children from the island. They'll assume you wanted revenge on the people who took you from the container. Who killed your parents. Simple, isn't it?'

Danilo took two steps back.

'You know the best part? You never suspected a thing! I told you that you should be careful. I told you. But you didn't listen to me.'

He pointed the pistol at Jana, ordered her to let go of Phobos.

She refused.

'OK,' said Danilo. 'Then I'll shoot you both.'

He aimed.

Fired.

As he pulled the trigger, Jana cast herself to one side and pulled Phobos down too. They landed on the floor. She rolled, pointed the Glock at Danilo and fired off a shot, but missed.

Danilo tripped over Gavril's corpse and dropped his gun. Before she could take aim, he ran out the door. Still breathing heavily, she got to her feet and looked around for Phobos. To her dismay, she realized he was gone.

She went out to the hall, her eyes peeled, listening for any sound. Keeping her body pressed against the wall, she pointed her gun up the stairs, then to the side, then up the stairs again. When she reached the first step she heard a sound: a door creaking. It came from behind her. She crept to the door and paused before turning the handle. It led down into a cellar. A lamp hung over the stairs. She hesitated. If she went down those steps, she would be a perfect target in the light. Then she heard a mechanical click by her side and glanced towards the sound. Behind the door was a fuse box.

She smiled to herself.

Now we'll play a game, she thought.

Jana Berzelius turned off the main switch and took a deep breath. Then she edged forward and found herself stepping straight into another world. Straight into a memory. She was transformed once again into the little girl in the cellar. The girl who wanted to survive. But this time she didn't struggle against the dark. She embraced it. Now she was in control.

She stretched up and listened for sounds. It was silent.

Numbingly silent.

She took a step forward, stopped and listened again. Yet another step, and still one more. After three steps she ought to be by the stairs.

Jana stretched out her hand to feel the banister. She counted her steps in her head. One, two, three. Now she felt the banister under her hand. In her memory, the handrail was rough and cracked. This one was polished and smooth. Her feet worked their way down the steps. On the last step she let go of the banister and felt with her hand in front of her. Then she heard a sound. Somebody was moving. Somebody was by her side.

Who? Danilo or Phobos?

She turned her head to be able to register new sounds. But there was only silence. It was far too quiet. Perhaps Danilo was waiting behind her back? The thought made her want to get out. To just get out of there.

Then she heard it.

The breath.

The signal.

She reacted instinctively and pointed the gun at the sound. A powerful blow slammed into her arm, sending her toppling backwards. She ended up lying on the floor. Knowing that Danilo was close now, she kept perfectly still, listening.

She tried to lift her arm and aim the gun, but the pain stopped her. And then Danilo kicked the gun out of her hand and she heard it skitter across the floor, coming to a halt behind her.

'You're not the only one who likes playing games in the dark,' he said, and kicked her hard in the side.

She groaned.

'It's fun, isn't it? It's good fun, right?'

He kicked her again, so hard that something broke in her forearm and she shrieked in pain.

'It's time to finish this,' he said and dropped to his knees astride her with his hands joined in a stranglehold.

Despite the pain, she managed to claw at his hands, trying to make him let go. But he didn't. He pressed harder. She gasped for air. A familiar sensation came creeping up on her; she knew that she was close to losing consciousness.

Her other hand was firmly wedged under Danilo's legs, and her fingers worked desperately to get a grip on the knife on her hip. With a final effort, she gripped the handle with her index and middle fingers, coaxed the knife out, and plunged it into Danilo's thigh. He cried out and loosened his grip on her throat. She took a gurgling breath and pivoted herself on one leg. Danilo was knocked to the side and she pushed herself up. She pulled the knife out of his thigh and put the point of the blade to his throat.

'I told you I preferred knives,' she hissed.

But she didn't have the advantage for long. He kneed her on the side and she was thrown backwards, landing on something hard. The gun! She picked it up with one hand and pointed it into the darkness. She heard his steps on the stairs and followed.

When she reached the hall, she heard him breathing. Although it was pitch-dark, she closed her eyes to focus. Then she fired a shot.

For a second, time stood still.

Then she heard somebody groaning.

Her arm was quivering with pain but she ignored it. She felt her way back to the fuse box, all the while maintaining her focus on the groaning. Then she switched the electricity back on and turned to see the victim on the floor.

It wasn't Danilo.

It was Phobos.

FIFTY-FIVE

WHILE GAVRIL BOLANAKI WAS BEING DRIVEN AWAY
from the police station under armed escort, Gunnar Öhrn
was standing in front of a crowd of journalists at a joint press
conference organized by the security services. The press officer
had read out a statement that gave much of the credit for the
arrest to Gunnar and his team, but even so he left the press room
feeling somehow deflated.

Then there'd been the fallout over Lena Wikström's suicide,
two days before she was due to appear in court. The rest of the
day had been spent debriefing security service personnel about
the case. Dumping all the papers in their lap and leaving them
to it was not his style. When they departed, and it finally sank
in that his involvement in the investigation was at an end, he
gathered the team together in the conference room. Henrik sat
up straight in his chair and stared hollow-eyed in front of him.
Anneli Lindgren was leaning with her arms on the table. Ola
Söderström chewed his pen. Mia balanced her chair on its back
legs. Unlike the others, she seemed delighted. As far as she was
concerned, it was a win-win scenario: the case was finished and
she would no longer have to put up with Jana Berzelius.

'It's a pity,' Gunnar said, and looked out over the room.

The victims' pictures had been taken down, along with the map. The whiteboard had been wiped clean, the projector turned off.

'There are a lot of questions that still haven't been answered. And it looks as though some of them will remain unanswered. Lena Wikström has taken her secrets to the grave. And I just heard back from Interpol: they say there's nothing in their database about missing people from Chile.'

This had come as a disappointment; Gunnar had hoped it would be possible to enlist Interpol's aid in identifying the victims from the containers. The only ray of light in this gloomy day had been the discovery that Anders Paulsson had committed suicide; had it been murder, Gunnar would've had to pass that case to the Security Services along with all the others.

'Why did he shoot himself?' said Ola.

'Moral qualms, presumably,' said Gunnar. 'Conscience. The same with Lena Wikström. Nobody can live with crimes like that on their conscience.'

Silence settled over the team like a lid.

'Well then,' said Gunnar.

'Thanks for everything,' said Mia, and got up from the table.

'Where are you going?'

'Aren't we finished?'

'No, we are not. There's still one thing left to do.'

Questioning looks were directed towards Gunnar.

'We're going to the docks.'

Five minutes later, Henrik Levin was back in his office, fidgeting with the ghost drawing Felix had made for him. It was a new drawing showing three small ghosts. But that wasn't what he was thinking about. He didn't know how to react to the fact he was to be a dad for the third time. Deep inside he was happy, but worries about the practical details overshadowed his happiness. He hadn't been able to sleep at all last night. And at the morning briefing he had struggled to concentrate.

He looked up from the drawing of the ghosts and out through the window. Even though the case was finished, his head continued to process the events. His mind kept returning to the dead children, wondering how he'd feel if his own children were kidnapped and trained as child soldiers.

Shuddering at the thought, he put the drawing to one side.

'What's the matter? You look dreadful.'

Henrik gave a start on hearing Mia's voice. She stood in the doorway in full winter gear.

'I'm going to be a dad,' Henrik said.

'Again?'

'Yes, third time lucky.'

'So you have fucked, after all! Well done!'

Henrik didn't answer.

'Anyhow,' Mia went on. 'Before I forget . . .' She dug into her pocket and pulled out a crumpled one-hundred-kronor bill. 'Here you are.'

'Keep it.'

'No, I want to pay my way. I owe you for lunch and coffee. Take it!'

'OK. Thanks,' said Henrik, taking the bill.

'Least I could do,' said Mia.

She wrapped her scarf round her neck three times.

Henrik pulled out his wallet from the pocket of his jacket, which was hanging on a hook behind the door.

He slid the hundred-kronor bill in with the other two already there.

Two?

Henrik was pretty certain that there had been three bills.

Mia noticed his surprised look and cut off his musings.

'Right, come on now. Let's get moving,' she said.

Phobos was lying against the wall, his chest heaving. He was taking short panting breaths. His dark eyes were like saucers and they stared in terror at Jana. He held his hand against his throat. The blood was seeping between his fingers and forming a growing red patch on his sweater. The Glock lay by his side.

In her peripheral vision she saw a silhouette. Danilo passed three metres from her, ran out of the room and into the next. She raced after him. The pain in her arm was forgotten. She would get him. He mustn't be allowed to escape. As she pursued him into the dining room, he was already running into the room beyond. She rushed after him. But he was too quick and with a couple of long strides he was out of the room and then throwing himself out of the back door. By the time Jana reached the door he was gone.

He had got away.

The bastard had got away!

She lowered the gun and put it into her waistband at the base of her spine. Her arm was throbbing and she felt weary to the core, but she forced herself to go back into the house.

Back to Phobos.

Henrik Levin stood on the docks and beat his arms to his chest but soon realized it was unnecessary. His down jacket kept him warm and he wore thermal underwear and heavy winter boots too. He stopped mid-movement and looked out over the quay. A large ship was approaching and now and then it released a muted signal. Large snowflakes fluttered down from the sky and formed a layer of white on the ground. The container area was cordoned off and the police ribbon danced in the wind.

'Shall we go closer?' said Mia.

She stood beside Henrik. Her hands were stuck in her pockets, her shoulders drawn up and her face hidden by a knitted scarf. Only her nose and eyes were visible.

'We'll wait until the ship docks,' said Henrik, then nodded to Gunnar and Anneli, who stood at the far end of the quay together with harbour staff and uniformed police officers.

They nodded back and everyone looked up at the ship as it made its way along the canal. The waves broke against the hull. Seagulls were shrieking loudly and circling above the stern. Several sailors wearing green overalls were standing on different parts of the deck with mooring ropes in their hands.

When the ship was right next to the quay, the first ropes were thrown down, followed by the others, each flying in an arc over the railing. The long ropes were picked up by the harbour staff who fastened them round short iron poles. All the workers were wearing safety helmets and had large emblems on their backs.

The unloading was under way.

Henrik looked up at the hull where the containers were stacked three storeys high.

Blue, brown and grey in turn.

'You're going to be all right,' said Jana.

She crouched down beside Phobos. He had sunk even lower

against the wall, his head now leaning on his shoulder. He had grown so weak, his short panting breaths were barely audible. His sweater was saturated with blood. The blood ran down on to the floor and formed a puddle. There was still a flicker of terror in his eyes, but already they were beginning to glaze over.

'It's getting lighter now,' he whispered.

He coughed and blood trickled out of the corner of his mouth.

'You're going to be all right,' Jana repeated, but realized how stupid it was to lie to him.

He looked her in the eye.

'Now it's all white . . . everything is . . . white . . .' he whispered.

And then his hand fell down.

He closed his eyes and took his last breath.

Jana got up from his side. She grasped the Glock and wiped it carefully before putting it into his lifeless hand. Then she went up to the fuse box and wiped all the switches. Next she went to Gavril's dead body. Taking care not to step in his blood, she ripped off the tracking device attached to his trouser pocket. She picked up the other gun from the floor, wiped it and dropped it next to him. Then she sat on her haunches and looked at him. And finally she did something she hadn't done for ages.

She smiled.

A genuine smile that spread across her face.

There was one more gun she had to get rid of. Wincing from the pain in her injured arm, she fished the Glock from her waistband. She must leave that there too. With a practised hand, she wiped off all the prints, lifted Gavril's fingers and put them around the magazine.

She was still not satisfied. An important detail was missing.

The knife.

She went back down to the cellar. It took her a while, but eventually she caught sight of the bloody blade sticking out from under a shelf. She slid it out and put it back in the thin sheath inside her waistband. Then she went up the steps and looked at Phobos one last time.

'I am so sorry,' she whispered to him.

Then she left the house.

CHAPTER
FIFTY-SIX

IT WAS IN THE FOURTEENTH CONTAINER THAT THEY made the miraculous discovery. The container was blue and rusty. The snowflakes landed softly on the corrugated metal and turned to drops of water which trickled towards the ground.

The team stood four metres from the doors. Four galvanized lock poles went from top to bottom and a dock-worker struggled to open the heavy padlock in the middle. In the end the lock gave way, and the dock-worker pulled open the doors. They were expecting engine parts, bicycles, boxes, toys – the sort of goods they'd found in the earlier containers. But in this one it was only darkness that met them.

Henrik Levin approached the container to get a better look. He screwed up his eyes. He took another step until he was standing with both feet on the edge of the doorway.

Then he saw her. The girl. She looked at him with her eyes wide open. And she hugged her mother's legs.

Jana Berzelius drove fast along the motorway. She turned the Volvo's heater to the maximum setting. The rhythm of the windscreen wipers was hypnotic as they cleared the slushy snow from the windscreen. Her eyes were heavy now that the adrenaline had worn off and she leaned her head back with one hand on the steering wheel. She rested her injured arm on her thigh.

Suddenly her phone rang. The display showed *Withheld number*. Jana hesitated, dreading the sound of Danilo's voice, but it was Henrik Levin.

'Gavril Bolanaki is dead,' he said.

When Jana offered no response, he continued: 'The Security Service couldn't get in touch with the policemen guarding the house. So they sent a special unit there and they found him dead. According to the first reports, they shot each other, him and his son. But the policemen are dead too, so we don't yet know how it all happened. It was evidently quite a bloodbath. The unit found three guns in the house. They also found a torn-open teddy bear, so the guns must have been inside that.'

'OK,' said Jana.

There was a pause, then Henrik said, 'I'm at the docks.'

'Yes?'

'We found them. Ten families with children. They're all safe.'

'Good.'

'I hope it was the last one.'

'Me too.'

'The case against him is over.'

'It is definitely over,' she said, and ended the call.

It was 18.59 when Jana raised her hand to knock on the mahogany door of the three-storey detached house. Then she changed her mind and rang the bell instead, letting the shrill tone signal her arrival. She took a step back and ran her fingers through her hair, still wet after her quick shower. In the windows the lamps with their cloth shades cast long shadows on the ground in front of her.

The door was opened by a grey-haired man.

'Hello, Father,' said Jana, and remained standing in the porch a few moments. So he could look at her.

Then she smiled her practised smile.

Nodded briefly.

And stepped inside the house.

ACKNOWLEDGEMENTS

This story is fiction. Any resemblance between the characters in the novel and real people is accidental. The same applies to the characters' names. The locations in the book are real, but I have sometimes altered their description so that they fit better into the action. Any errors that have found their way into the text are because of me.

I want to thank everyone who has helped me with this novel. All who have read and given me feedback, who have answered my questions and helped me with the facts, who have given me their commitment and time.

I want to say a big thank you to Mom, Dad and my younger sister, who have always listened to and encouraged me. Mother, your opinions have been important. And to my mother-in-law, thank you for your honest feedback.

Above all I want to thank my husband, Henrik Schepp, for your critical review, ideas and inspiration. Without you, there would be no book.

Keep reading for an extract from *Marked for Revenge*, the next book in Emelie Schepp's bestselling Jana Berzelius series. *Marked for Revenge* is available in eBook now.

PROLOGUE

THE GIRL SAT QUIETLY, LOOKING DOWN AT HER
*bowl of yogurt and strawberries. She listened to the clinking of silver-
ware against china as her mother and father ate breakfast.*

"Would you please eat?"

Her mother looked at her imploringly, but the girl didn't move.

"Are your dreams bothering you again?"

The girl swallowed, not daring to lift her gaze from the bowl.

"Yes," she replied in a barely audible whisper.

"What did you dream about this time?"

Her mother tore a slice of bread in half and spread marmalade on it.

"A container," she said. "It was…"

"No!"

*Her father's voice came from the other side of the table, loud, hard
and cold as ice. His fists were clenched. His eyes were as hard and cold
as his voice.*

"That's enough!"

He got up, pulled her from the chair and shoved her out of the kitchen.

"We don't want to hear any more of your fantasies."

*The girl stumbled forward, struggling to keep ahead of him as he
pushed her up the stairs. He was hurting her arm, her feet. She tried
to wrench herself from his grasp just as he changed his grip and put his
hand around her neck.*

Then he let go, his hand recoiling as if he'd been stabbed. He looked at her in disgust.

"I told you to keep your neck covered all the time! Always!"

He put his hands on her shoulders and turned her around.

"What did you do with the bandage?"

She felt him pull her hair aside, tearing at it, trying frantically to expose the nape of her neck. Heard his rapid breathing when he caught sight of her scars. He took a few steps back, aghast, as if he had seen something horrifying.

And he had...

Because her bandage had fallen off.

CHAPTER

ONE

THERE! THE CAR APPEARED FROM AROUND THE corner.

Pim smiled nervously at Noi. They were standing in an alley, in the shadows of the light from the streetlamps. The asphalt was discolored by patches of dried piss. It smelled strong and rank, and the howling of stray dogs was drowned out by the rumbling highway.

Pim's forehead was damp with sweat—not from the heat but from nerves. Her dark hair was plastered to the back of her neck, and the thin material of her T-shirt stuck to her back in creases. She didn't know what awaited her and hadn't had much time to think about it, either.

Everything had gone so quickly. Just two days ago, she had made up her mind. Noi had laughed, saying it was easy, it paid well and they'd be home again in five days.

Pim wiped her hand across her forehead and dried it on her jeans as she watched the slowly approaching car.

She smiled again, as if to convince herself that everything would be okay, everything would work out.

It was just this one time.

Just once. Then never again.

She picked up her suitcase. She'd been told to fill it with clothes for two weeks to make the fictitious vacation more convincing.

She looked at Noi, straightened her spine and pulled her shoulders back.

The car was almost there.

It drove toward them slowly and stopped. A tinted window rolled down, exposing the face of a man with close-cropped hair.

"Get in," he said without taking his eyes from the road. Then he put the car in gear and prepared to leave.

Pim walked around the car, stopped and closed her eyes for a brief moment. Taking a deep breath, she opened the car door and got in.

Public prosecutor Jana Berzelius took a sip of water and reached across the pile of papers on the table. It was 10:00 p.m., and The Bishop's Arms in Norrköping was packed.

A half hour earlier, she'd been in the company of her boss, Chief Public Prosecutor Torsten Granath who, after a long and successful day in court, had at least had the decency to take her to dinner at the Elite Grand Hotel.

He had spent the two-hour meal carrying on about his dog who, after various stomach ailments and bowel problems, had had to be put to sleep. Although Jana couldn't have cared less, she had feigned interest when Torsten pulled out his phone to show pictures of the puppy years of the now-dead dog. She had nodded, tilting her head to one side and trying to look sympathetic.

To make the time pass more quickly, she had inventoried the other patrons. She'd had an unobstructed view of the door from their table near the window. No one came or went without her seeing. During Torsten's monologue, she had observed twelve people: three foreign businessmen, two middle-aged women with shrill voices, a family of four, two older men and a teenager with big, curly hair.

After dinner, she and Torsten had moved to The Bishop's Arms next door. He'd said the classic British interior reminded him of golfing in the county of Kent and that he always insisted on the same table. For Jana, the choice of pub was a minor irritation. She had shaken her boss's hand with relief when he'd finally decided to call an end to the evening.

Yet she had lingered a bit longer.

Stuffing the papers into her briefcase, she drank the last of her water and was just about to get up when a man came in. Maybe it was his nervous gait that made her notice him. She followed him with her gaze as he walked quickly toward the bar. He caught the bartender's attention with a finger in the air, ordered a drink and sat down at a table with his worn duffel bag on his lap.

His face was partly concealed by a knit cap, but she guessed he was around her age, about thirty. He was dressed in a leather jacket, dark jeans and black boots. He seemed tense, looking first out the window, then toward the door and then out the window again.

Without turning her head, Jana shifted her gaze to the window and saw the contours of the Saltäng Bridge. The Christmas lights swayed in the bare treetops near Hamngatan. On the other side of the river, a neon sign wishing everyone a Merry Christmas and a Happy New Year blinked on and off.

She shuddered at the thought that there were only a few weeks left until Christmas. She was really not looking forward to spending the holiday with her parents. Especially since her father, former Prosecutor-General Karl Berzelius, suddenly and inexplicably seemed to be keeping his distance from her, as if he wasn't interested in being part of his daughter's life anymore.

They hadn't seen each other since the spring, and every time Jana mentioned his strange behavior to her mother, Margaretha, she offered no explanation.

He's very busy, was always her response.

So Jana decided not to waste any more energy on the matter and had just let it be. As a result, there had been few family visits over the past six months. But they couldn't skip Christmas—the three of them would be forced to spend time together.

She sighed heavily and returned her gaze to the man whom the server had just given a drink. When he reached for it, she saw a large, dark birthmark on his left wrist. He raised the glass to his lips and looked out the window again.

He must be waiting for someone, she thought, as she got up from the table, carefully buttoning her winter jacket and wrapping her black Louis Vuitton scarf around her neck. She pulled her maroon hat over her head and gripped her briefcase firmly.

As she turned toward the door, she noticed that the man was talking on his phone. He muttered something inaudible, downed his drink as he stood up and strode past her toward the exit.

She caught the door as it swung shut after him and stepped out onto the street and into the cold winter air. The night was crystal clear, quiet and almost completely still.

The man had quickly vanished from sight.

Jana pulled on a pair of lined gloves and set out for her apartment in Knäppingsborg. A block from home, she caught sight of the man again, standing against the wall in a narrow alley. This time he wasn't alone.

Another man stood facing him. His hood was up, and his hands were stuffed deep into his pockets.

She stopped in her tracks, took a few quick steps to the side and tried to hide behind a building column. Her heart began to pound and she told herself she must be mistaken. The man in the hood could not be who she thought he was.

She turned her head and again examined his profile.

A shiver went down her spine.

She knew who he was.

She knew his name.

Danilo!

Detective Chief Inspector Henrik Levin turned off the TV and stared at the ceiling. It was just after ten o'clock at night and the bedroom was dark. He listened to the sounds of the house. The dishwasher clunked rhythmically in the kitchen. Now and then he heard a thump from Felix's room, and Henrik knew his son was rolling over in his sleep. His daughter, Vilma, was sleeping quietly and still, as always, in the next room.

He lay on his side next to his wife, Emma, with his eyes closed and the comforter over his head, but he knew it was going to be difficult to fall asleep with his mind racing.

Soon he wouldn't be sleeping much at night for other reasons. The nights would instead be filled with rocking and feeding and shushing long into the wee hours. There were only three weeks left until the baby's due date.

He pulled the comforter down from his head and looked at Emma sleeping on her back with her mouth open. Her belly was huge, but he had no idea if it was larger than during her earlier pregnancies. The only thing he knew was that he was about to become a father for the third time.

He lay on his back with his hands on top of the comforter and closed his eyes. He felt a sort of melancholy and wondered if he would feel different when he held the baby in his arms. He hoped so, because almost the whole pregnancy had passed without him really noticing. He hadn't had time—he'd had other things to think about. His job, for example.

The National Crime Squad had contacted him.

They wanted to talk about last spring's investigation of the murder of Hans Juhlén, a Swedish Migration Board department chief in Norrköping. The case was closed and Henrik had already put it behind him.

What had initially seemed to be a typical murder investigation of a high-ranking civil servant had turned into something much more, much worse. Something macabre: the smuggling of illegal refugees had led the team working the case to a narcotics ring that had, among other activities, been training children to be soldiers, turning kids into cold-blooded killers.

It was far from a routine case, and the investigation had been front-page news for several weeks.

Tomorrow, the National Crime Squad was coming to ask questions about the refugee children who had been transported from South America in shipping containers locked from the outside. More specifically, they wanted to talk about the ring leader, Gavril Bolanaki, who had killed himself before anyone could interrogate him.

They'd be reviewing every minute detail yet again.

Henrik opened his eyes and stared out into the darkness. He glanced at the alarm clock, saw that it was 10:15 and knew the dishwasher would soon signal the end of its cycle.

Three minutes later, it beeped.

CHAPTER
TWO

HER HEART WAS POUNDING AND HER PULSE RACING.

Jana Berzelius breathed as quietly as possible.

Danilo.

A wave of mixed emotions flowed over her. She felt simultaneously surprised, confused, irritated.

There was a time when she and Danilo had been like siblings, when they had shared a daily existence. That was a long time ago now, back when they were little. Now they shared nothing more than the same bloody past. He had scars on his neck the same as she, initials carved into flesh, a constant reminder of their shared dark childhood. Danilo was the only one who knew who she was, where she came from—and why.

She had sought out Danilo last spring to ask for his help when the shipping containers filled with refugee children began appearing outside the small harbor town of Arkösund. He had seemed helpful, even favorably inclined, but in the end he had still betrayed her. He had attempted to kill her—unsuccessfully—and then disappeared underground.

Ever since then, she had been searching for him, but it was as if he had vanished into thin air. She hadn't been able to find a single trace of him in all those months. Nothing. Her frustration had intensified in proportion to her desire for revenge. She daydreamed of different ways to kill him.

She had sketched his face in pencil on a white sheet of paper, drawing and erasing and drawing again until it was a perfect likeness. She had saved the picture, pinned it to a wall in her apartment as if to remind herself of the hatred she felt for him—not that she could ever forget it.

In the end, she had given up on her search for him and returned to her everyday life with the belief that she would probably never find him.

He was gone forever.

Or so she had thought.

Now he stood fifty feet from her.

She felt her body tremble and stifled an impulse to throw herself forward—she had to think rationally.

She held her breath so that she could hear the men's voices, but she couldn't make out a single word. They were too far away.

Danilo lit a cigarette.

The worn duffel bag lay on the ground, and the man with the birthmark was crouched down next to it. He pulled the zipper, exposing its contents. Danilo nodded and gestured with his right hand, and both of them went with quick steps through the alley and disappeared down the stone steps toward Strömparken.

Jana clenched her teeth. What should she do? Turn around and go home? Pretend she hadn't seen him, let him get away? Let him disappear from her life yet again?

Silently, she counted to ten before stepping out of the shadows and going after them.

Detective Inspector Mia Bolander opened her eyes and immediately clapped her hand to her forehead. Her head was spinning.

She got out of bed and stood there naked, looking at the man whose name she had forgotten, who lay on his stomach with his hands under a pillow.

He hadn't been completely with it. For twenty minutes, he had paced the room and repeated that he was a waste of space and didn't deserve her. She had told him again and again that of course that wasn't true, and in the end she had convinced him to get into bed with her.

When he later asked considerately if he could massage her feet, she was too exhausted to say no. And when he had put her big toe in his mouth, she had finally reached her limit and asked straight out if they couldn't just fuck. He had gotten the hint and taken his clothes off.

He had also moaned loudly, licked her neck and given her hickeys.

That shithead.

Mia scratched under her right breast and looked down at the floor where her clothes lay in a heap.

She dressed quickly, not caring if she made noise. She just wanted to go home.

She'd only intended to make a quick stop at the pub. Harry's had had a Christmas-themed karaoke night, and the place had been packed with women in sparkly dresses and men in suits. Some had been wearing Santa hats and had probably gotten drunk earlier in the night at some Christmas party somewhere in Norrköping.

The man whose name she had forgotten had been standing at the bar, holding a beer. He seemed to be around forty and had straight, blond hair that was oddly styled—parted straight down the middle. She had seen a colorful skull-and-crossbones tattoo on his neck. He had otherwise been neatly dressed in a sport coat with overstuffed shoulder pads and a tie.

Mia had sat down a few stools away from him, fingering her glass and trying to get him to notice her. He finally had, but it took even longer for him to walk over and ask if he could join her. She had answered with a smile, again running her finger around the top of her glass. He'd finally understood that he should buy her another drink. Three pints of beer and two seasonal saffron-flavored cocktails later, they'd shared a taxi home to his apartment.

She could still taste the saffron. She went out in the hall, into the bathroom and turned on the light. She was blinded for a second and kept her eyes closed while she drank water out of her cupped hands. She squinted into the mirror, tucked her hair behind her ears and then caught sight of her neck.

Two large red hickeys featured prominently on the right side, under her chin. She shook her head and turned off the light.

She took his sport coat from the hook in the hall and rifled through the pockets. His wallet was in the inside pocket and only held cards—no cash at all.

Not a single krona.

She looked at his driver's license and saw that his name was Martin Strömberg, then she replaced it and put her boots and jacket on.

"Just so you know, Martin," she said, pointing a finger toward the bedroom, "you *are* a goddamn waste of space."

She unlocked the door of the apartment and left.

Jana Berzelius stopped at the top of the hill near Norrköping's Museum of Work and looked around. She couldn't see Danilo or the man with the birthmark anymore.

She surveyed all the street corners in front of her, but neither of the men were there. She didn't see another living soul, in fact, and was amazed at how deserted the industrial landscape could be on a chilly Wednesday evening in early December.

She stood there silently for ten minutes, watching. But she didn't hear a single sound or see the slightest movement.

Finally, she accepted that they were gone. She had lost him. The anger welled up inside her. There was only one thing to do now, and that was to leave, go home with the feeling of again having been tricked.

But what had she thought was going to happen? What had she been thinking? She shouldn't have followed him; she should just leave him alone and take care of herself.

There was nothing else she could do, really.

Walking along Holmensquare, she suddenly had the strange feeling that someone was following her, but when she spun around, the only thing she saw was a short man walking a dog off in the distance. She glanced up at the apartments along Kvarngatan and saw advent candelabras in many of the windows. The sky was pitch-black and still crystal clear.

Shivering, she pulled her shoulders up before continuing across the square and into the tunnel. Halfway through, she was again gripped by the feeling of being followed.

She stopped, turned and stared into the darkness behind her. She stood still, breathing quietly, listening.

Nothing.

She crossed Järnbrogatan with quick steps and rushed through the pink archway that marked the entrance to the Knäppingsborg neighborhood.

Then she suddenly heard a sound behind her.

There he stood, alone.

Thirty feet from her.

His chin was down and his jaw was clenched.

She met his gaze, dropping her briefcase, and prepared herself.

ONE PLACE. MANY STORIES

Bold, innovative and empowering publishing.

FOLLOW US ON:

@HQStories